THE ARENA

AMY PROKOPIS

Amy Prokopis

For the seven-year-old girl who used to sit on her bedroom floor writing in journals, dreaming about being an author one day.

CHAPTER 1

Red dirt rose into the air and made me cough, the only thing that kept me from stepping off the sidewalk and in front of the flat-top dune rider as it zipped around the corner. It was a rare sight outside of the capital. In the villages this far away, most people walked or rode on the backs of Aldierian wolves if they were rich enough. In Arro, we call them "dune dogs" and they might as well be legends as often as we see them.

"I never understood why they need so many soldiers for the ceremony," Jacob said, waving away the cloud, "Most of them don't even attend. No one attends. We have so few kids participate in the ceremony that the ones that do might as well travel to Brill to get the device." He was talking about the Ceremony for the Device. After finishing general education, kids went through the ceremony in which government scientists fitted them with the nationwide device. Years ago, the device used to be handheld. Jacob used to tell me stories when I was little about these small computers that people used to communicate. Now, these devices are no bigger than a silver dollar and are implanted behind the left ear where they remain until the wearer dies.

"I guess they think someone might try to steal one," I

suggested. It was impossible to steal another person's device, so taking one from the government was the only way to do it, not that I knew why anyone would want to steal what they got for free at eighteen. The ceremony was done in waves.

I was scheduled for the fifth wave, which would take place today at nine. We had an assembly on the last day of school to tell us what to expect, which only left us with more questions than we had before. We would go into the village community center alone. Jacob would have to wait outside for me like everyone else's family, though he swore to me he wouldn't be there. It was his last form of protesting my decision after his begging failed. They said we would be led into a holding room where we couldn't speak to one another until it was our turn. Then, we would have our devices implanted and we could go on our way, now adults, included in society where I had a chance at climbing out of the hellhole of this village.

"You are an adult now regardless of whatever you choose today, but by the end of the day," Jacob said, leading the way across the dirt street, "You will either be my apprentice in the forge to live free of government restraint or you will open yourself up to a world of President Grace's propaganda and control." We stopped at the end of the street, moving underneath the tent of a fruit salesman to make way for a family of five passing by. Jacob had always been a little paranoid about all the wrong things. He worried more about what the government was doing and how many Aldierians snuck into the city to attack it than he did the muggers and murders that hung around our street.

"You've always taught me to reach high, achieve more for myself so I don't have to live this way. I know I told you at graduation, but I hope you do understand that I am beyond grateful for everything you've done for me since my birth mom left. To reach higher though, the device is a requirement. Don't take this the wrong way. Hopefully, I'll do better than a blacksmith apprenticeship," I joked, flicking his leather apron. Jacob smiled, flashing me the silver tooth he'd made himself in his forge.

"Hopefully, you'll get approved for an academy apprenticeship," he said, squeezing my shoulder and patting the side of my face like he usually did before taking a swing. I took a step back and his left arm went whooshing past me. We both froze for a moment before breaking into laughter like we usually did between sparring sessions. He pulled me into a hug that lasted much longer than I had expected, and a single tear slipped from his eye when he pulled away, his expression etched with concern.

"I'm not even sure I want an academy apprenticeship," I said. It meant I had to go to more school while most of my class would already be earning money. I had been saving everything I could so poor Jacob didn't have to worry about how we'd eat next month. He did okay as a blacksmith. He was the only one in our region to have weapons deal with the government. He forged a certain number of weapons a month and shipped them to the capital to be used for the army, but they didn't pay as much as you'd think. Most months, we had just enough to afford the small house, bills, and food. I knew I'd never be able to attend an academy apprenticeship without his money and with the cost of tuition alone... I didn't even know what I wanted to do with the rest of my life. It seemed stupid to even take the offer if my tests were high enough to get approved. In another month, I would have enough money to get started on my own anyway.

"I wanted to give you something," Jacob said in my ear, "or rather, return it to you." I gasped when I felt something cool slide over the back of my neck. I pulled away just as he clasped the chain and let the pendant fall against my chest. I caught sight of the small blue stone, my heart nearly stopping dead.

"Jacob," I hissed, closing my fist around the pendant and quickly tucking the entire necklace underneath the collar of my shirt.

"You know what it is then?" he asked in relief, "It was

wrapped around your tiny ankle when I found you in the forge. That will be eighteen years ago come Tuesday."

"Yes, I know," I told him, leading him away from the fruit stand now that the owner had noticed us loitering. Ida stones were a precious commodity in Gallaterra, in the entire planet of Aldieria really. They were the whole reason for the war between us and the natives, so owning even the dust of a stone made you practically a millionaire.

"I kept it a secret until you were ready for it. It's yours. Maybe, one day, you'll find someone who can explain why the natives can make Ida stones glow," he said. Eighteen years ago, a woman came to the forge on a night Jacob was working late. She was injured and in the middle of labor. If she had gifted the stone to him, she must've been from an important family. Jacob didn't get a chance to ask her anymore, because he locked her in the backroom of the forge while he went for help and when he returned, I was the only one left. The name "Kenna" was drawn into the dirt floor at my feet along with the message to keep me safe, and Jacob had ever since.

"You shouldn't have put it on me like that," I told him, making sure the chain wasn't peeking out from my shirt.

"It belonged to your mother. You should be the one to have it," he said, "You could sell it and have enough to support yourself for your entire life, no government device needed."

"No, I meant you shouldn't have given it to me here," I said, "you couldn't have done that this morning over breakfast?" He laughed and led the way down the alley to the back entrance of the forge. He unlocked the door and went inside, but I stayed in the doorway. He pulled aside the iron doors on the front of the building and waved at the grocer across the street before turning to look back at me.

"What's wrong? You don't want to practice?" he asked, picking up one of the newly forged swords and tossing it towards me. I quickly stepped forward and caught it by the hilt to keep it from clattering to the floor. Jacob had picked up a second and turned to face off with me, our swords meeting with a metallic clang. I moved to the side and let his blade slide off mine and nick the floor, forcing him to stumble forwards. I moved out of range so he couldn't charge again and sat the sword back on the rack near the front of the forge.

"I wanted to do a few things before the ceremony," I told him, "I want to clear my head." I wasn't nervous at all, but I made sure to pause before adding the last bit to make it seem like I was. Jacob's expression faltered a little, but he nodded and lowered his sword.

"I'm behind on fitting the handles on a few guns anyway," he said. He joined me at the front of the shop, letting the sword rest at his side like a cane. "I have to say though, you normally like a good fight before big events like this. It's not like you to take a walk to clear your head. It'll all be fine. I promise you, whatever you decide." I nodded, keeping up the charade. I knew that there was nothing to fear from the ceremony. Rumors around my school were that getting the device put in hurt like crazy, but they assured us in the assembly that it was painless and simple. It was "like tucking a piece of hair behind your ear" according to the presenter.

"I know," I said, "I just wanted some time to think about it, is all. I'll see you outside the community center when it's all done." Jacob smiled and bent down to kiss the top of my head.

I started braiding my hair as I walked further down the street. Jacob didn't like when I wore my hair pulled up this way because it made me look older. This was exactly why I always wore it like this when I went pickpocketing at the bar on the east side of the village. It was an open-air bar, all the seating in a large courtyard with the small bar being at the back. This meant that you were only ID'd if you went up to the bar, not if you were just sitting in the courtyard. It was always packed, always had drunk people to steal from, and usually, these were capital soldiers or other undesirables that I didn't feel guilty for tricking afterward. Those men always let me approach, not because I was a girl that looked young, but not too young, but because my hair was such a rare shade of red that they always wanted to have a closer look to see if it was real or not.

The bar was filled exclusively with soldiers today, most of them men. Usually, I would abandon the hunt if there were too many soldiers, but my talk with Jacob about the future was too fresh in my mind not to take any opportunities. After pausing a moment across the courtyard to plan, I started towards the largest group packed around a table. I slipped my backpack onto my right shoulder as I got closer and pretended to fumble with the zipper and then my wallet. Just as I was about to chance a move on the largest of the men, they all burst into laughter. Thankfully, their exaggerated movements only made things easier.

"Sorry, sweetheart," the large man said as he leaned back into me, letting his hand linger a little too long on my left arm. I had already tugged the first thing my hand found from his pocket when he leaned into me.

"It's okay," I told him, ready to pull away when he did a double-take. His eyes went from my hair to my chest and back up again, his right arm slinking around my waist and making it impossible to slip the hard object I'd grabbed into my backpack.

"You work here, sweetheart?" he asked, a few of the other men chuckling. I shifted when I felt his hand press against my hip, giving me a better look at his face. He had shaggy dark hair and stubble on his jaw, making him the most unkempt soldier I'd ever seen. They usually had their hair cut short, even the women, and were well-shaved and groomed. This man was sloppy in comparison. His breastplate was gold, unlike the other men who wore silver, and it was unclasped at the sides so that he could sit with his feet propped up on the table.

"I was just on my way to punch in," I said, "I'll take those." I didn't care if it was obvious at this point. I tucked the object into my pocket and quickly gathered the empty glass bottles in my hands. The man laughed as I walked away. I only noticed now that there wasn't a trashcan in the courtyard, meaning I'd have to put the bottles on the bar. The owner figured out what I was up to, or at least that I was up to no good, a week ago. I turned to face the closest table when the burly man appeared behind the bar, but it was too late.

"Girl," he called out. I didn't wait for him to say anything else. I dropped the bottles on the table, a couple rolling off and smashing against the floor. I took off down the road, ducking into the first alley I found and coming out the other side. I slowed my pace to keep from drawing attention, continuing another block before I was sure no one was following me.

I started towards the community center early. The building was the largest in our village. It was a dome-shaped copper building set atop two flights of stairs on all sides. It took me five minutes longer than I had planned to reach it, causing me to rush up the steps and through the automatic doors with just a few minutes to spare before the start of my wave. The hairs on my arms and legs all stood straight up as soon as the cold air hit me.

The long hallway stretched from one side of the building to the other, the only light coming from the glass sliver that was the ceiling nearly twenty floors above us. There were twelve of us in my wave, my eleven classmates sitting in chairs placed along one wall. Two soldiers were positioned in the hall, one just feet from me and the other near the opposite exit.

"Please, sit," the soldier near me said. I took the last empty chair, which was six feet away from Jameson Roberts on my left. He didn't smile when he noticed me, the nerves clear on his face. We sat in silence for a few minutes, the hall too quiet for being one of the largest employers in the entire village. At last, a pleasant ding sounded from an unseen intercom. The soldier to my right pulled me to my feet by my right bicep.

"Where are we going?" I asked, barely getting time to loop my backpack around my wrist before a panel in the wall slid away to reveal a small room. The soldier guided me into the dark space before backing into the hall again so the panel could slide shut and leave me in the silence again. Another ding sounded and the room filled with light, making me groan as my eyes adjusted.

"Please, remove all your clothes and place them in the receptacle. Shut the receptacle when you finish," a woman's voice said. I looked around the room for the voice, but I was alone. The room was too small for more than one person anyway. There was a click and a rectangular bin slid out from the wall behind me. I paused just a moment to calm my nerves before stripping. I froze when the last thing I had on was the Ida stone Jacob had given me. Was it safer to put the glowing stone in my backpack or wear it? Would they go through my things?

I tucked my new necklace into the pocket of my pants when I felt the cool steel of the stolen object there. I pulled it out, a gold cylinder that looked like a tube of lipstick. Almost. There was a small switch near the bottom. I pressed down on it and gasped. A small dagger shot out the top, tapered to a deathly tip. I tested my index finger at the very tip and was surprised when a bead of red blossomed on my skin. I didn't feel the sting until I wiped the blood away.

I tucked my new necklace into the pocket of my pants with the knife and shut the bin. As soon as I did, another one slid from the wall. This one had what looked like a pair of blue scrubs inside and a shower cap. I was already sliding my legs into the pants as the woman's voice began instructing me to dress. I shut the bin after tucking my hair inside the cap and another panel opened to my left.

"Step out, please," the woman said. I followed the masked woman into a small operating room. A giant halo light turned on above us. She led me to a reclining chair where she began prepping a metal trolley with utensils as I sat. I wanted to ask what she was going to do, but her hands moved so fast from one thing to the next that I knew she wouldn't answer me.

"Keep your head against the headrest, please," she said. I felt my heart skip as the chair began to recline. I took a deep breath and tried letting my body relax against the cushions. The woman adjusted a pair of glasses on her face before taking a silver instrument from the trolley. I didn't get a chance to look before she pressed her gloved hand to my temple, so I was now looking at the blank wall. A strange feeling swept over the skin behind my ear, just like the presenter at school said. The feel of the cool gel made me shiver. Then, I heard a loud crunch. Four holes punched into my skull and I saw stars. I felt like I was floating somewhere above the action. It hadn't hurt, but the feeling of being so out of control sent my heart racing in panic.

"Stay seated, please," the woman said and took a step back. I heard a panel open behind me and then I was moving. I could only tell because the chair began to vibrate underneath me. Through my hazy vision, I could see the stark white ceiling change to dark wood. After nearly a minute, my vision went back to normal and I could take in more of the room. There were twelve soldiers in the large hall, one for each of us. They stood before a raised platform where four government officials sat staring at us. My classmates were laying on chairs to my left, all looking around the room with apprehension. Jameson caught my gaze and opened his mouth to speak, but one of the officials at the table spoke first.

"When you feel able to, stand up and move to the right of your chairs," she said. None of us hesitated. The chairs slid along the floor behind us. "The guards will now activate your devices," she said. The soldiers started forward. Mine raised a small silver rod as he approached. I forced myself to stand still, despite something nagging me to raise my hand in defense as he pressed the end of the rod to my new device. Twelve beeps sounded out and then the guards went back to their posts.

"Your devices are now active. You can use it by pressing the button just behind your ear, using your thoughts to send calls and messages. You will receive a letter in the mail with the results of your final exams. If you have been accepted to the academy, you will then be allowed to tour and select your apprenticeship and begin your next stage of education. If you haven't been accepted, your letter will also have your work card so that you may begin earning your living," the woman said.

The room went strangely quiet and then all eleven of my classmates said "yes," in unison. The room was quiet again, so much so that I was sure the panel of officials could hear my heart beating. A man at the table leaned to the woman and soon the four were bent together in discussion. I looked to my classmates for an explanation. Was my device not working right? Was I supposed to say something?

"The guards will now escort you back to the hallway where you can join your loved ones," the woman said. The soldiers moved forward, taking their places behind us as the woman pressed a finger to the device behind her ear. I expected someone to say something or for the guards to lead the way out, but the room was quiet. All twelve of us exchanged confused glances, a few looking to the soldiers behind them who remained stoic. Jameson looked at me just before his body went limp. All eleven crumpled, caught easily by the soldiers behind them. Before I could question what had happened, both my arms were seized and held tightly behind me.

"What did you do to them?" I asked. The doctor who had installed my device appeared next to me, pushing my hair aside and inspecting the area. I tried to pull away from the guard, but he held on too tight.

"It's active, lieutenant," the doctor called out, "There's nothing wrong."

"But there is," the woman said, standing up from the table, "She's Aldierian, a spy. She's a traitor to Gallaterra. Take her to the ship."

"I'm not a spy," I said, "I've lived here my whole life." The woman didn't say anything else. The guard began dragging me past my classmates, some of them stirring as a panel opened that led back into the hall.

"Help me with the girl," the soldier holding me said. One of the soldiers from the hall came forward and grabbed my right arm. Before he could get a good grip, I wrenched free and ran for the exit. The doors opened before me and the small crowd waiting to receive us began cheering.

"Jacob," I yelled as loud as I could. The crowd quieted, all aside for Jacob who began pushing his way through the people. I started down the first flight of stairs, feeling something wrap around my ankles. They both snapped together and I collapsed hard on the landing.

"Kenna," Jacob said, appearing at the bottom of the last flight. Soldiers along the street began running towards the crowd, the people all looking around us in horror.

"They're both terrorists to Gallaterra," a soldier said as two men grabbed my arms and hauled me to my feet.

"I'm not a spy," I said.

"Kenna," Jacob said. He stopped at the bottom of the stairs, a sheathed dagger coming out from underneath his blacksmith's apron and a small throwing knife raised in his right hand. The crowd was deafening when the knife sunk into the soldier holding my right arm, the wet thunk as the blade lodged in his throat nearly paralyzing me. The other soldier let go of me in shock. Jacob tossed the dagger at me and I caught it by the sheath with no idea what I should do next.

"Grab him," a new voice said, this one deep and guttural. It cut through the screaming of the onlookers in such a clear way that it made me pause and look. The man I had pickpocketed stood on a flat-top dune rider, himself guarded by two soldiers.

The remaining soldier escorting me grabbed my sheath. I didn't think, I acted. I wretched the dagger free and drove it into his gut before he could get his stunning rod more than halfway from its holster. I crumpled with him, remembering now that I was still bound by my ankles. With my hand gripping the hilt of the dagger almost to the point of pain, I tugged it from the soldier's stomach and flipped to my back to free my feet. The blade of the dagger made an ugly squeal against the metal device wrapped around my ankles, sliding off and nicking the top of my bare feet enough to spill blood on the stone beneath me.

"Girl," the man in the gilded armor said. I glanced up at him while trying to tug free, my hands freezing when I saw him. Two guards had Jacob between them. The gold soldier pushed a button on his wrist and then pressed the metal glove to Jacob's forehead. He let out a terrible scream, the sound so terrifying that I held onto the dagger tighter and pointed it towards the two soldiers who had approached to arrest me.

"Stop. Stop it," I told the gold soldier. He smiled and lowered his hand. This time he drew a sword from his hip. He nodded for both soldiers to move aside. He took Jacob roughly by the hair and held the blade to his neck.

"Drop the dagger or I cut him to the bone," he said. The way he said it, with such hope, made my body feel light with adrenaline. Instead of stealing from him, I imagined that I'd gutted him when he snaked his arm around my waist and called me sweetheart. I tossed the dagger towards the stairs and watched it rattle down the steps. The approaching soldiers tugged me to my feet again, practically lifting me onto my toes. The gold soldier lowered his sword and stepped away from Jacob. Before he could take a step, the scarlet tip of the sword burst through his chest. My throat ached from my scream, though I didn't hear the sound. The soldiers held me tight, preventing me from running to Jacob's limp body.

"Take her to the ship," the gold soldier said. My feet barely skidded each stair on the way down. I spat towards the large man once I was close enough, but he wasn't at all bothered by the saliva clinging to his cheek. "Wait," he said, raising the sword to my neck before the soldiers could drag me past him. Warm drops fell against my skin and slid under the collar of my scrubs.

"You swore you wouldn't," I said, my voice hoarse. The man smiled.

"I told you I wouldn't cut him to the bone," he said, turning the sword and cleaning the blood off both sides using my chest, "I went through the bones first." He started towards the flat-top dune rider. The soldiers led me away from the crowd and towards a line of larger dune riders along the street. One of the soldiers removed a small metal bar from his waist. He pressed a finger to the black line around the center and then tapped it to my wrists. It snapped tightly around them like a bracelet.

"Get in," he said, opening the back door of the cab. The inside was small with no windows along the metallic walls, just a bench on each side. I had to sit on the floor before using my tied wrist to pull myself into the seat. The soldier slapped his hand against the red button just inside the door and my wrists were tugged to the short ceiling and my ankles banged against the bottom of the seat, both held in place by a magnet force. The door slammed shut and I was plunged into total darkness with nothing but the memory of Jacob's pained expression and the smell of blood to accompany me.

CHAPTER 2

The ship was just a larger version of a dune rider. I was only allowed a brief look at its exterior before I was led inside. We descended into the cargo hold of the ship. It was separated into two sections, one side full of crates that were strapped down and another side separated with iron bars. It was a large holding cell, large enough to accommodate many more people than the four already there. Three were women, all of them between twenty and forty years old and one with a fresh bandage around her arm and a cut just under her eye that had crusted over with dried blood. A man sat with his back against the bars and remained on the floor, unlike the women who all stood as I approached.

The soldier guarding the door raised a silver remote and a buzzing sound echoed around the large space. The women let out cries of surprise as the restraints on their wrists were drawn to the floor. The man eyed me while the soldiers switched the metal bar wrapped around my wrists for a pair of handcuffs with a magnet sandwiched between the wrists. The soldier tasked with guarding the cell led me into the center of the room where he activated my cuffs by swiping his badge along one side.

My knees went numb when they bashed against the floor from the force of the magnet. The guard returned to his post, exchanged a brief crack about how long he'd be forced to spend alone with us, and then the soldiers who arrested me took the elevator back upstairs. The door shut and with another click of the remote, the magnets were freed from the floor. All four of us girls rubbed our now bruised knees and wrists as we rose, causing the man to chuckle.

"Shut up," the bandaged woman told him. He only laughed harder.

"Couldn't help myself. It's funny every time," he said.

"So, you're the type of criminal who gets caught more than once then?" she asks.

"And you're the type that what? You get caught the first time you break the law?" he said with a laugh. Her face turned red, giving away the truth of her offense.

"At least I know when to stay out of trouble," she said, "I'm not some real criminal who makes a job of breaking the law." The man scoffed, his expression darkening.

"No, real criminals don't get caught. They get promoted," he said. The words echoed once in my brain. I thought about the people in charge who decided that what I am is a problem. I have never even seen another Aldierian, let alone know a thing about what they stand for. Yet, I'm the criminal.

"Open that door," a familiar, gruff voice said. The gold soldier was crossing the cargo area fast. My back curved as my chains magnetized to the floor again. The guard pressed his badge to the lock on the door and the gold soldier pushed it open. He came right for me, pressing his badge to the magnet between my hands and then yanking me to my feet by my bicep. He stood two feet taller than me and I'm no shrimp.

"Where are you taking me?" I asked as I stumbled beside him the entire way to the elevator. He pressed a button with his fist and let the doors slide shut before speaking.

"Your case has been expedited," he said.

"I'm a minor. I'm seventeen," I said.

"For two days," he said, "We aren't allowed to confine minors with adults, so you'll stay in my quarters." He sounded a little too pleased with the arraignment. The elevator slowed to a stop and he pulled me down a long hall. One side had windows, enabling me to see over my village as we rose from the ground. By the time we reached the door halfway down the hall, the domed community center looked like a marble in a sandbox.

He pulled me inside the room. The door locked behind us without him stopping to turn the bolt. His quarters were made up of two rooms. The one I stood in was large. It had two sitting areas, with a massive window that overlooked nothing but sand for miles as we zoomed past. The man went to the dinette for two glasses of water. He pulled both chairs out from the table and sat down in one, staring at me until I took the seat opposite him.

"I'm not allowed behind bars, because I'm underage," I said, "but they'll let me stay with a grown man, me, a girl, in his apartment." The threat in my voice didn't make a single dent in his serious expression. He took a sip of his water and settled back in the chair.

"How did you get in the village?" he asked.

"I'm not a terrorist," I said.

"You're Aldierian," he said without missing a beat. The chains around my wrists clanked as I moved them onto the table. I didn't know most of my background. I knew I was born in the forge, but I couldn't tell you my mother's name.

"I've never even met an Aldierian," I told him, "I was adopted as a baby. I had no idea until the ceremony, so the idea that I'm some terrorist is crazy." He scoffed, pushing the glass of water towards me.

"Calm down," he said, "You're not being interrogated. I'm just trying to have a little conversation here." I knew the soldiers better than most and I knew they never opted for interrogations over more sophisticated measures. I slid the glass from the table using both hands and kept my eyes on his face as it shattered on the floor. He was too busy watching the water spreading over the tile to notice me, so I bolted for the door.

He wrapped his arms around me from behind. I gave him a good kick between the legs, missing that sensitive spot with my heel. He let go of me and shoved me hard against the door. My nose smashed against the bolt, making my eyes tear immediately as warmth oozed over my lips and chin. I spun around to face him, spreading my wrists as far apart as my restraints would let me so that the metal rod he swung my way connected with the chains instead of my skin. I'd seen the soldiers in the village use the weapon enough to know to surrender rather than be zapped unconscious when he held it towards me in a threat.

"You want the public to find out you got a seventeen-year-old alone in your apartment and she walked away bloody and unconscious?" I asked. He let out a laugh this time and lowered the rod.

"You don't know who I am," he said in surprise, "foolish little bitch."

"I almost got away from you. Maybe you're the fool," I said. He moved back to the table, motioning for me to go. I hesitated. Were there guards outside the door? Did I need his badge to open the door? I wasn't sure what to do now, but I wasn't going to go back to that table.

"I like you. You remind me of my niece," he said. I moved to the couch just a few feet from the door. He leaned the chair back from the table so he could reach the fruit bowl on the counter. He took an apple, his teeth crunching loudly into it and juice sliding down his chin. "She was about your height, almost the same face, but she had brown hair like my sister. They were inseparable, I mean, they did everything together. That girl adored her. Once, she spent an hour trying to capture a little mouse they found in their home. Once she got it inside a little box, she took it outside and released it. She said it deserved to be free. Beautiful," he said.

"I'm not anything like her," I said. I wasn't some ethereal little thing in the slightest. I barely felt girlish most days. The soldier smiled and shook his head.

"No," he said, "she didn't fight me in the end." My head snapped to his face. His expression was burning with the memory, making my stomach turn and my heart pound with fear for the first time.

"The end?" I asked, my voice barely carrying across the room.

"You see, this world is about taking opportunities. Nothing is just given to you. Too many people expect things to just fall in their lap or be gifted to you, bows and all. No. You must take what you want," he said, leaning his forearms on the table and studying the craters he'd bitten out of the apple, "There are people who are too soft to take what they want. Dumb. Lazy. They don't fight when the real winners take their gifts. They go limp. They let the winners unwrap their gifts and they just watch as they do it, ribbon by ribbon. They don't do a thing, not that they could. They're weak, remember? They need the winners to clear the way so they can keep moving forward."

He took another bite of the apple and stood up. I was frozen in place as he approached me. The door was less than two feet from me. I could reach it before he was even halfway across the room, but I didn't. I just sat there, my eyes glued on his every movement. He stopped directly in front of me, taking another bite of his apple. I felt some of the juice from his chin land on my collar and slide into the space between my breasts.

"I like the soft ones," he said, "easier to fit in the mold." I refused to fit anyone's mold. I spat in his face, the ruddy saliva clinging to his cheek. He laughed, wiping away the spit and taking a bite of the apple.

"I'm not your niece," I told him. He nodded.

"No, you're not," he said, taking a final bite and tossing the apple towards the trash can.

"You're going to get caught and get exactly what you deserve," I told him.

"You look like my niece, but you're just like my sister," the soldier said, slipping his shoes off, "When that little girl let that mouse go outside, my sister never told her that a cat pounced on it minutes later. She protected her. You're a protector. The problem with people like you is that they don't care to protect themselves. There's a chink in their armor right here." The man tapped his chest, letting his eyes look over me once before he began to shed the gilded armor.

"I can protect myself," I said, "foolish bitches don't forge weapons without knowing how to use them." He clapped his hands together.

"I knew I liked you," he said, slipping out of his jacket so he was only in a tank top and his tan army pants, "but you're not a winner. You are a protector or else you wouldn't have let me take your precious father or whatever that blacksmith was to you. He tried to protect you and you still ended up in chains. You tried to protect him, and he still died and you ended up in chains. I don't normally do this, but I like you, Kenna Riley. You can't be a protector. You see, life is a great big game of chess and you're the queen. Sometimes, to cross the board, the other pieces have to move out of the way. Pawns, knights, rooks, it doesn't matter, they all fall at the end of the game anyway. If you aren't willing to take opportunities, you won't win."

My stomach hurt. My entire body was aching and I was starting to wish I had just taken my chances with the door before he ever started telling me his horrible story. He went to a closet and pulled out a navy blazer adorned with more military pins than I'd ever seen on a soldier. He slipped it on his shoulders and began pulling on a pair of dress shoes. I scrubbed at the blood that had dried and started to itch around my nose, remembering then that not all the blood splattered over my scrubs was my own.

"I'm not a protector," I said as he finished tying the laces,

"I'm not any of those things. You can't just toss people into categories. They can't be manipulated that way." He tossed a leather bag onto the floor. I recognized my jeans as they flopped out the opening and I found the courage to leave the couch to retrieve my things.

"Not a protector? Just a foolish little bitch?" he asked, passing me for the door.

"You can't fool me. You're not a winner. You're a cheater. You're the real criminal, not me," I said. I remembered what the man in the cell had said. Real criminals don't get caught, they get promoted. The gold soldier had been promoted to the top.

"If I'm not a winner, then you wouldn't have let me cross the board," he said, opening the door and looking back at me from the doorway, "Winners take their opportunities, remember?" He closed the door and I heard three distinct thunks, deadbolting me inside for the first time since I'd arrived.

————

Surprisingly, none of my clothes had been searched. I only knew that because the Ida stone necklace was still tucked in the pocket of my pants along with the knife I'd taken from the gold soldier. After dressing, I tucked the weapon in my pocket again. I hoped I wouldn't have to strip down before an opportunity for escape arose. I wouldn't be fooled this time.

I watched the sand turn to concrete as we finally reached Gallaterra. It looked like a bleak place, little to no color unlike the red dirt and sands of my village. Most of the buildings were made with gray stone or reflective glass. Many of them were connected by glass sky bridges. The roads were congested with dune riders, all floating over the concrete and gliding through intersections in neat lines of traffic.

A network of pods zoomed along the skyway, an intricately laid series of tracks that somehow kept the thousands of silver pods from smashing into each other as they merged and exited the tracks. The skyway cast a spidery shadow over the people walking the dirt streets below and made them look like tiny ants stuck in a web. They were probably merchants by the look of them, wearing worn traveling clothes like the people in Arro. They stood out against the sleek, modern design of the city.

Our ship rose further above the buildings, stopping once we were in line with the tallest of the buildings. It was a massive complex, coated in what looked like solid concrete and containing no windows at all aside from the pyramid-shaped glass that sat atop the four interconnected towers. A panel began sliding open in one of the towers as we approached. The floor of the ship shuttered a little under me as we docked. I sat alone for just a few minutes before the gold soldier returned.

He didn't say a word before clapping a new set of chains on my wrists and ankles. He led me back down the hall and into the elevator. I kept my mouth shut, my eyes glued on our reflections in the gilded door as we dinged along from one floor to the next. I remembered the necklace and the knife as I felt both slip deeper into my pocket, prompting me to move my hands closer together in front of me and use the right cuff on my wrist to ensure they would stay there.

The soldier smirked and then his face parted as the elevator doors opened to reveal what looked like a giant warehouse. Rows and rows of the same ship lined the large space. After a push to my lower back, almost too low to be considered a push, I started down the ramp. To my right, another ramp finished descending with a metallic whoosh and the other prisoners from the holding cell were escorted out.

Together, we made our way through the bowels of the building. It was medieval compared to the shiny, glass-laden towers I'd seen on the way into the city. The further down we went, the darker it seemed. We all fell into single-file lines as we reached a small hallway, passing a large picture of President Grace on the wall. He was a large man, a little puffy around the middle and in the face, and had light hair that faded to a slightly gray color at the roots. His blue eyes were striking, but not in a beautiful way. They almost seemed to watch us as we walked by.

At the end of the hall, there was a landing. A dark hole led to who knew where below it and only a metal platform served as a ferry between our hall to the next yards away. The gold soldier didn't pause. He led me straight to the platform. He kept close to me, tugging my right arm so that my back was flush against his chest. After a moment, the platform floated away from the landing and towards the opposite hall, which I could see now was nothing more than dark brick walls with old fluorescent lights.

He pushed me forward a foot before we reached the landing, forcing me to reach a little further than normal with my right foot to step onto the concrete floor. I held in my shock and didn't say a word though, moving away from him before he could get a chance to touch me again. Striding down the dark hall, I was forced to wait on the soldier again when I met a gate. I tested it against the lock once, before I moved aside for him to approach.

"Looking for opportunities this time?" the soldier said, casting me a sly grin before pressing his index finger to the device behind his ear. He ordered the door to open and it swung free with a squeak. The room was similar to the holding cell on the ship, only this one was the size of an arena and filled with what looked like nearly a hundred men and women. There were small openings against the right and left walls, the only bathrooms.

When we entered, a loud buzz filled the air and most of the prisoners dropped to the floor. The ones who hadn't were wrenched there by their restraints. The soldier shoved me and I stumbled feet into the room, several people groaning in anger. I backed up a few more as the man rushed me, a girlish squeal slipping past my lips as his hands started to rove. He slid them up and then down my arms before pinning them to my sides. More people started to grumble as he forced my feet apart with one of his own and let his free hand slide over the outside and inside of my left thigh. A new panic struck me. This wasn't just his lewd desires, this was protocol. This was a pat-down.

I fought harder now, almost slipping away for just a second before he readjusted his grip on my right hip. "I'm seventeen! I'm a minor," I told him, loud enough that some of the closest men started chanting in disgust.

Underage! Underage!

"Shut up," the soldier said, his voice echoing through the room over every chanting voice. I put six feet between us when he released me, frozen in my spot out of fear. He looked back at the door when the rattling of chains grew closer. He raised a hand to the other guards, stopping them from entering the room. Finally, he looked back at me and said, "hold out your cuffs."

I held both my hands up and he exchanged the thick iron for a set of silver bracelets, each three inches wide and maybe half an inch thick. As soon as he slid them on, they shrunk in size so there was no hope of sliding them off again. I lowered my arms and he tossed my old shackles aside, the metal smacking the floor nearly as hard as he slapped me seconds later. I saw a blur of color as I spun around, my knees meeting the cold stone.

"Turn it on," the soldier called out. I felt my wrists kink painfully, forcing me into child's pose. The scream ripped from my throat before I ever registered it as my own, the zap of electricity from the metal rod pressed to my back painful enough to leave me out of breath when it was gone. "Who helped you, Aldierian bitch," the soldier asked.

"No," a new voice said, I heard the buzzing of the electric wand stop just behind my ear. "Don't," the voice said again. I turned my head to the right. A boy about my age was sitting cross-legged, his wrists pinned to the ground before him. He kept his blue eyes trained on the soldier, dropping them to my face just long enough to communicate the message that relaxed my muscles. He would take care of this, as much of it as he could.

The soldier laughed above me and asked, "You're helping her?"

"I am now," the boy said, the strength in his voice almost funny considering we were all tethered to the floor by magnets. A round of laughter came from the hallway behind us, but the gold soldier put an end to it with a single order. I saw a pair of boots appear between us, keeping me from watching the boy for just a moment as the soldier stopped inches from my right hand. He looked directly at the boy before stomping on my hand, shifting all of his weight onto my fingers so they changed from a bright pink to a bony white. I gritted my teeth and managed only a whimper before he finished.

"I'll make sure to tell your father all about your chivalry," the soldier said, joining the laughing guards in the hall. I had to stay pinned to the floor for minutes while they got the other prisoners admitted, the boy staring back at me in apology the entire time. Once the loud buzz returned and I felt the pressure release in my wrists, he was at my side to help me into a sitting position.

"You know that asshole?" I asked, flexing my fingers just a fraction to test the tendons.

The boy paused a moment, looking at me as if thinking about how to explain what should've been obvious. "That's Sargent Don Marcus," he said, "He's kinda notorious for being…"

"I'm well aware of what he's notorious for," I finished for him. His eyes fell to the hand I cradled in my lap.

"Can I see?" he asked me, nodding towards my cramped hand. It was still getting all the color back, my pinky already turning purple and a splotch in the middle looking questionable. I let him. He was gentle, his fingers barely touching me as he looked at each knuckle in turn. "Kieran," he said, finally looking up at me.

"Kenna," I said and sat my sore hand in my lap. I could feel the spot on my back burn from where the wand had zapped me, but I tried not to make it obvious, smiling instead to mask the ache.

"Most of the people in here are real criminals," Kieran said, "I mean that they actually committed crimes."

"And you didn't?" I asked. He paused, glancing at the gate in disgust.

"Well, I am more of a criminal than you," he said, returning his eyes to me, "You're the only Aldierian in here." I didn't even know what it meant to be Aldierian, so I wasn't sure what to say to that.

"And I wouldn't be in here if it weren't for the device," I said, noticing the curious way he watched me now.

"I know what you mean," Kieran said, sitting back on his hands. The question must have been there in my face because he continued with "I'm a device tamperer," a moment later. I had almost forgotten about the device behind my ear, not that it mattered. It wouldn't work on me anyway. Turns out, Aldierians are immune to thought technology. I looked closer at him. Blue eyes. Boyish face. He must have tried removing the device shortly after he got it because he couldn't be much older than me.

"Thank you," I said.

"He didn't…" He sat up a little straighter, glancing for the gate where Marcus had disappeared just moments before. I shook my head.

"No," I said. Kieran relaxed a little more and our conversation grew more casual. I told him all about my village, Jacob, how he died. Kieran listened to me intently, as if he'd never heard a sadder story even though there were a thousand more of them worse than mine back home. I told him about the old woman I bought coffee from on the way to school each morning. Every morning, she'd tote her coffee maker with her in a wagon, paper cups at the ready, and a screw-top jar crudely glued to the bottom of the wagon so no one could snatch in as they passed. I told Kieran about my side-gig hustling money from drunk soldiers. If I stole a good amount, I always tipped that woman extra.

The guards left the fluorescent lights on at all times. When we noticed that most of the room had laid down to sleep, Kieran showed me his usual corner. It took me much longer to get comfortable on the stone floor, but after getting tired enough, I felt myself drifting into dreams of my village and Jacob pounding steel.

CHAPTER 3

The next morning, I woke up to a loud buzz and felt the pressure return to my wrists. I was pinned to the floor again, but Kieran sat up sleepily next to me. Realizing he was the only one in the room not stuck to the floor, his expression turned to stone. I looked towards the gate and was surprised to see Sargent Marcus and President Grace himself striding through the room straight for us. He was a stark sight in his navy suit, red tie, and gold pin glittering under the fluorescent bulbs. None of us, all still dressed in the clothes we were arrested in, looked nearly as dressed-up as he was.

"Stand up," he ordered, "You know who I'm here for." Kieran rose off the floor, his jaw tight as he walked to meet the man. The president didn't stop walking before he slapped Kieran across the face hard, hard enough to elicit a groan and spin him halfway around. Kieran lowered a hand from his face to reveal the angry mark. His expression turned from surprise to anger before he faced the president again.

"Nothing?" President Grace asked and let the silence hang in the air a moment, "I put you in here for rehabilitation and you become an Aldierian sympathizer?" Kieran didn't move or say a word. He just faced the president who seemed to grow redder in the face the longer he kept quiet. I got another chance to see Kieran's face when the man backhanded him. This time Kieran winced in pain. He bit his lower lip to keep quiet, blowing out a deep breath before facing Grace again.

"Sargent Marcus would be in here with us if I let him touch her," Kieran said, "You know how he is." Grace pulled him by the front of his shirt so they were inches apart and hissed something into his face that I couldn't make out before releasing him. Kieran stumbled back, still well in arm's reach.

"I'm the only one you hit growing up," Kieran said.

"You're the only one who deserved it," Grace replied.

"And it's illegal," Kieran said, "You've arrested people for it."

"You're not my son, not anymore. You're an inmate, a jailbird, and you'll take your beatings as you earn them. You'll be discharged once you've earned my respect." Something told me he never expected that to happen. He looked back at Kieran with such disgust, like he didn't recognize him as anything worth his consideration. President Grace waited just a moment as if daring Kieran to utter another word, before walking alongside Marcus and disappearing into the hall.

I never asked Kieran Grace about the argument, and we returned to retelling stories. This time, I made him share his own. Kieran had four siblings, he didn't have to tell me. All of Aldieria knew the First Family, though I had never seen Kieran in any of the posters hung around the village square and it made sense why now. I didn't meet anyone else in the room until the third day, a woman in her fifties who used pieces of cloth to weave my hair into a series of intricate braids that all merged into a high ponytail and clipped me hard in the eye when I swiveled around to face her when she spoke for the first time.

"Such pretty," she said with a smile that was three teeth short, "Gift?" It took a moment for me to realize the necklace was hanging out of my pocket. I made sure no one else had seen before tugging it out. The Ida stone glowed blue when it touched my palm. I closed my hand around it so I didn't draw more attention. "From boy?" the woman asked, pointing to Kieran who sat in our corner a yard away with his knees to his chest. The last blow had left a small bruise on his right cheekbone.

The gate flew open and Marcus returned. Kieran's eyes lifted to my face and I slid the necklace across the floor to him before I could think what else to do. His surprise lasted just a second before he tucked it into his jeans pocket. The buzz sounded and my hands were pinned to the floor. Silence filled the room. I was turned towards the wall too far to see what was happening over my shoulder. A deep voice cooled my skin.

"Jack Henry, Tonja Jackson, and the Aldierian bitch," Marcus said, "You all face the arena tomorrow morning." A full minute later and the buzz echoed around the room again and we were free. I scrambled back to Kieran and didn't give him a chance to speak.

"The arena?" I asked. He closed his mouth and removed his empty hand from his pocket.

"We aren't in a prison, he said, "It's a holding center, like for cattle." I should've known that's where I'd go. I was unknowingly at the top of the Most Wanted list and it was the club the arena loved to host above all others. All its rich Gallaterran guests, who paid enough money to solve all poverty on the planet to attend, would be waiting just outside to witness my fight to the death.

"Well, that sets the human race back centuries, doesn't it?" He let out a small laugh, but the dark humor didn't touch his eyes the way I'd grown used to. Of course, they wouldn't let me live. I refused to tell them any information, despite not having any to give, and I was a terrorist to all humankind on Aldieria according to President Grace's laws.

I spent the rest of the day thinking though every time I sparred with Jacob in the forge, forcing myself to focus when the memory of his death grew heavier. Kieran told me there were assorted weapons throughout the arena I could pick up, everything from swords and knives to the stun guns Jacob makes for the army. Made.

The next morning, Kieran gave back my mother's necklace and I slipped it over my head and let the stone rest against the skin between my breasts. Maybe the pendant would help me somehow. Either way, it didn't matter now if they found it on me. Kieran forced me to eat half of my breakfast before he was satisfied, arguing that I had a better shot if I ate well. An hour and a half after, the gate opened and four guards came in. I knew who mine would be.

The buzz sounded, but I was already on my feet. I knew it wouldn't confine me and as soon as I rose, the two other inmates did as well. I took them in, assuming we would be fighting each other. The woman was small, but the muscles in her exposed calves and biceps told me she was stronger than she looked, and likely fast as well. The man was huge, but his belly hung over his pants and I was sure I could outrun him if he did turn out to be a threat.

"What?" Kieran said behind me. He was looking at his hands, which were a foot off the floor unlike the rest of the prisoners around us. He looked up at me in shock, fear in his eyes for the first time.

"Those two fight first," Marcus said. I whirled around to see him point at the man and woman. Two guards hurried forward to lead them into the hall. The last guard started towards us. I attempted to meet him, but Marcus stopped me. "Happy birthday, little fool," he said and clasped shackles around my wrists. Kieran fell in line next to me and the soldiers led us back the way we came in, taking a different hallway once across the dark pit. This one had a glass ceiling that enabled us to see the top of the arena stands. Hundreds of people were cheering, all of them elaborately dressed like it was the social event of the season and it likely was for them. I didn't recognize them all, but the dozen I did were senators and big-wig campaign donors. The representative for Arro sat just above one of the gated exits to the arena floor, her scarlet lips matching the ad for luxury handbags that were draped above her seating section. A man came over the loudspeaker to announce the first woman and man, returning my attention to our circumstances.

It went quiet as we were led down a small hallway towards a patch of sunlight at the end. It was a holding area, Aldierian sand replacing the stone floor. A gate swung shut before us, corralling the competitors in the small arena. I could see just a few racks for weapons. There was a sword and a couple of heavy-looking hammers. Another had a couple throwing stars and another sword. That's it. I cast a nervous glance at Kieran before a horn went off. Drummers in the stands began pounding out a steady beat on big bass drums.

The man ran for the nearest rack, the one with the lone sword. He was slow though, and the woman got to the remaining one in time to launch a star his way. The first sunk into the rack between his hand and the hilt of the sword, but the second ripped open the flesh on his forearm and splattered blood over the sand. The crowd gasped with delight and then the cheering grew louder.

"Respect has to be earned," a voice said. President Grace walked out of the adjacent hall and into the sunlight, making his graying roots more pronounced. Kieran stiffened between us, keeping his gaze on the gory fight. "If you kill an Aldierian, it won't just be me you make proud," Grace said, gaining his son's attention at last, "You'll impress all of Gallaterra. You can open those doors for your career that you shut when you rotted your brain as a teenager with all those banned books." Grace pointed towards the cheering crowd, almost all of them on their feet now as the woman swung her sword at the man's neck, a killing blow.

"If they didn't care before, I doubt they will now," Kieran said, turning to watch as a swarm of guards came into the arena for the body. President Grace opened his mouth to speak, but a thin man appeared at his side.

"Sir, the Head of Engineering needs you to sign off on mining for more Ida stones in the west," he said. Grace turned to look at him, annoyed.

"And why did they send the Chief Scientist?" he asked. The man seemed to shrink a little.

"Sir, I've already seen the effects of over mining for the stones. There's a crater growing just outside Valentia and another threatening to break apart one hundred and twenty-three miles north from there…" the man said, following the president further down the hall.

"You've informed me more than once, Haggarty," he said.

"Yes, but sir, our studies show…"

"We've already started a twenty-year initiative to evacuate Aldieria."

"Yes, but the data…" Haggarty stopped speaking when Grace motioned for his guards to approach, one stopping at each of the thin scientist's shoulders.

"Tell the Head of Engineering that he has my approval," Grace said, turning to look at the scientist. He withdrew a pen from his breast pocket and signed his name across the man's forehead. "That is, unless you'd rather take your data to the Aldierians," Grace said, smirking at the fear on Haggarty's face. Grace patted his chest as he passed, calling for Sargent Marcus to escort him back to his office to meet with the Head of Engineering and ignoring the scientist as he hurried after them. Kieran sighed.

"Not even going to watch his own son's fight to the death," he whispered.

"I'm sorry," I told him. He shook his head. The gate before us opened and the crowd and the announcer introduced us.

"It doesn't matter," Kieran said.

The crowd erupted in cheers and four guards shuffled us into the arena and led us to separate sides of the sandy circle. The weapon racks were placed on both sides, halfway between us. This time, one held a heavy-looking club and the other a sledgehammer. It was rigged in Kieran's favor, I was sure. I was comfortable with a sword, but there wasn't a single one here. Kieran was almost a foot taller than me and muscular, but he didn't have the years of practicing with weapons in the forge that I had. I would have to outlast him, hope that I could get a clean shot in. My stomach churned at the thought of smashing that blonde head of his.

The announcer yelled something that got a deafening cry out of the audience and the horn and the drums introduced the start of the battle. Kieran stared back at me, not taking a single step. He had so much to gain from this. He could win easily. He could be discharged just as his father said. He could get out and go far away from his family and his abusive father. He could start an uprising because there had to be thousands of people like him and Jacob that didn't want to fight the Aldierians anymore. He could make a difference and all it would cost him was one life. My life.

I started walking, my eyes trained on him. He stayed still and I tried to make my intent clear in my face. I picked up the pace so I was jogging now. My heart was pounding heavily in my chest. It was fine. He didn't need any weapons to do it. He could kill me with his bare hands, suffocate me in front of everyone or break my neck with a quick twist. Still, he didn't move. Damn. Damn you, Kieran Grace. Kill me. Do something.

He met me in the center of the arena and I raised both my hands to my face out of instinct. I felt my knees giving out and I was sinking towards the sand when his hands clasped mine. He tugged me back onto my feet. I collapsed against his chest and he raised my left hand to his shoulder and held my right in his own. That's when I realized the pounding wasn't just coming from my chest. The steady boom boom of the drums pulsed through the sand under our feet and as I looked into Kieran's face, I felt grounded by the rhythm and the resistance in his expression.

Kieran led. He lifted me and spun me around. I drug the toe

of my boot in the sand as I turned in a circle, letting him take my arms and lower me in a dip. The crowd began booing and more guards appeared in the stands, mostly watching us and looking to each other for orders.

"Where's President Grace?" one of them shouted.

"The gate," I said as it swung open. Just four guards were positioned at the arena, the clean-up crew. They charged towards us with their metal stunning poles at the ready. I kicked sand up at the first one, stopping him long enough for Kieran to appear with the sledgehammer. He crushed the first's skull and swung a second blow into another guard's side.

The way to the gate was free, so we ran. Kieran led the way down the hall his father had taken. We were back inside the main building in minutes before we ever heard anyone pursuing us. After taking a few more turns, we burst into a large lobby full of businesspeople. They stared as we ran past, not reacting until at least five guards came yelling after us.

"Left. Right. Up the stairs," Kieran told me between breaths.

"Up the stairs?" I asked as I rounded the corner, "We want to go out, not up." I followed his directions anyway, taking the lead so he could knock over a shelf full of files behind us so that it settled against the wall at an angle. Just like he said, a short flight of stairs took me to a landing before a door labeled for emergencies only.

"Go in," he said when I stopped. I pulled the door open and he slammed it shut behind me. The floor felt bouncy and I soon realized why as I continued down the ramp. Another door slid open automatically for us. Inside was a small pod with a giant control panel before the windshield. We were going to fly out of the capital.

"These pods can be programmed to go anywhere in Aldieria, that way you don't need a pilot in an emergency," Kieren said as he pushed past me and hurriedly turned on the engine. He turned off the voice command, glancing back at me nervously, before setting the coordinate by hand.

"Can't the government track these things?" I asked.

"Only if a transmitter is plugged in," he said, passing me again for a tiny metal door at the back. The pod began to hum, the engines warming up fast by the sound of it. I'd never flown before being arrested, and these pods were fast, I knew that much. Kieran pulled a black square out of the small compartment and laid it on the floor. He stomped on it until it broke into three scratched-up pieces. Then, he looked at me, something in his eyes changed. He let out a sigh as if preparing to do something risky.

Before I could defend myself, I was thrown onto my back by the force of take-off. A second later, he was on top of me. I let out a scream and tried to kick between his legs, but he pinned me down and wrenched my head to one side. Remembering the knife in my pocket, I focused instead on digging it out. I had just found it with my thumb and index finger when he shoved something sharp against my head. I screamed in pain, the feeling growing worse when he ripped the device from my skin and tossed it aside.

"Shit," he screamed when I swung the knife his way, the tip of the blade getting him just above the brow. "It's tracking us," he said, scrambling to his feet and smashing the device to dozens of glittering pieces with his heel. "Do me," he said, "quick." He laid on the ground next to me, taking a deep breath and turning to look towards the opposite wall. The device was a rectangle with a screen, dimly lit, that sat over the skin behind his ear. The space mine once inhabited still stung fiercely and I could feel blood seeping into the collar of my shirt.

"Here I go," I said, the words more for myself than for him. I used the edge of the knife to get under the device. He muffled his scream the best he could as I dug the four prongs from his flesh, blood running from the raw skin and into his hair. While he recovered from the ordeal, I used the butt of the knife to smash the screen apart.

"Where did you get a knife?" Kieran asked, lowering his

hand from the cut on his forehead and smearing blood down his temple.

"Marcus," I told him, "I stole it off him in a bar back in my village before the ceremony." Kieran shook his head.

"He didn't search you?" he asked.

"No, surprisingly," I said. I looked around the pod for anything I could use to clean up the mess of blood and found a first-aid kit clipped to the wall. I nearly lost my balance when I stood to retrieve it. I took out the supplies and laid them on the floor next to me after sitting across from Kieran.

"Sorry for jumping you," he told me, taking a wad of gauze and pressing it to the holes behind my ears. It stung, but I focused on his cut. It had mostly stopped bleeding, so I used an alcohol pad to clean off the remaining mess and then taped a gauze patch above his eye.

"Sorry for nearly shaving your eyebrow off," I told him, moving onto the still bleeding holes behind his ear.

"Shaving?" he said, "You could've poked my eye out." He winced when I pressed the gauze to his skin.

"I'm good with knives. If I had wanted to poke your eye out, I would've," I said. I knew what I was doing. He clearly understood all this Gallaterran technology better than I did. I needed him alive, but more than that, I wanted him with me. I'd never had a partner in crime. I'd been pick-pocketing soldiers for years and never had help, but Kieran and I needed the same things despite our huge differences. He was kind, noticing me on that prison floor with bold blue eyes seeing me at my worst when everyone else had abandoned me. I was suddenly a traitor, a terrorist, but Kieran placed himself beside me anyway.

I wiped away a fresh patch of blood and a new drop of scarlet replaced the thickness I'd swiped away. I watched the drop slide down the side of his neck and under the collar of his shirt, appearing again as a dark splotch spreading on the gray fabric. He swallowed as I began cleaning again, the muscles in his neck relaxing under my touch. I paused with my hand there as I felt the tension in my own body melt away at the realization of safety. It might just be temporary, but I was safer now than I'd been since Jacob died.

"That old woman did a good job with the Aldierian warrior hair," Kieran said, "It looks good." He glanced sideways at me, his expression boyish in comparison to the strong persona he'd worn during our time in prison. He bit his lower lip, chewing it between his teeth as he waited for my response. I wanted to tug it free with my own. I turned his face to mine and pressed my lips to his. They softened after just a second of the kiss and let it grow deeper. I took his bottom lip between mine before pulling away. He smirked and as I took in the single dimple that formed on his right cheek, I realized I had only met Kieran Grace four days ago. It might have felt like I knew him for years now, but still… Four days.

"God," I said, "I didn't mean to give you…" I felt my cheeks burn. He let out a little laugh that only made the dimple more noticeable.

"I can give it back if you want," he said. My entire body was warm now and I couldn't contain my smile. He leaned in and kissed me, his hands finding their way to the base of my neck. Mine were on his chest. I could feel the curve of the muscles under the fabric. I don't know how long we kissed, but I pulled away when my hand grazed the wound behind his ear.

"Let me finish," I said, wiping the scarlet smear from my fingers and unpackaging another alcohol wipe. He smiled the entire time I worked, not even wincing at the sting as I finished cleaning him up. I sat back on my hands once I'd taped the gauze to his skin. The room filled with the humming of the engine as we sped through the air, fast enough that the sky was just a blue and white blur as we moved.

"Do all Aldierians learn how to use knives like that?" Kieran asked. The question pulled me out of the aftershock from our kiss and back into the reality of our situation.

"I don't know," I said, "They didn't teach us anything about

Aldierians back in my village school." He looked away from the front window and at me in surprise.

"Wait. What do you mean, you don't know?" he asked, "You are Aldierian. It's why that old woman did your hair that way. It's how warriors wear it."

"I didn't know that until you told me. Yes, I'm Aldierian, but I was left in Jacob's forge as an infant. I didn't grow up with Aldierian culture." He gasped in disbelief, putting me on the defensive.

"I set the coordinates for the pod to stop in the Silent Sands. I thought you could get us to the East Sea and the Aldierians so they could help stop my father," Kieran said, "and you're telling me that you don't know the first thing about being Aldierian?"

"You never asked me," I said, "I thought you could get us there. You're the president's son. Don't you have some kind of insider knowledge about this stuff?"

"Hell no," he replied.

"Then why do you know so much about Aldierians?" I asked.

"Because I grew up getting caught looking up the truth," Kieran said, "My father thought he could beat it out of me and get me to see his vision by sending me to military schools and boot camps, but all it did was further prove that we're the ones who slaughtered them. The Aldierians aren't a threat to us, they just wanted us to respect and share their planet." I only knew the truth because Jacob told me all his conspiracy theories, not that I believed them at the time. He told me a lot of history about the Aldierians that I never learned in school, about how they lived in our cities in the east before we forced them to move out. He framed those battles much less victorious than school had, like we stole something and not that we had won it.

"We know that the East Sea is past the Silent Sands," I said, "We'll start there." He let out a sigh and nodded, surely feeling the daunting task ahead as heavily as I did. After a pause, he got to his feet and went to the control panel at the front of the pod.

"We still have about two days of flying," he said, going to a metal door against the wall. A twin-sized bed pulled down, complete with sheets and a wide pillow. He looked back at me and I could see in his eyes that he was going to offer it to me.

"I only slept on that stone floor for three days," I said, "You were there weeks longer." He shook his head, pulling the extra blanket from the foot of the bed and taking it to the opposite side of the pod. I didn't press him, sinking into the sheets a second later and feeling how sore my muscles were then. I could already feel my eyes growing heavy. My eyes were closed for not even a minute when I felt Kieran's body sink into the mattress behind me.

"I'm sorry I..." he whispered into my ear.

"I can give it back, if you want," I said. I didn't need to turn my head to know he was smiling. A second later, we were both laughing. I pulled his arm around my middle and we both melted into the softest bed I'd ever laid on and were asleep in minutes.

CHAPTER 4

was jostled awake. It was early, six according to the clock on the control panel. Out the front window, I could see the tan sand stretch towards the horizon and nothing more. I slipped Kieran's arm off my hip and pushed his shoulder until he woke.

"We landed," I said, "finally." I reached for my pants at the foot of the bed and quickly tugged them on. I was fumbling with the control panel when Kieran reached me, a single arm in the sleeve of his shirt when his hands kept me from pressing what I thought was the button for the door.

"That's the emergency button," he said, "press that and you'll send a message back to Gallaterra." I lowered my hands and, realizing now that I was barefoot, focused on finding my shoes while he worked. His lower back hung halfway out of his shirt, covered just a second later as he pulled his shirt the rest of the way on. It's not like I hadn't seen what he looked like by now. The pod had warmed up significantly, so much so that I woke yesterday to discover that I'd taken my pants off at some point in the night and tossed them halfway across the room. Kieran had been a gentleman about it, turning away when he caught me tiptoeing across the space for them. Another day and neither of us were embarrassed by our bodies. Kieran had no reason to be embarrassed as I had found out last night. He was sculpted like God had done it himself.

"What?" he asked. I hadn't realized he'd turned around until then. I wasn't normally the clumsy type, but I fumbled for my shoes as I tried finding an explanation.

"Damn you, Kieran Grace," I said after my brain failed me.

"What did I do?" he asked, looking for his shoes now.

"Nothing," I said, "and you better hope you keep it that way." My face burned, so I forced myself to focus on the laces of my boots. He snickered and began searching for his shoes.

"I know," he said, finally finding them under the bed, "You're good with knives." We finished dressing in our dirty clothes and then Kieran released the door. With a hiss that startled me, it began lowering. The sun pierced through the seam in the door and blinded me. I didn't recover until the door settled. There was nothing but sand. I led the way out of the pod, confirming that we were in the middle of a desert.

"I guess we walk from here," Kieran said when he met me outside. It took a moment for him to adjust, making me wonder if he'd ever been outside Gallaterra and its streets of steel.

"In what direction?" I asked. At least the device had a compass, something neither of us did. I remembered my history class from school, triggered maybe from the desert scene before us. Aldieria was particularly hard to navigate without technology. At least on Earth, the sun was reliable. On Aldieria, it changed positions every year and made it difficult to track if you didn't know its movements. I had written a paper about the subject for my senior year science project. "It's not much later than six," I said, "and the sun will rise from the west. The East Sea is that way." I pointed behind us and looked at Kieran. He closed his mouth and nodded.

"You're right," he said.

"Gallaterra isn't the only city with good education," I told him and started to walk around the pod. He followed me, sinking in the sand in a way only Gallaterrans ever did. I'd grown up playing in the Aldieran sand, trudging through it during the hottest seasons of the year, and running across its ridges on the rare occasion that some drunk patron at the bar caught me stealing. He adjusted quickly though, falling in stride with me just paces later.

"Last night, you told me about Jacob Riley," Kieran said, "So, what about the woman that asked him to watch over you, your birth mother?" I told him the same story Jacob had told me a thousand times. A woman ran into the forge after hours. He was just an apprentice then, so he was just as surprised as she was. She was in labor and asked him for a place to give birth without being discovered. She passed him the Ida stone he later gave me as a sign of good faith. It revealed the truth to him. She was Aldierian and on the run. She was lucky that she stumbled into the forge the night he was tasked with closing duties because the head blacksmith was far from sympathetic.

Jacob agreed to help without asking any questions. He helped her through labor and was there during my birth. He even bathed me and clothed me in his smock. The woman never told him her name and he had never thought to ask her. She told him to name me Kenna and that was all. He let her sleep after that. Jacob told me that he thought it was strange that she never asked him to do anything else. Before falling asleep, she had named me, told him to watch over me and not tell a soul about my heritage, and that was all. Jacob slept in the corner of the forge and when he woke to the sound of my crying, the woman was gone.

"I don't know anything about her," I said, "but you know more about her than I know about you." Kieran hesitated, long enough that he had to take double my steps to catch up. I could see in his profile that I had touched a nerve, but I wasn't sure if I had gone too far or not. My stomach felt heavy like I'd eaten rocks instead of nothing at all since we'd escaped. Finally, his body relaxed.

"I'm not my father's son," he said with a sigh.

"I'm sure somewhere inside his black heart, there's a place for you," I said, "You can't honestly believe that someone could cast his son out to his death." I thought about the arena, all the weapons so obviously placed there for his strengths.

"No," Kieran said, "I mean that I'm not his son. My mother had an affair." It was my turn to stop. Maybe that was the real reason Kieran wasn't featured on the posters of the first family. There was more against him than his rebellion against his father's politics.

"My father, the president," he said, "he must have found out right after I was born. I snuck all the records about a year ago. He had my biological father killed. He framed him for the fake terrorist attack on Valentia and had him executed. My biological father was an Aldierian sympathizer, but he hadn't orchestrated the attack. The whole thing had been planned by the president as an excuse to force the last of the Aldierians into the East Sea." I remembered the stories from history class. A series of bombs had exploded in Valentia the year I was born, killing hundreds. The reporters said it was a miracle more lives hadn't been lost. After our military forces marched further east than ever before and the Aldierians were forced into the sea, providing us with a sense of security we'd never had before. Well, so we thought.

"I'm sorry," I said. Kieran shrugged.

"He was an upcoming politician," he said, "He could've undone and exposed everything my father ever was."

"Why do you still call him your father?" I asked, unable to contain myself. It was disgusting what the president had done not just to the Aldierians, but to the planet and all the people who had left Earth centuries ago in hopes of a better future.

"He abused me and I'm sure he threatened my mother to keep her quiet," Kieran said, "but he's all I've ever known. He's not my father and I won't ever think of him that way, but he is... He's in that house with my mother and I wish... More than wishing I grew up somewhere else, I wish she could escape the way we did." He looked sideways at me. His expression was pained, but not sad the way you'd expect. It was like he had hope now that we were on our way. Maybe, he was right. Maybe, for now, being out here was enough.

"I'm sorry," I said, "I didn't mean to bring up bad memories." Kieran nodded, forcing a smile onto his face.

"No worries," he said, "We should be worried instead about what we should do next, aside from heading east." I knew what he meant. We hadn't eaten since breakfast the day of the battle and my stomach ached and my throat felt raw at the memories of the humble meal.

"Well, there are villages out here," I said. Kieran got a funny look on his face.

"You're thinking of the desert to the south. It's called the Silent Sands for a reason. Nothing lives out here," he said. I shook my head. Kieran hadn't done as much research as he thought. Little had been recorded about the villages in the east and that's because the Aldierians lived in the east, or they used to before they were driven into the East Sea.

"The villages in the desert aren't just sitting abandoned," I said, "Haven't you heard of the Conduit?" Kieran snorted.

"There's not a conduit out here," he said, "Any water those villages got was sent from the East Sea on ships. There weren't enough villages to even discuss building a conduit."

"Not that kind of conduit," I said. Clearly, he'd never heard of the religion. I only knew of it, because there was a small faction of them in Arro, missionaries that tried bringing the more conservative of us to their village in the desert.

"The Conduit of Christians from Earth was formed before Earth completely collapsed. It was supposed to be a way to honor God and keep living the word of the Bible even though all the biblical places were left back on Earth. It's not exactly the same religion as before. They reject most of our technology, so they wouldn't be getting any messages about us escaping Gallaterra," I told him, "And their largest village is west."

"Which is not east," Kieran said, pointing east as I started to walk.

"Trust me on this," I told him, "We need food and water. We won't make it to the East Sea at this rate. We'll die of thirst first. We aren't going to just come across water. It's like you said, there aren't any rivers or anything out here. We have to do this first before making our way any further east." He hesitated and I could tell that he knew I was right. I continued walking west, not pausing even when I heard the swish of his feet running across the sand to join me.

"Now that you brought up water..." he stared. My throat hurt as much as his surely did. I set my mind on the western horizon and focused on nothing else, worried that hallucinations would set in from lack of food and water and distract me from navigating.

We walked for hours under the blazing sun, both of us fading fast. I was glad when we came upon a farm. The house was small, maybe only a couple of rooms. A man was riding a camel, heading in the opposite direction ahead of us.

"Kieran," I said, looking back at him. His eyes met mine, but they were dead. A moment later, he was lying unconscious in the sand. There was no discussion now. We had to stop here. I ran towards the house, several of the camels behind a large enclosure looked in my direction. I knocked on the door several times, but no one answered. I tried opening it, but it was locked and there wasn't anyone else here besides me and a couple of dozen camels.

I unlocked the gate after befriending one of the smaller camels. I looped a rope around its neck and guided it back to the spot where Kieran was laying. The camel was trained for this, as I soon discovered. It knelt next to Kieran and with all the muscle I possessed, I draped him between the animal's neck and hump. I led the camel back to the house and once I had lowered Kieran into the shade next to the porch, I started looking for water.

The only source was a large pool just inside the enclosure.

Inside the attached shed, I found a leather pouch designed with an inner bladder for water. I hoped the camels were accustomed to people enough as I went to fill the sack. It was heavy, heavy enough that I knew we would have to take turns carrying it. I drank until I was full and then refilled the sack to the top and took it to Kieran. He was stirring, a moan coming out of his mouth before he opened his eyes and squinted under the sunlight.

"Here," I told him, lifting the spout to his mouth and tipping it before he was ready. He coughed a few times before accepting the water and drinking for a full minute. He took the pouch from me and sat it in his lap as he took in our surroundings.

"Where are we?" he asked, "How long was I out?"

"Not long. I found a farm, maybe a few miles from the main village. The man who lives here left on a camel, so it can't be far. He didn't look like he had anything with him," I said. I noticed the clothesline stretching from the corner of the house now as a light breeze came through. There was a large load of laundry nearly dry and just hanging there like welcoming flags.

"Is there something you could cover your hair with?" Kieran asked, "Red hair isn't exactly common, and it'll be a huge give-away if the word about us has come this far." I doubted that the technology-hating cult in the desert would hear about us within the day, but he was right about my hair giving us away. If someone came asking, I'd be easy to describe. Thankfully, I knew that the women in this cult covered their hair thanks to the missionaries I'd seen in my village. They wore silk scarves of all kinds of colors wrapped around their heads and tied in a variety of ways. The one that was known for casting disgusted looks at the girls on the way to school always wore hers tied in a kind of topknot I thought I might be able to recreate.

I found a couple of scarves draped at one end of the clothes-line. I decided to take the brown and hope that it served a little as camouflage over the brighter pink and yellow scarves. I chose a pale blue dress and a matching pair of opaque tights. I quickly pulled the dress and tights on before pulling down a pair of brown pants and a white shirt I thought would fit Kieran.

"We'll have to make do," I told him and handed off the clothes. He looked over me as I adjusted the ribbon around my waist. I turned my attention to the headwrap as he began checking the size of the new clothes against his body. It took me a couple of tries before I figured out how to contain my ponytail in the fabric. I was halfway done wrapping when Kieran pulled off his shirt. I'd seen him nearly naked every night we'd been together, but it always made my heart beat faster. He must have noticed me because he moved to the back of the house.

Shadow Kieran pushed his pants to his ankles and stepped out of them. His calves were rounder than I'd thought for a rich boy who didn't walk the town square the way the boys in my village did. He stepped into the new pants and tugged them upwards, angling his hips just so to get the fabric around his ass.

A curse slipped past my lips when the scarf slipped from my fingers and the entire thing was carried by the wind a few feet. I hurriedly stumbled in the sand to catch it, my face heating as I began rewrapping the scarf around my hair until I was left with just enough to tie a knot at the base of my neck. Just as I thought I avoided the embarrassment of getting caught staring, my eyes met Kieran's.

He came from behind the house in just the pants. He smirked and went to the far side of the clothesline for a different shirt, this one an army green. He neatly draped the white one back on the line and I knew now that he was making a show of the display just for me.

"Don't pretend to be modest, Kieran Grace," I said, making sure every wisp of hair was tucked into the headwrap. He snorted and slipped into the clean shirt.

"Don't pretend not to look," he said. I felt my face heat. "Where are you going to stash that knife?" he asked when I lifted the retractable weapon from our small stash of belongings on the ground.

"In my boot, like a proper lady," I said, dropping it into my right boot. He smirked and shook his head. Kieran refilled our water and slung it over his back while I ditched our dirty clothes in what looked like a trash bin in the corner of the shed. Looking as clean as we could without actually showering, we started the direction the farmer had. It took us just thirty minutes to reach the outskirts of the village. The entire thing was a complex made of stone walls and made me hesitate a moment as my thoughts went back to being imprisoned in Gallaterra. Those walls were there for a purpose, either to keep the people in or keep undesirables out. I tried to remember that we had come from worse, and I led the way towards the entrance.

It was an unguarded archway with the words, "All are welcome thanks to God" etched into the stone above the village name of Ariadne. A large road stretched before us, lined with tents much like the merchants that set up shop in my home village. There were women selling scarves, wrapped similarly to mine, I was pleased to see. A number sold fruits and vegetables, and in a courtyard off to the left was a man before a wooden cross who spoke to a small group of people.

"Okay," Kieran said, "Now what?" I wasn't sure. The sun was hanging just above the top of the furthest wall. We had just hours before all the people along the streets went home for the night. Two people walking the streets would surely draw attention.

"Maybe there's a hotel or something," I said, looking further down the road. Kieran elbowed me and I looked up at him and then in the direction of the man making his way towards us. He was dressed in a white shirt and tan pants and had a large cross dangling from a chain around his neck.

"Let me guess," he said, "You're from Ro'al." Kieran masked his surprise quickly with a smile.

"What gave us away?" he asked. They shook hands and the man inclined his head to me instead of taking my hand.

"Your uncle has been expecting you. He said he never thought his brother would return since he left the compound and when he said you wanted a Conduit blessing on your union… I was honored to be chosen," the man said. Union? Kieran laced his fingers with mine and raised the back of my hand to his lips.

"I've always wanted to meet my uncle," he said, "and I only want us to have the best start that we can in our marriage together." He winked at me. The man was too excited to notice my surprise because I'm sure it was obvious to Kieran.

"Your uncle is a good man, Zander," the priest said.

"Can you take us to him?" I asked, "I'm sure he's waited on us long enough, don't you think, Zander?" Kieran smirked, a funny look I recognized now thanks to all the times he poked fun at me.

"Of course," the priest said, "He has a room for you both. Now, I know you've already married, so it is within your marital right to share a room, but I do ask that we do the blessing after dinner just to keep a sacrament with God."

"Absolutely," Kieran said, "I swear on the Bible that aside from a kiss here and there, we have been chaste despite our marriage according to Gallaterran law." I elbowed him as soon as the priest turned to lead the way.

"Then you have kept more than a few promises to God," the priest said. We followed him down a side street and past one last road of merchants before we encountered another archway. This one had the family name "Reed" engraved over the top. Houses lined the road beyond and led to a large estate at the end.

"Seems like my uncle has done better than I thought," Kieran said. The priest began telling us about each house as we passed, drawing attention from a few. We found out that they were all members of the Reed family. This was a compound and Zander Reed's uncle was at the head. The estate was two stories tall with windows that cast a ghostly glow over the empty courtyard. A dinner party was already in full swing inside. There were people everywhere and in minutes, it seemed as though they were all pressed together in the large entryway to greet us. We met more aunts and uncles and so many cousins that I could barely keep up the charade much longer.

"Let me get a look at you," a man's booming voice filled the space. The crowd parted and a thickset man with a dark beard pulled Kieran into a tight hug. "You're taller than I'd expected," the man said, "You must take after your mother. My brother Paul was a short guy, bless him." The man led us past the dozens of guests and into a dining room. A large table was set up buffet-style and empty plates and glasses were already stacked next to the sink.

"-Not your only uncle Roger," the man continued his speech, "No, I got the best of the Reed genes. Your father always was the soft and kind-hearted one though. It's not a surprise that he let that Godless woman steal him from the flock. I am so thankful that you saw the truth and want to rejoin our family here. Take a plate and help yourselves. I'll come and get you for the ceremony in a moment."

Kieran and I both accepted the plates and stood in awe for a moment before laughing. The food drew my attention first. I filled my plate twice with turkey and potatoes and rich dressings and casseroles. I ignored how heavy I felt until I noticed the slight bulge of my belly. If I ate any more, people would wonder if our upcoming nuptials were inspired by more scandalous reasons than our love for one another.

The party seemed to grow quieter once we both settled into seats in a corner, my sore legs like jelly once I relaxed. Uncle Roger returned and led us back through the house, most of the people were gone now and we found out soon that they had all converged in the backyard. The stone pathways were broken up by marble fountains and green bushes, metal torches evenly spaced out casting a warm glow over the guests.

The Reed family were gathered around the largest white veil I'd ever seen. It covered almost the entire back patio. The priest was waiting for us at one corner. All the women in the family knelt to take an edge of the fabric. Together, they brought their arms up and the veil floated upwards to create a beautiful dome above the patio. The priest motioned us both forward and we walked to the center. As the priest joined us and told me to take Kieran's hands, the veil floated down around us. He removed a red, satin scarf and wrapped it around our hands.

"This symbolizes two bloodlines becoming one," the priest said, "two families converge to make one. Out of love, new life is formed. Just like this veil, may heaven clothe you in righteousness and shield you from harm. Zander, state your intentions." Kieran looked anxiously back at me now. I expected him to devote his life to me, express his undying love for me, all the classic words I'd heard uttered at the few weddings I'd attended.

"You're not just a pretty face. I've never met anyone with the intelligence and the boldness to stand up for what's right in the face of the ultimate punishment. Through everything you've endured, your entire life… I know that I can never measure up to everything good and kind and strong that you are, but I promise that I will help you in every adventure. Take me with you on every grueling quest so that I can use my privilege to bring just a little more hope to those who need it most. I swear to you that I will help you to…" Kieran paused, glancing at the priest for a moment before looking back at me, "I swear to you that I will help you to heaven. You may be stubborn, but I am a man of my word. You may not always want me and I know I ask a lot of your trust, but I pledge all of my own to you now. I trust you with my body and my heart. If these are our last days on Aldieria… I can't imagine spending them with anybody else."

"Genevieve, you may state your intentions now," the priest said. I wasn't aware of how tight my grip on him was until now. Kieran made a real promise to me, not some scripted spiel about love and marriage. He pledged his body and heart and his entire life to get me to the Aldierians and to do whatever it is I will do once I get there. Why not just spout the usual flowery drivel? Why the sudden passion?

"Zander," I started, clearing my throat and looking straight into his blue eyes, "I swear to you that I will keep you close to me always. There is no one I trust more in the entire universe. I know it hasn't been that long, but I feel like we've lived a whole life together already. I wish I could explain it better, but you… I think I need you, Zander Reed," I looked up from our hands and straight into his face now. There was something sincere, yet strong in his eyes. From the first moment I looked into their deep blue pools, I was pulled under and when I went into that arena on my own to face my death, I felt like I came back out as a new person, baptized almost. Somehow, I feel more like myself because of him. "I'm not that good at making speeches. I think that's it." I looked to the priest and hoped I had said enough. He smiled at me and continued with his speech about love conquering all, inserting Bible passages conservative enough that Kieran and I barely masked our cringing.

"With a kiss, and the honor bestowed by our God, may heaven bless this union," the priest said. The courtyard erupted in applause and whistles. I hesitated before raising my lips to Kieran's. All the awkwardness I had felt at his words faded now. Everything about him felt right, so easy.

After making our way from under the veil, the priest served a communion of bread and wine and then we were free to go to our rooms. Uncle Robert showed us the wing, which consisted of a sitting room, a small office, and a single master bedroom and bathroom all to ourselves. The bedroom was larger than Jacob's whole house was and the bathroom had a shower and a tub with jets. I went to the bathroom to shower first while Kieran asked if more food could be sent to our room.

"Send two of everything. I want to try it all," he told a confused-looking Uncle Robert. I laughed and ducked into the bathroom. Under the warm spray of water, I relaxed for the first time in days. I stayed in the warmth long after I'd finished washing, not emerging until Kieran knocked on the door and called out, "save some for me."

I ate another round of dinner while he showered, amazed that I could still be hungry. Anything that could be saved, I wrapped back up in the tin-foil it had come to us in and stuffed it inside a silk laundry bag I found in the closet. Kieran opened the door and walked into the bedroom out of a cloud of steam. I opened the large bay window to chase it away and sat on the sill with my legs crossed. A firework exploded outside and startled me, red sparks lighting the sky.

"Can I braid your hair?" Kieran asked behind me.

"You know how to braid?" I asked, turning to look at him. He handed me the strips of fabric the Aldierian woman had used back in prison to tie my hair up the first time. I sat it on the seat next to me and turned back to watch as more fireworks exploded against the sky.

"Not all of my family members are monsters," he said, combing his fingers through my damp hair. "My sister taught me years ago," he said and started twisting the hair on the right side of my head.

"Jacob taught me when I was little," I said, "He used to make jewelry out of the extra strips of leather in the forge. He could do all kinds of braids. I can hardly do any on my hair." Kieran laughed.

"I tried growing my hair out once when that trend went around when we were like twelve. My father ambushed me with scissors and did a hack job. Kinda forced me to get it buzzed short," he said. I couldn't imagine him with hair longer than he had. It just wouldn't suit him. He finished the first braid and moved to a second on the opposite side of my head, two pigtails.

"I know we probably won't ever get a chance to be normal again," I said, "but what would you do for the rest of your life?" It was a big question to ask, though I wasn't surprised that he had an answer ready for me. Kieran always seemed to know what to do.

"I want to be a scientist. I love history and everything about how the world works the way it does. I want to study planets and help create cleaner fuel than the Ida stones, especially after learning about how they are destroying Aldieria. I would invent something that doesn't create any waste. They'd probably name it after me, Kieran, not Grace. Maybe I'd change my name or just take my wife's maiden name when we marry," he said with a laugh. Kieran Riley. The thought made my head feel light on my shoulders.

"And you'd live happily ever after with your dog and two blonde children," I said.

"Yeah," he said, "maybe one's a redhead though. You can never be sure." We both laughed. I let him finish the last braid in silence. He wove the two pigtails together, using the remaining strips of fabric to tie them in place at the nape of my neck. The last of the firework display faded to gray smoke and the Reed family cheered for the last time tonight, the ant-sized figures saying their goodbyes and scattering down the main road.

"Kieran, why did you say all of that during the blessing?" I asked, "You could've said anything."

He sat down next to me, facing our room instead of the stars. "I know that, but I meant what I said. I made that promise because I'd rather be a wanted man with you than what I was before." I felt light, the air in my lungs thin from holding my breath.

"We may only have a few days or just hours before we're caught," I said, "you would rather spend them on the run with a nasty Aldierian than taking down your father from the inside?" He snickered.

"I've never been this free in my whole life and I never would've been if it hadn't been for you and that arena. I want to walk this path as far as we can. Life can't happen behind bars, not really," he said, "and you showered." I slapped his hand away when he tugged at my braids, hardly able to hold in my laughter.

"I don't know if I can last even five more minutes with you," I said.

"Whatever," Kieran said, his boyish smile fading as he looked at me. His hand slid across the bench towards mine. "Five minutes is enough for now," he said. His fingertips brushed mine before he looked out the window again. He looked at peace, like any other boy I'd gone to school with and so much more.

I scooted closer to him so that our arms brushed, close enough that he looked back at me, surprised to find that we were just inches from each other. I could see more in him than before, like when you stare up at the stars and notice a constellation that has been there the whole time just waiting to be noticed. Different than the rest, but just as beautiful.

His lips came down on mine, or maybe I raised mine to his. It didn't matter, because neither of us protested. His hands ran over the braids trailing down the nape of my neck and down to my waist as I let mine comb through his blonde hair. A particularly loud firework exploded just above our window and a lady let out a hysterical scream of surprise. Laughter erupted just below as the woman began scolding whoever lit the firework. We both pulled away, all smiles as the humor relaxed the moment and we returned to stargazing, keeping our hands entwined the entire time.

CHAPTER 5

Falling asleep had been easy but waking up from the dreams of a perfect future was hard. Kieran and I gathered our sack of food and our water bag, and we crept out of the house without any trouble. We passed by a young couple on our way to the main road and I wondered briefly if they were the real Zander and Genevieve Reed.

When we got to the main road, it was full of people. Shop owners were setting up for the day and posted at the entrance were five soldiers in their silver suits, shining under the morning sun.

"Kieran," I said, slowing my pace. Two of the soldiers remained at the entrance while the other three started down the street. I steered us closer to the line of fruit stands. One of the soldiers approached a woman under a tent full of scarves. He pulled two papers from his weapon's holster. Photos, maybe?

"I see them. We can't stay here. The Reeds may know we weren't who we said we were by now," Kieran said, his tone growing more urgent as he spoke. "I don't know what to do."

"We're going to walk right past them," I said. Kieran tried to stop next to me, but I wrapped my arm around his and pulled him along.

"How?" he asked.

"I'll take care of them both," I said, "You gave me your trust." He let out a deep breath. I led us past a tent of cacti and onto the sidewalk between the tents and the storefronts.

"What do you need?" Kieran asked. I picked my right foot up a little higher as we walked so I could slide the retractable knife from my boot. I hid it just underneath the sleeve of my dress.

"Another knife," I whispered, "two more if we can get them." A moment later, Kieran snagged a paring knife from a cutting board at one side of a tent selling melons. He handed it off to me as we passed the first cutting station and I hid it inside my other sleeve. One of the women stocking the tallest display looked our way before one of the soldiers demanded her attention.

"Shit," Kieran said. I didn't stop him this time as he quickened the pace. He snagged a large butcher knife from the last cutting station and tried handing it off to me when the guard yelled.

"Terrorists! In the melon tent."

I launched a melon at him before he could move. He ducked and let it soar by, the melon exploding with a squelch against the tent post. The soldier sent a knife flying towards us and I pulled Kieran down to his knees behind a display. The knife cut through the center of a melon on the display rack and lodged into the wooden crate behind us. I plucked it free from the wood and sent it whizzing right back at him, hitting him full in the chest as the remaining two soldiers charged towards the tent.

"Whatever you do, don't throw that knife," I told Kieran as I bolted behind the next tent and sprinted down the sidewalk, hoping he kept close behind me. I saw the feet of the next soldier behind a tent flap before he struck, swinging a tent post at me. I ducked under it and turned around, sinking the paring knife into his gut before he could even face me. I sliced him open and left him to bleed into the sand, urging a stunned Kieran to run.

"The two at the entrance have stunning poles," Kieran said. I saw them now too, both on the defense and waiting for us to come to them. I was pretty confident that I could take one, but probably not two with stunning poles. Could Kieran handle the other while I took on the first?

Not seeing another option, I sprinted to the front. The woman was tall and her reach was longer than I'd expected, forcing me to dodge when I wanted to jab. I was light on my feet, but I didn't gain any ground and the thought of the last soldier just behind us spurred me to work fast. Kieran let out a yell and ran to the second, a man no larger than he was, with the butcher knife held high. Before he could even bring it downwards, the man drew something across Kieran's middle. For a split second, I thought it had missed him, but Kieran screamed in pain and went down to his knees.

Before the soldier could make a killing blow, I sent the paring knife spinning. It sunk into his neck and I backed up to avoid the woman's stunning pole. Kieran yelled for me to duck and I did as I was told. He threw the butcher knife and I heard a muffled scream just feet away, the last soldier crumpling to the sand behind me. I had the retractable knife in my right hand now and I aimed, jabbing it as hard as I could into the woman's stomach.

"Let's go," I said and ran to help Kieran before I was even sure the woman was dead. He had his hand clapped over a spot in his chest, a red splotch spreading across his green shirt. I tugged him to his feet and he groaned the entire trek past the arches. Four large dune riders with domed tops were parked just outside. My heart sunk as I saw them. You could comfortably seat four soldiers under the canopies.

"They're outside," the woman screamed, confirming what I'd feared. I helped Kieran into the front seat of the nearest dune rider and began searching under the remaining seats for a first aid kit or more weapons. I found the former as we began coasting away, gaining such speed that I had to brace myself against the back of the seats to keep from sliding from the flat top. Four more soldiers ran from the arches and got into two dune riders, both starting their chase yards too close for comfort.

"Can you lose them?" I asked Kieran after minutes of speeding.

"Where?" he asked, pointing to the sand around us. We were out in the open now. So long as we didn't run out of fuel, we could continue racing, but as soon as we ran out it would be two against four. Kieran was likely too injured to even try and fight.

Something to the left of one of the dune riders drew my attention. A tan-colored animal leaped onto the dune rider, sending it crashing into the ground. Sand exploded onto the second. It swerved out of the way, but grazed the top of a hill and lost control. It rolled several times, a soldier flying out of the top and into the air too high for survival. It finally settled in the sand upside down.

"Dune dog," Kieran said.

"Are you sure?" I asked, turning to face the front of the dune rider. A large Aldierian wolf slammed its paws into the nose of our dune rider. Kieran and I ejected out the front. Sand scraped painfully up and down my arms and legs as we slid across the ground. I stopped just feet away from Kieran who was clutching at his bleeding chest with his face screwed up in pain. I heard the snarl behind us and I scrambled to my feet, feeling helpless with just my retractable knife held before me.

"Kenna, don't move," Kieran said between groans. The dog was large, one of five that were now closing in on us. The one just a yard from us was the largest, its body covered in dusty short hair with large, pointed ears that folded down against his head as he skulked towards us. I held both hands up in surrender, not sure how to get out of this. No one had ever told me what to do when faced with a pack of Aldierian wolves. He sniffed the air between us and his posture changed. He shrunk a little more, his teeth not nearly as exposed as he scurried forward.

A squeak escaped me when he pressed his wet nose against

my hand and inhaled so forcefully that my fingers slipped into a nostril. He nudged my hand again with a whimper and I relaxed a little. I reached out to his downcast head, the entire time chanting in my mind. Please go away. Don't hurt us and go away.

My hand was in his fur for just a moment before he turned and ran, taking with him the other four large dogs in a shower of sand. I stood, stunned, with my right hand still raised. Kieran let out a gasp behind me and I remembered the first aid kit I found earlier. I searched the area and found it half-buried in the sand where the dog stood.

"What hurts?" I asked, sinking to my knees next to him.

"Where all the blood is, Kenna," Kiera said. I cut open the front of his shirt with a pair of scissors and relaxed once I saw the extent of the cut. It was almost a foot long across his chest and just deep enough to need suturing, but the bleeding had mostly stopped now.

"Such a smartass," I said with relief and slowed my pace as I looked over the contents of the kit. My hands still shook as I rummaged for something to close the wound. After manipulating it a bit, I decided it wouldn't do anything more than scar if left open. So, I cleaned it with every available solution and made sure to wrap it as tight as I could.

"Don't get it dirty," I told him.

"Aye-aye, captain," he said. "tell me I'll at least have a cool scar after this. It hurt enough that it has to scar, right?"

I laughed, more out of relief that he was fine than at his concern. I kissed the top of his head and stood up, pulling him to his feet with both arms.

We gathered our things and checked to see if any of the dune riders worked. Not a single one hummed to life, the one we'd commanded too smashed apart in the front to even have a distinguishable control panel.

"I guess we'll walk and hope we have food and water for the trip," Kieran said. Knowing we only had a limited amount of time before the scorching days turned to frigid nights, we started walking and only went twenty minutes before spotting a shining blip on the horizon.

"Are you seeing something right there?" I asked, pointing at the shiny button in the sand.

"That pod, yes," Kieran said. We exchanged brief looks before sprinting the best we could in the thick sand. My excitement faded when we got close enough to see that it was our pod, the one we'd escaped on. We had simply come full circle.

"This doesn't help us at all," I said, "The most we get is a safe place to sleep unless another troop of soldiers finds us here." Kieran shook his head, his excitement growing.

"No. No, this is just what we need," he said, "I can take the fuel from that dune rider and we could use it to get as far as we can to the East Sea. I doubt it will get us there, but it will save us some time. All I have to do is set new coordinates." The idea of relaxing while the ship did the traveling was enough to convince me to at least try moving the fuel.

Kieran knew enough about the pod to find the fuel compartment quickly. He decided it would take both of us to carry the fuel and likely the rest of the day to walk the thirty minutes with it depending on weight. Once we walked back to the wreckage, I helped Kieran dismantle the correct hatch and remove the fuel tank. It was just the size of a large backpack, but it easily weighed fifty pounds. Kieran was glad to find out that it was mostly full.

We took turns carrying it, Kieran making most of the trek himself. We both sat inside the shade of the pod until near sunset to regain our strength. My legs felt like jelly as I helped him fill the tank. To our relief, the pod came on with a simple press of a button. I pulled down the bed and kicked off my shoes as Kieran set the new coordinates for the East Sea.

"The coordinates put us five days away," he said.

"Five days isn't all that long," I said. Kieran looked back at me from the control panel, disappointment on his face.

"That's five days if we travel by pod," he said, "We only have enough fuel to make it maybe a day."

"Can we go at super-speed?" I asked, knowing it would still mean a long hike on foot.

"If we go at super speed, as you put it, we would be sick for days," he said, "That kind of speed is meant for short bursts. Even a few minutes of it is enough to turn your stomach." It had taken us a day to find and gather the food we had. I wasn't too keen on the idea of throwing it all up.

Kieran finished setting the pod and joined me on the bed as we began moving, rising into the clouds and away from the sand below. He raised the hem of his shirt again to look at the bandage. I let my hand rest against my own chest as I watched him inspect his, feeling the lump of the pendant under the fabric. I wondered what it was about the Aldierians that made Ida stones glow. They didn't do that on their own.

"Why can Aldierians use the Ida stones and other people can't?" I asked. Kieran lowered his shirt again and shrugged.

"I tried finding that answer in the libraries in Gallaterra and I never found it," he said, "but Aldierians can use the stones to communicate through their minds. Pretty cool, right?"

"What? You mean it's like their own device but from nature?" I asked. He smirked, clearly excited by the information.

"Pretty much, but the Ida isn't destroying them to power their cities like Gallaterra is."

Destroying them. Something about that seemed familiar. I wanted to ask Kieran if there was more to just destroying Ida stones for energy, but he began talking before I got a chance.

"You can talk to other people by touching them, but only as long as you possess the stone. I don't know if it works on all living things or…" he was staring at my chest now, the spot where the necklace disappeared under the dress. He turned a light shade of pink and focused on untying his shoes when I caught him.

"I wanted the dune dogs to go away," I said, "When I

touched the big one, it took off. Maybe it works on any living thing." I reached out and touched his hand, feeling a little silly as I let my first thought come to the front of my mind.

You can look at them. It's not a big deal.

Kieran sat straight up, shock written all over his face. My entire body grew hot with embarrassment. I knew I wanted to say it. I wanted to tell him a million things, but I hadn't wanted to tell him *that*. I mean, not really. I'd never say it out loud. Kieran was laughing now, bright red in the face and the tips of his ears.

"I'm sorry. I shouldn't laugh," he said, "and I shouldn't be looking either."

"We change in front of each other every night," I said, "Don't be embarrassed." I wasn't shy about nudity or sexuality, even though I'd never had sex before. We get the sex talk in elementary school and I got my period earlier than most of my friends, so I was well acquainted with my body. Kieran though looked back at me a little anxiously. He stole a glance at my chest again, relaxing a little when he saw me watching. I slid my hand across the bed to him and he met me halfway, curling his fingers around mine. I remembered the feel of those fingers in my hair, his warm breath on my neck as he worked on the braids. He must have too because we were suddenly a foot closer than before.

"You know," I told him, "I've heard that beds are for more than just sleeping." He blushed and my words snapped him out of the trance. He let go of my hand and scooted to the foot of the bed, shaking his head.

"Believe me. I want to," he said.

"It's okay. I haven't ever either…" I said, my chest growing heavy. Why did I even bring it up? "Forget I said anything," I said.

"No. No, it's okay, Kenna," he said, hesitating a moment before scooting a little closer again. He let out a deep breath and relaxed. "I didn't mean… I really want to. What I mean is, that I want to know you first. We've only known each other for a little while now but it also feels like I've known you forever somehow, but I still… I don't want to just do it like…" He didn't have to finish for me to understand. The ceremony last night and everything we shared felt so real. Still, though, was it too soon to really know him? I felt like I did, especially after fighting for both our lives, but was it truly possible?

"Do you think that you can see things I want you to see? Like, if I can use the Ida stone to talk to you through my mind, maybe I can use it to show you memories," I said, offering my hand again. After a moment, he took it and I laid back on the bed with my feet dangling from one side. I closed my eyes and I focused on the first memory that meant something to me, meant enough that sharing it with just anyone would be embarrassing. As soon as I started to remember what it felt like to get jumped by that man and have to go to elementary school without the only pair of shoes I owned, I heard Kieran gasp. He laid back on the bed beside me, turning his head to look at me.

"Why didn't you tell anyone?" he asked. When my teacher asked me where my shoes were, I told him I lost them. I managed to hide the truth from Jacob, or at least I thought I had at the time. The first day of school was the only time I ever got a new pair of shoes. It didn't dawn on me until I was older that he lied about the Christmas bonus that supposedly enabled him to buy me another new pair of shoes.

Thinking about Jacob made my skin go cold. I remembered the hopelessness I felt when I surrendered on the steps of the community center, Don Marcus holding Jacob to his chest with a dagger at his throat. Tears slipped out of the corners of both my eyes as I remembered the sight of Jacob crumpling to the ground, the bloody sword sliding from his back. I opened my eyes again when I felt Kieran's finger wipe my temple. He didn't say a word and I'm glad for it. It wouldn't matter anyway.

As I remembered more things about Jacob, trying to focus instead on the Christmas dinners and sparring sessions in the forge, I realized that there was a giant silver lining in all of this. After his death and my arrest, I wouldn't have survived prison without Kieran. I wouldn't have known what to do, even if I had survived the arena without him. I hadn't grown up Aldierian. Jacob was all I had before. More than the device outing me to the entire nation and Jacob dying, my life, everything that I am now, was so different because I met Kieran Grace.

My cheeks were wet now that I stopped transferring the memories and I must have made all of my emotions clear using the Ida stone because his expression had changed. It was intense. He looked straight into my face with such desire that it made my stomach clench with excited nerves.

"Forget everything I just said," he said. He cupped the side of my face and brought his lips down to mine. We fumbled with the buttons and zippers of our clothes, but everything felt instinctual once we were free of the Conduit garb. It was strange in a good way, like discovering something earth-shattering. When we laid back down to rest, the stars were beaming down on us from the front window of the pod.

"Do you feel like you know me now, Kieran Grace?" I asked. He elbowed me, smirking.

"In more ways than one," he said, folding both hands over his stomach and letting out a deep breath. He kept his eyes on the windshield, a giddy look on his face that had nothing to do with the stars.

"They're beautiful," I said. The elation faded just a little as he came out of his thoughts and glanced at me.

"Yeah. Yeah, you're right," he said and looked back at the window, "You can't see them very well with all the lights in Gallaterra, not like this anyway." I snuggled a little closer to him, resting my head against his bare chest. He relaxed his own against my forehead and snaked his arm around my waist. We laid like that for a long time and I nearly drifted off to sleep at the sound of his breathing.

"I think it's my turn to share now," he said. I was so curious that I almost gave in, but the soreness I felt growing in my muscles won out.

"Tomorrow," I said, "I'm not done enjoying the present yet." He smiled, kissed my forehead, and returned his gaze to the stars. I watched the specks of light zip by for just a moment before relaxing into a dream of normalcy, Kieran, and a city by the sea.

CHAPTER 6

t took much more time for Kieran to tell me all of his stories than it had for me to do so using the Ida stone. He told me all about his parents, his three sisters, and his brother. His sisters had both married rich, one marrying a politician and becoming a doctor and the other marrying a lawyer and becoming one herself. His brother was the prized jewel of the family, already a lieutenant in the army and earning two awards for valor.

He told me about his childhood, from the few times he could remember receiving his father's praise, to the time he took the fall for his eldest sister, which resulted in a beating that made his body tense from memory. Not all his memories were grim. He had a lot of special moments with his mother. She was kind and countered his father's powerful rule with compassion and mercy. He spent most of the day telling me about her.

"I want to be the one to do it," Kieran told me as he started eating the last of our food from the Conduit blessing meal.

"Do what?" I asked him. He sandwiched the remaining pieces of ham between a roll.

"Take down my father," he said, "We find the Aldierians, explain everything, and we go take down my father in Gallaterra with their help. That's the plan, right?" I guess we'd never talked about it before, but yeah. That was what we had to do. It was that or continue running forever.

"Okay," I said, "but I want to be there when it happens." He nodded and we raised our ham sandwiches in a toast.

It was nearly evening when the pod's autopilot system alerted us that we were out of fuel. We began descending slowly, prompting Kieran to go to the controls to make sure we wouldn't land anywhere public. It didn't look much different than the last time we landed, sand as far as I could see from the front window and not much else. We made sure the pods were secure and settled in for the night, as it was too late to try walking anywhere.

My stomach ached the next morning as we get ready to leave the safety of the pod. Kieran's expression dimmed when he handed the water bag off to me and I could see why as soon as I took it from him. There was just enough water for me and nothing more. We exchanged nervous glances before I finished the bag and slung it across my shoulder.

"Any idea how far from any towns we are?" I asked him as he finished checking the cabinets in the pod for anything we might need. We tucked the first aid kit inside the laundry bag that held our food before last night. He opened two of the compartments beneath the control panel and found a map.

"I can use the coordinates in the pod's system and find where we are on the map," he said, moving back to the bed. I helped him flatten one side of the map over the sheets. He went back to the control panel to search for our location. I could narrow it down a little just from the map. We flew east from Gallaterra for several days. Small dots represented the Conduit villages in the Silent Sands, one of them labeled Ariadne. From there, we had flown almost exactly twenty-four hours more eastward.

"Here," Kieran said, placing his finger over the spot I was eyeing. I looked around for anything to mark it with, resorting to pricking a tiny hole through the map with the end of a safety pin from the first aid kit. I felt a glimmer of hope as I realized we were closer to the East Sea now than Gallaterra.

"Do you think Grace will have soldiers follow us that far?" I asked.

"They sent five soldiers to Ariadne," Kieran said.

"I know that, but we have a few options here and the likelihood of us being arrested is higher in one than the other," I said, pointing at the map. We were still pretty far into the desert. We had no food or water and it will still take us weeks to get to the East Sea. We had to stop somewhere for food and water and possibly another change of clothes since the soldier I stabbed likely survived the attack to describe us.

"I see what you're saying now," Kieran said, pointing to the largest dot on the map. "We can walk to the city or we can go a little further and stop in Elien, which would have a whole lot less policing. We have to go to Elien. We can't risk going to another city."

"I agree, but if we aren't careful and make good time then we risk not having enough water to make it there," I said, "We have to figure in the travel time, yes, but there's also the heat and water lost through exercise." Kieran relaxed a little.

"You're right, but we have to try going further," he said. I wanted to ask if he thought there would be soldiers looking for us, but I was already sure there would be. He's the president's son and he was with an Aldierian. He could potentially give important information to Gallaterra's enemies. That part mattered more than his relationship with President Grace.

"Okay," I said, folding up the map and tucking it into the band of fabric wrapped around my waist. "We better start walking then," I said, "and hope for a breeze."

There was no breeze. The sun pounded down on us so hot that Kieran's neck was turning bright red by the minute before me. I wrapped the scarf around my head and neck to keep from getting too burnt. It was a terrible balance of sweltering under fabrics or burning exposed skin. As we walked late in the afternoon, I pulled off the Conduit dress I was wearing and adjusted the long-sleeve undershirt.

"Here," I said, tossing the fabric over his shoulder, "Put that over your head. Your neck looks like it's ready to blister." Kieran draped the fabric over his head. He looked back at me and smirked, his expression changing fast to horror. He let out a yell of pain and fell onto his back, bringing his knees to his chest and scooting backward. I jumped back as well, only seeing what got him just in time.

The fangs of the serpent stopped a foot from where I had been standing moments before. I'd never seen a snake like this, but I'd heard about them from the merchants in our village. It was no bigger than a water snake, the scales across its back rigid and the color of the sand around it. It coiled up, ready to strike again if either of us ventured closer. He flicked his tongue into the air, the wide scales along its body rising and looking strangely like plates of armor.

The merchants said that these snakes like to burrow partway into the sand and wait on prey to wander past. When it was in striking distance, it would sink its teeth in. It was a snake you didn't want around and a hard one to kill thanks to its reinforced body and scales that were as sharp as razor blades and coated in the same fatal poison contained in their fangs. My racing heart nearly got away from me at the thought of Kieran being injured.

"Don't move," I said, trying to remember what the merchants told the children in the village to do if they found one while playing. I couldn't remember, but I knew that you didn't want to make sudden movements regardless of the type of snake.

"What? You plan to win a staring contest with it?" Kieran asked. I wasn't sure what to do, but the snake quickly slithered away a moment later and was six feet from us before I could give it much more thought.

"Did it bite you?" I asked him. Kieran sat up, his hand going to his ankle. There were two small holes punched into his skin and a small pool of scarlet forming in the sand beneath him.

"It's really not bad," Kieran said.

"That snake is poisonous," I said, my body going cool despite the blazing sun above. Kieran's face lost most of its color.

"Are you serious?" he asked. I didn't explain any further, already going to work on his ankle.

"Kieran, I think we need to go to the city," I said. Kieran shook his head.

"We've walked a whole day and the map says just one more day…"

"You may not have a day," I said, "You may not even have an hour." I wish I hadn't yelled at him now as I realized he too was beginning to panic. We'd been corralled into an arena for the only purpose of fighting to the death and yet survived. Dying from a tiny bite would be the dumbest way for our journey to end. I could feel my breath hitch in my chest as I thought it through. I couldn't lose him. I didn't know what I'd do next. I would continue to the East Sea, but then what? Kieran was the diplomat. He was going to be the spokesperson. I was never good in front of a crowd and I wouldn't know what to say.

"Okay," Kieran said, his voice surprisingly even. "We go to the city" He gave me a firm nod, but I could tell it was for my benefit only. He was as scared as I was. I worried just how far we were from Lyle. It could be an hour. It could be two. Kieran may not even have thirty minutes. I swallowed the thought and got to my feet.

"How do you feel?" I asked him as he rose. He started to walk ahead of me as if he'd never been injured at all.

"I feel fine," he said, "Maybe it works slow." I followed him, every step feeling like mere inches as we walked towards the skyscrapers in the distance. My muscles felt weak as I calmed down the best I could, my heels chafing against the back of my boots. I remembered that we didn't have any water when I noticed the blood dried and cracking in spidery patterns along Kieran's ankle. The realization made me aware of the dryness at the back of my throat and I wondered if Kieran felt the same as his panting grew worse.

"We should stop for water when we get into the city," he said.

"We have to get you to a hospital first," I said. He turned to face me now and I nearly ran into him, stumbling in the sand.

"If we go to a hospital, we're both done for sure," he said, "They'll arrest us."

"If we don't go to a hospital, you're dead."

"What do you think they'll do to us if we do?" he said. I wanted to argue with him, but I knew he was every bit as stubborn as I was and we had so little time for a debate.

"We'll use fake names or find an outpatient clinic." Kieran wasn't satisfied with my answer.

"You think a clinic won't report us?" he asked, "It's like you want us to die."

"What? No. Why would I want us to die?" I asked.

"So, just me then. You never did give a damn about me," Kieran said. It was like something in his brain had just flipped, sending him into an overdrive of anger. The snake.

"Kieran, this isn't you. It's the venom," I said. I took a step back when he approached me.

"You always favored Eli over me. You never raised a hand to him," Kieran said.

"Kieran, listen to me," I said, "It's me, Kenna. I'm not your father."

"All you've ever done is lie to me. You said you did it all for my benefit, to make me a true Grace man. You have always and will always see me as your bastard son," he said, taking a swing at me. I dodged but was so stunned at the sudden attack that he was able to land another blow to my jaw. It knocked me to the ground, my vision blurring so much that I was worried the lack of food and water had finally caught up with me.

"Get off," I said and aimed a kick at his gut. It caught his lowest ribs and nearly threw him off. I tried rolling away and I thought I was free just as a hand kept me from crawling to my knees. I let out a yell as he tugged me from behind, managing to drag my body through the sand. He pinned me to my stomach and began digging for the knife tucked in the band at my waist. I tried to fight him off, but after I was sure he had it, all I could do was twist to defend myself. The blade sliced across my raised forearm, sending warm blood dripping onto my face.

"Kieran," I yelled, something changing in his face. He paused with the blade held above me. I was quick to snatch it away from him, keeping it tightly in my grasp. My head spun again, and I knew this time it was from a dangerous combination of dehydration and shock. Kieran was injured. The venom from the snake had progressed far enough to drive him mad and there was no telling how much longer he'd last. As if reading my thoughts, he slumped to one side.

I heaved my body onto my hands and knees and mustered enough energy to crawl to him before my vision darkened again. He didn't move. At least, I don't think he did. Everything was spinning. My face felt sticky now with warm blood and I smeared a scarlet streak over Kieran's cheek as I tried turning it to get a reaction. It was no use. His head was heavy in my hands. I was sure I could hear the soft shushing of something over sand. Feet maybe? No, several feet? It was a rhythmic pattern like the hooves of the camels from the farm in Ariadne.

I began pushing the sand over Kieran. If I hid him, maybe he would come out of his stupor and get help. Maybe he could get himself to a hospital. My eyes burned with frustration as I realized my delusions. If I left him here, he'd die.

The sound grew louder, but it seemed further to my left than before, like the rider would race right past us without ever noticing Kieran dying in the sand. One rider. Maybe it was just one. A friend, I could force to help us. A foe, I might be able to fight. Might.

I let out a scream and began running towards the stranger.

CHAPTER 7

woke up to the crackling of the fire and sat straight up when I saw the dune dog laying just feet from my head. It was the same large wolf I'd faced days ago, but this time he wasn't threatened. He looked my way before lowering his head back to the sandy floor of the cave, watching me with sweet eyes.

"Before you ask," a woman's voice said, "you're in the meeting place for the Aldierian Peace Alliance and you are safe here." The woman sat across the fire from me, bent over Kieran with a rag and a bowl of water. She never once looked up at me. She was so wrinkled that she could easily be a hundred and yet she had youthful hair bound in a single braid down her back and moved with so much skill that I was sure she was a doctor or at least used to dressing wounds.

"Who are you?" I asked. There were barrels in the darkest side of the cave, a spot where it seemed to fade into a black hole and stretch for miles. I noticed now that a strong smell of meat and rice hung in the air, and I found the meal on the floor before me along with another bowl full of water. I lifted the bowl to my lips and drank mouthfuls of it before even questioning.

"You may call me Mama Abraham," the old woman said. She was looking at me now, her face illuminated by the fire so that I could see not only the many wrinkles there but the leather eyepatch over her left eye. She returned her attention to Kieran, scooping a thick substance from the bowl before her with a cloth and packing it to the bite at his ankle.

"What are you doing?" I asked, my head pounding so much as I tried getting to my feet that I abandoned the effort.

"This will relieve the swelling and bruising," she said.

"He was bit by a venomous snake," I said.

"Yes, for which I gave him two doses of an antivenom, one intravenously and another by mouth when he was conscious," she said. My mouth hung open for a moment, all memory of my next retort gone at the mention of Kieran awake.

"He woke up?" I asked her.

"Yes," she said, "and I won't say a word more unless you eat." She continued working, draping a wet cloth over Kieran's forehead. I obliged.

The rice and beef were dry, but somehow exactly the juicy meal I needed. I scooped it into my mouth with my fingers before I realized she'd given me a wooden spoon to use. After several bites, she seemed satisfied and began to explain.

"I'm a kind of middleman between the cities and villages in this region and the Aldierian rebels that work the area," she said, continuing with her explanation after seeing the confusion in my face, "The Aldierians have been making efforts to stop the mining of the Ida stones since their people were driven into the East Sea. There was a hope for increasing awareness of the reality of Aldierian life. It's the reason this area has become more active in the last five years. The APA was able to get a sympathizer elected to the local government, but after he mentioned the Aldierians in a speech, he was killed. It was framed as an Aldierian attack on a shipping center that housed pods used to ship Ida stones nationwide. He was the only hope for halting current mining practices until you and Kieran Grace made such a scene in the arena."

"Everyone in that arena was on the president's side, so the

public shouldn't have found out that we even escaped. President Grace made me out to be a terrorist and he didn't want to attach himself to Kieran," I said.

"I think the president sees your escape as the final act of rebellion for Kieran. He spoke on the national news broadcast the same day of your escape from the arena. He named you both," she said, her expression grave. "I wander the dunes from time to time with the dogs. I noticed an increase in air travel, military air travel, I should say. I kept track of it, which led me to Ariadne where I saw the soldiers. I tried covering your tracks by sending the dogs after the troop. From there, I have been following about a day or so behind until you started walking the desert. You're lucky I was close enough when the hallucinations set in or he might have killed you," she said. I scoffed, a small mouthful of rice falling back to the floor.

"Kieran doesn't have the knife skills I do," I said. The woman smirked. The largest dog scooted closer to me to lick up the scraps of food I'd dropped and settle his fuzzy head against my knee.

"Perhaps he's just lucky you were walking within range of my hideout then," Mama Abraham corrected. I reached out to pet the dog but froze with my hand out as I remembered his teeth bared and the snarling sound he made the last time we were this close. I touched him last time and he left as if on command. Before I could decide what to do, the dog raised his head to meet my hand. He was warm, like a soft blanket freshly laundered. When I looked up again, the old woman was watching me with a smirk on her face.

"Do you know much about Aldierian wolves?" she asked, gathering her supplies and getting to her feet. Her maxi dress flowed around her bare feet as she rounded the fire to sit in front of me. I shook my head as she sat aside one bowl of brown water and sat the clean one between us. I had almost forgotten about the cut along my arm. Specks of sand were embedded in the dried blood. Mama Abraham took my arm into her lap before I could do any more prodding of my own.

"Aldierian wolves can get large. They are native to the planet and like all native things, they can interact with the Aldierians," she said. I gasped when she poured a cleaning solution over the cut, the antiseptic stinging for a second.

"What do you mean they can interact?" I asked. She sat the glass jar aside and returned to flushing the wound with water. She eyed me curiously and I remembered then that I hadn't explained myself. "I didn't grow up with the culture," I said. She nodded slowly, the curious expression still on her face.

"Have you found out why Ida stones are so precious to the Aldierians?" she asked.

"I can use it to speak to Kieran in my mind," I said. She nodded and looked back down at my arm.

"Dune dogs are a lot like people. They like some people better than others, but dogs are dogs too. They have senses we don't. They can smell things from far away, can track familiar scents to find missing people... From what I'm told, you can communicate with a dune dog the same way using the Ida stone, but only if that dog is willing to accept you. It's unusual for a dog to have the same amount of loyalty to communicate with anyone other than their Aldierian companion," she said, deftly wrapping a bandage around my arm.

"So, the dog recognized me as Aldierian," I said, petting the dog at my knee.

"Only that dog recognizes you," Mama Abraham said, "His name is Dimas." The dog raised his head a little at the sound of his name, looking at the woman.

"Dimas," I said, getting his attention now, "Hi, Dimas." He laid his head in my lap and rolled onto his side, a cloud of dust rising from the sandy floor. I could feel the happiness radiating from the dog as my hands combed through his thin fur and then I heard a man's voice echo in my head.

Naja. Naja. Naja.

"What's Naja?" I asked. The woman's smile faded in surprise. A groan across the room drove the thought out of my mind. Kieran sat up and leaned back against the wall. Mama Abraham scurried to the barrels and filled a clean bowl with water and took it to him.

"Drink plenty," she said before turning to the fire and filling another bowl with the rice and beef from the pot. Kieran didn't need her permission and downed the entire bowl of water so quickly that it left him breathing heavily.

"What happened?" he asked.

"Before or after you sliced me open?" I asked him. He looked back at me in horror. "We're in a meeting place for the APA. I forgot what it stands for, but they help the rebels," I said. Kieran didn't need a definition. He looked away from me and at the woman who was bringing him a fresh bowl of water.

"It's real, the APA?" he asked, "My father told me it was a fake organization that sympathizers made up to make it seem like there were others like them." Mama Abraham chuckled.

"Of course, he told you that, always spreading his propaganda," she said, "It's a real organization, though we don't do much more than stealing back Ida stones."

"My father said the rebels blow up the mines," Kieran said.

"There have only been two recorded mine explosions that were purposefully caused and both of them were coverups President Grace ordered," the old woman said, a bitterness in her tone that I knew she hadn't meant for Kieran.

Kieran looked at me, his eyes going to the bandage around my wrist.

"You were hallucinating from the venom," I said, "You didn't hurt me." He snorted.

"Don't lie," he said, taking my arm and looking it over. I managed to contain my groan when his finger brushed over the cut. "I told myself I was going to grow up and be the one saving everyone else," he said under his breath.

"Kieran, you did save me. I wouldn't have even escaped the

arena without you. I have a future only because you stepped up when Marcus hit me," I said. We'd been attached ever since.

His shoulders relaxed a little and he accepted the water when Mama Abraham offered it. I sat in silence while Mama Abraham told him the same story she had told me, glad when Dimas moved to our side of the cave when a cool breeze moved through.

"You can talk to dogs now?" Kieran asked me.

"Not talk exactly. I can communicate with him, but he doesn't say anything back. I can just feel him. Like, he feels at home now. He likes me. Although, I heard a voice saying Naja earlier," I said, turning to Mama Abraham now, "What does that mean?" She hesitated, looking from both of us to Dimas. Finally, she let out a deep breath and answered.

"Naja is his companion, his rider," she said.

"Wait. These dogs aren't yours?" Kieran asked. She shook her head.

"The rebel troop that works in this area leaves their dogs here with me so they can venture closer to the villages and cities unseen. I help clothe them so they look less Aldierian and I watch over their dogs while they are away. Sometimes, I house Ida stones as they steal them until they can take them back to a safe place where they won't be mined," she said, "Naja leads this troop." Did I look like Naja? Is that why Dimas felt so comfortable with me?

"Can you take us to him?" I asked. The woman nodded slowly as if measuring what to say next.

"Yes," she said, "I can help you. We will go tomorrow, but you will have to help them with the mission. It's a dangerous one that they weren't sure they could complete alone. They can use extra people on their side." Kieran looked a little nervous, but he nodded.

"Yes, please," I said, hoping that their mission wasn't so dangerous that we'd end up dead or captured instead.

"Their troop plans to blow up a crane at a mining site on the other side of the city," Mama Abraham said.

"I thought you said the Aldierians have never blown up a mine on purpose," I said. Kieran elbowed me.

"Sometimes the ends justify the means," he said, motioning for the woman to continue.

"We're not committing eco-terrorism," I said, "Someone could get hurt."

"They are planning the attack at noon when all work ceases," Mama Abraham said, raising her voice over our arguing, "And it's a small explosive. It should only blow apart the base of the crane. From there, gravity can smash the rest. They were worried about keeping security low after the explosion. They have to be close enough to denote the explosive they're using. I know a guy who can get me a sedative. You two can get it to the security guards. There are only three of them."

"How are we supposed to sedate three guards?" Kieran said with a sigh. My brain was still stuck on the exploding mine news. Maybe there was a way to help that didn't involve destroying the mine at all. Sure, the Ida stones would survive a blast, but even with the workers on break, they could be injured.

"We can do it," I said, placing a hand on Kieran's shoulder. I passed on the silent message using the Ida stone, making it clear that I had a better plan. His expression went from surprise to one of trust, giving me a single nod.

"Tomorrow," he agreed. Mama Abraham was happy for our help. She gave us both another helping of the meal and began making her arrangements for tomorrow as we settled down to sleep. Dimas snuggled next to me, his thick front paw making a nice pillow. With a final dose of anti-venom, Kieran thanked the old woman and joined Dimas and I by the fire.

"Care to explain," he whispered to me as the woman moved to her makeshift bed across the cave.

"Not really. Too tired," I said, hoping I sounded sleepy enough. Thankfully, Kieran didn't press me for an answer. I didn't have one yet.

CHAPTER 8

The next morning, Mama Abraham dressed us both in brown pants and sleeveless tops. The billowing jackets she gave us had hoods, but I wrapped the scarf around my head again to make sure I concealed my hair. Dimas groaned deep in his throat when we left him and his pack at the cave. The three of us crowded into the back of a rickety cart pulled by a mule. The cart smelled sweet, a smell I couldn't place until we stopped at a greenhouse a few miles outside of the city.

Kieran and I helped Mama Abraham with a few barrels full of dried plants. They looked like saucers, almost like cacti, but these were a dusty rose color and wrinkled like jerky. Kieran and I worked together to load them into the back of the cart while Mama Abraham strapped a metal money box to the mule.

"What are these?" Kieran asked.

"Drugs," I said, "She's a drug dealer."

"They are legal," Mama Abraham said as she urged the mule forward, "and they are used medicinally for aches and pains. It works faster than aconite. It's what I used on you for that snake bite. That venom feels like fire in your veins otherwise." Kieran's eyebrows lifted.

"Yes, but you can also induce hallucinations if you smoke it,"

I said and added, "which you didn't," when I noticed how surprised Kieran was.

"How long does it stay in your bloodstream?" he asked.

"Why? Are you planning on taking a drug test?" I asked. Mama Abraham laughed. Kieran calmed down a little, smirking.

"How do you know so much about the stuff?" he asked me. It was my turn to smirk with embarrassment. It was a long time ago, or it felt that way. It had been just three years ago.

"I got caught at school smoking it," I said. Kieran laughed, the sound so infectious I couldn't help but join in.

"I thought I was the rebellious one."

"That's up for debate," I told him, swinging my hips further to the left when he tried slapping my butt. "You're not the dexterous one, we all know that," I said.

"You like me for my good name," he said with a wink.

"Oh, yeah. Totally. Kieran is a good name."

"I'm not getting a cent from my father, and I didn't have anything of my own, so I'm about as broke as you can get," he said. Jacob tried his best to save away money for me. He had big dreams of me graduating and getting a good internship, maybe even getting a degree that meant I'd never worry about not affording dinner again. I was used to scavenging the way we were now. Kieran, for a boy who grew up in luxury, hadn't complained about a thing. He was almost comfortable with the idea of living this way. My stomach dropped at the thought of what life with his father must have been like.

Compared to all the walking we'd done, the trek into Lyle felt like nothing. The skyscrapers rose high into the air, metal bridges decorated with the flag of Gallaterra connecting several of the buildings at varying heights. There was a market along the road where we entered. Mama Abraham led the mule to one side of the street and stopped, greeting the basket merchant under the tent a few feet away.

"This is where we part ways," she told us, pulling two thick coins from her pocket. "Those will block the sensors on the skyway just long enough for you to send for a pod and take it to Anvalt. Go left to Downsbury. You want Rox." She pushed my hands away when she passed both coins off to me, her good eye motioning over her left shoulder. I saw the soldier down the street, too busy talking with a woman selling coffee to notice us.

"Let's go find the skyway," I said, grabbing onto Kieran's arm and steering him down the street. He pulled his hood a little lower on his face. We slowed our pace a little after a few blocks. I glanced back to make sure no one was following us, relaxing my grip on his arm when I confirmed we weren't being watched.

"This city is beautiful," Kieran said, "It's like a jungle of steel." I knew what he meant, but I didn't think it was very beautiful. The city was always a place too busy and congested. In Arro, it was hard not to miss those of us working the streets, but here people walked by them like they were common features, a part of the scenery, not real people trying to earn their meal of the day.

Lyle was like a single reflective surface from all the metal. The further we walked towards the skyscrapers, the busier it got. Dune riders began taking over the streets and we had to move to the sidewalk. Above us was a canopy of metal bridges, people walking them on their morning commute. Flashy billboards advertised for fast food restaurants, diapers, and the newest TV shows. A web of steel framing twisted and branched off in all directions, pods attached on top. I scanned the structure for an entry point.

"Do you see a sign anywhere?" I asked. Kieran pointed to one almost immediately. It led us down a side street to the left filled with more merchants. Kieran stilled next to me. There were two soldiers positioned halfway down the street as if waiting for unrest. Both had steel crossbows in one hand.

"If you act like we know what we're doing, they won't stop us," I said, tugging him forward.

"You better be right," he said as we walked. I kept us on track to walk right by the tent selling "oddities" and hoped that we wouldn't need to bolt before I got my chance. The shopkeeper was busy entertaining a pair of children with a blue crystal, probably a fake Ida stone, when we finally reached the tent. I carefully opened the laundry bag and scooped an animal skull into the top, the artifact sliding in as smooth as butter. Kieran didn't even flinch as I did it, keeping our pace even and casual.

Neither of us spoke as we passed the guards, the one on my side of the street not seeming to notice. My chest felt full of air as we rounded the corner like I hadn't taken a full breath since laying eyes on the soldiers.

"I should've snagged a weapon from one of those tents like we did in Ariadne," Kieran said, keeping his voice low.

"No, a fight wouldn't help us now. We need to make sure we don't attract attention before we get to the dig site." We followed the next sign for the skyway. The entrance was a set of stone stairs encased in glass. We took them two at a time and joined another couple and a businesswoman on the landing.

"I've never signed in for one of these before," I whispered to Kieran. He shushed me at the sound of an incoming pod. It was egg-like in shape, almost entirely surrounded by a seamless window. It came to a stop and a door near the front opened. The couple made their way forward, the door folding flush with the pod. The man tapped a button on the control panel and the windows began tinting so deeply that you couldn't even see a shadow of a figure beyond. The pod slid away a moment later, following the ramp to the busy system of metal roads.

"Wait," Kieran said. We didn't have to wait long before another pod came for the businesswoman. With her gone, we went to a TV screen against the far wall. I tapped the button labeled "call pod" and a symbol to insert a coin came onto the screen. I lifted the coin Mama Abraham gave me. It didn't look like the coin in the picture, but it was the same dimensions. I slid it into the slot next to the screen and it beeped twice before dispensing the coin into the bowl mounted below.

"Nothing happened," Kieran said, pointing to the screen. It

was back to the main menu, an advertisement for whitening toothpaste sending flashes of blue and white color over Kieran's confused expression.

"Should we try again?" I asked. Our answer came in the form of a pod sliding into the loading dock. The door lowered with a soft hiss. I led the way into the compartment. It was nothing like I'd expected. It was more like a hotel room than any kind of transportation system you'd expect. At the front was a large screen like the one on the loading dock. Further into the room were two long padded benches on both sides of the pod and a table with four chairs in the center, all bolted to the floor. At the back was a closed door, a small bathroom.

"Hello, my name is Celina," a voice said when the screen turned on at the front of the room, "You may set your destination by saying my name and your destination or finding it on the map provided." A map of the city appeared before us. Kieran looked at me.

"She told you where to go," he said, "What did she say?" It took me a moment to remember. The words were strange. Only the first part sounded like any location.

"Celina," I said, "Set destination for Anvalt." A moment after I spoke, there was a ping and the map zoomed in on a suburb on the other side of Lyle. A time of two hours appeared at the top as our total travel time.

"Destination is set for Anvalt," the voice said, "Press the button on the screen to begin transit." I nodded and Kieran pressed the red button when it appeared. The pod began moving, making me stumble a little as we began gaining speed. I settled into one of the chairs at the table while Kieran played with the screen.

"There's a food and drink option," he said, "and we can both shower in the back." He came back a few minutes later with a plate of French fries and another with mixed vegetables. He handed me a plastic fork and went back to the front. When he returned, he had two plastic cups of water and another filled a fourth of the way with a dark liquid.

"That coin must be some kind of ghosting device," he said, "It let me order whiskey." He took a sip and held it out to me. I'd never tried any alcoholic drinks before, but if there was a time to check items off a bucket list the time was now. It burned, but in a warm and tingly way that felt good. We finished the food and took turns showering while we waited.

"You shaved," I said when he returned from the back room. His face was smooth, a small nick still bleeding along his jawline.

"I only did, because my beard grows thinner on the left side," he explained, handing me a handheld device I discovered was a hairdryer. "I found it under the sink," he said. I gladly took it and finished drying my damp hair while he checked the screen for the estimated arrival time.

"So, how long do we have left?" I asked.

"I knew you stole something," he said. I turned around to see him holding the skull in his right hand, "Why?" I sat the hairdryer down.

"I have a plan," I said.

"To do what? Are you going to sell it for money or..." I pulled it from his hands and tucked it back into the bag.

"No, and it pisses me off that you think I'm a criminal just like everyone else does," I said. He let out a sigh and followed me to the bench. The anger that flared hot in my chest surprised me at first, but in a way, it also felt overdue. It was like I'd been unconsciously suppressing it each time we had to keep moving or problem-solve the current plan. Maybe this was exciting for Kieran to break the law, but I was so used to it that it was tiring. When, if ever, would I finally be settled?

"I didn't mean that," he said, "I just wanted to know why you took it. I trust you, Kenna. You're the one who's gotten us out of all the trouble we run into, not me. Whatever you wanted to do with it, let me help." I knew he was telling the truth. You could always see it in his eyes.

"I don't want to blow up a crane. I think it just legitimizes your father's conspiracies about the Aldierians wanting us all dead. I was going to plant it at the dig site. It's the only thing I could think of to halt the expedition. If there are signs of archeological finds, then they can't mine the area until it's been fully explored. It's the law," I said. Kieran smiled and laughed in disbelief.

"That's genius. God, there's a new reason I love you at every turn." We both froze at his words, my stomach knotting up so tightly that it made it hard to breathe. Before he could grow any redder, I leaned over and kissed him on the cheek. A smile spread across his face and he leaned in to kiss me, only we were interrupted by another ping from the screen at the front of the pod.

"You have arrived at Anvalt," the voice said, "Thank you for traveling with Skyway." The door opened with a hiss and we exited onto another platform, this one packed with people.

"She said to take a pod to Anvalt, go left to Downsbury, and that we want to look for Rox," I said, "Do you think Downsbury is another suburb or a neighborhood?" Kieran joined me at the stairs and we made our way down to the street. It was busy with businessmen and women on their way to work or gathering in the streets around restaurants for lunch. None of them looked our way as we passed, despite the conspicuous hoods over our faces. It was common to see people from the villages and other rural towns shielding their skin from the harsh sun.

"I should've asked the pod before we got off," Kieran said, "No, wait. I think Downsbury is a street." He pointed to the nearest intersection, the sign pointing left saying Downsbury. We followed it down a street lined with industrial business. There were a few hardware stores, then lumber yards, and finally warehouses the further we walked.

"I bet Rox is the mining company," I said, ignoring Kieran's scoffing at the irony. We kept walking, scanning the name of every building or gated yard as we went. I started watching the time as I realized it had been at least twenty minutes since we last saw anyone.

"What's he up everyone's ass about anyway," a man said, appearing around the corner a second later. Another man came after him, both still dressed in thick work pants and steel-toed boots.

"I don't know, but I'm about ready to kick his ass if he keeps ordering us all around like we don't know what we're doing. I've been working the Rox two years longer than that guy," the second said. The name drew my attention down the street they came from, the road leading to a gated area that stretched to the mountains beyond. We kept close to the sidewalk as we walked towards the gate. A security guard manned the open entrance from a covered patio, taking a break just as the miners were judging by how comfortable he looked sitting in his chair with a tablet resting on his knees. We moved closer to an abandoned bodega and sat amongst the rusting dumpster and old tires.

"Merrick," a woman yelled, approaching the awning. She was dressed in the same blue uniform as the security guard. "I brought you a cup of coffee," she said, handing off the paper cup, "The foreman said there's an issue with the equipment, so he's going to stay behind and take a look at it over lunch. He told me to tell you not to worry about locking up the gate." The man took the coffee, and the woman followed the other workers down the street and off to lunch.

"Did you get that sedative from Mama Abraham like she talked about?" I asked.

"No, she shooed us away before her guy could find us," Kieran said, "It's just us and that skull now." The skull wouldn't matter unless I got the opportunity to plant it at the dig site. He sat and watched the gate, occasionally suggesting terrible ideas of how to sneak past until someone else took care of the problem for us.

"Kenna," Kieran said, pointing towards the opposite side of the street. Two girls came around the corner of the gate, hiding behind the final wooden panel. They both had dark hair, pulled back into the same braided updo that the woman in prison had done for me. The girl in front reached behind her and the girl behind took her hand. They were communicating using the Ida stone.

"Should we get their attention?" Kieran asked. I shushed him. The girls inched closer to the opening of the gate. The one in front pulled a round ball from her pocket. With a twist, it split in half and she tossed both ends around the gate. The security guard lowered his tablet to look at the ground, tossing it aside a moment later and getting to his feet in a panic. It was too late. A loud humming sound echoed through the air. The man went limp and fell to the wooden floor of the awning. The first girl made sure he was unconscious while the other took the used halves of the device and tucked them away in her pockets.

The first girl let out a whistle. I heard the pounding of feet over dirt and three boys came running around the edge of the gate towards the entrance. They spoke in a language I'd never heard in Aldieria before, the words sounding like a mixture of Spanish or Italian and an island language. Together, the five of them began running further into the gated area where the dig site must be.

"Let's follow them," I said, turning to look at Kieran. He wasn't next to me anymore. Kieran was laying in the dirt, his head lolling against the side of a tire. The device must not work on Aldierians. I tried waking him with a gentle shake, but he remained unconscious. I stacked a couple of the tires in front of him to keep him hidden and turned back to the gate. I guess I was on my own from here.

CHAPTER 9

nside the gate looked exactly like a construction zone. There were abandoned machines parked at the front just behind the large building that served as headquarters. As far as I could tell, everyone had gone for lunch aside from the one worker I passed who looked like he was taking a nap on a bench behind the building when the Aldierian's device went off.

I hoped that was the foreman the woman had mentioned on her way to lunch. He was supposed to be here somewhere to check the equipment at the site. That's what I was concerned most about. The last thing we needed was for the nation to see another report about the Aldierians killing a Gallaterran, especially not a real attack.

"What are you doing back here?" a voice asked, startling me. I turned around and nearly walked right into the thickset man. He was dressed like the other workers, except his orange shirt had the words "supervisor" printed over the left breast pocket. I thought about the skull still concealed with the laundry bag.

"I- I heard about the site," I said.

"The site is closed to the public," the man said, grabbing my bicep and towing me back the way I came.

"No. No," I said and tugged free, trying to think fast, "I

mean, I heard about what this place actually is. The rumors are true, aren't they? There are not just Ida stones here." The man's expression changed, his annoyance flaring to anger. His patience had worn out already and he changed directions, nearly dragging me towards the door to the headquarters building.

"I don't know what you heard or who told you, but we can't excavate an area with artifacts. The site has to be cleared first and this one was," he said, "So, you can wait here with your crazy ideas for the police to come and take you home." He pulled me into the small building. It was one giant room, a couple of messy desks set in the corners with two other men sitting together at one, reviewing something on a screen mounted to the wall.

"What's this?" one of the men asked. His shirt identified him as the foreman. He was tall and as he stood up, I noticed the radio at his hip. One call and more security could flood this place.

"This girl came looking for artifacts," the man holding me said, "I told you those rumors were worth addressing."

"Addressing them would make people think they're true," the third man said.

"Well, no one will find anything anyway, if they can get past security that is," the foreman said.

"I found something," I told him. The supervisor let me go and I stepped far enough away to dig into the bag. I had barely pulled the skull out before the foreman snatched it from me, the jaw of the animal snapping off and falling to the bottom of the bag.

"You found that here?" the third man asked, out of his chair now.

"What is it?" the supervisor asked.

"Bullshit," the foreman said, looking up from the skull and at me, "You expect me to believe you got past security before and found this at our site?"

"I got past them today," I said, "That guard you have up front was too busy playing games on his tablet." The foreman cursed under his breath, looking closer at the skull. He scratched at the surface and took a sniff.

"It was buried in red clay," he said in defeat. The others groaned.

"I still don't believe her," the supervisor said, "She's dressed like a freaking desert merchant. She probably stumbled upon the site, got past that idiot out front, and thought that maybe she'd find money or food or something here."

"Where do you think merchants get their goods, asshole," I snapped. The supervisor raised a hand to slap me, but the foreman stopped him. He shoved the supervisor aside and took his place before me, straightening up to his full height and adjusting the tools at his belt.

"What do you mean?" he asked.

"I heard the rumors about this site, that it might have arti-facts buried here. I found that skull at your site. It dates back five hundred years at least," I said. He shook his head with an amused laugh.

"I think you wandered in here looking for food and got caught."

"Why would I carry around a skull with me?"

"Beats me. It doesn't matter anyway. Rumors are just rumors."

"Until they're proven as facts," I said, my heart leaping into my throat when he removed the radio from his belt.

"Yeah. You just try proving that when the cops get here for you," the foreman said.

"Okay. You can show them your site permits," I said. Bingo. All three men paled at my announcement. The radio static died instantly, and the foreman sat it on the desk behind him. If I just kept him away from that radio, it would buy us time to get out of here.

"I told you," the third man said. The foreman cast him a glare that kept him quiet.

"Want to know where I found it?" I asked. The foreman let out a laugh.

"Sure. Show me where all the other artifacts are that you buried here, you little liar," he said, kicking open the front door. The supervisor kept close to my side as we walked. A few minutes later, we were in an area where the crane was positioned. I saw a foot disappear behind a tree to the right of the crane. They wouldn't be hiding so close to the crane if it was rigged with explosives. Maybe we got here just in time. I turned the laundry bag upside down and the jawbone slipped out and into the dirt. I stopped walking just long enough to kick some red dirt over the top of it.

"It was here," I said, pointing to a spot on my left. The three men stopped walking ahead of me, the supervisor already heading for the spot I'd pointed at.

"This is a waste of time," he said, brushing away the top layer of dirt with his gloved hands, "We're halting production all because of some teenage girl and a wild rumor."

"She has a damn skull," the third man said, "It's illegal to mine anything until a crew comes to confirm there aren't artifacts here and if there are..." He was cut off when the foreman spat loudly in the dirt between us.

"There," I said, pointing a few feet from me. I pushed the dirt with my toe before the supervisor pulled me away by my arm.

"No way," he said, brushing the dust from the bone.

"Shit," the foreman said when he lifted the jawbone.

"I think it's human," the supervisor said, dropping it back to the ground with a grimace. The foreman kicked the dirt, sending a shower of red dust into the air around us.

"We have to call it off, call it all off," he said, reaching for his hip. His hands fingered where his radio would've been, causing him to look down. A movement to my left caught my eye. The Aldierian girl who had thrown the first device was back with another, twisting it apart and lobbing it at us from behind a trailer full of dirt.

"Terrorist," one of the men yelled. The hum filled the air and the three men dropped around me. All five Aldierians were on their feet now, staring in shock at me as the humming finally died out.

The girl who'd thrown the device yelled to the tallest of the boys. While the others had their hair tied back in ponytails at the nape of their necks, his was pushed back in a mohawk. He yelled at me in Aldierian, waiting for an answer.

"You can't blow up the crane," I said, pointing to the crane. He yelled at me again, this time starting forward. The other four followed after him, withdrawing knives from their hips. I dropped the laundry bag and pulled the retractable knife from my waistband. He ran at me when I raised it, nearly landing a punch to my face. I had only practiced hand-to-hand combat a few times with Jacob growing up. I was usually armed with whatever weapon he was working on at the time, so I wasn't used to being so close to my opponent and it showed in my speed.

The boy missed my face a second time with his fist, but an open hand landed exactly on target across my right cheek and sent me stumbling backward. Just when I thought I had my footing, I tripped over the unconscious foreman and fell flat on my back. The boy was on top of me, prying the knife from my hand and raising it above his head. He looked up when something whooshed over his shoulder. I lifted my head to see Kieran standing yards away with a metal crossbow.

The boy leaped off me and started running towards him. Kieran tossed the bow aside and began searching himself for another weapon. I was running, feet pounding against the dirt for just moments before I was tackled to the ground. The girl and I skidded to a stop and my face was pinned to the dirt a second later. Kieran raised his hands in defense as the boy approached, knife raised high.

"Mama Abraham sent us," I said, my voice sounding hoarse. I coughed as I inhaled red dust. "Mama A-Abraham," my voice cracked. The boy stopped, the knife still raised. The remaining two boys grabbed Kieran, each holding an arm. The boy, the leader, whatever he was… He turned back to face me and said something to the girl pinning me down. I was tugged to my knees, both hands confined behind my back.

"Why did she send you?" he asked.

"To help," I said, "We escaped from the arena at the capital," I said.

"I didn't ask for help from the sympathizers," he said.

"She's not a sympathizer. She's Aldierian," Kieran said, groaning when one of the boys tugged on his arm to keep him from wiggling away. The boy looked straight at me. The girl holding me hostage tugged my hood from my head and roughly yanked the scarf from around my hair.

"Aldierians don't have red hair," the girl said.

"Why else would that device not work on me?" I asked. The boy paused, his eyes going past me to the girls and then back on me.

"A real Aldierian has a stone," he said. Before I could react, two pairs of hands were tugging at my clothes.

"Stop! Leave her alone," Kieran said, pulling so hard against the boys that they pinned him to the ground. The girls ripped the jacket off me and I was able to slip away, pulling at the chain around my neck to reveal the pendant. One of the girls got to me first, pulling my arms behind my back as the pendant finally fell from my collar. The boy's face went from surprise to anger. He stepped towards me and pulled me the rest of the way by the chain.

"Where did you get this?" he asked, his hand shaking.

"My mother gave it to me," I said.

"Liar," he growled.

"I was adopted. She gave birth to me in my adoptive father's forge. He was a blacksmith." His stony expression softened a moment at my words.

"Blacksmith," he said, his grip relaxing. He kept the pendant in his palm, looking down at it.

"Yeah," I said, "a blacksmith. He made weapons with steel and worked with leather and…" He nodded. He didn't need my explanation. There was something else he realized. He stepped back from me and looked me over, making my stomach knot. He held his hands up and waited. The girl holding me let go and I felt like a deer in a wolves' den. Should I run or should I press my hands to his? I did the latter.

He showed me a little dark-haired boy playing on the floor in his bedroom. A tall, slender woman stopped in the doorway. She lifted the boy high in her arms, snuggling him to her chest and taking him into a living room. A red-haired man was sitting on a couch, his smile growing wide when he saw the little boy. He took the boy from his mother, spinning him around in a circle and tossing him in the air. The boy giggled wildly.

The images faded and a new one formed. This time, the little boy was a few years older. He was maybe three by the size of him tottering next to an elderly woman. They were just outside of a compound much like Ariadne. The dark-haired woman and the redhead man came out of the entrance to meet them. The woman bent down to allow the little boy to kiss her, his tiny hands fingering the Ida stone hanging from the chain at her neck, the same necklace Jacob gave me. The boy moved to the redhead next, hugging his leg hard before the man knelt next to him to embrace him. The elderly woman had to hold the crying boy to keep him from running when the couple mounted the backs of two dune dogs.

The scene dimmed and another one returned. It was the same setting, the sun halfway sunken beneath the horizon. The woman was alone, riding one dune dog with another trailing after her. She slid from its back and the elderly woman surged forward. The woman collapsed into her, head buried in the old woman's chest and body heaving with sobs. The little boy tugged at her pant leg until she lifted him onto her hip, the boy joining her in tears.

The boy stopped projecting his memories and we were left staring at each other in silence before I heard his voice echo in my head, saying my name.

"Kenna?"

"Yes."

The boy's eyes glassed over, and I felt my own burn as he pulled me to his chest. He spoke to the troop around them in Aldierian and they all looked back in astonishment.

"My name is Naja Petrek," the boy said.

"Can I join the party?" Kieran asked. Naja nodded and told the boys to let him go. Kieran massaged a spot on his forearm and joined us. "What did he show you?" he asked me.

"My mother," I said, "Naja's my brother." Kieran's mouth parted. After the surprise passed, he shook Naja's hand.

"I'm Kieran Grace," he said, "We wanted to help."

"We were hoping you would take us to the Aldierian city," I said. Naja nodded.

"You want to speak with the Ida," he said, "our leader."

"Yes," I said, "We can help stop Gallaterra, well, stop the president." The girl to my left said something under her breath, a curse no doubt.

"We just want the president to leave us alone and stop drilling holes in the planet," Naja said, leading the way to the front of the complex, "That's all we want from Gallaterra. I'll keep leading my troop on missions to stop him until he does."

"We know that, but it's not the only thing he's doing," I said, catching up at his side.

"He's not going to stop even though the planet will crumble and die in forty years," Kieran said, "The scientists in Gallaterra are sure the planet will collapse if we keep mining the stones. He doesn't care. He plans to evacuate a certain number of the people and leave the rest to die here, along with the Aldierians. We can stop him from mining the stones. Some scientists have found alternatives to the Ida stone that won't destroy the planet. I know how we can stop him."

"How do you plan to do that?" Naja asked, stopping at the front gate to make sure no one was around to follow us out.

"I'll get close to him and kill him," Kieran said. His words sent a chill over my skin. It was the first time he sounded so sure of the task. He looked strong now, ready for battle even. Naja let out a laugh and led our group around the gate and towards the mountain beyond.

"How are you going to get close to the President of Gallaterra?" Naja asked. The boys following us laughed.

"I'm his son," Kieran said, "Kieran Grace?" Naja stopped and turned to look at him. We were still out in the open, exposed to any security that was surely on their way at least.

"It's true," I said.

"You'd kill your own father?" Naja asked. I had wondered the same thing when he told me, but I'd been too afraid to ask. I couldn't imagine the amount of pain and rejection he'd felt growing up. His father was mentally and physically abusive to him and his mother. He led the nation with tyrannical force and openly admitted he would allow millions to die instead of changing the nation's energy use.

"Yes," Kieran said, "I want to be the one to do it." Naja's face bore a hint of sadness.

"Welcome to the troop," he said, "and welcome home, sister."

CHAPTER 10

We set up camp high in the mountains before it grew too dark to see that night. Naja introduced us to his troop, who didn't turn out to be his troop at all. When Kieran asked where his normal troop was, the rebels all looked anywhere but at us or Naja. Naja stood up as if he'd never heard the question.

"I'm going to gather more wood for the fire," he said, "I'll take the first watch." The boys didn't hesitate before laying their heads down on their packs and pulling blankets over themselves. The girls did the same but continued their conversation in Aldierian.

"You think he's upset?" I asked Kieran as he made our bed in the grass. The only possessions we had with us now were the retractable knife and the water bag. One of the girls loaned us her blanket after they'd agreed to share one. Kieran glanced towards the bushes Naja had disappeared into.

"Something about the troop hit a nerve," he said.

"I'm going to go talk to him," I said. Kieran looked like he wanted to go with me, but he started smoothing the blanket over the grass again when I tucked the knife in my pocket. I followed the path Naja took, surprised by how far he'd walked after being gone only a few minutes. I nearly walked past him until I heard a sniffle.

Naja was standing on the ledge of the hill that overlooked the city, his tall strong silhouette a strange contrast to the sobs. He turned a little from the view, the light from the moon making his quivering lip clear. I walked slowly towards him, not sure if I should announce myself or just let him catch sight of me on his own. I didn't have time to debate the two, because he saw me a second later. He wiped his face and sent me a little smile.

"I needed a moment away from those..." he said, letting out a long sigh, "We'll be home in just a few days. Mother won't know what to say when she sees you." I stopped next to him, looking over the skyscrapers and twinkling lights from the skyway.

"What's wrong?" I asked him. He opened his mouth to speak but closed it a moment later and let his eyes go to the slope of the hill with a quivering lip. I offered him my hand the way he had earlier today. After a moment, he took it. I could feel his sadness immediately. It was heavy, but empty somehow. Something was missing. Something he loved was gone. Then, his voice echoed in my head.

I can't say it aloud. I think he's dead. He must be. The task was designed for his failure. If I say it aloud though, that makes it real.

"Who?" I asked aloud, still not used to using the Ida stone. He looked at me, using his free hand to wipe his face again.

Illya. His name is Illya.

I wanted to know more, and I was glad I didn't have to ask. Naja kept our minds tethered using the Ida stone, so I was suddenly immersed in his memories. My mind was flooded with images of a grand room full of people. They were all dressed in long black jackets with silver pins in the shape of ocean waves on the lapel. A boy walked down the aisle towards us, escorted by two women with swords. The boy had long dark hair that was pulled into a ponytail, the sides of his head buzzed short.

He stopped on the black rug positioned at the front next to Naja. They were both dressed in white.

My view shifted from Illya to the raised platform. Sitting in high back chairs were three women and a man, all dressed in the same long black jackets and wearing headpieces of metal spikes. One of the women began reading off a list of charges, all military crimes, naming both Illya and Naja. When the charges were read, Naja was seized by both women and a man stepped forward to hold Naja's arms behind his back.

A man came forward with an electric razor and began shaving Illya's hair. Naja screamed for them to stop, but the man just held him tighter. Once Illya was left bald, the woman on the platform announced that he was banished from Aldierian society unless he could return with an Ida stone converter from a Gallaterran city. Naja began screaming again, falling onto his knees and begging for the judges to send him instead. Illya didn't do anything but stare at the floor.

Naja was too busy fighting for Illya's freedom to care when they told him he was being temporarily demoted for his part in the mission. He would be assigned to training troops and small missions no further than a hundred miles from the East Sea. The women held Naja while the man escorted Illya out of the room. The scene faded and I focused my gaze on Naja's face, which was glistening with a new wave of tears. He tried to brush them all away, but new ones silently rolled down his cheeks to replace them.

"I'm sorry," I said. Naja squeezed my hand.

"I was the reason Illya was involved with the plan," Naja said, "I knew it would never get approved, but the shipment was going to be so large. He was the one who stole the ship, but I blew the hole in the desert that caused the Gallaterran ship to crash. We used our own ship's cargo hold to bring back the Ida stones. We thought we would be welcomed as heroes, doing what no one else had done before. She was furious that Gallaterrans died. She didn't want to risk starting a war."

"I can understand that much," I said. Naja blanched, stepping away from me and forming a fist at his nape.

"We have been at war since the humans arrived," he said, "We've been pushed out of our homes. We watched all these years while the humans ruined the planet with their trash and mining. We have been killed by them. Two Gallaterrans died in that crash, just two, and she sends Illya to his death and leaves me behind to…" Naja was in tears again, taking a deep breath to control his sobs.

"I'm sorry, Naja. I can't even imagine…" I thought about Kieran. He was so smart and always knew how to fix any problem we came across. He was also inexperienced with weapons, new to facing battle, and had never fought without me by his side.

"I'm afraid it will take a huge attack and lots of death of our people before the Ida sees this for what it is," Naja said, "Tell me, what do you think is President Grace's plan?" He looked straight at me, his strong exterior back. As far as I could tell, the president was just concerned about staying in power. In Gallaterra, a person can be elected to any branch of government so long as the public doesn't vote him out. President Grace led his platform to the public as the only person who could keep us safe. Most of the nation saw the Aldierians as a threat and he was the only politician with plans that kept us safe from them. It's fearmongering supported by false evidence as the sympathizers could prove. That's why Grace quietly dispatched them.

"I think President Grace would like it if the Aldierians were all dead," I said, "but I don't think he wants it to look that way to the public. That's why he's framed attacks in our own cities as if the Aldierians committed them. It's an excuse to kill Aldierians that the public will accept as a lesser evil. No one wants war, but no one wants to die either." Naja nodded. I knew I had confirmed the way he saw it as well.

"Do you trust that guy, Kieran Grace?" he asked, "You're sure that he's not a spy or won't feel differently about killing his father once he's standing before him?" I had no doubts that he wanted his father dead. That wasn't the doubt making my muscles tense now.

"Kieran is a huge asset to the mission against the president. He knows things I don't know about Aldierian culture, and he knows the capital and the government better than I do. Most importantly, he is the only one who could get us close to the president," I said. Naja was studying my face, I was sure based on the curious look in his eyes.

"You're worried about him," Naja said, "You love him." My lip a little quiver and I knew he was feeling the same devotion for Illya. I'd never said it aloud. Kieran told me he loved me on the skyway and it felt so obvious and so natural to hear him say it that I almost missed the meaning of the words.

"I do," I said, "and I won't do this without him. I can't do this without him, but still..." Naja and I stood there for a long time before either of us spoke. We discussed what a mission would look like and how we would need to showcase it to the Ida to get her approval. Naja said that we would need to come in with proof that whatever we would do in the capital would put a firm halt to the entire mining operation across Aldieria. She wouldn't risk a war for anything less. We thought hard, but I had no idea how to cut off all the power the Ida stones provided. I didn't know the first thing about where the stones even got converted into power. I was sure Kieran did though. So, we decided that he needed to be the one to present the plan.

The days following our discussion, Naja would take time to walk next to me and hold my hand. He'd channel the Ida stone he wore around his wrist to show me memories from his childhood. I saw the first time he went to school, the day he was accepted into the military, and the day he was promoted to captain. Most of his missions had been for the sake of causing equipment malfunctions on dig sites, usually going unnoticed. The one time his troop was caught, his second in command had been killed. The event hit Naja hard, but the man was replaced with Illya.

Illya wasn't the military type. He was what the Aldierians called a specialist. He was trained in politics, medicine, and all the science behind the powers of the Ida stones. His purpose among Naja's troops was to plan for all the possibilities of failure during their missions. He was the last hope for success and for that reason, he replaced the man as Naja's second in command. They worked closely together and much like Kieran and I, their relationship grew fast.

My feet had blisters by the time we were done walking. We met Mama Abraham in a field, the dune dogs gathered around her. Dimas surged forward immediately to greet Naja, the earth around us shaking when he rolled over for a belly rub.

"As always, thank you for helping," Naja told Mama Abraham as the rest of the troop found their dogs. She smiled and her eyes went to Kieran and I.

"Good to see you again," she said.

"Thank you for helping us find them," Kieran said. I turned my gaze from Naja and Dimas back to the woman. She had been so strange about Dimas back in the cave.

"You knew we're related, didn't you?" I asked her. She shrugged.

"I had a suspicion. Dune dogs aren't loyal to just anyone." The girl that had loaned us her blanket let Kieran ride with her. I climbed onto Dimas's back and settled into place behind Naja. We thanked Mama Abraham one more time and then the dogs started into the forest again.

The trees were much thinner here than on the mountains, making it easy for the dogs to navigate. We ate leftover berries and dried meat as we traveled, not stopping until we reached a gorge. A steel bridge stretched the mile-long gap from our end of the forest to the opposite end. There weren't any trees on the other side, the dirt between the grass a light tan.

"Is that sand?" Kieran asked. The dogs came to a stop feet

from the bridge. No one spoke for a long time and something about the way Naja's body stiffened set me on edge. I met Kieran's nervous gaze. Naja let out a yell, startling me, and the pack of dogs sprinted ahead. I held tight to Naja's waist as we sped along. A few yards past the end of the bridge, the land began to slope. I could see the ocean stretch behind it and when we reached the ridge, the waves were in full view as they softly lapped over the shore.

Dimas skidded to a stop and my heart slammed against my chest. A giant domed tube descended from the shore into the water, a steel door sealing off what I was sure was the entrance to the Aldierian underwater city. Dead bodies were strewn across the sand around it, Aldierian soldiers dressed in plated armor with bloody pools soaking their uniforms. Several dogs were gutted close enough to the water that red foam was floating in and back out again with the tide.

"And she says we aren't in a war," Naja said under his breath. The rest of the troop looked on in anger, one of the dune dogs whimpering. We were the first to start down the slope. I noticed more bodies the closer we got. There were at least fifty men and women stationed here, all dead. A dune dog whimpered behind us as the rest of our troop followed, one of the girls shushing him. Dimas growled, the sound vibrating my entire lower half. My body went cold when I felt his emotions flood my mind, urging me to move with such intensity that it felt like everything stopped when Dimas did. I leaned closer to Naja and pressed my hand against his forearm to pass the message when I finally saw what had Dimas on edge.

There's something buried near the entrance. A bomb?

Naja stiffed, looking at me over his shoulder with his stony eyes before directing the girl behind us to move closer. He put his hand on her bare shoulder, the gesture was so casual that anyone unfamiliar with Ida stone power would've missed the true nature of the touch. She nodded and looked back at our troop, sending the silent order onto them as well. Naja reached back and laid his hand on my knee. Since the stones only work on skin-to-skin contact, I laid my hand over his to hear his message.

Can you fight or do you need a cover?

I can fight.

He pointed at the dagger strapped to his right thigh and I gripped the hilt. He steered us near one of the bodies, leaning down to pull a metal spear from the woman's chest. I finally looked up at the rest of our troop, drifting further and further away from us and pretending to inspect the carnage. Kieran met my gaze from his seat behind one of the girls. The confusion on his face told me that he was the only one amongst us who hadn't gotten the message.

Naja let out a yell and launched the spear into the air. Dimas lurched under us, and I barely got my left arm around Naja's waist. All the dune dogs sprinted away from the entrance of the tube, Kieran and two of the other Aldierians went the opposite direction. When the spear sunk into the sand, the bomb buried at the entrance went off with such force that my eardrums popped, and I hadn't heard the yells from the attacking Gallaterran soldiers.

The sand was still settling around the unscathed tube as the soldiers charged towards us on foot. Where all fifty or so of them had been hiding was a mystery, but it was clear that there were too many of them for us to fight off. Dimas began running back to the tube, the other dune dogs doing the same. Naja pressed his hand to a panel on the left side and the doors began sliding apart. He shoved me off Dimas's back and into the tube before the doors had fully opened. I tossed myself against the clear wall so one of the dune dogs could launch itself inside along with the man on his back. Two more came in right after it. Kieran and the last girl made it inside just as I saw Sargent Marcus leading the way across the beach, his deranged expression clear even from a few yards away.

Dimas and Naja slipped inside last, pressing the panel on the inside of the door. The steel doors barely slid shut in time, the loud pounding of metal on metal and fists echoing loudly in the space. They went quiet after just a moment. Armed soldiers, faces concealed behind silver helmets appeared outside the transparent walls. Some of them tested their best weapons against the tube despite its superior strength.

"They won't break it," one of the men said, "It's Aldierian made." I didn't care about the soldiers surrounding us now. Marcus came through the crowd and stood outside. He was maybe a foot away from me. I had forgotten just how large he was, muscles seeming more pronounced than I remembered them. Kieran tried slinking comforting hands around my waist, but I pushed them away and strode forward. I pressed my lips to the plastic or glass, whatever it was separating us, and stepped back. With a wink, I turned and led the way further down the tube where the waves were too high for them to follow.

CHAPTER 11

Once Kieran finally came out of his shock, I let him pull me to his chest in a tight hug. The Aldierians had all dismounted from their dogs and were assessing themselves, making sure that no one had been shot or somehow hurt from the blast of the bomb.

"Are you okay?" I asked Kieran when he pulled away. He let out a deep breath, looking me over.

"Yeah. Yeah, I'm fine. Are you?" He took the dagger from my grip and held it out for Naja without ever taking his eyes off me.

"Yeah," I said, "Yeah, I think we'll be fine now." It was dawning on me now how close we were to reaching help. Getting to the Aldierians had seemed like such a huge task before and here we were, standing in a fortified tunnel that led straight to their capital city. I pulled his face to mine and kissed him, so overcome with excitement that I felt light as air.

One of the girls said something in Aldierian that got a laugh out of everyone. I didn't care. Never in my entire life did I think I could do anything this worthwhile and I never dreamed that I would meet anyone like Kieran Grace.

"It's still a few hours walk from here," Naja said, "Since no one is hurt, we don't have to worry about rushing." He led the way further into the sea. We walked probably an hour before switching to the dogs again. Kieran and I shared Dimas while Naja opted to continue walking.

The ocean was mostly peaceful aside from the occasional school of fish and a pair of dolphins that swam around the tube to inspect us before darting back into the blue. I shared more of my memories with Kieran, this time focusing on the happy ones. Most of them featured Jacob. There was Jacob and I sparring in the forge, then Jacob and I on the only trip out of our village to deliver weapons to Gallaterra. I showed him the games I played with my childhood friend, the happy moments before she moved away. Kieran sat in silence behind me, the soft hum of a laugh his only response as I continued through my memories.

The memories drifted to Kieran. I went through our entire journey, showing him every moment through my eyes from the second I saw him on the prison floor to the kiss we shared in the tube. Maybe we could make a life here when this was all over. I could finally learn about Aldierian culture. Kieran was so keen to learn that I knew he'd pick up the language before me. I wondered what "I love you" was in Aldierian and his lips against the back of my neck reminded me I was still transferring my thoughts.

"I love you too," he whispered. I pulled his arms tighter around me.

After another thirty minutes, we could see the city. It was like Gallaterra with its tall, metal structures. The biggest difference was all the windows. The steel was broken up on almost every building with transparent panels. Instead of sky bridges, clear tubes connected the buildings in a crisscrossing web. They went on forever, connecting to more underwater skyscrapers and wide compounds far out of sight. There was no way to tell just how big the city was or how much of it was considered the capital city versus other towns. There were ships, much like the one I was on when I arrived at Gallaterra, that glided softly through the water around us. I could see people in the windows sitting in rows like they were on a bus.

"Welcome to Varillia, our capital," Naja said, "Varillia means home away from home."

"Varillia," Kieran said, saying the word a few more times under his breath as if testing out the syllables.

"What should we know before we get to the city?" I asked. Naja slowed his pace, moving aside so that the girls and boy could move ahead towards the entrance.

"You don't speak Aldierian, but you can communicate using the Ida stone just fine. Most of us know English though and people will be eager to try speaking it with you," he said, petting Dimas, "We learn it in school in case we need it." My mind couldn't help but think that they learned it out of fear for the moment they're overtaken by Gallaterra. It made me even more excited to speak with the Ida.

"What else?" I asked.

"We call our leader Ida. Ida is an old word for mother in our language," Naja said. I remembered the dark-haired woman from the memories he showed me. I've never had a mother before. Jacob never married and he hadn't even dated, not that he had any free time to. The closest thing I had to a mother was the old lady who sold coffee on the streets every morning.

"What is our mother's name?" I asked. He smiled back at me.

"Imara," he said, "Imara Petrek."

The entrance led us into a large holding room. Several other round metal doors were encircling us, a few letting Aldierians out of one of the busses we saw outside. Some of the Aldierians in the room were dressed casually in pants, dresses, some men and women in skirts. Others were dressed like Naja and his troop and after watching the others mill from the busses to other tubes around the room, it was clear they were soldiers on patrol. Two women were manning our tube. Three others were finishing checking the girls when we approached.

"Captain Naja Petrek," Naja said and nodded towards Kieran and I, "with travelers from Gallaterra."

"Travelers, Captain?" the man that approached us asked.

"Travelers," Naja said, "Sympathizers with valuable information for the Ida." The man eyed us curiously for a moment before standing aside and passing on the message to the women behind him in Aldierian. Kieran and I slid from Dimas's back and let the girls pat us down. Naja dismissed the girls and boy who stood to one side, waiting for his order, and then he led us towards one of the tubes with the most amount of traffic.

"How welcome are we here?" Kieran asked. I elbowed him. "I only mean that Gallaterra thinks of Aldierians as enemies and kills them on site. I wouldn't imagine Varillia would throw a party in our honor."

"Where are we going?" I asked. Naja ignored Kieran's question and focused on me.

"I want you to meet mother," he said, "We won't be allowed an official meeting with the Ida until they know why you are here and what you have to offer. My word may be enough for them to call a meeting." My stomach felt light like I hadn't eaten in days. I had to remind myself to keep walking before the people behind us could bump into me.

"Okay," I said, "Home it is."

We took one of those underwater busses, which I learned were called subs, for a twenty-minute ride further into the city. We got out and walked through another two tubes before we entered a large structure. The inside looked almost exactly like the cities we passed through on our way here. It felt strange to say they were under the sea, the only reminder was the clear ceiling that acted almost like the sky. There were roads with dune dogs and dune riders. Aldierians walked outside of different shops.

Naja led us past what had to be the rich part of the city. The stores got fancier and the streetlights were made of gold. The Aldierians that walked here looked like they could be important politicians or businessmen, dressed up extravagantly. Naja spoke to the two soldiers guarding a door and they both moved aside so we could enter. Behind the door was a marble hallway with gilded sconces to light the way towards another door at the end. Beyond that door was a large hall. It was rounded, with a circular stone platform in the middle and raised golden thrones around the outskirts.

Naja passed the grand hall for another hallway that led to a set of stairs. We climbed several flights, took a few more halls, and greeted another guard at a door before we moved into what had to be the living quarters of the palace. The last hallway we took was abandoned, a wooden door with a golden doorknob at the end. Naja took a deep breath and paused.

"Why are you so nervous?" Kieran asked, "She's your mother." Naja nodded.

"I disappointed her," he said, reminding me of the events that led to Illya's banishment and his demotion.

"She can't be mad now," I told him, giving his arm a comforting squeeze. He didn't look any less anxious, but he led us towards the door and knocked. After a moment, a man dressed in military attire opened it. It was strange, not the way I imagined being introduced to my mother. I figured she was important judging by the beautiful building, but even the senators in Gallaterra relaxed at home without guards. It made me feel guilty as if I was somehow at fault for the violence and cultural destruction the Gallaterrans did to the Aldierians all those years ago.

"Captain," he greeted, the word more pointed than respectful. Naja spoke to him in Aldierian and he moved away, motioning for us to sit in the massive living room. He went to the door opposite us. One side of the living room was completely transparent, a slight dark tinge on the glass telling me it was tinted for privacy. It overlooked the most beautiful and busy section of the sea. In the center was a garden of colorful coral that was alive with sea life. The subs cast warm light over the sea as they glided past, the lights of the buildings a mile away glittering like underwater stars against a night sky.

"Imara," Naja said, his voice urgent. He stepped away from us and got on one knee before the dark-haired woman. She was tall and slender, her hair loose around her shoulders. She was dressed casually compared to the Aldierians we saw on our way here, wearing a simple blouse and a pair of tights. She said something to Naja, her expression dismissive. Naja raised his voice and I heard him say my name. After I heard Jacob's name, I knew he was retelling the story of my birth. The woman relaxed and drew closer to Naja, letting a hand rest on his shoulder. Finally, she looked up at me with a gasp. A smile formed on his lips and she laughed in disbelief.

"Red hair," she said. She took just two steps before I crashed into her arms, my eyes burning. We hugged for a long time before breaking apart, mother sinking into the blue sofa.

"They found out that I'm Aldierian," I said, "I was arrested." My voice squeaked and she shushed me.

"Your brother told me. He told me everything, but I want to see it as you endured it." She made a space for me on the sofa and I sat down, letting my head rest against her shoulder as she took my hand. I let the entire journey replay in my mind, the room silent through the whole thing. She was happy to meet Kieran, whom she embraced tightly and thanked for his support. She said that if he couldn't be a son to President Grace, he would be like a son to her. I was so overcome with happiness that I cried again, my eyes sore by the end of it all.

"Do you think we can get a meeting with the Ida?" Kieran asked her. She looked to the guard and nodded, waving him towards the door.

"Absolutely," she said, "All of Parliament will want to hear this. Let's dress properly." Before Kieran and I could disappear into the side room with her, Naja spoke.

"Imara," he said, still standing in the middle of the room with that anxious expression on his face. It was an almost questioning look, one that begged for forgiveness.

"Come," our mother said, "You've been punished enough, Lieutenant."

———

Naja was dressed exactly as we arrived except for the silver pin at his breast. That silver pin had made all the difference to him, putting him in better spirits than I had ever seen him. Our mother dressed in a jade gown that flowed to the floor and was sheer in some spots, showcasing the dark tights she wore underneath. A woman helped braid her hair in the same warrior hairstyle the woman in prison had done for me. When she was done, she did my hair the same way and brought me a gown like hers. Kieran showered while we got ready and was surprised to find a new pair of pants and a white dress shirt waiting for him when he got out.

I caught my mother staring at me as I put the Ida stone back around my neck. She joined me in the mirror and lifted the necklace, the pendant rested in her palm.

"You'll know soon how important that necklace is," she said, "It's why I left it to you." I didn't fully understand, but a kiss on my cheek put an end to any questions I had. I wanted to enjoy every minute of this, the luxury of it all, having family around me again, and sharing my happiness with the man I loved. Kieran smiled at me as he finished buttoning the collar of his shirt.

With us all ready, we left the apartment and followed the way back to the main hall only this time we went into a room down the hall from the circular room. Mother didn't follow inside, staying in the doorway.

"After the general briefing, someone will come for you," she said, "You can share your story then and why you're here." She didn't wait for any answers, shutting the door behind us.

"This room is…" Kieran started. I turned to take in the space now that the three of us were alone. It was dripping in gold. The gold crown molding popped off the deep blue walls. The claw-foot sofas, of which there were four, were upholstered in the softest velvet I'd ever felt. I was too nervous to sit though. What if Parliament didn't believe us or worse, didn't care any more than Gallaterra did about the over mining of Ida stones leading to the planet's collapse?

"Everything will go fine," Naja said, "Nothing matters more to Aldierians than preserving the planet. We would go to war over that, I'm sure." I hoped he was right because war is exactly what we were presenting. There was no way around it. President Grace sent soldiers after us, killed dozens of Aldierians on the beach, and he had framed the Aldierians in attacks that led to the deaths of his enemies. He was too powerful. He bore too much influence to let live.

I looked at Kieran. He stood tall, determined. My heart picked up pace in my chest. I was in love with him, so deeply that I couldn't stand this. I wouldn't.

"Kieran," I started, almost letting his sincere blue eyes ease my resolve, "I don't know about this."

His expression changed, brow furrowing. He glanced at Naja as if he would have an answer, and in some ways he likely did. Understanding crossed my brother's face and he looked at me now soberly and gave a nod. Kieran blanched.

"You don't think I can kill him, do you?" he asked.

"No. No, that's not it. I know you want him dead, but-"

"But what? You think I'll chicken out?"

"No, Kieran," I stepped towards him and tried taking his hands, but he stepped out of the way. "Listen to me," I said.

"We had the plan straight," Kieran started after taking a deep breath, "We're all going to go together. I know the capital. I know those buildings and I'm going to be the one to get us into them. There's no other way."

"You can draw us a map. We can take down the coordinates and we'll be fine," I said, trying again to move towards him. I had taken half a step before he closed the gap. He held my face between his hands, keeping my eyes raised to his intense gaze. My heart skipped in my chest.

"You won't go without me," he said, emphasizing every word. "Kenna, you grew up with love and family. I didn't. Yours is the only love I've felt clearly. Don't do this to me. Please. I can't watch you leave and not know when, if you'll ever come back to me."

"Kieran," I started. I could hear the weakness in my voice, barely holding on. I watched as Kieran's eyes glassed over.

"After everything… We can't be apart now. Let's finish this the same way we started it."

I raised a hand to one of his but didn't have the heart to pull it away. His fingers were soft on my cheeks. He trailed the pad of his thumb across my skin. My hand was against his cheek before I realized it, brushing the tear that had spilled over before he had controlled the emotion behind it. I took a deep breath and pulled both his hands away from my face and held them low.

"You don't have the weapon skills to protect yourself," I said. He groaned.

"I can learn that along the way." He pulled his hands away from mine.

"What if I spread myself too thin in a fight trying to protect us both. It could kill me. It could get us both killed."

"Not if I learn the skills myself. I could do it, you know I will. We'll be stronger than before."

"You aren't strong, Kieran," I yelled over him, "Not that way. It's taken me years of practice. Naja has formal training and spent years doing that. We have a month, maybe, for you to get that good and you just aren't that skilled."

Kieran shook his head, looking around the room again as if

someone would come through the walls to his aide. Naja kept his eyes focused on a spot on the far wall, purposely avoiding the fight. Finally, Kieran looked back at me. His anger was gone, replaced with a plea that nearly broke me.

"You won't go without me," he said, "I won't let you. That's not the plan. I won't present it to the Ida if it doesn't include me."

I knew he meant it. He would do whatever he needed to stay included. I was also right about having him there being a risk. I wouldn't let him fight alone. I would try to defend him, even if he did increase his abilities. I couldn't even imagine a battle where he was more than feet away from me. He couldn't imagine it either and I didn't know how else to keep him away.

"I don't want you there, Kieran," I said, "I don't want you."

The words were painfully drawn out, barely making it past my lips. I saw his expression fall, the pain crossing his face. I hadn't intended on this being easy. I meant for the words to hurt. They had to. There was no other way to keep him safe in Varillia without making him question my feelings for him. He shook his head, letting out a gasp of disbelief. He didn't believe me one bit.

The door opened and a woman announced that Parliament was ready to hear our case. I tried to think about Kieran, forcing my feet forward and leaving the room ahead of the boys. Every chair was filled, the members of Parliament dressed in the black jackets and wave pins Naja had shown me from his disciplinary hearing. They all wore spiked crowns, but my mother's was the largest. Unlike the others that were silver, her pin and crown were made of gold. The elegance alone made her stand out among the crowd. I stopped before the stone platform when she rose from her seat. The woman escorting us moved to one side and extended a hand towards us in introduction.

"Ida," she said to my mother, "Kenna Riley and Kieran Grace are here to present valuable information about Gallaterra with you."

"Thank you," mother said, nodding to us in acknowledgment

before taking her seat, "You may speak." I was stunned to silence now, all confidence in my plan chased away by the shock. My mother was the Ida. She was the leader of the Aldierians.

Kieran stepped onto the stone circle and began retelling our story from the beginning, all the way back to my account of getting the device. I could barely focus on the room, my brain still far away in that gilded room. I always did right by others, that's about all I was good at, and it usually meant letting them go.

"-that's what we have to do to stop my father," Kieran finished, "I don't have weapon skills, but Kenna does and Naja is trained. I know the government buildings of Gallaterra more than anyone, even Gallaterrans. I can get us through them with less risk of being seen and I can get access to the power supply where the Ida stone converter is. That one converter is responsible for all the power in Gallaterra." I knew he wouldn't present my new plan to her. Surely we could amend that part later.

"I thought there were thousands of generators across Gallaterra," a man said across the room. Kieran turned to address him.

"There are, but the main converter sends a secondary power source to those generators," he said, "There are other Ida stone converters, but without the power generated from the main converter in the capital city they are useless. It's a one-of-a-kind converter. It would take them millions of dollars and fifty years of work to recreate it exactly." A woman laughed.

"Then, we've only bought the planet fifty years then," she said, "They will rebuild it. There's no way around it. It's what Gallaterrans do. They destroy, rebuild, and then destroy again. Their time on Earth is proof enough."

"Not if it's cheaper and better for the planet to use another source," I said, "Many of the scientists in Gallaterra prefer other resources. They see what is happening to Aldieria. They know we can't survive here just like we couldn't survive on Earth."

The woman started protesting again but stopped when the Ida stood. She raised her hands towards the man and the woman, a signal for silence. Then, she scanned the room and addressed us all.

"The sun is the ultimate source of energy, is it not?" she asked. No one spoke for a long time, many exchanging confused looks.

"It is, but solar energy only works as long as the sun shines directly on receivers," Kieran said. She didn't look down at him, still addressing the room.

"The sun is older than any of us, any of the planets, even this universe," she said, "It is one of the few renewable energy sources. It's because of the sun that we have Ida stones. The heat it provides enables the chemicals and pressure deep in the Aldierian sand to solidify into the stones, but there is another element that enables the stones to grow stronger." A soft mumble went through the room.

"You're describing a hybrid," Kieran said, "you're saying that by changing an element, you can change the power of the stone without corrupting the basic structure. Do you have hybrid Ida stones?" She finally looked back at us, a hint of a smile on her lips.

"It is called the Heart of Aldieria," she said, "and it is created by taking fully formed Ida stones and putting them on the floor of the East Sea. After a million years, the stone grows harder and stronger. Like the sun, it can't be fully harnessed or broken down. It survives every effort to destroy it, yet it still provides power. My husband discovered them." The room was buzzing with excited murmurs now.

"How long would this stone power an entire planet?" a man finally asked. Mother laughed.

"According to my husband's research," she said, "infinitely. He was unable to calculate a final power estimate. It never decreased or increased. The numbers stretched on and on."

"Like pi," Kieran said under his breath. A few more people laughed. Some were congratulating her.

"That's great, but we can't get to the bottom of the East Sea so easily," a woman said, "The last time it was done, the ship returned with the dead crew. None survived, despite your husband's research."

"It was a tragedy, but it wasn't all for naught," the Ida said, "The ship returned with a single stone. One stone that could power the entire planet for a million years at the least, easily twice the amount of time it takes for new stones to form." She looked at me now and I was suddenly very aware of the Ida stone around my neck. Just a moment later, a man asked the question I already had the answer to.

"And just where is this stone now?" he asked.

"Why did you leave it with me if it was so important?" I asked, taking the stone from under my dress and holding it up for her to see. Soft murmurs traveled the space around me as other officials made the connection.

"I was afraid I would die or be captured before I could get back to Varillia with it. I left it with you hoping you would grow up with all the knowledge of a Gallaterran citizen. Jacob swore to remind you what you truly were. I hoped you would come back home with that knowledge and share it with us. You've provided us with far more than just that," mother said, nodding towards Kieran. Cheers erupted through the space. I couldn't believe the gamble she'd taken eighteen years ago for this moment, a moment that very nearly hadn't happened. I looked to Kieran who was looking back not in shock, but in relief.

"If we can put that Ida stone in the converter, it will get stuck in a spiral. It will stay there for millions of years, powering all of Gallaterra. We won't have to mine the stones anymore, at least not to the point of collapse. It's sustainable," he said. He moved to embrace me, but he paused just inches away. His expression fell, sadness overtaking the excitement.

A moment later, guards could be heard yelling. A boy ran

into the room. He had short dark hair and was covered in bruises and cuts, his shirt hanging off one shoulder. He rushed forward, stopped in the middle of the room, and sat down a boxy metal object with wires exposed on two opposite ends. He moved towards mother, dropping to one knee and withdrawing a dagger from his hip. The soldiers stopped approaching. I had just taken two steps forward with the retractable knife ready in my hand before Naja tugged me backward.

"It's the Aldierian Courtship Rule," he said, his eyes glazed over and trained on the boy. I could hear his voice in my head now, telling me that the boy wasn't a threat to anyone. It was Illya.

Illya pulled his shirt off and turned the dagger so that the tip was positioned directly over his heart. He let out a couple of nervous breaths before speaking to my mother in Aldierian, the end of his speech sounding less confident and more pleading. He lowered his head and let the hilt rest in his open palm. My mother gripped it, her expression tight as she looked over the boy and then at Naja. The room was so silent that I could hear Illya's shaky breaths.

"It's a marriage proposal," Kieran whispered to me. "You ask to be accepted as family and ask that your companion's parents allow their love to live or die. If she rejects their marriage, she will kill him." I glanced at Naja, who had silent tears slipping down his face as he waited with shaking hands. Our mother looked back at Illya on the floor and stepped down from her raised seat, dagger still poised at Illya's breast. At last, she tossed the dagger aside where it skidded into the stone circle.

"Rise," she said, "and let me welcome you as my son." Illya was in tears now, his shoulders heaving when he got to his feet and accepted a kiss on the cheek from my mother. The room applauded and the cheering grew louder when Naja surged forward and wrapped his arms around Illya. They kissed, the way you do when no one is watching, and spoke in Aldierian.

I felt Kieran's fingers graze mine like he was still deciding if he should take my hand. I looked sideways at him. His expression was soft, a small smile faltering at his lips. It was forgiveness. He was Kieran from the pod that devoted himself to me and our journey to find the Aldierians, our entire plan to keep the planet from collapsing. His hand had nearly clasped around mine when I let go.

CHAPTER 12

At the insistence of my mother, I joined Naja and Kieran in an advanced combat class within the military outpost. The first week had been basic, boring if you asked me. The second and third were less so because I was allowed to showcase how much I already knew. Kieran struggled to follow along. By the sixth week, our instructor made a habit of letting me demonstrate the moves. Not long after that, I was teaching alongside him. It took just a week later, a private meeting with the training board, and a formal initiation for me to become the Advanced Combat Trainer.

ACTs got paid. It was three times the amount Jacob made at his forge each week. After our training class, Kieran and I would awkwardly part ways. He would go study under Varillia's top scientists and ecologists, and I would teach more classes and occasionally sit in meetings with Naja. After a month of training, mother set up a meeting that would hopefully clear us to begin planning for the mission back to Gallaterra.

I felt a rush of adrenaline as we all packed into the boardroom. Naja and Kieran were there, of course, but so were the regular members of Naja's troop and many other soldiers. The scientists and ecologists Kieran worked with were also seated around the large domed table. The top was a touch screen that showed one-half of the planet. Mother swiped her finger across it to place the East Sea and Varillia in the center.

"Everyone will get their turn to speak," she said, "I want the heads of the departments to sit at the table. The rest of your team can stand behind you." I looked around the room as we all began moving. Two men in blue coats sat at the table on the opposite side, Kieran positioned just behind. Three political representatives sat near my mother. Naja took a seat and pointed for me to take the last empty chair at the table.

"We have science, politics, and military here at the table," mother said, pointing at each group, "In that order, I want each team to explain possible issues within their domain that need to be addressed moving forward with the original plan that consists of Naja leading his troop and other soldiers towards Gallaterra to replace the converter with the Heart of Aldieria. Science?" The men in blue coats adjusted in their seats before the man with curly hair spoke for the group.

"We don't anticipate any scientific problems moving forward," he said, "The Heart of Aldieria functions just as you said, as far as we can tell, and should jam the converter and work on a continuous rotation to provide power. The science is more than assumptions, it's absolute." Mother nodded and looked next to the woman sitting to her right who would speak for the political side.

"The only issue we are concerned with is the possibility of starting a war with Gallaterra. We have already been chased entirely underwater. We would likely be sitting ducks in an attack," she said.

"Thoughts?" Mother asked those at the table. Naja was quick to speak.

"We are already at war with Gallaterra and have been since it was established on Aldieria. We just never actively fought back. If they do begin attacking us, our cities are fortified and protected from underwater attacks and with just one entrance, a breach is not only unlikely but would be easily contained. It would be like trying to suck pudding through a straw. They won't attack us here." The woman paused, considering his words.

"What about how President Grace has poisoned society against us? He spreads lies and frames us to control the sympathizers," she said.

"We're already called terrorists in Gallaterra," I said, speaking over Naja. When no one objected to me speaking up, I continued. "This mission won't change their thoughts of us, but even if we fail, it could embolden the sympathizers to act within Gallaterra." She nodded slowly and then sat back in her chair.

"Military?" our mother asked Naja and I. Naja looked to me first, but I nodded for him to lead.

"I am concerned that we are taking too many men and women into this mission," he said with a sigh. This was not at all what we had planned on presenting. I could tell he purposefully kept his eyes on everyone around the table but me.

"How many would be sufficient?" mother asked.

"Only the best should be allowed to go," he said, "the fewer the better. We are more likely to be noticed with more manpower. We need to include only assassins." Assassins? What exactly did that mean?

"What would that look like?" I asked, surprising everyone around the table. Now, they all knew that Naja was going off-script. He glared back at me.

"Assassins are the final defense," he said, "It means a mission could consist of one or even just two people. Sargent Marcus is positioned on the beach. He's Gallaterra's best, as far as we know, and we are more likely to slip past him with one or two people than a whole troop."

"Who do you suggest should go on this mission then?" I asked him, making sure he saw me look back at the twelve soldiers behind us who prepared for over a month with this mission in mind. His expression softened a little and he looked away from me and to our mother.

"I think we need to pair the troop down to six soldiers that meet assassin qualifications," he answered, "We can't sneak a troop of twelve into a government building. It's too obvious." I didn't know what to say to this. I agree that we didn't need a lot of help. Kieran and I had barely made it this far, but we had done it on our own. No one in the government building had thought to stop us as we ran past during our escape. Twelve people would be suspicious, running or not.

"Agreed," I said when our mother looked at me. She nodded.

"Then we will go through the twelve soldiers' credentials now and you two will approve or deny them. You are their trainer and Naja is their lieutenant," she said to me. We sorted through the twelve, not finding an issue until the Ida counted out for number six.

"You forgot me," Kieran spoke up. I felt my muscles tighten, preparing for the fight.

"You aren't sitting at the table," Naja said. At that, the curly-haired man spoke.

"Kieran is capable of serving as the mission specialist," he said, "he knows the science needed to replace the converter with the Heart of Aldieria better than anyone because he also knows every inch of the government building where the power supply is located."

"I drew a map," Kieran said. My mother lifted her hand in warning at him, keeping him from defending himself any further. She looked at the rest of the group.

"Any issues?" she asked. No one spoke for a long time until there was a shifting of papers, and the politician lifted a hand.

"The documentation lists Kieran Grace at a basic level in combat training," she said, "Basic would make him a liability more than an asset on a mission of this level. He should hand off his map and train the approved soldiers on how to access the supply room."

"That documentation was created before my assessment," Kieran said.

"It is still a liability," the politician said.

"I've improved a ton since that was created and it was inaccurate to begin with. Kenna and I handled five Gallaterran soldiers within Sargent Marcus's rank all on our own," he continued. The woman didn't even look his way.

"Not only would he be gambling his own life on chance but protecting him could cost the mission. I don't trust Kenna to sacrifice him over the mission," she said.

"Hey," I protested, "I'm an ACT here. I trained him when he first got here. I'm not denying that his skills are basic."

"That's bullshit," Kieran yelled over us all. Mother stood up and the arguing ended. Her armored glance at us nearly quelled my anger. After shooting us all stern looks, she sat again and asked for each group to weigh in. It was quiet for an awkward moment. No one wanted to be the person to sway the argument in the wrong direction, I was sure.

"His value is too high to leave behind," the curly-haired man said.

"We dismissed soldiers a few minutes ago who met advanced-level training," the politician said, "If we had documentation that he was better than basic…" My mother looked at me now, skipping Naja entirely.

"You are the ACT here," she said, "You trained all the men and women present. Is Kieran's documentation incorrect?"

"No," I said, "Well, maybe it is out of date, but I know he's not assassin-level."

"You haven't been present in any of my training since the first week," Kieran said, not looking at me as he spoke.

"What is his combat level?" my mother asked, point-blank. Her eyes bore into me so deeply that looking anywhere but at her would give away the truth.

"Advanced," Naja said, "easily." The room was quiet. I couldn't believe it. I could feel the anger hot in my chest. Naja understood what it meant for Kieran to go on this mission better than anyone. I stood with him as he cried over the mission that led to Illya's banishment. How could he agree to this? Why?

"Any other concerns not listed on the agenda?" she asked, moving on.

"Kieran's combat level can't be advanced. There hasn't been enough time," I said. Naja stood up abruptly and withdrew a folded sheet of paper from his pocket. He flattened it out in his hands before setting it down on the table before me. It was an evaluation of skill, the very same document I had filled out dozens of times for students in my classes. I knew every line and every requirement. Kieran's name was signed at the top and the document was filled with so many detailed notes that more of the page was handwritten than the original printed text. At the bottom was the official seal of the military along with Naja's signature of approval. Kieran would go on this mission.

"Kieran tested well within the advanced level yesterday. He also possesses valuable information about the mission, and no one can deny that first-hand knowledge serves the mission better than sending his notes and maps along. He did the work. He earned his spot. More than that, we need him as the specialist," Naja said, sliding the document away from me and towards our mother. She barely looked at the document, glancing at the bottom for the seal before sliding it to the politician beside her.

"We will meet in another month to hear drafts of a plan of action," Mother said, rising from her seat, "We could all use some time to de-stress and my son needs a while to enjoy married life before he deploys on this mission." She smiled and cheers filled the room. Naja's usual serious expression broke for a moment, the happiness undeniable on his face.

I skipped the line of people that had gathered to congratulate him and moved into the hallway to wait on him. Kieran brushed past, pausing awkwardly after apologizing for bumping me.

"I guess I'll see you at the wedding tonight," he said, raising a hand for a moment as if to take mine. I wanted him to. I did, but I didn't want him to think I was happy about the decision, like I would just back down and let him come aboard. Kieran's smile faded and after a beat, he walked down the hall. Naja joined at my side.

"You should talk with him about the fight," Naja said through our thoughts, *"I can feel how sad you are and it's ruining my wedding day."*

I let go of him, wishing his teasing could keep me from remembering. I didn't speak until we had moved further away from the boardroom. The main street of the gated government complex was busy with people on their lunch break.

"Why did you lie about his skill?" I asked.

"I didn't. He's improved," Naja said. I scoffed. "Listen," he continued, "He is the best specialist for this mission. That's my decision. It's mine to make, not yours, but I understand your concern. I do"

"Then how can you let him come?"

"Because I know you are both focused on the mission. You both want the same things. You want what's best for Aldieria, Varillia, Gallaterra, all of it. You're doing this for different reasons than the rest of us, more reasons than just protecting our people. For Kieran, he needs to be there for personal reasons. I don't know that he could handle anyone else killing his father. It's not about just killing him. It's about making sure it's done a certain way. That's still his father."

"This mission isn't all about killing Grace. It's about the Heart of Aldiera too. If we don't get it in the converter, then it doesn't matter if he's dead. Aldieria will still collapse because Gallaterra will keep mining Ida stones." Naja took my hand, stopping me from walking.

"He's earned his spot. I know you're worried about him, but he wants to do this, Kenna."

"And he wants to do a lot of things like have a family that loves him and become a scientist and invent things that will change the world," I said, turning to look at my brother.

"He already is a scientist," Naja said, "You both have jobs here now and a life to come back to. He's prepared for this. He knows the risk to you both. I didn't let him be a part of our troop just because he's advanced his skills and he's got the knowledge of Gallaterran technology. This is the last thing he needs to do before he can move on with his life, with you. He knows you're worried about him, but he's worried about you too for all the same reasons. You're so concerned about protecting everyone. Have you ever thought that maybe you need protection too? Now that he's able to, as I swear to you that he is, let him."

I'm a protector. The words made me shiver as I remembered the story Don Marcus told me. Jacob had protected me from the beginning. He kept my identity secret. He tried keeping me from the ceremony. He tried protecting me and he died as a result. I knew that I would take a knife to the heart for Kieran the same way.

"The problem with people like you is that they don't care to protect themselves. There's a chink in their armor right here."

I felt like stone. Maybe protecting Kieran wouldn't save him. You can't protect the people who don't want to be protected. You couldn't force them to lie low. If Kieran and I spent this mission trying to protect each other, neither of us would survive. He needed to trust me just like I needed to trust him, no matter how scary that would be.

"You're right," I said, "but that doesn't mean I hope he'll stay behind." Naja smiled and gave my hand a firm squeeze.

"I bet if you sleep with him he'd stay," he said.

"Believe me, he won't," I thought.

"You must not be any good at it then."

I shoved him away and he laughed.

"I'm kidding. I just don't want you two to spend all tonight avoiding each other. We are friends. We will be on this mission together. Talk to him so it's not awkward for you and everyone else going with us." I hated that he was right. I could barely be in that boardroom with him. How did I expect to travel across Aldieria with him and just four other people?

"I will. Just not tonight," I told him. He didn't press me, leading me into the apartment we shared. It was small, with a tiny kitchen and living room with two bedrooms and a shared bathroom. It was nothing like the apartment our mother lived in, but it was practically luxury compared to what I was used to. Naja gathered his clothes from his bedroom, promised to talk to me at the wedding, and left to dress at the venue.

The loneliness hit hard now that he was gone. I tried keeping busy in the apartment, but there was nothing to do aside from getting dressed for the wedding, which I did at a snail pace. Aldierian weddings were like Gallaterran weddings except they were less extravagant in the ceremony. Naja told me that weddings usually came just days after the Aldierian Courtship Rule. I thought that Illya had asked for our mother's blessing to be with Naja when he had put his life on the line. It turned out that you only needed your family's blessing to form a life-long union with your significant other.

After an hour, I finished my makeup. I wore much more than I normally would, probably more than I ever had. Not that I didn't care about makeup. I loved looking at the beautiful women on billboards and that flashed across the displays at the grocery store. Makeup was expensive and when you can afford just one pair of shoes a year, makeup is reserved for very special events. Weddings. Graduations. The Ceremony of the Device.

The memory of the device being ripped from my ear made me shudder. There was still a square-like patch of pink skin behind my left ear that I knew would never fade away. My first thought was to smooth my hair over it, but I started a French braid there instead. Kieran loved my braids. The thought stilled my hands for a moment. I tied the end of the small braid off and pinned it to the nape of my neck and focused on styling the rest in loose waves that cascaded over my right shoulder and down my back.

Maybe our fight was stupid after all? I wish it had been. All this time, we were living in the moment, just along for the ride. Now that we reached our destination, was there really anything left to us? It didn't matter how loud the voice in my head called yes, our futures diverged. What the hell was I going to do when all of this was over?

I was tired of stalling. I chose the first of four white dresses and pulled it on before getting a good look at it. I was surprised when I didn't step into a skirt, but a pair of white pants. They were surrounded by a lace overskirt. The bodice was a jeweled halter that scooped in the front of my navel. The back was missing, not even a layer of lace or tulle as coverage. This was an elaborate dress and in white... Who was getting married here? Jesus.

I decided not to look at the other dresses and just go with it, not doing anything more than slide into the strappy heels my mother loaned me and start back towards the capital building. At first, people stared, but the closer I got to the expensive side of Varillia, the more men and women I saw dressed in similar white finery. I didn't look so out of place as I joined the small crowd that had gathered in the courtyard. I scanned the area for anyone I recognized before going into the building.

I followed the flow of traffic down a couple of halls and into a large ballroom. One wall was open to the coral garden of the sea, a whale gliding by as if not aware of the onlookers standing at the glass. A woman and a man sang in Aldierian in a corner, accompanied by a small orchestra. On the far side of the room was a gorgeous marble staircase, the gold railings weaving their way to the second-floor balcony where a woman stood in a coat, the white version of the coats the politicians wore in Parliament.

Still, I didn't recognize anyone in the room. I took a red glass from a tray when a server offered it to me, a cautious sip of the sweet liquid telling me it contained alcohol. I finished a glass as I stood awkwardly before the window, the room growing more crowded by the minute. I was nearly halfway into my second glass when applause drew my attention to the balcony. Naja and Illya appeared at the top of the steps, both dressed in red. I'd never seen Naja look so relaxed, more overjoyed than even Illya looked, staring back at him as he waved to the crowd. They shared a deep kiss, which sent the crowd cheering, before joining the party on the main floor.

I leaned towards the nearest server to ask, "Did I miss the ceremony?" when I noticed Kieran standing just feet behind him. The server saw him starting my way and he scooted past me to offer drinks to the next couple. Kieran had on white slacks and a white long sleeve shirt with a high collar. His blonde hair was pushed back. Hanging around his neck on a silver chain was an Ida stone still in its original form. It looked like a crystal, the rough edges glittering in the blue light from the sea.

"Who gave you a stone?" I asked, a little taken aback at the sight of him. He probably dressed like this all the time in Gallaterra City, attended tons of fancy parties, drank far more fancy cocktails in a single year than I knew how to name.

"Ida Imara," he said, addressing my mother by her title. He nodded towards Naja and Illya who were swaying happily to the music in the center of the room. "Aldierian wedding ceremonies take place between the couple in secret. I sort of like the privateness of it.".

"That sounds..." I started, feeling a blush rise to my cheeks as I thought about the only private ceremony that happens between the couple at Gallaterran weddings. Kieran let out a laugh and joined me at the window, resting against it.

"More than that happens behind closed doors," Kieran said.

"It's not that much of a ceremony if no one else is allowed in," I said. He shrugged.

"When you declare your love for someone," he said, keeping his gaze on the newlyweds when I looked sideways at him, "It matters most that the special person is there to accept it and to make their vow in response." It sounded like he was making his own promise.

"That's more beautiful than making your deepest felt promises before a crowd of people," I said, looking back at my brother and Illya when Kieran turned to me. Illya laughed as Naja spun him around and around before pulling him into an awkward dip. My mother interrupted them, holding her hand out to Illya as an offer. After a moment of surprise passed over his face, he accepted, and they began to waltz and left Naja to chase after a passing server.

"Yeah. Beautiful," he said under his breath. We stood there in strained silence for a long time. "You know, in Aldierian culture, you address the Ida with her title only, not her name. It's that way no matter who the Ida is. The same goes for the Ida's family. So, you have a title, Idava Kenna Petrek," Kieran said.

"I'm just Kenna Riley," I said. I could feel him staring at me.

"No, you're not," he said, his tone sharp. I turned to look at him. His expression was intense, a hint of anger in his eyes. Maybe it was frustration. Whatever it was, it sparked a fire in my belly. I opened my mouth to tell him off when Naja approached us.

"I don't know how I'm going to leave him this time," Naja said, handing a glass to Kieran and looking back at his groom as he sipped his own. "Illya is usually the specialist on the missions I lead," he said. His smile dimmed a little and I felt my stomach sink as I remembered vouching for Kieran. He had improved since his first evaluation, but he was nowhere near advanced in combat. I was lucky that he did his training after hours when Naja and I brushed up or else there would have been witnesses to call my bluff in the boardroom. That woman's voice still echoed clearly in my head.

He is a liability... I don't trust Kenna to sacrifice him for the mission...

My eyes burned and I raised a hand to swipe at them when I realized Kieran was watching me. I lowered my hand to the Heart of Aldieria hanging around my neck instead and cleared my throat. The chain was cool against my bare chest and I focused on my breathing and turning the stone on the chain until I felt in control again.

"I started training extra in the mornings, "Kieran said, "I know I'm the best specialist and not the best soldier, but I swear to you, Naja, that I won't slow down the mission." It sounded more like he was speaking to me. Naja turned to look at him, his jaw tightening as he looked from Kieran to me and then back at Kieran again. He nodded slowly.

"We really shouldn't make this day about the mission," I said, my voice still sounding thick. I cleared my throat again before adding, "It's your wedding day." Naja smiled and looked back at Illya again. He was still dancing with our mother in the center of the room, a new slower-paced song beginning and causing them to break apart. Illya began looking around the room, kissing my mother on the cheek before she greeted an elderly couple a few feet away.

"She's right," Kieran said, "Go celebrate," Naja smirked.

"I guess, I do have some dancing left to do," he said, pulling Kieran into a hug. He reached for my neck, his hands warm against my exposed back. I could feel his mind open to me, keeping me in his embrace a little longer to hear his thoughts.

"Kieran has something to say," Naja said, "Let him speak."

"I know what he's going to say."

"No," Naja said. His voice echoed so loudly in my mind that it nearly triggered a headache. *"I said let him speak, not talk to him. Listen to what he has to say. Just listen."*

"Sure thing, Lieutenant."

Naja pulled away from me, a forced smile on his face. Kieran didn't seem any the wiser about our silent conversation as he sipped from his glass, the red liquid fizzing.

"I'll talk to you both later," he said and dove back into the crowd before either of us could reply. I didn't want to talk to Kieran. I didn't want to hear any more about how much he's training for the mission or how he's studying with the Aldierian scientists or any of his other attempts at proving he would be fine during our mission. Naja was right though. I supported him this far. Now I had to trust that he knew what he was doing. I had to listen to him.

I let out a sigh, my chest relaxing as I accepted the coming conversation. "Kieran, we should…" I started, my words trailing off when he grabbed a hold of my hands and pulled me towards the dance floor.

"Dance with me," he said, positioning one of my hands at his shoulder and holding the other aloft. His hand sliding around my waist nearly made me melt. I let him spin me around, leading the dance that I vaguely remembered as being the Aldierian dance we did in the arena. He told me once that it was a traditional dance, but he hadn't elaborated any more on its meaning. It must have been some kind of dance of celebration because the rest of the couples on the floor were turning in the same way.

"Kieran," I started. He startled me by lowering me into a dip, breaking the uniformed dance the entire party was doing.

"It's your brother's wedding," he said, forcing a smile, "Let's celebrate."

"We can't avoid this forever," I said.

"But we should for now," he returned, spinning me around and pulling me to his chest. We fell back in unison with the other couples, the orchestra swelling again to the chorus.

"We can't," I said as the song finished. I tried backing away, but he caught me by my waist and pulled me to him as a new, slower song began. His expression was soft, a little sad in those blue eyes that threatened to capture that voice in my head that wanted to drag him into the nearest closet. He took my hands and draped them on his shoulders, the gesture bringing my face closer to his.

"I know you want to talk to me about that dumb fight and I don't want to hear any more of your reasons why you aren't helpless, but we have to talk about it before the mission," I said. Kieran let out an annoyed sigh, turning his gaze from me. I cupped the side of his face with both my hands, wishing I hadn't after I felt his strong jaw and his blue eyes were focused on me again.

"You don't have to worry about me, not anymore," he said.

"Yes, I do." He groaned.

"Naja handed the proof in, so it doesn't matter what anyone thinks now."

"So, you're mad at me for that now, not admitting that I had it all wrong in front of all those people? Oh, Kieran's so strong and muscular. He's so manly, too manly to need protecting from some girl," I said, letting my hands slide to his neck when he shook his head in disbelief.

"That's not what this is about," he said, "Not anymore, at least"

"We shouldn't do this here," I said. He held me tight by my hips, preventing me from backing away.

"I'm not going to let you do this anymore. You can't run away from me like you've been to avoid your feelings about us."

"I'm running away from you because of them, asshole," I said, lowering my voice before continuing, "You got what you want. You're going to go on the mission, but I can't just go back to the way things were. You can't storm ahead like you should if I let myself be with you."

"You're being so distant because you think you're weighing me down?" he asked, surprise etched into his face.

"I'm trying to support you by letting you go on this mission, but you're making it really hard, Kieran," I said.

"Letting me?" he said, "Just admit that you're jealous."

"Of what?" I shot back, feeling hot despite the amount of skin this top showed off.

"That I'm smarter than you, have a future planned out, get to be the big bad hero by killing the president and you don't get your usual role of protecting me this time," he said. I pressed my hands to the sides of his neck, pulling him another inch closer before letting my threat transfer through the Ida stone.

"If this wasn't my brother's wedding, I'd slap you so hard right now."

Kieran stared back at me in shock. His eyes burned into mine and his jaw formed a tight line. I could feel his hands stiffen at my waist before he lowered both arms to his side.

"Okay," he said, backing away a step, "I'm ready to talk." I didn't wait, leading the way from the dance floor and down an abandoned hall where a set of stairs were. I quickened my pace as I heard his steps fall closer and closer to me with each stair. Another hallway and I could no longer hear the noise from the party, just the sound of blood rushing in my ears.

The hall I turned down was a dead end, a painting filling most of the wall space at the end that depicted wind turbines that once stood tall west of the Silent Sands. The only door halfway down the hall was labeled as a mechanical room, so I felt confident that no one would interrupt or overhear us. So, I turned around to face him. He was lucky he was out of arm's reach.

"You said it yourself when we were waiting in that lounge to present our plan to my mother," I started, "You've had it worse. I can't imagine what your life was like and I don't want to think about everything you've been through. I want you to have everything you never had. I want you to feel love and success and use all that random knowledge you have about Aldieria and cultures and sciences and shit to save the planet. You're the one who's going to keep Aldieria from crumbling, not me. I'm trying to support you and get you back to that power supply room in Gallaterra so you can make things right, but I can't do that while I'm with you."

"Why not?" he said, his voice loud in the small space, "I get it, Kenna. I want the same things."

"No. How can you? You're right about me," I said, angry tears burning my eyes, "I'm not smart like you and I don't have big ambitions, but I've never had the opportunity before. It's always just been me, the streets of Arro, and a plan to survive the day. Then you come along, all shiny and perfect... I'm scared, Kieran. For the first time in my whole life, I'm scared for a life that might not include you. I feel stupid that I can't see anything more for myself than you right now, not a career path or any kind of future except for you. I know you need to go on this mission for yourself, but I am so afraid that us together is going to ruin everything for you." Kieran had both hands in his hair, combing his fingers through it so roughly that it ruined his perfectly suave look.

"I don't want to be a scientist," he said as if admitting some big secret, "Not after the things we've been through and seen. It's not enough."

"Don't be stupid because of me," I told him, moving further from him and leaning against the wall. I looked up when I heard something whoosh past me and then a soft thunk. A small throwing knife was stuck into the center of one of the wind turbines in the painting. I looked back at Kieran. He stood tall, taller than normal somehow, and looked strong. Maybe he had been training more and I hadn't noticed until now, but he was muscular in places I don't remember him being. His shoulders were rounder and a tendon twitched in his forearm when he raised his arm, another knife positioned between his fingers.

"I want to go on this mission with you, kill my father, replace the converter with the Heart of Aldieria, and come back. I want to come back here with you, that's all I know for sure. My big ambitions don't mean anything to me if they don't include you," he said. He sent the second knife flying down the hall and then a third, both landing dead center of two other wind turbines in the painting. Where did he have those stashed all this time and who taught him to throw knives anyway?

"That's not what you want," I said, turning away from the painting.

"Yes, it is, you stubborn girl" Kieran said, "This whole time with you, you showed me that I can do more. Because you were with me, I realized I was stronger than I always thought. I'm not some fatherless boy hiding behind books, I'm a man who fights fiction with facts and finally has the guts not just to say all the things I've felt but take action. I've seen my file. I'm the most improved in our troop in combat. I may not have your knife skills and I'm not going to pretend that I'm assassin-level, but I'm not weak and I will only get better and fast as my records have shown. I can do so much more for this planet by going on this mission and becoming an assassin than if I become just a scientist. I want more in my future than just science experiments in a laboratory. Plus, I get you, Kenna. That's what I want. I'm not giving up science. I'm not giving anything up. I want more. You're more."

My stomach was in knots, and I was caught in his gaze, unable to look away, breathe, move in any way without feeling like I would crumble into a heap of emotions. I felt more girlish than I'd ever felt before. The tears were burning angrily in my eyes, threatening to tank any resolve I had left. But if he meant what he said, Kieran wasn't settling. He wasn't accepting his place as his father had always tried making him.

Kieran crossed what little space was left between us to meet me, hesitating before taking my hands as if I might push him away.

"We are going to keep my father from destroying Aldieria and after that, we are going to come back here, to Varillia. I'm going to keep working with the scientists and training with the military. You're going to be whatever it is assassins do when they aren't out killing off evil. With my father gone, the politicians who sympathize with the Aldierians will start coming out. We will help them show Gallaterra what the Aldierians are and be the ones to ally. Varillia is the best place to do that. It's what your father and your mother were trying to do with their mission, right? It must be. I can be the human among aliens like he was. I can continue his work and educate both sides about the other's culture," he said. The way he spoke eased the tension. His eyes were alight with such hope, and I could hear the passion in his voice. It was the Kieran I fell in love with, the one who always seemed to have an answer even when everything went wrong.

"God, I hate you sometimes," I said, tasting salt as a tear slipped down my face. He laughed, pulling me closer. His hands moved to my face, one finding its way into the loose waves that hung over my shoulder.

"Because I'm right?" he asked, "and it's what you want too." And he was perfect. I pressed my lips to his, pulling myself to his chest by his shirt. His hand was warm on my lower back, the other combing deep in my hair. I took a step backward towards the mechanical room, pulling him with me. The door opened when I tried the handle. I didn't look inside before I ducked into the darkness. The only light came from the large window on the opposite side. The remaining walls were filled with screens, displaying everything from security cameras to graphs and other surely important data. It was late, so the dozens of desks were empty.

His lips met mine again as I continued to back further into the room, stopping only when I felt the cool surface of a desk behind me. Kieran lifted me onto it, his hands fumbling at the small of my back while his lips kissed from my cheek, my jaw, and down my neck.

"As much as I want to be the one to peel you out of those pants, I think you'll have to do it," he said, moving his hands to my thighs. I pulled back just a little and behind his blue-eyed stare, I noticed my face flash across one of the screens.

"Wait," I said, getting to my feet and squeezing past him. His face came across the screen next and I noticed the words "The Heart of Aldieria" displayed in the top left corner and the word "approved" in the left. I looked around the room. Some of the desktops were screens as well, smaller versions of the giant map in the boardroom. A sweep of all the screens confirmed that this wasn't a control room for the heat and A/C. The screen flashed through the members of our troop before restarting the rotation again with me.

"Our mission must've gotten approved today," I said, "Maybe a date is listed here somewhere." My hands were already skimming the surface of the closest desk, the largest screen on the wall projecting a random report on invasive coral and then a video of the steel bridge outside the main tube to the Aldierian underwater cities.

"Stop! Stop," Kieran said, brushing my hands away from the control panel before I could switch it. He pressed a few buttons to zoom in the camera and then another made a recording message flash red on the corner of the screen. "Look," he said, pointing to the middle of the bridge where a flash of light hinted at something moving. It was hard to make out the steel armored soldiers against the silver surface of the bridge, but the gold suit leading the way was an obvious giveaway. I remembered the look of absolute loathing the gold soldier gave me before we descended into the waves. His being here was personal or else President Grace would've ordered him back.

No, we had something important keeping the president in power and it wasn't some escaped Aldierian. We had the greatest weapon against President Grace, the only one that could spark real change after his death. I looked at Kieran, but his eyes were trained on the awaiting soldiers. I didn't say a word.

CHAPTER 13

"We have to tell someone," I said as Kieran finished recording once the last soldier walked out of the frame. We counted fifty soldiers. Fifty against six made for dismal chances for success right out of the gates.

"Your mother?" Kieran suggested. She would cancel the entire mission.

"Naja," I said, "It has to be my brother." He followed me back into the hall, noticing the signs that my anger had blinded me to earlier. We were in the military wing of the government building.

"On his wedding day?" Kieran asked as we walked. I wish the answer was no.

"Yes," I said, finding my way back to a familiar hall that led back to the party. The room had thinned out a little, signs of a party ready to end. Naja and Illya were nowhere in sight. I grabbed a passing waiter by the arm.

"Where are the newlyweds?" I asked. He seemed taken aback by my English but recovered quickly to answer.

"They left over an hour ago," the man said. I turned to face Kieran who scanned the floor for what I could assume was my mother. She wasn't among the party guests either and I was glad. Naja needed to know what waited for us outside the East Sea, but my mother did not. Not yet.

"They probably went home," Kieran said. Together, we left the party passing the exhausted guests in the streets. I stepped out of my heels after a block so we could move quicker, not the only one with the same idea. A drunk girl yelled something in Aldierian at Kieran as we rushed past them, her barefoot friends bursting into fits of giggles.

"Don't worry," he said to me as we rounded the corner, "I'm still yours."

"Kinda wish I hadn't noticed my face on the wall," I mused, loving the smile it brought to his face.

"Oh, I still plan on getting you out of those pants after this," he said, a man looking back at us in surprise as we passed, "If I can find that damn zipper." I resisted the urge to pull him down each alley we passed as we moved into the clear tubing system, deciding it would be quicker to run a couple more blocks than wait on a sub among the rest of the nightlife crowds. I led the way again when we reached the military housing.

Our complex was quiet in comparison with the boisterous wedding party. My heart seemed to pick up pace as we got to our floor of the building. I left Kieran on the landing to run down the last stretch of the hall for the white door, trying the knob before my key. To my luck and surprise, the door was unlocked.

"Think about what you might walk in on," Kieran called down the hall as I swung the door open. Naja stood just a few feet away with a bowl of chips, dressed only in his red pants from the wedding. He looked up at me as he walked towards the couch in our small sitting room, eyeing me with a confused expression.

"Did you run here?" he asked. Movement caught my eye down the hall.

"Woah," I gasped when I saw Illya, averting my gaze to the

floor and waiting until he was behind the kitchen counter to look up, seeing a little less skin than seconds before.

"Illya, are you naked?" Kieran asked as he joined me in the doorway. I shut the front door with a snap behind him. Illya opened the fridge and pulled out a blue bottle before turning to face us again. He didn't seem bothered by us being in the room, looking from Naja's calm expression back to us.

"Yeah," he said with a shrug, "Does my being nude offend you? Is that one of those Gallaterran things?" He started to move towards the end of the counter, but Kieran and I both raised our hands in protest.

"No, nudity is fine," Kieran said, "It's just that... We aren't exactly so..."

"Just stay there, for now, Illya," I said, tossing my shoes next to the front door. I went to the sitting room and stopped in front of my brother. "We have to talk about the mission and before you argue that it's your wedding day, it's important," I told him. The annoyance replaced the amusement in his expression. He let out a long breath and fumbled through the heap of clothes on the floor for another pair of red pants. He brushed past me and slid them over the counter to his husband. While Illya began dressing, I explained what we had seen in the control room. I ignored Illya's groans behind me, but Naja couldn't. He kept his eyes on his husband as he listened to me, the look in his eyes growing more nervous the longer I talked.

"Illya," Naja said once I'd finished, his tone alone pleading.

"I just got back and I won't lose you again," Illya said, joining us in the living room now.

"You won't," Naja firmly said.

"I'm your specialist," Illya said, pointing at Naja's chest, "My job is to calculate risk and solve problems. There is a huge amount of risk here and you don't need me to point it out. I don't see many options that get you safely across the bridge."

"I see one," Kieran said, cutting off the argument before it could begin. "It's a possibility," he added, moving to the tablet resting on the side table. He began typing, the glow highlighting his serious expression as the screen on the wall across the room lit up.

"I didn't want anyone to find out we knew just yet, so I didn't send the video. I did memorize the code though," he said, pressing just a few more buttons until the video of the bridge was projected on the screen.

"There are so many of them," Illya said.

"Fifty," I said. Naja squeezed my wrist, a silent plea to not make things as bad as they were.

"It's a small area between the beach and the bridge. I mean, it's large enough for fifty soldiers to hide in the trees around it, which puts the distance between the tube and the bridge pretty close in comparison. If we are moving fast, like on the back of dune dogs, we could make it to the bridge before any soldiers reach us. The risk in that plan is that we could be shot down if we aren't quick enough," Kieran said, playing the video at double speed.

"Dimas and the rest of our dogs are the top of their rank," Naja said, "They're trained to run through the maelstrom."

"The fifty soldiers are going to chase after you, not to mention testing your dog's finite speed and endurance against military-grade dune riders," Illya said, crossing his arms over his bare chest.

"The dune riders are hidden in the tree line here," Kieran said, pointing to the video where the bridge met the forest. I could just see the line of silver on one side. That meant the soldiers would be fighting on foot on the beach.

"You can't outrun them," Illya said.

"We can if they can't follow," Kieran said, pulling even Naja out of his serious expression. Kieran had a smirk on his face, the same look he had whenever he announced a plan that would save the day.

"We ride fast, straight out of the tube and over the bridge and..." Naja started.

"Blow it up after we cross," Kieran finished. Of course. They would be stuck on the beach, at least for a while. It would be long enough for us to gain a day between us.

"It's one plan with little room for amendments, no room for a plan B," Illya said at last. Naja stood up, positioning himself in front of his husband.

"This mission is for the future of the planet. One possibility, a strong plan even, is better than taking no action at all out of fear," he said. He reached out for Illya's hand, but he moved away before Naja could touch him.

"Then take me with you. Two specialists are better than one and you have two of the best in this room now." Two? The surprise was evident on Kieran's face, a blush creeping up his neck from the compliment.

"No," Naja said, "You're not going. You may be a top specialist, but you don't have the combat training for this. You're just a rank above the basic level. Only those with assassin-level skills were cleared." He spoke with enough venom in his voice that it stung. I pushed back all my worries about Kieran and the mission.

"I know," Illya said, "and I know that we took oaths to Aldieria and our people and the Ida. I know that. I don't want to lose you again." Naja cupped the side of his face and pressed his lips to his forehead. He spoke a few words of Aldierian, and they stayed connected by touch for a moment, their eyes staring far off even though they were just inches apart.

"I love you," Naja said, kissing him again.

"I love you too," Illya said. His shoulders relaxed a fraction, enough that he settled into an armchair while we went through the plan a few more times. Each time we reviewed it, all three of us felt more confident. Kieran would stay close to Naja and I for help and the three of us would lead the way across the bridge. After doing a little research on explosives and using Kieran's computer skills to hack into a database to find more information on the bridge, we determined what explosive device was needed to do the job.

"All that is left is to decide what we tell mother and the board," I said once we had tired from reviewing the details. The room was silent. I kept my gaze on Naja and he stared back at me, his expression telling me he had the same idea.

"Mother will halt the mission if we tell her," he said, "If we don't, she will be angry when she finds out we knew."

"There's no reason she has to know that we knew beforehand," Kieran said. I nodded.

"I think we lead the other three Aldierians without telling them. They are trained well and they are ready for last-minute changes if the need is there. I don't think we need to tell them," I said. I had seen all of them train before, so I knew they were prepared and advanced enough in skill that a change wouldn't be a huge setback for them. They were trusting in us to make the best decision for the mission and Aldieria. My skin cooled as I thought about the risk we were putting them in. It was all on the three of us. I was responsible for so much more than just myself. I was responsible for so much more than just Kieran's safety.

"I'd like to get back to my wedding night," Naja said, standing up from the couch.

"Round two," Illya said with a smile. I felt the embarrassment burn in my cheeks. They were cute though and Naja looked like a different person when he looked at Illya, the way I felt when I was with Kieran.

"Stay hydrated," Kieran said, pulling my wrist towards the door. I snagged my heels on my way out, using the hallway wall to balance myself while I slipped them back on my feet.

"I guess, I'm staying with you tonight," I said. It hadn't occurred to me this whole time that I wouldn't get to sleep in my bed, not that I wanted to sleep at all. Naja was right about needing the best skills for this mission, and I knew Kieran wasn't advanced enough. I didn't want to be away from him since we talked in that hallway. I wanted to be as close as I could.

"Don't expect anything fancy," Kieran said, "My apartment is smaller than yours."

It was smaller, by a lot. Kieran"s apartment was one room with a kitchenette on one side, a bed in the corner, and just enough room near the front door for a couch that sat just six feet from the screen bolted to the wall. He used a tablet on his bed to turn on the screen, the menu displaying his most recent searches. They were all learning apps, history lectures, and even one that connected him to a language class that denoted him as being thirty percent into the level two course.

"You're learning Aldierian?" I asked him. Kieran settled onto the couch, scooting over to make space for me to curl up next to him.

"Yeah, aren't you?" he asked, "I'm going to live here. I want to learn all the ins and outs of the culture." Of course. Kieran was always learning something. I, on the other hand, tried learning off and on with Naja, but I didn't practice often enough to retain more than a few words.

"How long have you been studying this?" I asked him, looking back at the screen.

"Since we got here. I told you I knew what I wanted." He pulled my hand so that I had no choice but to settle onto the couch next to him, his body warm and the cushions soft.

"Say something in Aldierian," I told him. He smirked and began searching the app for food delivery.

"How about I order some burgers in Aldierian? I'm hungry," he said, dialing the number listed. He stumbled through a few words as he spoke to the voice that projected through the small space. After he finished paying using the tablet, he told me a drone would arrive with some kind of Aldierian sandwich in thirty minutes. The package was here within twenty, an automated voice from the big screen on the wall alerting us that the drone had left it outside our door.

"Shit," Kieran said from the front door. I had just finished showering in the only other room in the apartment and emerged wrapped in Kieran's white robe.

"In my defense, the word for two sounds super similar to the word for seven," he said, turning from the door with two large sacks. Once I stopped teasing him about the mix-up, we ate dinner. The sandwich was similar to a burger but had the taste of seafood and a crisp tanginess in the sauce I'd only tasted in Aldierian food before. It was delicious, so I ate two and we split a third and stashed the extras in the fridge for later. We were both so full that we laid in bed and watched an Aldierian TV show, with the subtitles on for me, until we both fell asleep. I don't think we spent a moment apart after that night.

Illya moved into our apartment with Naja, which was the perfect excuse for me to move in with Kieran. He told me we could get a larger apartment, but now just wasn't the time with our mission so close. We got our official date the day after the wedding. Getting clearance so easily only confirmed our decision to keep the soldiers waiting on the beach a secret.

We didn't see Naja in the remainder of the month before deployment. Kieran and I didn't see much of anyone. Outside our jobs, we stayed in our tiny apartment. I studied Aldierian culture and history with him and he was sweet not to point out how truly abysmal my Aldierian was. In a way, it was like there would be no mission at all. I felt so well adjusted in Varillia, more so with Kieran by my side, eagerly navigating the cultural differences and injecting his usual positivity into our new life. When we finished packing out military-issued backpacks and looked up at each other, I saw something different in his eyes than before. He looked strong but in a forced way. Kieran always had answers, a plan, a way out if things were to go wrong and that assurance kept him in control at all times and made sure there was a kind of positivity between us. Optimism wasn't my thing. With so much responsibility on us for going forward with the mission, I wished to see anything other than the nerves in his expression now.

"We, um, should get to the center," he said, slinging his pack over one shoulder.

"I guess so," I said and did the same. His hands moved slowly on the knob of the apartment as we locked up. Then, we were off to the deployment center. It was located close to the main tube, so it took us a forty-five-minute walk and a silent sub ride to reach it. We were on a schedule once we set foot inside the doors. It didn't look like a military building at all. It looked more like an inviting five-star hotel or an upscale hostel even. An elaborate buffet was already in full swing through the doors of a large dining hall. Four identical backpacks were strewn at the doors.

We dropped our bags at the door with the others and joined the small party. Illya and Naja were at the end of the line, piling their plates with foods I couldn't name. The smell made my mouth water despite the fact. I blindly followed Kieran to the beginning while I watched my brother and his husband walk past a few full tables to join my mother at the head table.

"What's that?" I asked Kieran as he spooned a helping of some kind of orange noodle dish onto his plate.

"I don't know, but it looks fantastic," he said, "and smells rich."

"Fancy," I said with an awkward giggle, failing to make a joke of the matter. He looked at me, a forced laugh coming from his mouth a second after. We filled our plates in silence and took the remaining two seats with my mother. Illya looked nervous. We ate in the quiet for long enough for it to be unsettling. The little conversation we had felt forced until Naja came right out with it and promised the safety of the entire troop to our mother, taking Illya's hand to pass on a silent message to him as well.

Kieran squeezed my thigh under the table and I cast a blushing smile at him, the assurance in his expression easing my anxiety a fraction. He smirked a little and leaned over to kiss my cheek before going back to the noodles, which turned out to be my favorite dish of the night. I felt the nudge again as I raised my water to my lips, this time feeling cool toes press to my exposed ankle.

"Do you trust that he's skilled enough for this?"

Cool water dribbled down my chin in surprise. No one noticed except for my mother, who was staring across the table at me in anticipation of an answer. I lowered my glass to the table and was careful not to let the wrong thoughts pass through the Heart of Aldieria around my neck.

"Yes. He says he's advanced and I believe him."

"But that's not the risk the board worries about," she said, *"You already know that, don't you?"*

She glanced up at me for just a second with raised brows, the gesture so subtle that no one but me would ever notice the true meaning. I wasn't careful enough. My emotions gave me away and her posture relaxed a little as she reached for her wine glass.

"I know I can watch his back if I have to just like I trust him to watch mine," I said.

"Yes, but are you willing to let him die to save the mission?" she asked.

I stopped with my fork halfway to my mouth, smiling at Naja when he noticed me hesitate. I tried playing it off by reaching for my napkin and he returned to explaining why he chose Dimas as a puppy and not the stronger puppy in the litter. Kieran listened intently as he explained the traits that make not just for a good companion, but a great military wolf.

"Yes," I said.

I projected the message before I could think of the words. My feelings flowed easily. I knew my mother had felt my anxiety and the memory of all the nightmares of Kieran's death that I'd been having for weeks now. I cut them off before she could sense anything more and I made sure I looked straight into her face. She stared right back at me, her expression so serious that it highlighted the lines around her mouth and eyes. No one else at the table seemed to notice us, thankfully. The idea of masking my emotions with a lost appetite seemed close to impossible. I focused instead on making sure my mother understood.

"I know what is at stake here. It's bigger than me, Kieran, all of us. I don't want to, but if I have to make that call…"

I didn't finish the message, not because I was trying to make a point. Mostly, I couldn't bear to say the truth. I made sure my eyes were sincere, hoping the strength I felt burned through the rest of the emotions the Ida stone was passing back and forth between us. She looked down at her plate again and began slicing her steak, pressing her toes harder against my ankle.

"When it comes to those tense moments in battle, the bone-crushing decisions, I trust you to do what's best."

She looked at Naja for a moment and then back at me before withdrawing her touch. She still didn't trust him. It took me just a few seconds to understand why. Naja swore to Illya that he wouldn't lose him again. The expression on his face showed such raw emotion that I knew he meant the words. Naja was more dedicated to his military obligations than any of us, dedicated enough to know what he risked if he broke those obligations to keep his promise to his husband. As surprising as it seemed, he was the emotional one in this mission. At least, that's how our mother saw it.

"Is it too late to go back for seconds?" Kieran asked, looking around us to see if anyone else had risen from their chair.

"It's our final meal," I said, this time the dark joke getting a real laugh from him.

"You're right," he said, "Might as well taste everything then." He stood up. I notice now why the room was so silent. At the remaining five tables, the soldiers were holding hands or otherwise touching the various loved ones around them, passing silent messages before we deployed in the morning. After our grand dinner, all six of us would be sharing a bunker located further in the building. Together, we would review any last plans like sharing with our troop what we had discovered was waiting just outside the tube. We would relish in luxury and sleep in the finest beds before being plunged into the dangerous mission ahead. It was supposed to be celebratory, a show of deep gratitude before we pledged our service and possibly our lives. Despite the grandeur I've never dreamed possible of experiencing, I wanted more to be back in that simple apartment with Kieran. I wanted the hot desert where we shared stories. I wanted the cluttered pod with the barely padded twin bed.

"Friends and family," my mother spoke, raising her voice and stature so it was high above everyone in the space. "I want to formally thank the soldiers deploying on this mission, but also extend my gratitude to their loved ones. You too are going to battle and for that, I feel your pain. I understand your fear. Know that what you are sacrificing and what your soldier is undertaking is so much more important than just us. It's not about Aldieria or Gallaterra. It's about both. It's for us all," she said and raised a glass of wine from the table. The room followed suit, waiting for her to speak.

"Falle etwva," she cheered, raising her glass.

"Etwva Ida," The room cheered in response. Everyone drained their glasses, and the party was over. All six of us lingered in the entryway with our backpacks as we said our final goodbyes. Mother didn't say a word to me, just kissed me on the forehead and sent me a serious gaze as a reminder of our conversation. I nodded at her and moved to Illya, promising to look after Naja. He pulled him into the tightest hug I've ever had and kissed me on the cheek before letting go.

Naja gave an order in Aldierian and the six of us fell into formation as we followed two uniformed women down an adjacent hallway. It sloped downwards for what felt like miles as we walked in silence. Finally, we reached a heavy-looking metal door that took a finger scan from all six of us for entry. Once we were all checked in, the door opened with a hydraulic hiss and the women closed us inside.

One of the men in our group said something in Aldierian as we took in the space, translating it a second later for Kieran and I as, "holy shit." The bunker was cabin-esque. The walls in the main space looked like trees, a few oaks ever-growing from square cutouts in the stone floor throughout the room. The ceiling was domed with half of it transparent and flowing into a large window on the far side of the room that overlooked the ocean. There was a pool at this side, so clear that you could see the bottom where the clear glass met the stone floor.

The rest of the living space was communal, though just as ostentatious. The bathroom was dripping in gold and polished stone, the Aldierian's openness about nudity clear when it came to the various showerheads along the walls. The bedroom was a long room with gold four-poster beds. Kieran, Naja, and I went there first to drop our bags. Rather than taking one of the open beds, I dropped my bag next to Kieran's by the first bed. A loud cheer echoed through the entire bunker, a splash from the pool following shortly after.

"This place is amazing," Kieran said, turning from the bed to look at us both in turn. His smile faded. I was sure my nerves showed on my face, but I didn't want to hide that anymore. It was all too real. I felt myself sinking back into my dreams, the terrible versions of the mission that had me waking up the past few nights sweating. I came out of my thoughts when Kieran slipped his hand into mine.

"We should tell them," Naja said as more cheering came from the main room. Kieran shook his head. He let go of me and backed towards the main room.

"We could all die tomorrow," he said, pulling off his shirt.

"That's exactly the point," I said as he unbuttoned his pants.

"You're the specialist on this mission," Naja said, "You're supposed to counter any risk you calculate."

"Yeah, but we could die tomorrow," Kieran said again, tossing his pants aside and kicking off his shoes, "So, I'm going to enjoy today." He kissed Naja on the cheek, slapped my ass, then ran back down the hall. A splash sounded and so many cheers filled the air that Naja and I recovered from our shock quickly just to go see what was happening.

Kieran emerged from the water. Two girls from our group, also submerged to their waists, both gave him high-fives as he floated past them. Kieran swam to the edge to face us, water dripping from his hair and onto my shoes.

"Come in," he said, "both of you."

"This is so far from military obedience-" Naja started. I grabbed onto his arm and shifted my weight. We went crashing into the water, my clothes heavy when I floated back to the surface. Naja came up beside me. I expected him to be angry that I pulled him in, but he laughed. He laughed so long that we all joined in from the sheer ridiculousness of it.

Kieran pulled me through the water by my arms, guiding me towards the window that overlooked the sea. We were far enough from the network of tubes and glittering lights of the city that more marine life glided through the water than we'd seen during our time in Varillia.

"Will you hold onto this for me?" he asked, handing me a small, sealed bag. Through the clear surface, I could see a folded piece of paper and a silver ring. Sandwiched in the middle where two ends of the silver band met were the rough edges of an Ida stone similar to the one he wore ever since the wedding.

"What's this?" I asked, a little breathless from the knot twisting in my stomach.

"A promise," he told me, "I won't ask you now, but when we get back... You'll have to give it back to me later so I can get on one knee and do this the right way." This was the right way. Nothing about our relationship had been planned out. It happened despite our fears and regardless of our backgrounds.

"Do I get out and read the note?" I asked, my heart beating fast and my surprise making it difficult to swim and talk.

"No," he said, "You'll know if you're supposed to read it." My heart skipped. The note was a precaution. I felt my excitement dim. I turned the bag between my fingers, watching the stone glitter in the light. He lifted my eyes to him with a finger under my chin.

"I'll keep it safe," I said, my forehead resting against his.

"Every Aldierian needs an Ida stone," he said, "and you're losing yours in this mission."

"And I've gained so much more," I said, pulling his lips to mine by the nape of his neck. I don't know how long we kissed, but when we pulled away, we were the only two left in the pool.

CHAPTER 14

Unlike the rest of our troop, Kieran and I dressed behind the curtains of the four-poster bed. I kept the ring and note safe in the buttoned pocket over my breast. Kieran kissed me before we left the bed, the kiss lasting forever and just seconds all at once.

"Everyone remembers the plan?" Naja asked the troop when we joined them in the main room. No one protested. We told them about the video late last night, walking through the plan at least four times before going to bed. Like I had anticipated, none of them seemed surprised by a sudden change or were nervous about facing the soldiers on the beach. At least, not any more concerned than before.

"I'll push the button?" I asked, my hand wavering over the spot next to the entrance of the bunker. Naja nodded, his expression serious the way it had been when we met at that dig site months ago. I pressed the button and a red light emanated from it. After a few minutes, the doors opened with a mechanic hiss and the same two women greeted us from the night before.

"Lieutenant," one spoke and started leading the way down the hall, "We will take you and your troop to the armory on our way out of the military compound. They have prepared the weapons you requested."

"Thank you," I said. Naja translated the words in Aldierian, and silence fell again. The armory was a giant room full of shelves of weapons, some of which I'd never seen in Jacob's forge. Soldiers met us all individually to outfit us. I was fitted with a belt with a gun, a dagger, and a pouch with bullets. Before I could join the soldiers who were finished being outfitted, the man grabbed onto my belt and began attaching a thick pack.

"I got everything registered to me," I told him. He shook his head.

"This was reassigned this morning," he told me. Reassigned? Meaning it was someone else's?

"What is it?" I asked him as he finished clasping it to my belt, tugging it to make sure it was attached well and that the buttoned flap would undo itself.

"Tug hard when you open it," he said, showing me how and pulling out a sphere I recognized from the dig site. One of the girls had used a similar device to unleash the terrible sound that rendered the security guards unconscious. This one was larger, with a small button on one half of the sphere. "When you are ready to use it, press this button, twist the halves apart, and throw both of them to your target areas. Both will explode at the same time, so make sure you account for that when you throw them," the man said. I felt a jolt go through my body, but not about using such a dangerous device. Naja was supposed to be the one to blow the bridge.

A sideways glance his way confirmed that it hadn't been his decision. He looked away when he caught my gaze, his jaw going tight as he adjusted the sleeves of his shirt and joined our troop near the exit. I thanked the man that outfitted me and went back to Kieran's side, no one saying a word about the explosive as we continued on our path.

I let Naja lead the way back to the main tube, our route occupied only by the occasional military personnel. He relaxed a little when he reunited with Dimas. I forgot how large dune dogs were. The plan would go into action from here. Since the dogs don't trust humans like they do Aldierians, Kieran would ride with me. We mounted the dog I'd chosen a month ago, Reign. He was the puppy of the group, young and playful but nearly as fast as Dimas.

We started up the tube, the silence so loud it was deafening. I felt a need to fidget or run or cheer. I wanted to jump into the fight. I imagined myself plunging the retractable blade I'd stolen from Sargent Marcus into his chest. Kieran's arms around my waist centered me. I slowed down my breathing, not realizing how fast my heart was beating until now.

Naja slowed our pace once the tube had gone bright with light from the surface. We stopped entirely when we could see the end of the tube and the tide gently rising and falling along the transparent walls. No one spoke. I positioned myself next to Naja. After a deep breath, he looked at me. For a moment, I expected him to offer a hand to me and use the Ida stone to speak, but instead, he nodded. I nodded back. He looked at the woman and the man behind and did the same.

Dimas took off and the rest of us jumped to action behind him, speeding towards the closed doors. Reign gained on Dimas after a yard and continued to run faster as we barreled towards the metal at the end. Right on cue, the doors split and Dimas moved so he could squeeze through the opening. We were halfway across the beach when I heard the first whistle of an arrow. A gasp behind me told me it hit its mark. I turned just in time to see the man go down, the arrow electrifying and zapping whatever life was left of the poor man lying in the sand.

"Forward. Always forward," Kieran said in my ear, reminding me of the bridge ahead. Reign's claws clacked against the steel. It felt like sunlight on bare skin on a cool day, a brief relief. Reign let out a muffled yelp and dropped, the force sending Kieran and I flying forward. I tried not to brace my fall with my hands and instead rolled the minute I hit the steel, feeling dozens of bruises forming along my spine and knees with each bounce. Kieran groaned as we both pushed ourselves from the ground.

"Go," I yelled to Naja who had turned around and was staring at us in shock. He looked up and drew a gun, aiming past me and pulling the trigger with a bang. I got to my feet and started to run, passing Dimas and towing Kieran with me until he recovered enough to run on his own. Dimas kept pace with us until we had gone another yard, then sprinted the last two to the grass ahead where we would put an end to this battle.

Arms wrapped around my middle and something heavy plowed into me from behind. I barely got my arms up to keep from smashing my nose against the steel. The soldier on my back gripped my braided hair and tugged, a knife appearing before my eyes. I twisted so I was under him and pulled my knees high, kicking him off just enough to scramble back.

Marcus flicked the knife at me and I tried to dodge, letting out a cry when I felt the bite of the blade just catch my shoulder. Warmth leaked down my chest under my shirt and before I could assess how bad the cut was, he was on me again. I spit in his face and he backhanded me, my head smacking the ground hard enough to blur my vision for a second.

"I won't gut you like I did that idiot blacksmith," he said, "No, I have other plans for you." He gripped the hem of my shirt and tugged, ripping the fabric up to my navel in one go. The memory of Jacob's death reminded me of the gun at my hip. I unholstered it and pulled the trigger without consulting my training. My lack of aim sent the bullet through the very top of his shoulder and made him howl. My hands shook as I recovered and took aim this time, pointing the vibrating barrel at his chest. Through his scream of pain, he pulled my boots and I fell flat to my back again, the shot going skyward.

"Foolish bitch," the man growled, launching himself onto me again and pulling the gun from my hand. He tossed it off the bridge and looked back down at me just in time for my fist to connect with his nose. A crunch confirmed I had broken it and blood poured hot onto my face and neck. I hit him again and he rose to his feet. I got up just as Kieran ran at the soldier with a knife held above his head.

"I prefer knives anyway," I said, removing the dagger from my hip and hoping he kept his eyes on me. Instead, he turned and caught Kieran's wrist, twisting it so the knife fell to the metal beneath us with a clank. Kieran cried out when a punch met his jaw, sending him staggering backward. I ran at Marcus when he turned to me again, my first two attacks blocked by his armored forearms. I landed a cut on his left cheek and went in for a jab.

The soldier dodged, grabbing my arm and pulling me towards him so that my weapon slid underneath his armpit, completely missing him but sinking into someone else instead. Kieran cried out and I realized whose weight was on the other end of my arm. I released the knife in horror and the soldier shoved me backward. I stumbled and fell to the metal again, my head hitting softer grass. Marcus turned to seize Kieran by the shoulders.

I withdrew the retractable knife and the soldier laughed at me.

"What do you expect to do with that toothpick?" he asked.

"Kill you," I said and ran at him. He shoved Kieran to the side where he landed hard against the guardrail. We fought for just minutes, both of us sustaining punches to the face before I jammed the knife into the soldier's eye. I pulled it free with a disgusting pop and he roared, reeling backward and scrabbling at the front of my shirt. I stepped back, but only after his hand wrapped around the chain around my neck. It snapped as he fell and I gasped in horror, my expression giving its value away.

He rolled out of reach and held the necklace aloft, looking at the pendant a moment and then back at my surely terrified expression.

"This matter to you?" he asked.

"Give it back," I stupidly said. As if my wide-eyed face hadn't given it all away. He snickered. Before I could take another step, he yanked Kieran to his feet by the front of his shirt. I let out a scream when he pushed him over the guardrail, holding him in place by a fistful of his protective vest. Kieran panted heavily, gripping the soldier's thick wrist with his one good hand while the other was cradled at his side from the wound I was responsible for. I froze in place. The soldier held up the necklace.

"Kenna," Naja yelled behind me. I held a hand back to stop him from advancing. If we weren't careful, we could lose both the stone and Kieran.

"You can save just one," the soldier said with a laugh, "Gallaterra is a democracy. Cast your vote." Kieran looked at me, his hand slowing on the soldier's and his breathing more even. He nodded his head, his eyes gentle as if to tell me that it was okay. His face blurred before me as the tears came. Shit. Shit. Fuck.

"The stone," I said, "Give me the stone." My voice was strong when I said the words, though my body sagged, and I barely stayed on my feet. The scream ripped my throat raw. Kieran fell like a rag doll, feet going over last. I opened my hands to catch the stone, but the soldier changed directions and tossed it over the side after Kieran.

"Oops," he said, sending me the nastiest smile. I was going to blow it off his face.

The device was in my hands and the button was pressed. I twisted the halves apart and threw them at the soldier's chest with a scream that felt like it would rip me in two. Naja yelled behind me, and something yanked me hard from behind. I was being dragged at high speed over the grass, the explosion sending Dimas and I both skidding over the dirt. My head connected with something hard.

CHAPTER 15

opened my eyes, the sun making me squint. I looked to the left as an ear-splitting sound of steel scraping steel rang through the air. The section of the bridge where Kieran and I had been fighting Don Marcus was completely gone, the last half of the bridge breaking free from the cliffside and slowly falling into the ravine. Kieran was at the bottom of that ravine with my knife stuck in his shoulder. Kieran fell from the bridge and into whatever lay underneath. Kieran was...

I felt my heart speed up and I sucked in a breath of air that didn't completely fill my lungs, another breath coming in sharply after it. I clawed at the ground to raise myself when Naja slammed both of his hands onto my shoulders and held me down. His eyes were glassy for just a second, a quick blink returning the military manner I was growing to hate about my brother.

"Calm yourself. You have to calm yourself."

"K-Kieran," I got out between breaths.

"You did your duty. His plan worked and they can't follow us now," Naja said, pressing me into the grass as I started to fight back. "Stop. Kenna, stop," he said, his tone growing more urgent each time he repeated. "STOP! KENNA, STOP." he leaned back on his knees to reach for his hip. I sat up straight, eyes trained on the dust still hanging in the air from the explosion. I choked as Naja slammed me back to the grass by my throat, cutting off what little oxygen was in my lungs. They burned for a moment while he twisted the cap off a small vial with his teeth. I gasped when I felt the pressure at my neck let up, a cold liquid flowing down my throat before I could even taste the sweetness. I spluttered, sitting up and pushing myself away from him as he got to his feet. He watched me anxiously, replacing the vial in his pocket.

"W-what did you do to me?" I asked him. My body slowed in response to the drug, my heart rate returning to normal, and my breathing evening out. My brain was still racing, replaying the moment Kieran fell from the bridge over and over and trying to find explanations for what it meant for him other than the obvious. I knew I was panicking, but my body was calmer than it had felt in months.

"It's a drug that works against panic. It mellows you out," Naja said, "but you have to get a hold of yourself because you can only have two more doses of it." I noticed that his own hands shook as he opened another vial and took a dose himself. I looked over him for any sign of injury and found none. I felt for the cut at my shoulder, the bleeding already slowing. The gash needed stitches but should heal cleanly.

"Do you have the medical kit," I asked him. He shook his head.

"Only half of it," he said, "Ky had it." We both looked back at the sandy side of the ravine. A few Gallaterran soldiers were still there, some looking over the edge of the cliff. Maybe our troop had been too small. Maybe we should've told mother about the soldiers on the beach so we could increase our numbers. Maybe it didn't matter. It didn't now.

"The Heart of Aldieria is in that ravine. We have to find it," I said. Naja shook his head, staring off towards the west. A tear slipped down his face and that was the moment I realized my own was slick with moisture.

"There's a river at the bottom of that ravine. The explosion can't destroy the stone, but it could send it flying miles away. There's no way to know where it landed and it could take us months or longer to find it," Naja said, shaking his head. He let out a breath, then a groan, he kicked at the ground and ripped off his belt. He sent it flying towards the trees, the heavy belt smacking the trunk of a tree and sliding to the dirt. Neither of us spoke for a long time.

"Did that make you feel better?" I asked him. I wanted to do the same, but I hardly felt the emotions. He didn't look at me.

"I don't feel anything at all," he said, "damn drugs." I sat motionless as he started the walk to retrieve the belt. A breeze came through the path, blowing away the haze in the air in minutes. Another gust and I heard a funny whistling sound further down the road. I noticed a shimmer in the tree line and remembered the dune riders concealed there.

"We can continue the mission," I said, "the part that might matter the most." Naja had returned with his belt clasped around his hips again.

"You want to kill President Grace?"

"We are assassins," I said, though I didn't feel like it right now with the retractable knife as my only weapon. "Since it's just you and I, we can go undetected in the city. We can navigate our way through the government buildings and get close enough to kill him, I'm sure," I said.

"Stop," Naja said, the words barely audible.

"We are trained for exactly this mission," I said and stood up.

"Stop," he said more firmly, finally looking at me. "We don't know how to get into a government building, not to mention how we can get close to the best-protected man in the nation." I lunged for him. My fisted landed hard on his jaw. It caught him off guard and sent him stumbling backward. An expression of shock was on his face just long enough for him to hit back.

I dodged his fist and swept his feet out from under him with a well-placed kick. I was on top of him, eyes blurred by tears from the heartache I couldn't feel. He blocked punch after punch and finally landed one of his own. I fell off him, tasting rust in my mouth. We looked up at each other and froze, just feet apart. I spat a mouthful of blood on the grass.

"Kieran wanted to be the one to kill him," I said, "If he can't do it, then I will."

"In a few months maybe, but not like this. We aren't going to go in blindly, without a plan, because we hurt," Naja said. I stood up as he did, both of us eyeing the other as if another attack was imminent. "Kieran told his team. He drew them a map of the building where his father works," Naja said, "We go home because it's too close not to. We get that information and then we go to Gallaterra to kill Grace, you and me." I hated him for the logic, more so because he was right. It felt like we failed. We lost. We lost the mission, and I lost the only person who ever made me feel like more than a poor village girl.

"Fine," I said. We didn't move for a long time. We didn't do anything. When we did, it was to hug. He was nearly the same height as Kieran was, and he felt similar in my arms except Naja was muscular. The difference made me long for the warmth of Kieran's embrace.

"We can stay concealed better going through the forested side in the south than the thinner forest of the north," Naja said when we broke apart. I agreed and we planned out the rest of the day. Naja had been this way once before with a troop after a mission, so he knew the way and the lay of the land and the best places to stop for the night to keep unseen.

We took turns riding Dimas. When I felt the stiffness of riding set it, I got off to stretch my legs and walk. A bruise had appeared on Naja's jaw from where I punched him. Neither of us talked about the fight and I was glad for it. My emotions hadn't come back yet for me to gauge our situation. I knew the minute the drug wore off that everything would come crashing down. In my brain, I feared what it would feel like to know Kieran was gone.

Naja stopped our trek before the sun started setting, leading me towards a low section of the forest where large boulders and brush could conceal us and Dimas. After deciding that the risk of running into any soldiers was small, we built a fire and sent Dimas out to hunt. I stoked the flames as Naja settled in against one of the boulders, propping his feet up on his pack.

"Setta," Naja said. I looked up at him as he laid out a blanket next to him.

"What does that mean?" I asked him. He rolled his eyes, and I knew he was annoyed with how little I studied Aldierian. He'd told me as much a month ago.

"Sister," he translated, "come here." I finished adding enough wood to the flame to keep it hot for a while and joined him on the blanket. The blanket, despite being thin cotton, felt like thick wool after the day we'd had. I relaxed immediately to the sound of birds chirping. The trees rustled as a breeze came through, making the fire dance.

Naja took my hand and gave it a gentle squeeze. Before I realized he was doing it, I was in his head. He showed me his bedroom in our apartment. He was laying on his back in his bed, Illya curled up asleep next to him. A knock came at the door and Naja rose, adjusting the shorts on his hips as his bare feet slapped across our wooden floors. He paused when he opened the door halfway, only fully opening it after a moment of hesitation to reveal Kieran standing there awkwardly.

"My mother took Kenna to meet one of the combat trainers," Naja said, starting to close the door. Kieran caught it with his hand and moved partway into the room, the warning on Naja's face keeping him from stepping any further.

"I came to talk to you," he said.

"If you're asking me to get involved in that fight you had with her-"

"No. No, it's not about that. Well, not really. I don't care about that," Kieran said, following Naja into the apartment and shutting the door behind him. "I need to talk to her and make her listen," Kieran said.

"That's your problem." Naja pulled a glass from a cabinet and filled it with water in the sink. "You can't make someone listen. If you think that then you probably didn't even hear what she was saying."

"Oh, I heard her loud and clear.".

"You're a smart guy, like a really educated person, but you're acting pretty stupid," Naja said, taking a drink.

"You don't like me. I know that," Kieran said.

"No, but she does," Naja said, pointing at the door, "and you're too stupid to listen and see that you both are fighting over the same things. She's not denying that you can go through with the plan to storm Gallaterra and kill your father. She worries that it might kill you just like you're afraid she's going to leave you if you're not man enough to follow through." Kieran stuttered, turning bright red. He let out a long breath.

"I'm not strong the way she is, but that doesn't mean I'm not strong," he said. Naja let out a laugh.

"It's funny because she thinks you're stronger than her," he said, "You're the brains of this whole plan and you know best how to execute it. You have so much mental strength and she loves you for it, but it scares her." Naja went to the couch and sunk into the cushions.

"How do you know all of this?" Kieran asked.

"You can tell when she looks at you and how she talks about you," he replied, "The problem is that both of you are letting your fear get in the way of telling the other person what's bothering you." Kieran blanched at that and sat back in the seat.

"You said it yourself, she doesn't think I'm man enough to"

"No, dumbass, *you* think that," Naja said, glancing back at his room in case he woke Illya. When only silence greeted him, he continued. "She doesn't think you're trained enough to go on the mission. She's right, you aren't, and you are too afraid to admit it because you don't want her to think you're weak."

"How is she right?" Kieran asked, the defensive edge in his tone less than before.

"You aren't as physically strong as her. You aren't good with weapons. You aren't trained to go on a mission like that and you probably aren't skilled enough to do the deed of killing your father, even if you are mentally prepared to do it," Naja said, "You refuse to admit that because you're stubborn for one, but also because you want to be the man in the relationship. You want to be man enough for a girl like that." Naja was pointing at the door. Kieran looked like he'd been punched in the gut.

"I know I'm not… man enough," he said. Naja finished the last of his glass and sat forward, resting his elbows on his knees and rolling the glass between his hands.

"Humans are so dumb," he said, "Am I man enough?" Kieran snapped to attention, eyes on Naja.

"How can you, of all people, question that? You're a leader in the military. You have thighs as big around as my entire body and your abs…"

"And I sleep with a man," Naja said, "The human standard is made up. It's not real. You can be man enough for her by being honest with yourself and her. So, she has more muscle than you. So, she has to protect you in hand-to-hand combat. Who cares? Be man enough by admitting that she's right and do better." Kieran stared at the floor for a long time, thoroughly beaten. He seemed small, like a child facing punishment.

"I get it. I messed up. I have to apologize," Kieran said, "but I don't know how I can do better. I want to go on the mission back to Gallaterra. If anyone is going to kill my father, I want it to be me. I need to be the one to do this. I can't just become the best guy for the job." He looked up at Naja, his expression changing when he did. His mouth parted slightly, and his eyes widened as if he suddenly made some kind of connection.

"I'll help you train," Naja said with a sigh as if he was

taking on a momentous project. "You have to do more than that though. I can teach you what you need to know, but I can't make you perfect all the moves. That's on you." Kieran smiled, the excitement barely containable. Before he could finish thanking Naja, the scene changed, or rather, the people changed

It was still Naja's apartment, only this time Naja was fully dressed in his military training uniform and our mother was sitting at the kitchen bar. She wore her hair down, the first time I'd seen her so informal. It flowed thick and dark over the back of the chair. Then, I noticed what she was wearing. It was the same all-black she wore the day of the board meeting, the day Naja agreed that Kieran should go on the mission with us.

"You told me you've been helping him," she said, sitting back from the counter.

"I have been and I mean it, mother," Naja said, "He's gotten good."

"And this changes things?" She asked, sending him a very pointed look. "You were against Kieran going on this mission the last time we spoke. You haven't expressed to me any reason why he should go except that you say he's gotten better in his combat classes."

Naja moved behind the counter, taking a bottle from the fridge and twisting the top off. "He has more knowledge than anyone about Gallaterra, even more than Kenna about the government and technology. The only reason I told you he shouldn't go is that he didn't have the skill to fight, but now he does. You know I don't take anyone into my troop that can't pull their weight. We don't need any risk, especially on a mission like this."

"I know. You calculate risk almost as well as a mission specialist," our mother said, "but you're known to let your emotions affect your missions-"

"One mission hardly makes it a known fact."

"Two people died."

"Gallaterrans who tried to kill us," Naja said, sitting the bottle aside.

"People, Naja," mother said, her tone sharp. Naja's jaw tightened, probably to keep from saying anything more. "And that's my point. You let your emotions cloud your judgment. You say this boy is ready, that he's earned his spot thanks to all his knowledge and scientific skill."

"I know because I trained him myself," Naja said, his tone more even than before.

"Why train him?"

Naja froze and I could feel his surprise through the memory. Naja had never told me why. He told me he and Kieran spent long hours outside of the normal training sessions preparing, but he'd never explained why he suddenly felt a desire to help Kieran.

"I want to say the words, Naja," our mother said, "and I think you need to hear them more than I do."

Naja spun the bottle between his hands, keeping his eyes on the counter. He let out a deep sigh and looked up, the serious expression on his face so forced it was easy to see the pain behind it.

"Kieran's dad has done terrible things to him, mother. He deserves to die for what he's done to him and Gallaterra, but Kieran deserves to look him in the eye and ask him why." Naja's hands shook as he fidgeted, so much that he finally held the bottle with both hands to keep them still. Mother shook her head and leaned over the counter again. She reached over and raised Naja's head with a finger under his chin.

"Your biological father did terrible things, son," she said, "but he's not your father, not really. Aaron was your father, that's why we are all called Petrek, and that man is not. You can help Kieran get justice for what his father did. If you think he's earned his place on this mission, I will sign my name beside yours, but don't live vicariously through Kieran's fight with his father. You won't find closure in that battle, and I hope for your sake that you don't bring tragedy for your sister."

Naja stood up and looked away from our mother, staring off to one side in what I was sure was an effort to restore his stoic demeanor. Before either could change the conversation, the vision blurred and Naja let go of my hand. His breath hitched and tears rolled down his face.

"I'm so sorry, Kenna," he said, his voice a small whisper.

"It's not your fault. It's not your fault," I said, crying now too as I wrapped my arms around him. We stayed in each other's tight embrace for a long time, my eyes sore when we both had recovered and laid back against the rocks. It was quiet for a long time, giving me time to replay both memories in my mind again, remembering a name.

"Aaron Petrek was our father?" I asked. Naja glanced at me and nodded, then looked back down at his palms as if he could read his fortune there.

"Aaron practically adopted me from day one. He's probably the only reason I'm not more of an asshole than I already am," he said.

"Your birth father…" I didn't know what to say. Did it even matter what that man did to my brother and mother? Naja dried his palms on his pants.

"He left," he said, "had a whole family and wife before us. Mother was just a soldier at the time, transitioning into politics, but just a soldier. He left when he found out about me and never looked back." I'd heard that story a thousand times back in Arro, only there it was a little more complicated. Sometimes children were left behind because they were better cared for where they were than with their parents.

I took Naja's hand as the memories of the village came flooding back. I started with the earliest memory I had of Jacob, the time he closed shop early and took me to walk the traveling markets with him in Arro. He bought me a bracelet, which I lost an hour later. He wasn't even mad, insistent that we would find it and we did after walking a stretch of the market multiple times. That was one of my favorite memories. It was before the thief knocked out his front tooth and he forged the silver one. It was before life in our neighborhood caught up with him and carved wrinkles into his face and started graying his hair despite his age. Way before I started participating in the life of the streets.

I showed Naja as much as I remembered, from those happy memories, the few times Jacob had gotten angry with me, even the sad ones. It was cathartic to know I had so many memories of him, and the scenes seemed to ease Naja's guilt as well because he smiled and even laughed a few of my funnier tales.

I dropped his hand when I heard feet over grass, turning to see Dimas proudly walking our way with a horned pig held in his mouth.

"Finally," Naja said, his eyes red and face glistening as he moved to dress the animal. I remembered the ring then, the moment Kieran handed me the plastic bag with the ring and note and promised me not to read it unless something happened. I pulled it free from the pocket of my shirt and dumped the contents into my shaking hands. The ring fit almost perfectly on my finger, the fact almost crushing me again. I unfolded the note while Naja began spearing hunks of meat onto a stick.

The note was short, the paper alone a small sliver. It only said a few words. *If I can't do it, then I want you to do it. I love you. I love you so much.* Under the words was what looked like a code. It was separated with periods and after realizing it didn't look anything like the letters and numbers he'd typed in to access the security footage, I realized what it was.

"Naja. Naja, where's your tablet?" I asked, already digging through his backpack for the device. I found it before he could ask any questions, turning it on and accessing the GPS app. I typed in the coordinates. The overview was a point within Gallaterra City, a government building. When I zoomed in, the red dot was placed inside the building. It was easy to see, the walls marked out and the doors easy to find.

"Hell yeah, Kieran," Naja cheered.

"We can do this, Naja. We have to do this," I said, crying for a new reason now.

"Yes," he said, "We can do this."

CHAPTER 16

KIERAN

I woke up to excruciating pain on the left side of my body. When I glanced over, I felt bile burn its way up my throat. A giant steel brace was crushed so far into my leg that I couldn't make out anything other than metal past my thigh. The same had happened to my left arm, pinned to the gravel at the elbow. My vision began to fade, and I only kept conscious thanks to a splash of cold water lapping my face.

A look to my right and I inhaled cool water and had a new reason for panic. I kept my face turned upwards as the water of the river rushed past me, an occasional ebb and flow rising to my ear and threatening to drown me as I lay there. There was no other choice but to die and hope it happened fast. The pain in my arm and leg was so intense that I didn't know which to focus on, making it impossible to try and control my panic. I let out a scream that echoed off the cliff, the sound cut out by a sob.

Kenna probably thought I was dead and here I was, not dead yet, just miles beneath where she stood. She had to have survived the blast. She was too far away when it happened. All thoughts of the attack vanished when the slightest movement sent a fresh wave of pain through my entire left side. This time, I did pass out.

When I woke for the second time, I was laying on the steel floor of a dune rider. Two men sat at the front, both outfitted in brown pants and jackets with old-style bows and silver arrows propped against the seats. I couldn't feel anything, my left arm and left leg so numb that I wondered if they were even there. I didn't get a chance to check before my vision blurred, and everything went dark.

This time, I woke so completely that my entire body jolted into a panic. My heart beat heavy in my chest, and I sat straight up in the stark white hospital room. The two men sat across the room from me, a rolling cart between us. My weapon's belt was sitting on top along with the Heart of Aldieria glittering in the light from the window.

"Woah there," one of the men said, both rising from their seats across the room and moving to restrain me. The smaller of the two looked over his shoulder and called for help while the large man shushed me and eased me back into the pillows. A man in scrubs came in the door followed by a woman dressed identically and another wearing enough badges and devices that she had to be the doctor.

"You had an accident," the large man said, "my buddy and I found you while we were hunting." The doctor rounded the man and raised my bed with a mechanical hum until I was sitting up.

"Can you tell me what you remember, sir?" the doctor asked.

"Um…" I remembered the blast, the pain of the steel crushing me, and Kenna. "Free climbing," I said, looking left at the nurse who had taken my arm. I gasped and felt like I might pass out again. My forearm was missing. The thick bands of white bandages stopped where my elbow was.

"Can you tell me your name, sir?" the doctor asked me again, turning my head to her with a gentle hand. She took a tablet from her pocket and positioned a finger over the screen. How did she expect me to answer any of her questions after realizing my arm is gone?

"W-W-" I started.

"What was that? William?" the doctor asked, looking up from her tablet.

"Y-yeah," I said, "William" Good enough. I didn't care right now. I cared more about what happened to my arm.

"What is your last name, William?" she asked me after she'd finished typing onto the tablet. You saw me notice my arm was gone. Why not start there?

"B-Baden," I said. The doctor began typing again, lowering her eyes enough that I began taking in my surroundings. Past the big window on the right, I could look over the parking lot and down several blocks. I knew enough about the area near the East Sea to know that any towns were still within a day's travel of the larger Gallaterran cities and there wasn't enough traffic for this to be a large town.

"Alright, Mr. Baden," the doctor said and lowered her tablet, "You were in pretty bad shape when these two men brought you in. We took you to surgery. Unfortunately, we were unable to save your left arm and your left leg. Both had been crushed beyond repair. However, we already did the prep work to fit you with robotic prosthetics. If you consent to the final surgery, we can fit your leg and arm with those this afternoon." My leg? Did they take my leg too?

I moved to flip back the sheets with my left arm before I remembered that it was no longer there. The nurse slipped the sheets from my left leg instead, revealing the same white bandages from my mid-thigh to my knee where my leg now ended.

"This afternoon?" I asked, repeating the last of the words I could remember. The doctor nodded, handing the tablet to me.

"We can have you fitted this afternoon. We'll keep you overnight for monitoring and check that you have normal usage before releasing you in the morning," she said.

"If I don't have the surgery?" I asked, my finger already poised over the digital line.

"The robotics function just like normal limbs, so little therapy is needed for you to learn how to use them. Without the robotic prosthetics, it would take a few more days for you to heal and get used to the missing limbs," she said. I had already finished signing the tablet, so she didn't go into any further explanation past that. My right arm felt strangely cool, and the nurse told me she'd given me more pain meds.

"We will come back in for you later this afternoon," the doctor said, giving me a sweet smile. No identity check? Robotics was pretty straightforward, so I understood going ahead with the surgery, but did no one care to check my story?

"Where am I?" I asked, not realizing that the doctor and nurses had already left the room. It was just me and the two hunters now. The larger one moved a rolling tray towards me where a giant plastic cup sat with a bendy straw.

"Chesney," the man replied as if I should've known it all along. Maybe I should. If my story was that I was free climbing, then I probably would know the surrounding villages.

"Got it," I said, groaning as I struggled to adjust myself with just one arm.

"Is there anyone we could call? You didn't have any identification on you, so the hospital said they'd take your name and put it into the database for missing people and check the area in case anyone called looking for you," the smaller man said. The idea of anyone looking for me made me anxious. No one would be looking for me, at least no one I wanted to find me. All the people I cared about thought I was dead, and I was sure of that. I remembered the note and ring I left with Kenna. In it, I asked her to take out my father. How stupid. She wouldn't go back to Varillia to raise an army. She would continue the mission. Kenna didn't like to accept a loss. She wouldn't scrap the mission, especially if she thought she had my blessing in my death to continue it. She needed to know I was alive. She needed to wait.

"Don't stress, man," the large man said. I followed his gaze to the monitors on the other side of the bed. The beeping began to slow as I focused on it. There had to be a way to get a message to Kenna somehow, but I didn't know how I could do that here. I could probably figure out how to send one by hijacking a tablet somehow. Maybe. My head hurts too much right now to think about it.

"Can we help contact someone?" the man asked again. I lowered my hand from my head and sunk back into the puffy pillow, the papery case letting out a hiss from the force.

"I think I just... I need to figure out..." I started, trying not to ham it up too much, "I need to be alone before." The men looked more than happy to give me space.

"You got it, mountain man," the big man said, patting my good knee and then motioning for his friend to follow him out the door.

"Thanks for helping me," I said before the small man could leave the room, "I wouldn't have lived long if you hadn't brought me here." The smaller man paused at the door. He had blonde hair that flopped over one side the same way my brother wore his and when he looked back at me, his blue eyes almost made me ache for my blue-eyed sister who was still trapped at home.

"You'll feel more than alive after that robotic surgery," he said, "You can thank me then. They asked us to stay until the MP could come and ask us some questions. Turns out all that metal that squashed you came from some kind of terrorist blast." He let out a laugh of disbelief before letting the door swing shut. I was glad he left because I was sure the panic was painted across my face. My eyes stung. How cruel could life be? I knew there was a high chance of dying just going on this mission, but surviving an attack like that and knowing that Kenna was out there on what might now be a suicide mission... I couldn't live the rest of my life behind bars now.

I tried to control my breathing, but my chest just heaved more the harder I tried. Instead, I closed my eyes and laid back against the soft pillows. I was there long enough that I must've calmed down and gone to sleep because when I opened my eyes again it was because the medical team had returned to prep me for surgery.

I focused on taking deep breaths as they worked, mostly because I was afraid of the surgery. My nerves got the best of me for sure, drowning out their words as they explained to me how the surgery would go and all the drugs they began administering into my IV. I was glad when we began to move down the hall, but it made things worse also. So, I closed my eyes and imagined Kenna.

"You doing okay, William?" a man asked. I just nodded, exaggerating the gesture to make sure they knew.

"Are you nervous, Mr. Baden?" A woman asked. I nodded again and I felt her hand cover mine and squeeze it as she promised to take care of me. I imagined that hand was Kenna's. Her hair was tied back in a series of red braids, the signature of an Aldierian warrior, the strong picture of my Kenna.

I felt groggy. My eyes were heavy. My vision was blurry when I finally woke enough to open them. It took a moment to realize I was in my hospital room. A nurse stood to my right, his face vaguely familiar. As I took in more of the room, I recognized him from earlier, when I first got here.

"The surgery was successful, Mr. Baden," he said, "I'm just here to make sure you're doing well. The doctor will come in just a few to check that the robotics are operating as they should." The man fidgeted with a tablet for just a moment, probably sending a message to the doctor, before he began checking my vitals. I reached for the blanket over my legs, realizing after the fact that it was my new left arm that clasped around the hem. The forearm connected almost seamlessly to my elbow, the contour of the metal resembling a normal arm so much that it was surreal to even look at, much less acknowledge as my own.

I raised my arm and flexed my fingers one by one. It wasn't my old arm, but in a lot of ways, it was. It looked almost like someone had dipped my arm in silver, it was so realistic. I pulled back the sheets and what I saw was less realistic. A metal bar was connected to my knee. A curved running blade sat even with my other foot. I felt weirdly compelled to get out of bed to try it out, see if it was as springy as it looked.

"Mr. Baden," the doctor said as she walked into the room, "You seem to be doing well." She looked from me to the nurse, and I knew her silent gaze was asking him a list of questions. Was he doing well? Are all his tests normal?

"When can I try it out?" I asked, lifting the new leg off the bed an inch. She smiled and began looking over the monitor for herself.

"That's what I came for," she said, comparing the monitor with her tablet for a moment. I noticed movement outside my door, a flash of silver sending a pit into my stomach. I remembered the soldiers that chased Kenna and I through Ariadne. Maybe I was just paranoid. I'd been through enough to be.

"Is there anyone we can call for you?" the doctor asked me, looking down at her tablet again as she typed.

"Am I being discharged?" I asked. She hesitated for a moment, completely frozen mid-type before restarting a moment later. If that wasn't confirming every paranoid thought going through my mind....

"Yes," she said, her voice different than before. I hadn't been imagining it or triggered by the silver of someone's watch then. There was a real soldier outside my door and there was only one reason for that. They wouldn't have an armored soldier to question me. They knew exactly who I was. It took me far too long to realize how they'd figured it out. I should've known when I was admitted to the hospital. The wounds behind my left ear were far too old for them to have happened from free climbing. The entire nation knew the president's son was AWOL and a blonde-haired boy with blue eyes and a missing device fit the profile too perfectly. Shit.

"Can I borrow your tablet to call a pod?" I asked. The doctor didn't look my way. She finished checking my new arm. The nurse removed my IV. Did I have a chance at running?

"I need to make sure you can walk to get to a cab first," the doctor told me, offering me her hands. I took them and slung my legs over the side of the bed. If I could stand like normal, should I run? I couldn't imagine pushing this woman who had been so nice to me. She took my hesitation as nerves and tugged a little on my hands in support. I stood up without shifting my weight onto her. It felt natural, not exactly normal, but not overly difficult like I was worried it would be. I tried taking a step and that's when I felt my momentum shift.

I collapsed onto the floor, taking the doctor down with me. The nurse gasped, the sound alerting the guard at my door. She was outfitted in the signature military garb of Gallaterra, a pair of metal cuffs already coming away from her hip at the sight of me. I tried to scramble away, but she had me pinned onto my stomach halfway out the door, my face turned towards the shocked eyes of the nurses and a few other amputees who were walking the halls.

"Kieran Grace," the woman said as she cuffed my wrists," You are under arrest by the nation of Gallaterra. Anything you say now can and will be used against you in the high court." I didn't struggle as she finished shackling me and I even helped her when she tugged me to my feet. The people in the hall gave us a wide berth like I was a serial killer or someone dangerous. I kept my eyes on the halls before us as we walked, not once fighting, not even in the brief moments when the guard let go of me to open the door to the stairs.

CHAPTER 17
KIERAN

After leaving the hospital, I rode for a long time in the dark compartment of a police pod. When the back door opened, the light was nearly blinding. It gave the guards enough time to unchain me from the seat and pull me out before I realized we were outside a prison. I was in the fresh air between chain link fences just moments before being ushered into a new building. The first space looked like the waiting room of a doctor's office, only there were minimal chairs and more security officers than the space needed considering I was the only person in it.

The soldiers around me, all three of them, led me past a gate and into another compartment where I was photographed and my fingerprints were scanned into a tablet on the wall. I was ordered to say my full name along with a few basic phrases into a tablet and recorded them several times before I was allowed to pass onto the next area. This one had racks of the same orange jumpsuit. Once I was given the right size, one of the security guards put it through a machine where it came out the other side with a number and my name stamped across the back. The material felt unlike any piece of clothing I'd ever felt. It was almost plastic-like or what I'd imagine a parachute felt like.

A woman shoved me into the middle of the room and ordered me to strip. I shivered once I removed all my clothes, every article promptly snatched from the floor and searched as I stood shielding myself with the strange jumpsuit. I slipped into a new pair of boxers, my new leg catching on the fabric as I tugged them on. I slid into the strange fabric of the jumpsuit that swished as I was led into a long hall. We took a few turns before I was pushed past a guarded door. The room was huge, with dozens of doors on every side. There were picnic benches bolted to the floor in the middle of the room and a single screen mounted high on one wall that displayed the evening news.

What a coincidence. My face was emblazoned across it along with the word "captured alive" and a news ticker at the bottom encouraging viewers to stay tuned to hear the full story. I was ushered to the far side of the room before I could listen to much of the report. The new guard fitted my wrists with the thick magnet bands I remembered from the prison in Gallaterra and with a press of her hand on the tablet mounted outside the cell, she unlocked the door and I was shoved inside.

The cell was almost entirely dark aside from the dim light from a single recessed light. There was a blue waterproofed mattress on the floor and a combination toilet and sink in the corner. The top of the mattress was scuffed up, so I flipped it over to see if the other side was any better. It was worse, but I stared at it long enough to take in the words "Gallaterra Maximum Security Prison" that were spray-painted near the foot before I flipped it back over.

I hadn't just been arrested. I was fully imprisoned. There would be no trial. I was sitting in G-Max, the last prison stop for the highest-profile convicts in the whole nation before the arena. There was no telling who was locked up here with me, but it was likely they would all know who I was before I could even ask for names tomorrow.

I settled onto the mattress, which was so thin it practically sank straight to the concrete, and I tried my best to sleep. A buzzing woke me hours later and I could hear the lock in my door slide open. People groaned and called out for breakfast in the space beyond, prompting me to get to my feet and open the door. The room was full of people now, some as young as me and some nearly seventy, and guards dressed in tan uniforms were scattered along the walls. A line had formed on the opposite side of the room where inmates received breakfast on paper plates.

A group of women at least twice my age looked up as I passed, not even trying to hide their stares of surprise. I heard someone to my right say my name and I turned towards them to see that two other tables of people had stopped talking to look. Most of the inmates were turning to watch, making me pause a moment before I walked past the tables for the line. I saw a leg kick out in front of me, barely catching my footing as I stepped over him.

"Oops," the man said. He had to be in his late forties. He looked like an old rock star with his long hair and the tattoos peeking out from under his jumpsuit at his wrists. The corner of his mouth pulled up in a smirk for just a second. "I saved you a spot," the man said, sliding his plate of orange slices, oatmeal, and sausage to the empty seat opposite him.

"You eat it," I told him. I took one step before I felt his hand on my wrist.

"Go along with it and we'll be outta here," the man said in my ear before twisting me around and landing a punch to my jaw. The room burst into gasps and groans as I tried blinking away the stars that were obscuring my vision. I felt him on my wrist again, tugging at the cuff despite my attempts to push him away. Finally, a buzz sounded and cries of pain rang around the room as the inmates were pulled to the floor by their restraints.

All the inmates except for five of us.

The long-haired man and I stood in the middle of the room amongst the tables. A blonde girl stepped out of the breakfast line, her slender frame making her confident walk amongst the burly guards comical. Near the main entrance stood a wide-set man as tall as the door. He seized the first guard who ran for the door and slammed him into the wall, knocking him unconscious before taking his place to guard the control panel on the wall. Two guards groaned behind us and I turned to see an Aldierian woman attempting to take on two men.

The larger of the two guards finally got her arms pinned to her back. The second began punching her. The long-haired man tried pulling him away, but another guard tossed him to the side. The woman screamed when her attacker pressed a stunning pole to her neck, holding it there even after subduing her.

"She's not fighting back," I yelled at him, shrugging out of a guard's arms and starting forward.

"Lay down," she yelled after me as I advanced.

"I said stop," I yelled and grabbed the back of the guard's shirt. I tugged, harder than I thought. She fell to her back and skidded into one of the tables. The Aldierian propelled herself back into the wall, sandwiching the guard detaining her. Once released, she turned and smashed the man's head into the wall until he fell over limply.

"Damn you, Barker. You should've stuck to the plan," the Aldierian yelled, her eyes on the long-haired man.

"Don't make me regret freeing you," Barker yelled, his gaze on me. I ran at the guard holding him before she could free her stunning pole, surprised by the force of my punch. My new hand smashed into her face so hard that I could hear the bones crunch. Lots of bones. She crumpled to the floor where blood trickled from her mouth and ear. Dead.

I stood there for a long while in shock while the rest of the group fought the last three guards together, the rest of the inmates pinned to the floor remaining silent until not a single guard was left standing.

"You're not just gonna leave us here," one of the men called out.

"They're staying," Barker said as he grabbed my forearm and

tugged me towards the far side of the room where the big guy was searching one of the guards laying on the floor. "You're coming with us," Barker told me.

"Why him?" the big guy asked, straightening to his impressive height with a stunning pole in one hand.

"You don't know who he is?" Barker asked, looking at the rest of the crew. Only the blonde girl acted like she understood. The Aldierian ignored them all and finished dragging one of the women to a door next to the breakfast counter. She pressed the woman's hand to a tablet and opened the door to reveal the kitchen.

"He's the president's son," the blonde said, "There's no telling what he may know."

"So?" the big guy asked as we all crossed the room for the kitchen.

"So, he may be useful," Barker replied, looking around the room. He groaned when he found a clear case holding knives of various sizes, a padlock still in place. "Come here," he said to me with a whistle. I didn't know what else to do, so I stopped next to him and took the lock. I put aside the memory of what I'd done to that guard, and I tugged on it. I was surprised when it snapped into two halves with minimal effort.

Barker began taking knives down from the case, handing a few off to the blonde girl, then to the big guy, and hesitating before handing a single paring knife to the Aldierian. She scoffed and brushed past him, taking a butcher knife and a serrated bread knife from the case. She pressed the flat side of the paring knife to Barker's chest and muttered something in Aldierian before starting across the kitchen.

"Take your pick, Grace," Barker told me.

"Kieran," I corrected and pulled an assortment of the smaller knives from the case, "not Grace." I found an apron with a small pocket large enough to hold the knives. I was halfway done tying the band around my waist when the Aldierian pushed open the back door. Light streamed into the space and my heart fluttered in my chest as the possibility of freedom, a chance to find Kenna and put an end to my father's rule.

"The kitchen pod is still here," the woman said. As she said, a large pod was backed to the loading dock.

"Where's the crew?" the blonde asked, hesitantly peeking her head out the door. I noticed three men standing yards away from where the fence backed to the forest. All three were in the middle of a smoke break, deep in conversation and oblivious to what had happened in their absence. I pointed them out and the big guy let out a laugh, the humor on his face fading when Barker and the Aldierian glared back at him.

"Let's take the pod," the Aldierian said, starting towards the open cargo hold.

"No," the blonde said, beating her there. She stepped in just far enough to tug a large metal ladder from the wall, teetering a little under the weight before handing it to the big guy. "The pod can be tracked and easily seen. Sneaking over the gate might buy us a little more time, even though we'll be on foot."

"The crew is right there. What if they see?," the Aldierian groaned, motioning to the kitchen crew.

"Make sure they don't," the blonde said simply and led the way around the pod and towards the nearest stretch of the barbed-wire fence. The Aldierian kept watch as the big guy raised the ladder the full twelve feet and stepped aside. The blonde quickly climbed to the top and jumped down to the grass, bailing into a roll to absorb the shock of the fall.

"After you," the big guy stuttered to me. I climbed up and jumped down just like the girl had, a sensation like pins and needles shooting through my feet despite the roll. Barker came next and after a short argument, the Aldierian followed. The big guy climbed much slower than the rest of us, but not due to his size so much as his nerves. The ladder shook under him each time he moved up a rung until he stood crouched at the top.

"You expect me to jump down?" he asked.

"August, get your fat ass down before someone sees," the

Aldierian said.

"I'm not fat," August said, "just got a lot to love." Barker groaned and turned his back on the scene, starting further into the forest. Finally, August jumped down with a yelp and held his knee as he got to his feet. The rest of the group started into the forest ahead of him, keeping a brisk pace. I lagged behind with August until he recovered and then we jogged ahead to join them.

"No alarms yet," Barker said with a laugh. Just a few days ago, I wasn't sure I would survive the blast, let alone survive and escape again. I couldn't help but laugh at how ridiculous it all was. It felt like my entire life was a big joke at my expense. I was alive, sure, but I lost my arm and my leg and maybe my fiancée.

"What are you laughing about?" the Aldierian asked.

"I've officially escaped from every high-profile prison in Gallaterra," I said, letting out another laugh of disbelief. August and the blonde girl were both looking back at me in awe.

"And I thought all of us getting out of G-Max was impressive," August said.

"I can't believe you actually got out of the arena," Angel said past the laughter of relief, "How?"

Our pace slowed, everyone suddenly more interested in my story than our reality. I didn't speak, my throat suddenly thick at the reminder of Kenna out there somewhere.

"That's where we were all supposed to end up someday, the arena," Barker said. The Aldierian scoffed.

"Everyone but you," she said, "You know why." No one asked what she meant. They were all too focused on me again to care.

"So, Grace," Barker said, the mention of my last name sending a jolt of irritation through me, "How did you do it?"

"I had help," I responded immediately, looking away from them. No one pressed the issue for a long moment.

"I always knew I would die in the arena," August said. I looked back at him, and he shrugged before continuing. "That's how the neighborhood I grew up in was. It was full of rough people, basically, a revolving door of poor people turned criminals and shoved into the arena instead of prison. No one goes to prison unless they have money or some kind of fancy connection with the government. I thought I'd go that way until I got lucky. It's funny because I thought getting a professional wrestling deal was my ticket out of the arena," he laughed, "Maybe it's fate. My trainer always told me that you can't talk the talk until you walk the walk. You gotta step into the ring first. When you come back out, then you can have your say."

"No one comes out of the arena though. That's the problem," the Aldierian said and started walking again, forcing us all to follow after her.

"No one except Kenna and Kieran," Barker corrected with a laugh, "and would you believe that one has a fancy connection to the government?" Barker smirked my way before patting August on the back.

"Lucky me," I said.

"Now don't tell me you got survivor's guilt," Barker said, elbowing me. I didn't know what I had. I survived. Kenna and I survived, but I wouldn't have made it to this point without her. I'd never done anything like this myself and when I tried to stand up to my father alone in the past, I never ended up the victor.

"I only survived that because I had Kenna," I said, "I told you, I had help. I would've died there without her."

"She would've too," Angel said. It was the first negative comment I'd ever heard her say and it must've been the first she ever said by the way the group turned to stare at her in surprise.

"Fight alone, you die. Fight together..." Barker whistled. "We may all be destined for the arena, but I won't be fighting alone and you won't either." Barker looked straight at me this time, eyes screaming his message of solidarity.

I gave him a nod of agreement and somehow, with that one look, I knew he'd help.

CHAPTER 18

We departed from the original plan and continued our journey towards Gallaterra City through the forest instead of the desolation of the Silent Sands. We knew it meant that the journey would take longer, but that only gave us more time to better plan out our attack. We alternated between riding Dimas and walking, setting up camp whenever we found a tighter section of the forest or a low section of the ground that would keep us hidden. It was a smooth trek until about three days in.

I stopped walking and I grabbed onto Naja's arm, gripping the bare skin at his wrist.

"Do you hear that?"

He didn't need to reply, because we could hear the voices perfectly over the next ridge. Naja patted Dimas once and the dog followed as we moved through the brush, hoping the sound didn't draw too much attention. Thankfully, laughter masked the noise.

"Screw Thomas," a man said, "He can hunt for himself. We got berries and leftover venison." Naja and I stopped behind a thicket of trees. Just between the branches, I could make out four men, minimal armor telling me that they weren't there on the beach. They were dressed more like the military police that gathered in our village only during the Ceremony of the Device.

"He's just pissed off that he didn't get picked to join the troop to wait on that Aldierian girl and the Grace kid," another man said, pocketing the gun in his hand. I looked over all four men. Each had at least one gun and the other pouches at their hips suggested maybe a few knives. I pressed my hand to Naja's, but he spoke first.

"We need their weapons."

I nodded in agreement but froze as the men began talking about children. The youngest man said he and his wife were thinking about having kids soon, the elder of the group jumping into the conversation at last.

"You just wait, brother. My first didn't sleep until he was three," he said, lowering his raised gun a little. That's when Dimas launched into the hunting troop. His teeth sunk into the shoulder of the younger soldier. Naja ran after him, stabbing one man through the back and jabbing the other in the stomach. I joined him late, late enough that Dimas had killed the last soldier in the party.

"You still with me?" Naja asked, looking up at me with questioning eyes before kneeling to search the nearest man. I forced all thoughts aside and began stripping the elder man of his gun, finding two knives at his hip.

"Is it worth taking their clothes?" I asked, already clasping the man's forearm guards around my own. Naja stood up from the last soldier, struggling to find space on his belt for the last gun. He tossed it to me instead.

"No," he said, "A soldier in a city would draw more attention, don't you think?" I hadn't thought about it. In my village, yes, we watched the soldiers in anxious anticipation for sure.

"You're right." I clipped the gun to my left hip. Naja paused and decided to steal one soldier's guards like I had, eyeing the rest to make sure we hadn't missed anything. I emptied all their packs while he inspected the area, gathering the food and tucking it into my backpack as I went.

"Dimas," Naja said, patting his leg to draw the dog close to him.

"One of them said something about other soldiers," I said, "So, they can't be far off." Naja agreed, motioning for me to mount Dimas after him. I did and together we began running through the trees, a steady pace that made it difficult to do more than hold on to Naja's waist. We rode for hours, stopping for only brief moments until the sun began to set and the forest floor grew dark. We had done our best to travel without stopping to hunt, but the GPS put us too close to civilization to risk running out of food in the next few days.

I was sure the temperature hadn't dropped at all, but it felt strangely cold to me as the sunlight faded and only our campfire lit the area. I moved to sit with Dimas after he returned with his catch, glad that Naja was still energized enough to cook for the both of us.

"You seem far away," Naja said. I felt strangely out of practice with keeping a conversation, realizing how long we'd gone without speaking about anything more than directions. My brain seemed to have memorized the men, hanging on to every word of their conversation about family.

"I've killed before, you know that," I said after a long pause, "but today was..." Naja's hands slowed over the fire, letting the meat he'd skewered hang there in the flames just a little too long.

"I know what you mean," he said, his expression somber, "When I thought I'd lost Illya... Part of me feels like a monster each time I have to kill." That's exactly how I felt standing by while Dimas and Naja gutted those men, despite who they were working for. After feeling the immense weight of Kieran's death and reliving that moment every time I shut my eyes, how could I do that to someone else? Did it matter what those men have done to others or that they pledged their service to President

Grace? How were we any different taking what was likely a loving father from his son? What was the justification for that?

"Does it get easier?" I asked, already sure of the answer. Naja shook his head.

"You just do it," he said, finally removing the overcooked meat from the fire. He stabbed the end of the skewer into the dirt next to him and started jabbing raw meat through a fresh skewer.

"That sounds…" I let the words hang in the air for a long time, Naja not looking up from his work. "Too easy," I finished. I was starting to understand what he meant though. When not killing means not seeing the people you love again, you do what you must. It becomes a game not of politics or us versus them, but survival. It was a kind of arena.

"I don't think it makes us terrible people that we kill others," Naja said, "I think the fact that we have to flip a switch off to do it proves we understand that life is valuable and the true consequences of our actions." I didn't speak until the meat had finished cooking and he offered the skewer to me. I took it and blew on it, the steam hot over my fingers.

"You know, I would've killed him the day I stepped foot in the arena," I said, "but Kieran chose a different option. That's the way he is. You offer two doors and Kieran uses his brain to dig a tunnel or something." Naja and I both laughed, but the gesture was almost painful. Kieran would see a different way.

"Kieran embodied that whole not letting anything limit you thing," Naja said. A ship passed over us, a small spec against the night sky. The green light on the bottom blinked just once before it vanished behind the treetops.

"Since I stepped foot in that arena, I don't feel like I ever really left. I think that, in a lot of ways, nothing mattered until I did that. We all think we know what we would do if we had to make the choice, but there's no way we possibly can until we are face to face with it all. The voice of truth can only come from the person who stepped foot in the arena. Am I making any sense?"

I asked. Naja nodded slowly, looking at his half-eaten burnt meat. He looked at me now, for the first time his expression free of pity or worry.

"I've spent so much time in the arena that I know every rock and tree," he said, "I also know who I'll be when I walk out again. Who will you be, Kenna Riley?"

"Not Kenna Riley," I said with a sigh, pulling the last hunk of meat from my skewer, "but I think I will be Kenna Petrek. At least I'll be that."

———

Another day of riding put us too close to civilization to take Dimas with us. Naja promised me that he knew the way home alone. I'd grown too fond of Dimas to help but feel a pang of guilt as we left him in the tree line and started into the desert. This was the part of the trip that would've been nice to have a dune rider for, but I understood Naja's concern about them being traceable when we argued about taking two the first time.

"Mama Abraham has a contact in the suburb Divez," Naja said. I stopped walking for a moment. Divez was known for being a rich alcove outside of Gallaterra City.

"Divez?" I asked him. He nodded, clearly not realizing how huge this was. Mama Abraham's contact must be a big shot.

"I've never met him, but I bet we can use an Ida stone to show him everything we need to," Naja said, stopping at the bottom of the hill. He dropped his backpack and began taking off his weapon belt. "I'll go into the city and come back in a few hours with disguises. The merchants that come through the desert wear large cloaks and we can hide our guns underneath," he said, "We can't get around going through the city. I think Covas can get us transportation."

"That sounds familiar," I said. I didn't know anyone named Covas, that much I was sure of.

"I have Gallaterran money," I said, digging into the zippered pocket of my bag and pulling out the small wad of bills. It was the only thing left that tied me to my old life. "Buy something for dinner? All we have left are the berries and one moldy slice of bread," I said. Naja hesitated but took the money from me in the end. If we needed more cash, surely Covas could loan us some once we found him.

"Four hours puts the sun there," Naja said, pointing to the spot in the sky, "If I'm not back by then, start heading towards Divez without me." I nodded and began unpacking my blanket and laying it in the sand. I watched Naja walk towards the city a couple of miles away until his figure was blurred by the heat rising off the sand. I was startled awake in what felt like just minutes later, Naja standing over me. He was wearing a large rust-colored jacket that stopped at his knees, a second tan coat draped over his shoulder. He didn't look happy.

"What?" I asked him. My stomach growled when I saw the sack in his hand. He set it down on the blanket and I began unpacking paper boxes of noodles.

"I can't believe you thought a nap was a good idea," he said, taking a seat across from me.

"I didn't exactly try to take one," I told him, handing him a container and a fork. We finished dinner in record time, setting up the last of our camp and getting a small fire going. In the distance, we could see merchants setting up their fires, small plumes of smoke going up into the air.

"I'll take the first watch," I offered, pulling my weapons belt closer to me while keeping it concealed under my blanket. Naja didn't give it a second thought and settled into his makeshift bed. I had too much on my mind to sleep now, so I never woke up Naja for his turn. Instead, he woke up as the sun was rising and I was tossing sand onto our campfire.

"You should've woken me," he said. I ignored him and finished packing.

"I think I can get us to Divez, but you'll have to be the one to find Covas," I told him. Naja looked a little anxious, but he told me he could do it. We strapped on our weapon belts and pulled on the jackets. Once buttoned up, you'd never know we were carrying enough to take out more than twenty soldiers between us.

We went unnoticed in the city until we got off a public dune rider near Divez. No one in the suburb needed public transportation, so the dune rider let us off six blocks away. The houses changed from small one-story compounds to three-story so fast it was almost comical. They were raised off the ground and then overlapped each other going upwards like a modern version of a child's toy blocks all stacked in a tower. Transparent bridges wound upwards between the houses, a highway of pods zooming past us overhead.

I noticed that we had slowed down after I'd taken in all the buildings, but Naja wasn't staring in awe at them the way I was. He was staring at the road ahead of us and then the entrances for the pods as we passed each station. My body felt heavy, and I was suddenly aware of how sore my thighs were from walking.

"You have no idea where to start, do you?" I asked.

"It's just that merchants this far into the city stand out," he said, "We should've stopped for new disguises."

"And you have no idea where to find Covas," I added. He glared back at me and then continued scanning the entrances for the pod stations. I led the way down a side street and away from the pods. This street was lined with luxury stores for everything from handbags and shoes to a custom pod shop where a couple of men in suits and shiny shoes were trying to sell a woman in a velvet mini dress a gold pair of doors.

"Do you have any money left from dinner last night?" I asked him. Naja dug in his pocket and came away with a handful of silver coins, maybe a few dollars.

"Well, it will buy us a cup of coffee," I said, looking down both sides of the street at the intersection. A to-go cup was painted on the sign of a place called *21st Street Coffee Bar*. String lights hung from the outdoor patio and the rooftop lounge area, both abandoned. Naja followed me down the street and into the shop. It was pretty standard as far as coffee shops went. Leather couches and armchairs were set around the space over concrete floors. A patch of turf the color of emeralds was tucked in the back corner of the shop, a small sign on the floor asking patrons to clean up after their dogs. A Great Dane was sleeping on a plaid blanking in the floor-length front window.

"Welcome," a man dressed in slacks and a button-up said from behind the bar, "What can I get for you?" His hands slowed as he polished the wooden countertop, looking over both of us. Maybe Naja was right, and we should've ditched the dusty traveling coats.

"Water is fine," I told him as Naja lifted himself into a barstool. The man shook his head.

"Get out," he said, motioning to the door with the dirty cloth.

"What?" I asked.

"Merchants don't come this far into the city that often, but they never pay up when they do," the man said, "and they always smell like dirt." I opened my mouth to yell back when a thunk down the bar drew our attention. Naja had dropped a coin purse onto the table, he pulled the strings apart without looking our way and removed a blue bar the length of his thumb.

"Whatever the best beer is you serve here," Naja said as he looked up at the man, "We each want a glass." They stared at each other for a long time, the man's mouth parting in shock.

"I need an ID," he said. Naja let out an annoyed sigh and removed another blue bar and sat it next to the second. Without another word, the man began working the bar. I slunk into the seat next to Naja, looking down at the blue bars. They were Ida stones, refined and shaped in a way I'd never seen them before. I grabbed one with my thumb and forefinger, surprised that it was light in my hand. The bar was larger than the Ida stone in the Heart of Aldieria and it weighed twice as much. Naja placed his hand over mine and slowly lowered it to the counter.

"They are fakes," he said, "He won't know the difference."

I removed my hand and Naja drew the stones closer to our side of the table, his expression remaining stoic as the man returned with two glasses of amber. He sat one in front of each of us, eyeing me long enough that I adjusted the scarf concealing my hair under my hood.

"I've never met an Ida stone miner before," the man said.

"Dumbass," Naja said, kicking me. I gasped a moment later, trying to mask my pain as disgust like the expression he wore as he glared across the counter at the man. "She owns half the mines in the east," Naja said, "No miner has this many Ida stones handy and we only travel like this so we aren't robbed when we stay in the desert towns."

"My apologies," the man said, his face turning red. "Do you live in Divez?" he asked, trying to hide his embarrassment as he finished cleaning the counter.

"Sometimes," I said, "I stay here to get away from the heat in the east and meet with my business team."

"And it better be the last time we have to talk with Covas," Naja said, the name making my heart skip a beat. The man dropped the cloth to the counter.

"You do business with Covas?" he asked, confusion taking over the surprise on his face. "Wait. What kind of business are you doing with Covas?" Naja tensed beside me.

"You could say we are on the legal side of things with Covas," I said. Naja was already slipping his hand into the bag for another Ida bar when realization dawned on the bartender's face.

"I'm sorry. I'm an idiot. Of course, you're fighting Marcus Covas. Every mining company in Gallaterra is trying to fight his bill to try restricting mining expansion," he said. The weird feeling returned as he spoke, the same one I felt the first time Naja mentioned Covas. Andre Covas. Senator Andre Covas. He was a senator and not just that, he was one of those secret Aldierian sympathizers Kieran talked about in the government.

"The senator agreed to meet with us, but he failed to tell us where his office is because of course, he did. So, we have been walking around this district for hours hoping to stumble into the right building," I said, taking a sip of the beer. Despite pickpocketing at the bar in my neighborhood back home, I'd never tasted beer before. It was weird. Bitter, but foamy like whipped cream. I tried not to act surprised when I lowered the glass.

"You have to go further into Divez to get to the government offices. He works in the same building you go to to get... I guess you probably have a private pod and don't need transportation credits," the man said, yet again providing us with the perfect cover.

"Can we walk from here?" Naja asked and took a long drink.

"Oh yeah," the man said, "You just keep going down Addison Boulevard and you'll run right into the steps." Naja drained the last of his glass and pulled another fake Ida block from his bag. He left all three on the counter and took me by the hand. I thanked the bartender and followed his lead back into the street.

Looking down Addison Boulevard, we could see the dome of the government building with its marble stairs. The streetlights flipped on halfway there and I worried that Covas wouldn't even be at his office anymore. Senators worked long hours though, right? I quickened our pace just in case.

The area around the building was beautiful, complete with a fountain out front with a statue of none other than President Grace raised on a pedestal in the water. It was obvious that the building was shut down for the night when we walked inside, the two security guards on duty not even paying us any attention as they locked up the doors at the back of the grand entryway. A woman sat at a three-sixty-style desk in the middle of the floor.

"We were supposed to meet with Senator Covas this afternoon," I announced.

"He just left," the woman said, her eyes darting towards the doors to her left.

"You don't understand. He didn't give us the right meeting place," Naja said. I tugged on his arm, making sure to grab his bare hand.

"He went out the side," I said, "We can find him if we move fast."

"Thank you anyway," Naja said, his tone much calmer. The woman sent an apologetic look our way before slipping into her coat. I led the way back to the front steps and then down a ramp to the left. I could see the lights come on for a dark pod waiting in a loading zone, an abnormally tall man in a suit starting towards it with four well-dressed men following him.

"Senator Covas," I yelled, drawing his attention. The four men turned out to be his security and they were reaching for unseen weapons at their hips. "Wait," I yelled, starting into a run.

"Damn it, Kenna," Naja said, catching up to me as I reached the grass. The men were all pointed guns at me. "Falle etwva. Falle etwva," Naja said, freezing in place and raising his hands in surrender. The men looked back at the senator who stared at Naja in shock. His expression tightened and I felt panic rising in my chest. We hadn't come this far to be arrested this easily.

"Etwva Ida," Covas said and moved aside, motioning for us to get into the pod.

CHAPTER 19

"Not a word until we get to the house," Senator Covas told us when the pod door slid shut. So, we all sat in silence while we zipped through the skyway. Andre Covas was a middle-aged tall man, but he wasn't just tall. He was tall like a professional basketball player, which it turned out he had been before stepping into politics. The entryway of his ginormous house displayed framed posters of the various teams he played on, two championship rings beneath glass domes, and the jersey with the number he retired.

The rest of the house glittered with gold and polished chestnut floors. The living room was larger than Ida Imara's entire apartment. It was the epitome of money for the sake of money on display. Covas led us to the sitting area in front of the fireplace, which came alive with a whoosh that startled me. The entire security team followed us, stationed around the room and making me fully aware of how easy it would be to end this mission if the wrong things were said.

"Who do you work for?" he asked us.

"No one," I said, a knee-jerk response that made the security team draw feet closer.

"My mother, Ida Imara, of Varillia. The leader of the Aldierians," Naja said, removing his jacket. The security team rushed us at the sight of the guns at Naja's hip, stopping only when Covas raised a hand to them. Naja unclipped his belt and tossed it onto the floor near the closest security guard. He motioned for me to do the same and I did, the guard taking both our belts and inspecting the weapons.

"She sent you to see me?" Covas asked.

"We were sent on a mission to Gallaterra. We had a way to stop the mining of Ida stones and keep the planet from crumbling," said Naja. Covas kept his expression stern.

"Had?" he asked, "What happened to your plan?"

"Gallaterran soldiers attacked our troop and we are all that's left," I said.

"Why did they attack you? Who are you?" he asked, looking directly at me.

"I'm Naja Petrek, the Ida's son," Naja said, but it wasn't him the senator was asking. He kept staring at me, waiting for me to answer. It was an intimidation strategy. He was making sure that whatever we came for, whatever we asked, we were prepared to go through hell to get his help. He was a high-profile senator. He wouldn't just help anyone, and he couldn't afford to do favors without getting something in return.

"My name is Kenna Riley. I was caught for being Aldierian during my device ceremony and arrested," I said, not needing to explain the rest. The severe exterior had faded away and he looked much more human now.

"You're the girl who escaped with the president's son," he said. I nodded. "Was he part of your troop?" I felt my eyes burn and my throat close. I nodded, fighting to control myself. The senator didn't respond this time. He relaxed his stance, sitting back in his chair. At last, he looked to the four members of his security team. He asked one to open a bottle of wine and bring in some glasses. He asked another to see if the cook was still in the kitchen to prepare a late meal. The third was sent to make sure his daughters were in their rooms for the night and the fourth was asked to wake his wife. In a matter of seconds, we were left alone with one of the richest men in Gallaterra.

"You'll help us?" Naja asked, his hand moving awkwardly to his back. He must have stashed a knife there. Covas had seen the reaction as well.

"Absolutely. So there's no need for that," he said, nodding towards Naja. My brother relaxed on the sofa next to me. "Now that we are alone," Covas said, "Not that any of my team would alert the authorities... I employ Aldierian sympathizers only so I can help people like Mama Abraham whenever they need it. This is a different matter though. I assume you two are planning to assassinate the president." He said it so casually, so easily that there was no need to ask his feelings on the subject.

"That's the idea," I told him, "That part was supposed to be Kieran's mission."

"I don't blame the kid," Covas said, "Politics aside, the president is a vile man who holds himself above the law. He also manipulates it so he can't be brought to justice. I tried once and he's kept me on the outskirt of political decisions as much as he's legally allowed. I don't go to Gallaterra City anymore after what happened to the last senator to speak against him."

"You mean the explosion?" Naja asked.

"No," Covas said with a laugh of disbelief, "Genevieve Lance died of an allergic reaction to peanuts. It wasn't peanuts. Her cook would know not to use peanuts and the woman was a health nut. She knew what was in the food she ate." Wow. Who else had the president and his administration killed off that we didn't know about?

The security team returned all at once and it was almost comical. All three of us were offered glasses of wine, our choice of red or white. I didn't know which to choose, so I took a glass of red as Naja had. The senator's chef was still in the kitchen and had started preparing a meal of leftover turkey and mixed vegetables. The remaining two guards came into the room together along with a beautiful woman that made even the sweatsuit she wore look fashionable.

"Before you get mad," Covas told her as she crossed the room, "I knew you'd want to be here for this, baby." Her brows furrowed and she accepted a glass of white wine from one of the guards. She settled onto the arm of his chair and looked back at Naja and I, expression growing more confused as she took in our merchant garb.

"I assume you both are Aldierian?" she asked.

"Not just Aldierian," Covas spoke before we could even nod, "the Ida's kids." The woman looked at her husband in surprise. "Dawn, they want our help to save the world," he said. She let out a sigh of relief and looked back at us.

"We've been waiting for years for the Aldierians to finally make their move on Grace," she said, "What took so long?"

"We didn't have a good angle until Kieran Grace mapped one out for us," Naja said, "The president's son is the only reason we can do any of this, but we need your help to get there. Mama Abraham told me once that you had the resources to do the big stuff. We need transportation to the capital." An elderly woman waddled in with two steaming plates of food. She sat them on the coffee table in front of us and left without saying a word.

"I can't implicate myself or my family in this kind of a plot," Covas said, taking his wife's hand, "but I can arrange for you both to take a stolen pod to the capital. Would that be enough?" It was exactly what we needed. It saved us days of travel and the possibility of being noticed on foot.

"Thank you," I said, completely in awe that someone could have the kind of reach that this man did.

"Let them eat, Andre," Dawn said, patting her husband on the shoulder and rising from her seat. "I'll see what extra clothes I can gather from upstairs. You can get closer to the government plaza if you're well dressed," she said and went back to the entryway.

Covas shared with us how the political climate in Gallaterra had changed in the months I'd been gone. The arrest and escape of the president's son had become public knowledge and he put forth laws that came down harder on Aldierian sympathizers to put up a strong front against Kieran. According to Covas, it made the leaders in the sympathizer movement nervous. Like he had said about Genevieve, people had started vanishing and threats were being made clear to the most influential people in the movement. Covas said he could hide all the evidence that he ever helped us, but he and his family had already received threats from President Grace's administration about leaving Divez. He hired more security since he'd been ordered to stay in the suburb and said that he had spies around the city for the sake of keeping himself safe and making unseen moves to try undermining Grace's power.

"If people, even the citizens, have strong suspicions that Grace is manipulating the government and abusing his power then why can't they just vote him out?" Naja asked. That showed just how little he knew about the Gallaterra political system. It had followed the American system from Earth, though loosely. Every citizen was allowed to vote after receiving their device, but there was no limit on the number of times a person could run for any office. The idea was that if that official was doing a good job, then there was no point in appointing someone new who may not do as well. President Grace has been in office for four terms and despite not being exactly well-liked by most, he always seemed to win the vote by a decent margin. Covas had also informed us how he runs his smear campaigns so there's little chance of him losing.

"If there is proof of him working outside of his legal duties or proof of him breaking any laws, then the High Courts can decide to take him out of power whenever they want," Covas told us.

"And there is no proof," I added, though no one in the room needed the explicit details.

"From everything the sympathizers have gathered, his death

is the only sure way to take him out of power. He has such a tight grip on his administration that there are bound to be some within it that disagree with his ways," Covas said. He looked up from me. I followed his gaze to his wife, who had returned with our weapon belts.

"I can show you to your rooms if you want. It's getting late," she said. Her husband looked like he wanted to protest and so did Naja when I looked at him. I was sure he was ready to hop into the next pod and go to the capital, but I was exhausted. We'd been traveling by foot for so long I had blisters and we hadn't eaten a proper meal until tonight. If we were going to fool anyone in the government plaza with our dress clothes, then we would at least need a shower.

"Thanks. That would be great," I answered and stood up with my wine glass in hand. Dawn smiled and showed the way up the stairs. We stopped on the second of three floors, going down the left hall which opened into another large living space with several bedrooms open at the back.

"You can take any of those, but I already put some clothing options into the first two bedrooms," she said, pointing to the four bedrooms, "They each have their small bathrooms and are stocked with soaps and towels. Just use the tablets in the rooms to let someone know if you need anything." She left us in the living room alone and I hadn't felt so safe in weeks.

"We leave at five?" Naja asked. I nodded and he started for the second bedroom, tossing his weapon belt onto the bed inside and shutting the door behind him. It was strange being alone. I hadn't had a second alone since we started this mission. Before that, I was always with Kieran.

I walked past the gray couches and the massive window that opened onto a patio light with twinkling lights. The first bedroom was huge. The bathroom was not small by any normal person's standards. I don't know what Dawn Covas thought was small, but a clawfoot tub, a shower with enough room for four, and a double vanity and walk-in closet were not considered small.

I got into the shower in such a daze that I had forgotten to pull my hair from my ponytail and take off my jewelry. My fingers stilled over the engagement ring and I left it on, not recognizing the sound of my voice howling off the granite and polished stone of the bathroom. I looked worse when I stepped out of the shower, eyes red and face sore.

Dawn had left several different outfits in the closet. I pulled on a pair of designer sweatpants and a hoodie so soft it was surely worth months of my salary. I wanted to choose a pair of jeans and a t-shirt for tomorrow, but the most dressed-down I could go was a pair of black slacks and a jade green blouse. Thankfully, she had provided shoes that would be comfortable to run in. There was no doubt that there would be running.

I tossed the clothes and the shoes onto the desk in the corner, feeling guilty enough that I went to politely fold them a moment later. The bedroom was the size of the entire apartment I shared with Kieran in Varillia. The bed was a massive king with a fluffy white comforter and champagne-colored pillows. There were two armchairs in the corner, the same gray color as the ones in the living room outside. The lighting fixture over the bed was an intricate cluster of clear globes, though I never turned it on. Just to the left of the bed was a large window that looked over the busy highway of pods below. There was a padded bench in front of it that reminded me of the window in Ariadne.

I sat there and watched the pods for a long time, braiding my hair into the traditional Aldierian hairstyle the best that I could. When I was done, I undid the do and started again. I thought seriously about slipping into Naja's room and asking to sleep on the floor, but the bed was so soft and I didn't want to bother him anymore with the sadness I felt. He'd already offered me another vial of that numbing stuff, reminding me that I could still take a few more doses before I was cut off. I didn't want to go numb, despite how lost I felt. In a lot of ways, I felt like I was that poor village girl again with no idea how she would ever be anything more.

My thoughts went to Naja next. He wanted to go home. He wanted to abandon the mission, but Kieran's note stopped him. He hadn't changed his mind, because it was Kieran. I wasn't an idiot and I knew he was doing this for me, but what about him? I'd learned that he was a lot of things and selfish didn't seem to be one of them. He loved Illya and he loved him enough to go on this mission with me to make sure that there was an Aldieria in the future for him. He knew just like I did the way this mission would likely end.

I was sure that with a little careful planning and Covas's help, we could get into Gallaterra and get close enough to kill President Grace. That was the entire mission now. From there, we would be arrested and executed, if not killed on the spot. I had accepted that once I read the note. This is what Kieran wanted and I needed to do this for him, for all of Aldieria. Naja didn't need to be a casualty in this. Naja had Illya. He'd made a promise to him to come back. I could make sure that he did if I was careful. Suddenly, I didn't feel so sad anymore.

CHAPTER 20
KIERAN

We kept going until we had just enough light left to find a place to camp. We were lucky. We found a low stretch of land with boulders to hide it from view. Charred remains of a campfire sat in the dirt.

"Aldierian soldiers traveled through here," the Aldierian woman said, dropping her butcher knife so it sunk into the dirt blade first. She sat next to it, leaning back against the boulder. The camp looked a little too fresh to be Aldierian soldiers. I knew for a fact that Varillia wasn't deploying anyone to prepare the way for our mission. Even after the blast, they wouldn't have sent anyone and there was no way they could've come this far so soon with the bridge out.

For a moment I wondered if it could've been Kenna's. Maybe she and Naja continued on their own. Of course, they would. Kenna promised and I encouraged that in my note. Stupid.

"This stretch of forest is patrolled by soldiers," Barker said, "I used to be one of them."

"You mean a knight," the Aldierian said, her words sharp, "You were a knight." I didn't know what she meant, and I wasn't the only one. August was the first to dare ask more. The

Aldierian woman didn't look at anyone but Barker, waiting along with the rest of us for him to answer.

Barker's expression was unreadable. He didn't look upset but he wasn't happy. After a moment, he nodded as if agreeing to explain.

"I was a member of the Knights of Earth," Barker said.

"And your rank?" the Aldierian interrupted. "I saw it," she told him. Barker smirked as if not surprised.

"Sargent James Barker," he said with a little lazy salute to her before looking at the rest of us, "The Knights are a kind of organization that developed out of the training camps. Gallaterran soldiers train in these forests on mock missions. The goal varies but killing any Aldierians we come across is a part of the job. The Knights are the soldiers who opt to stay behind to help train soldiers. The mission of the Knights isn't training soldiers so much as it is killing Aldierians. You can raise your rank quicker in the military by killing Aldierians. Each knight has a tattoo with the insignia," he said as he began shrugging his shoulders out of his jumpsuit. He pushed the top down to his hips so his chest was bare. In the middle of his chest was a tattoo of a shield with the Earth in the center. The tattoo was the size of a fist. At the top of the shield were smaller badges I recognized from army uniforms, the different ranks he'd earned over time as a knight.

"You ranked up three times after becoming a member," the blonde said under her breath. None of them aside from the Aldierian knew Barker's whole story.

"That was twenty years ago," Barker said, his mouth pulling into a frown of disgust. Cries echoed off the boulders when the Aldierian charged and shoved his back into the stone. I was the first to attempt to grab her.

"Let her go," Barker yelled. I took a step back and looked at August, giving her the perfect opportunity to snatch the stunning pole from him. She ran at Barker who did nothing to defend himself as she pressed his neck to the boulder and shoved the end of the stunning pole to the tattoo on his chest.

Barker gritted his teeth as the sizzling sound filled the stunned silence. The Aldierian held the stunning pole steady for nearly a minute, Barker's face scrunched with pain the entire time. He didn't let out a sound until she released him. He groaned and crumpled to his hands and knees. He stayed there for another minute as he recovered, deep breaths coming out from between his teeth like steam from a kettle. He sat up, relaxing against the boulder.

Where the tattoo should've been was a bloody mess of burned skin, making it impossible to see that there had ever been a tattoo at all. Barker looked up from it and smirked, letting his head lay back against the stone.

"I won't let anyone with that damned mark be a member of this troop," the Aldierian said.

"Don't worry," Barker said, "This suits me better." Stripes of blood were reaching the jumpsuit at his waist now, pooling in the folds and rolling off the strange, apparently waterproof, material. The Aldierian moved to the opposite boulders and sat down, seemingly satisfied now that the mark was removed.

I shook the knives out of the apron and balled the fabric in my hands. Barker didn't say a word as I sunk to the ground next to him and began sopping up the mess. The burns were bad but manageable enough. He wouldn't die from them anyway, but he'd be in pain for a while and bear the scar of the event after. He kept surprisingly quiet considering how his back bowed and body writhed under my touch. Once the bleeding stopped, I left him alone.

The rest of our troop was gathered around a fire away from Barker. I gathered the knives and sat them next to me once I joined them. I wondered what other kinds of threats were hiding behind the trees. Animals. Poisonous bugs. I'd studied enough of the area back in Varillia to know the forest was plagued with poisonous plants. Preventing a killer rash might be the only perk of wearing the jumpsuits.

"Kieran Grace, right?" August asked me, extending a hand. I

took it and gave it a shake, his hand so thick that it made me feel like a child.

"Just Kieran," I told him.

"I'm August Merkwood," he said, "I was serving a life sentence for conspiring against the government. I'm a sympathizer, used to be a professional wrestler." That explained it.

"Good to meet you," I said. The blonde sat forward next to him, the firelight highlighting all the sharp angles of her face. She didn't look like the type to ever be in prison. She was beautiful without needing to style her long hair or add any makeup to her face.

"I'm Angel Torsney," she said. Torsney?

"Like TED? Torsney Engineering Development?" I asked. She nodded.

"I'm, at least I was, going to take over the company before I got arrested for being a sympathizer," she said. I had a suspicion that most of our wing of the prison was full of sympathizers. You couldn't be arrested for your opinions though, no matter how much I was sure my father wished he could. You had to act on them.

"What happened?" I asked.

"She hijacked the government," August said in astonishment, patting her on the back. She smiled but shook her head.

"I hacked into a government database and got access to some military records. I found a report that connected the killing of business mogul Grant Jackson to President Grace. It was a text message Grace sent giving out the location where Jackson was when he was stabbed. The proof was deleted within the hour and I was arrested," the girl said, picking up a twig from our pile of extra firewood and turning it between her fingers.

"She's the one who got us out of prison," August told me, "She knew that magnets could offset the cuffs and she knew where to find them around the prison. She's the beauty and the brains." Angel's cheeks turned pink. The Aldierian sat up a little and tossed a clump of dirt at August so it exploded against his chest and sent dust raining down on his lap.

"She's not into you," she said.

"What's your story?" I asked before the dust had even settled. She looked at me, eyebrows raised like she couldn't believe I even asked.

"I'm Aldierian," she said, "I was arrested for being Aldierian."

"That's Sissa Tamlot," August said, "She was arrested while on a mission with her troop." Sissa glared back at him.

"Your troop was captured?" I asked.

"Killed," she corrected, "all but me. Execution style by a bunch of knights." She glanced at Barker who was still sleeping against the boulder with his head lolling to one side. No wonder she hadn't even looked our way when she burned Barker. I felt a pang of hate in my chest, not so much for who he was as what he'd done. He seemed like a different person now than twenty years ago when he was arrested. It made me remember that I had no idea what he'd done to be arrested in the first place.

"I'm sorry. I understand how hard that is," I said, all the sharpness gone from my tone now.

"Sure," Sissa said and then muttered in Aldierian. I knew enough of the language to know that she was calling me a liar. More than that, she was taking a jab at my privilege.

"I'm not," I told her, repeating her words and adding a few of my own. She stared back at me in surprise for just a second before her stony stare was back.

"How did you learn Aldierian?" she asked, tossing another log into the firepit and focusing on moving it around with her butcher knife.

"I learned in Varillia," I said. She looked up, knife hanging in the flames and slowly changing from silver to red.

"You've been to Varillia?" she asked.

"Yes."

"How did you even find the entrance, not to mention get past the gate?"

My brain flashed through the first battle on the sand. It looked much the same as the one just days ago, only devastating in a different way. The bodies were strewn around the beach still gave me nightmares, but now when I closed my eyes, they weren't faceless like before. Now, when I let my mind wander to that dark place, the bodies were of my troop, Naja, and even Kenna laying in the sand with the tides of the East Sea swirling her red hair around her lifeless face. I felt cold even thinking about it.

I must have been out of it for a long time because all three of them were looking at me with concern now. I realized when I relaxed that I had gripped my right forearm hard enough with my robotic hand that it was numb.

"When my father imprisoned me in the arena, I met this girl," I started. They sat silently while I retold the entire story. I felt better the more details I divulged, not even embarrassed to tell them about our night in Ariadne or every raw emotion I felt for Kenna when I realized in Varillia that I didn't want to untwine my life from hers after all of it. Angel offered me her condolences when I told them about the explosion and August got a little emotional as I explained that their mission was suicide unless I could get to Naja and Kenna and help.

"I'll go with you," August said, "I didn't know what I was going to do if I ever got out of prison anyway." Angel nodded.

"I can still hack into any government records online. I bet I could help get you guys into whatever building you need to kill your father. Finding your girlfriend may be the hard part," she said.

"I knew I busted you out for a reason," Barker said. None of us realized he was awake or for how long. He winced as he got to his feet and moved closer to the fire, sinking next to me.

"You didn't know a thing about me," I said.

"I know more about you than you know about me," he shot

back with a smirk, "So, you have an ex-soldier, the best hacker on the planet, and heavyweight over there. I don't have the damn knight's mark anymore." Barker looked at Sissa expectantly.

"Falle etwva?" I said, offering her my hand. She looked down at it, her entire body relaxing a little.

"Etwva Ida," she said and gave my hand a single shake.

CHAPTER 21

KIERAN

After identifying bush after bush of berries as poisonous, I finally convinced the group to let me hunt for game using the paring knives like throwing knives. It was successful the first time, immobilizing a horned hog so that Barker could deliver the death blow. Sissa and Barker worked together to dress the animal, reluctantly, but they were able to have meat prepared to cook over our fire quicker than the rest of us could've.

"I'm done with you for the day," Sissa declared, rose to her feet, and stalked off into the trees. I was drawing buildings in the dirt, showing Angel and August what the government plaza looked like where Kenna was surely headed.

"What did you do?" I asked, getting up. Barker didn't look up and continued to shove hunks of raw meat onto sticks. I stalked towards him and gave him a shove, repeating my question.

"I told her not to forget what she is," he said. I grabbed the front of his shirt and pushed him against the boulder.

"Why? After everything she went through, the stuff you did…"

"Because they're right," he said between his teeth, "and I know that loss."

"How could you know what that feels like?" I asked, not seeing the hurt in his face until the words had slipped out. He did know what that was like. I let him go, but I didn't step away from him. "What happened?" I asked.

Barker brushed past me. He went back to stabbing hunks of meat onto the sticks, calling us all over after Sissa returned. We gathered around the fire again like the night before, all holding our skewers of meat into the flames until they were cooked through.

It was the first meal I'd had since being arrested, rousing a burning hunger I hadn't realized I had until the food was placed before me. I devoured the first skewer and barely could contain my impatience while I waited for the second to cook.

August told us stories from his days as a professional wrestler. Angel nearly stopped eating when he detailed his worst injury, but none of us could deny a meal. August was by far the best humored in the group. He took everything in jest, not even offended when Sissa commented on how idiotic a sport was that didn't involve fighting to injure.

We ate for hours, eating a surprising amount of the large pig. After we were all full, we tossed dirt on the fire and started to hike again despite the tightness of our bellies. We were sluggish at first, only picking up the pace when Sissa pointed out how much daylight we likely had left in the forest. I moved ahead of the pack, steering us towards the largest city where I hoped we could get some kind of transportation to the capital. If we didn't head off Kenna or at least run into her along the way, stopping her once we got to the capital would be difficult.

"I fell in love with an Aldierian girl too," Barker said to my right. I hadn't noticed him until then. The rest of the group was almost a yard behind us. He was relaxed, not walking with his normal sauntering gait. It made him look old, middle-aged.

"There's always a girl," I said under my breath.

"That'll do it," he replied, "I didn't mean to love her either."

"Never do," I said, "How did it happen?" Barker took a deep breath and for a moment, I wasn't sure he was going to tell me.

"She was nothing like what the Knights said they were," he said, "Smart. Nice. Civilized. My team was attacked by a couple of mountain dogs. Some of the soldiers ran back to camp, but most were mauled and died in the forest. I didn't think I'd make it. I was with her when I woke up. I was in pretty bad shape and she and her troop nursed me back to health. They were nice, despite what I was, and I learned about their culture and the way we abuse the planet. When I was healthy enough, she asked me to stay with them. I wanted to, but I was afraid. So, I went back to the camp. They all thought I was some kind of hero surviving in the forest for months like that. I told them I scoped out an Aldierian camp while I was out there, told them a few things I learned. I didn't tell them anything important that might put them in danger."

"I bet going back to that life after was hard," I said, "My father always hated that I couldn't just keep my mouth shut about the things he did." Barker nodded.

"I was in a position of power with the Knights, which made things dangerous. First, I pretended to be rusty on my aim when we would try killing Aldierians in the forest. I faked an injury to keep out of the action for a few weeks. That gave me a lot of time to research things using the military database. While I was on leave, my second in command dragged back an Aldierian woman. I heard about it late, so I was at the back of the pack of soldiers at our camp when they brought her back and…" I was glad he didn't finish.

"Was it her?" I asked. He shook his head.

"No," he said, "I found that out when I finally saw the body. I was so sure it was her though. I started meeting her in the forest after that to leak information to her and the Aldierian troops. I told them about our methods to capture Aldierians and that completely stopped our success in that area. I got pretty bold about what I was sharing, making it obvious that someone was leaking our secrets to them. I didn't care. I said to hell with the Knights. I told her that I couldn't do the double-life thing anymore. I would have to kill myself or join her somehow. I was almost finishing making arraignments when I was followed by my troop to meet with hers. They slaughtered them. My second in command dragged her into a tent after it was over and…" Barker's voice shook. He sucked in a deep breath, his knuckles around his knife going white.

"Bastard," I said, feeling my muscles tighten.

"He brought me her head when he finished," Barker said, his voice loud enough that I glanced behind to check if anyone heard. August was telling Sissa and Angel a story behind us with a smile on his face.

"I know exactly what I did to the Aldierians and troops just like Sissa's," Barker told me, taking a swipe at his left eye, "I taught my soldiers to be ruthless because I thought you had to be. I didn't even question everything we are taught in Gallaterra about them. I thought we were keeping the nation safe by taking out anyone who left the East Sea. The Aldierians are the only people on this damn planet that are doing any kind of justice."

"So, you were arrested," I said. Barker smiled a little.

"After I killed the bastard," he said, "I was sentenced to life imprisonment in G-Max. I was spared execution in the arena because of my military rank. They worried I would inspire others to act if a report got out about sympathizers in the military." And James Barker had been in that prison cell for the last twenty years since. The few days I'd spent in the arena's holding cell seemed like a joke now.

"I'm sorry about what happened to you," I said.

"It's not me you should be apologizing to," Barker said and patted me on the back, "but you know that already." We walked in silence after that for a few hours before it got too dark to continue. We set up camp where the trees grew a little closer together, though they would do little to hide us if someone walked within yards of our site. It was too dark to hunt for another meal, so we were all glad we'd gorged ourselves on that pig.

"I'll get some more firewood," Angel said after August lit what little we had for a campfire. She started back into the trees while the rest of us sat down and got as comfortable as we could on the grass.

"I'm gonna take a piss," Barker said, heading in the opposite direction from Angel. We sat for a long time in silence. August was the first to lay down, falling asleep flat on the ground with one arm under his thick hair and the other holding his knife. I laid back and stared up at the stars, the glowing lights I hadn't seen clearly past the Gallaterra City lights since I was a little. We'd gone on vacation, though my father and mother had an argument and he stayed home to work. It was glorious. I was almost asleep when August's deep voice woke me.

"I don't mean to get too personal, Kieran," he started, "and you don't have to answer, but I feel like I have to ask." I rolled onto my side and propped myself up on my elbow. August was laying in the same position as before and I was just able to see his eyes staring at the sky.

"More like you want to," Sissa muttered, propping herself up on her hands so she was in a reclining position. Her jab hadn't deterred August though, who I'd learned was always well-meaning and kind, but also gullible and forward.

"You can ask," I told him, sitting up. They both looked a little anxious now.

"I understand being okay with your father paying for his crimes and I can see how you could accept him being killed for it, but it's so personal to you. You said you wanted to be the one to do it. I just wondered…" August didn't finish, which was surprising considering how much he talked the entire trip. The man had a personality as big as he was.

"He smacked me around daily and I mean that literally. Unless he was out of town, I knew I had it coming. He made me feel like it was my fault like I earned it or something. In his eyes, I probably did, because I didn't go along with his rules when it came to his beliefs about the way things should be in the country. Sometimes, it was just a slap for saying something he didn't like. Sometimes, it was more. My mother didn't like it, but she knew better than to get on his bad side. Most of my siblings just saw it as me getting what I deserved. Old fashioned discipline. Traditional values bullshit. They are so brainwashed to his administration about the threat of the Aldierians and about his father being in power because the people vote for him. They don't know the truth, because father keeps it from them and he made sure to shut me up whenever I tried to present the facts," I said.

I could feel my hands shaking a little at the memories. I could feel the back of my legs ache from one of the worst of my father's so-called punishments. Even now, whenever someone raised their voice, I sometimes tensed in anticipation. I hated it. I hated that even now that I had escaped him for good he still had that hold over me.

"It is personal then," Sissa said, pulling me out of my thoughts. I wondered how long they'd let me sit in the silence.

"You could say that," I told her, "I think he deserves to die for it all. I want him dead. Nothing can change what he did to me or my mother or our family, but if I do it myself…"

"Maybe it will bring you closure, make it easier to leave behind?" August asked. I'd never made that connection, but yeah. That was how I felt.

"It won't," Sissa said, her voice firm, "It may seem like it, but it won't. He will be dead, but you will still have the memories of the abuse." August sat up and looked at her, open-mouthed.

"You didn't have to do that," he said, astonished. My hands shook enough now that I held them close to my side. It took a moment for me to realize I wasn't angry. I felt something else. Sadness? Loss? I don't know. It didn't matter what I felt, I knew she was right. I had to be the one to do it though, but not for revenge.

"I know it's messed up and it probably doesn't make sense, but he's still my father," I said, "It's like I can punch my brother for making me mad, but if someone else did it I'd be pissed. It's complicated." We were quiet until Angel returned with her arms full of wood.

"Where's Barker?" she asked. We all looked around the camp as if he'd suddenly appear from behind a tree.

"Ditching us, probably," Sissa said. I let out a sigh and stood up, plucking her butcher knife from her hand.

"I'll go find him," I said. August was the only person to offer me his nervous gaze and forced smile of support. The girls both went back to tending the fire and I stared into the trees. I was surprised I hadn't at least heard him after walking nearly ten minutes and I started to believe Sissa about Barker running off until I heard a thumping sound behind a thicket of trees. I pushed them aside and saw Barker leaning over the body of a soldier, three other men laying feet away.

"How did you..." I started, gaining his attention.

"Not me," he replied, "and whoever it was took their weapons."

"They, probably," I said, looking over the soldiers. They were low rank by the identifiers on their jackets, but not untrained. They had basic rank, so there was that. Surely, it would take two people at a minimum to take down this many soldiers, two people, or some kind of skilled assassin.

"What?" Barker asked, pulling me from my thoughts. My heart was still racing, however.

"I think she was here," I said, "Maybe both of them."

"Your girl and her brother?" Barker asked, halfway bent over another soldier in search.

"We didn't deploy any Aldierian soldiers in preparation for our trip, not that we could if we wanted," I said, "There were too many Gallaterran soldiers on the beach to get anyone out." Barker stood up again, empty-handed, and let out a sigh.

"If she's heading to the government plaza in Gallaterra City from here, she'll be going through Divez," he said, expression grave. Damnit, Kenna. She probably didn't fully understand what that meant and Naja definitely wouldn't. Divez was a suburb of Gallaterra City, a very rich and very well-protected suburb. There would be guards all over the place. Without a good disguise, they'd stick out traveling the streets.

"At least they had enough sense not to take the soldier's clothes," I said, "They'd be swept into some battalion or something."

"Yes," Barker said, his tone lifting in such a way that made me nervous. His eyes were alight with excitement, and they met my gaze for just a moment before he began sizing up the soldiers. He went to the medium-sized one of the group and began stripping the soldier until he was laying in just his boxers and undershirt.

"This is crazy," I said as he slipped out of the orange jumpsuit.

"No," he replied, "Getting sucked into some military building is exactly what we need."

"How is that remotely close to helpful," I said, not caring that my voice echoed off the trees, "I didn't come this far, survive everything I have along the way, just to get this close and walk right back into the hands of our captures."

"You heard my story, right? The nearest military outlet was mine," Barker said, already dressed from the waist down in the military garb. He slipped into the jacket and began buttoning it over the terrible burn marks on his chest. "I know every inch of that place," he said.

"Even after twenty years?" I asked, "And who's to say you won't be recognized while we're there? What about me? My face is all over posters and tablets and-" I was cut off when Barker tossed a boot hard against my stomach. I caught it against my knees as I doubled over, watching as he looked me over and then moved to the smallest soldier.

"Put his clothes on," he said and snatched the boot back from me, "that will take care of you." I did as I was told, not sure where his plan was going other than getting us out of the eye-catching orange jumpsuits.

"What about you?" I asked as I began pulling off the soldier's pants.

"I grew the hair after I was imprisoned," he explained, "and twenty years is a lot of time in the military." He smirked a little as he adjusted the collar of the jacket like he had been doing it for years. I ignored him as I finished stripping the soldier and climbing into his clothes.

"We can't dress all five of us," I noted, looking at the remaining soldiers, "one of us has to stay behind."

"None of them would go for that and Angel, while the least necessary of the crew wouldn't do well by herself in the forest," Barker said, "The girl is a genius, but she doesn't have the survival skills for this forest." I doubted his opinions about Angel, but maybe he was right at least about a part of this.

"How far is that military outlet?" I asked him. Barker's serious expression pulled into a sly smirk.

"So close that we're taking a risk by camping where we are," he said with a snort.

"And are there pods or anything we can use to speed this trip up?" I asked. Barker was smiling now, showing a whole front row of overlapping teeth.

"Can you handle a flattop dune rider, kid?" he asked. I let out a laugh at the memory of Kenna and I zipping over the Silent Sands as we tried to outpace the dune dogs.

"Can you keep up after twenty years?" I asked.

CHAPTER 22

KIERAN

We went back to the camp to finish developing the plan with the rest of the crew. Barker and I would head out before the sun had fully risen. The goal was to stay as unseen as we could in the military outlet so we didn't have to risk being discovered ourselves despite the uniformed disguises. The rest of the crew would hike to the edge of the forest where the terrain turned from humid jungle to arid desert. We would barely fit into one dune rider as is, so we hoped we could steal two so we would have extra space for Kenna and Naja, or worst case, one dune rider could be used to lead a chase away so the other could escape. At the rate, we were traveling plus the time saved thanks to the dune riders, we could head off Kenna and Naja or at least catch up.

The others agreed and we parted ways while it was still dark. Barker led the charge blindly, using his memory as our only guide until it grew light enough for him to note markers along the way. From there, we walked just a few hours until we began to hear machinery and the occasional call of orders.

"It's almost too…" Barker didn't finish, but he did slow his pace for a moment.

"We'll be quick," I said, patting him on the shoulder. He

seemed to come out of whatever memory he was reliving, and we walked until we could see the gates between the trees.

It wasn't a large outlet by the look of it. The main gates were swung wide with just a few soldiers guarding them as dune riders zipped in and out among the traffic of soldiers in the dirt street, some marching in groups and others walking as if on their way to a day's work.

"The dune riders will be parked to the right," Barker said quietly to me. I followed his lead, giving a guard at the gate a nod in greeting as we passed. The street was lined with dozens of buildings, two more rows behind those on both sides. After passing the final row of identical buildings, we found a large lot full of the exact flattop dune riders we had hoped for. The gates of the enclosure were thankfully open just like the main gate, though we wouldn't be allowed to pass as easily as we had there.

"Credentials," a man called out. I felt my skin cool at his voice, but Barker didn't seem the slightest bit worried.

"I lost my badge in the fight, but we're with the scout troop F6," Barker said without missing a beat. We both had the ID cards of the men who wore these uniforms, but after confirming that we looked nothing like either of them, we memorized everything listed on the plastic cards on the hike here instead.

"We didn't expect your troop back for another two days," the man said after confirming our details with his tablet.

"Our captain was injured in the fight along with another man," Barker said, "We came back for a dune rider." The man let out a curse and began punching buttons on his tablet again.

"I sent for a medic to escort you," he said, "and I can spare another man for the day, so he can drive you. The captain is the only person authorized to drive a dune rider." Shit. Of course.

"Can you bring the dune rider around to the road in the meantime? The captain was hurt badly, and he may not be alive if we don't move quickly," I said, the nerves in my voice thankfully came across as urgency based on the actions of the man. He barely glanced at his tablet before setting it aside and ducking back inside the small shack. He emerged a second later with a key fob and started towards the back of the lot.

"We have to get rid of the medic," Barker whispered as we moved back onto the main road.

"Maybe we can take the dune rider before he ever gets here," I suggested, realizing it wouldn't work as a man a few inches shorter than me and at least as old as me ran towards us dressed in the same military uniform. The red cross over his breast gave away his purpose.

"We have to get rid of him along the way," Barker said before the man grew too close.

"What are the injuries?" he asked, looking for the dune rider, only it wasn't a flattop dune rider that pulled into the road. The pod stopped before us, the red cross emblazoned next to the army insignia over the doors. They slid open and the man climbed out, another maybe Barker's age replaced him behind the control panel. The medic didn't wait for us to answer his question before scrambling inside.

"Where to?" our escort called as the medic began checking the drawers along the back of the pod. Two rolling stretchers were strapped to the floor at the back, enough space in the front left for Barker and I to sit on a long bench just behind the man punching the controls. I could see on Barker's expression that he didn't feel nearly as confident navigating a medical pod and I knew that I wasn't equipped to. I wasn't used to a control panel with so many buttons.

"Where to?" the man asked again, already moving the pod down the road and past the gates.

"East," I answered, ignoring the pressure of Barker's foot on my own. The man didn't question me and began punching buttons again. Our new companions were too busy falling into their roles to even glance our ways. We sat for a long time on the bench while both men worked. The medic never spoke to us as he clanged around the back, prepping the medical station.

"What kind of injuries are we dealing with?" he finally asked. I caught Barker's wary gaze before I looked back at the younger man.

"Stabbed in the chest," I said. The medic looked surprised.

"And he's still alive?" he asked.

"I hope so," I replied, noticing the way the medic turned a little pink and went back to prepping a station with materials. So he was inexperienced and easily manipulated. He wouldn't fight us if it came to that.

"Sorry to take you on your day off," Barker said to the man behind the controls. He was dark-haired with a thin bandage at the back of his neck.

"All I had today was my induction," the man replied, "and I got my tattoo early." he gestured to the bandage. Barker stiffened next to me, and I realized with a pit in my stomach why. This man was a knight.

"Congrats, man," I said, getting a brief smile in reply before the man returned his eyes to the forest ahead of us.

"Don't worry," he said, "I'll be on the job tomorrow to take care of those Aldierian terrorists who attacked you. I'm hoping to rank up fast." Barker sucked in a deep breath and slowly let it back out, his hand going to his waistband where his knife was stashed. I elbowed him and his knuckles turned white around the knife before he relaxed against the seat again. We couldn't kill them, could we? We shouldn't kill them. I was tired of killing. There had to be other options. These guys were just doing their jobs, right?

Barker counted down the hours until we would reach the point where we were supposed to meet the others. He flashed me two fingers across the seat and then one, at which point I was much more aware of my knife strapped to my hip. I was thinking through ways to avoid a fight when the pod began to slow. Our driver was leaning over the control panel and squinting at something.

"You see that?" he asked, looking back at us just as Barker's fist smashed into his face.

"Jesus, Barker," I cried out when he sunk the knife into the man's chest. He slipped from his seat limply and collapsed onto our feet. Before the blood could seep from his shirt to the floorboard, Barker hit a button for the door and shoved the dead man to the grass underneath where he rolled twice on impact.

"No," I said as Barker lunged for the medic at the back of the pod, the poor man raising a scalpel as a weapon.

"If the word gets out, we can be run down in Divez," Barker said, looking back at me while keeping his bloody knife aimed at the wide-eyed man.

"I won't say a word," the poor guy said, "I just want to practice medicine. I couldn't get into med school, so I joined the military and got assigned as an apprentice. I don't even like the military. I hate it."

"Shut up," Barker said, his tone firm enough to scare the man to silence.

"We aren't going to hurt you," I told him, "I swear. Right, Barker?" It was not even remotely a question, more of a threat. I won't let this man die. Annoyance flashed in Barker's face, but he lowered his knife and moved past the medic for the stack of white towels behind him. I motioned for the man to sit on the bench seat as Barker cleaned off the blade. The terrified man sat, practically flopping against the back of the seat.

"I swear we aren't going to hurt you," I said again, "You believe me?" He looked up at me, the color fading from his face. He nodded, which made the knots in my stomach ease a bit.

"What's the plan, Grace?" Barker asked, saying my last name in a hiss. I wanted to shoot an insult back his way, but what was the plan?

"Toss me that pillowcase," I said and pointed at the gurney. Barker pulled the case off and tossed it to me along with a pair of flex cuffs he found in a drawer. "Sorry," I muttered to the medic as I fastened the zip ties around each wrist. I slipped the pillow-case over his head and past his shoulders.

"The others are heading our way," Barker said, nodding towards the front windshield. Just like he said, Sissa, Angel, and August were all within yards of the pod now. "You better get out and explain it all to them," Barker said with a salute, "I'd say you're the one in charge here." I ignored the jab. I was a little satisfied that Barker agreed to let me take the lead. None of the others would likely contest the move, and Barker was the only person in the crew that worried me a little.

I pushed the button for the door and slipped out before it had even opened completely. August let out a cheer that he cut off as soon as I ran at him with a finger pressed to my lips.

"What's wrong?" he asked.

"I thought you were stealing a flattop dune rider," Sissa said, almost accusatory.

"We were, but things changed," I said, "and we took a hostage." Angel stopped walking and August sucked in a breath.

"Why?" Sissa asked.

"We aren't going to kill him," I told her, "We're going to just drop him off somewhere. His face is covered, so he won't know what anyone, but Barker and I look like." Sissa shook her head in disbelief and started towards the pod ahead of us. August and Angel exchanged nervous glances.

"I think you did the right thing, man," August said, patting my shoulder.

"Yeah," Angel agreed, "The pod may attract some attention in Divez though." I worried about the same thing. Military pods didn't travel through cities often and military med pods only did to make the rare trip to civilian hospitals.

"If we move quickly, the pod won't be reported missing for at least a day," I said, "We didn't technically steal it. It was given to us."

We all piled into the pod, startling the poor medic who

needed my reassurance that nothing would happen to him. Barker proved to be a capable navigator thanks to his military training, so I let him set the destination through Divez. We stayed mostly quiet as we traveled to keep the medic from hearing Angel, Sissa, or August's voices.

I woke up in a panic when someone smacked the side of my head.

"We're being followed," Barker said. It took a moment to get all my bearings before I was able to see things properly. We were in a city now, Divez based on the cleanliness of the streets out the window. I rose off the bench and moved to the passenger seat.

"Are you sure?" I asked, glancing behind us. About a block away was a dark pod, clearly a privately owned vehicle. A taxi or city pod would be marked and this one didn't have any visible distinguishers.

"I wasn't sure at first, but it's been a few minutes, so yeah," Barker said. My stomach churned so much I thought I might be sick. We weren't even a day from the government plaza. What if Kenna and Naja made their move before I got there?

"We have to lose them," I said, looking out the window again.

"If we make a break for it and they follow…"

"If they are following us, then they know we're up to something already. They won't just stop following us on their own," I said, my voice rising so much now that everyone in the pod was awake. Sissa stood up, bracing herself using the gurney.

"Just gun it, Barker," she called. Before she'd even finished, the pod lurched underneath them and the chase began. The medic let out a cry of panic, but we were all too busy watching the pod behind us to worry about him. The pod increased speed until it was keeping up with us again. There were no extra lights, no officers to be seen past the tinted windows, nothing at all that I'd expected a police pod to have or even the military.

"They aren't police or military," I said, hoping someone else had some answers.

"Federal agents?" August suggested. If they were federal agents, then they likely knew exactly who we were. Barker must've thought the same thing because the pod jolted again as we picked up speed. The screen to his left that displayed the speed in green numbers kept ticking up, the green turning to a yellow-orange color as if the pod was close to maxing out.

"Are we going to crash?" the medic yelled. Barker's eyes flicked to the rearview mirror long enough to glare at the restrained man.

"I swear I'll toss him out if he can't-"

"Barker," Angel yelled, hugging the back of the bench seat the best she could. I didn't look away from the mirror in time. My head sunk deep into the headrest as we came to an abrupt stop before the dead end. The seatbelt burned as it tightened against my skin and the only part of me that didn't feel sore were the parts made of metal. In some kind of a twisted bit of irony, the wall at the end of the street had been painted, a long time ago based on the amount chipped away, with a photo of my family. My father stood center and directly in front of the pod was the picture of me. It had chipped at the edges so only my shoulders and face were intact, not that it mattered. Someone had spray-painted a red X over my face and written the word "wolf" out to the side. Is that what they were calling me?

"Everyone okay?" Barker called out, breaking my thoughts. The gurneys were perfectly in place, though the rest of our crew had slid almost to the back of the pod. August was braced against the back door when it opened and he flopped out, revealing a man dressed in a black jumpsuit like the ones I'd seen at various galas at the capital. He was a federal guard. He had a dark gray patch over his breast that said his name, but I didn't get a look at it before two more guards opened the side door and ordered us out, each pointing guns at us.

Barker and I got out first while the others recovered from the stop. There were five guards in total, though none of them seemed too worried about us as we gathered in the street. The area was abandoned, but they worked fast anyway to round us up into their pod.

"What about the medic?" I asked, the last to stay behind. A single guard climbed into the driver's seat of the med pod and the doors slid shut.

"We'll take care of him," a woman told me, her gentle touch steering me back down the road as the pod turned and disappeared around the corner. Something about this was strange. If these were federal guards, wouldn't we be in handcuffs and subdued somehow? I expected a fight to break out with us being on the losing end, battered and broken.

"What's going on?" Angel asked as I finally got in. I felt my body relax. The pod was luxurious. The seats were tan leather and in the middle of the floor was a table with a tablet for a topper that displayed all our names and faces along with files for our arrests minimized behind the photos. Two of the guards got into the front seats and we quickly began our journey through the streets again at a leisurely pace.

"They work for someone on our side," Barker said with a little laugh, "someone important." The woman sitting next to me smirked but didn't say a word.

"Can't you tell us anything?" I asked her. She glanced at the man who sat opposite her, his amused expression glowing in the light from the tablet. "Got it," I said under my breath. Barker was the only one who was at ease with our capture, the rest of us sitting straight and silent as our surroundings turned more and more extravagant. The pedestrians went from wearing modest shirts and sensible shoes to satin dresses and heels so high it was obvious they weren't walking more than the block it took to reach their private pods.

Our pod slowed to a crawl as we were admitted into a gated residence. The sun glinted off the gilded gates as we moved to the end of the road where another gate was with a guard dressed in the same jumpsuit like the ones accompanying us. She spoke into a radio and the door opened. We drove on until the pod stopped in the circle drive, giving me the perfect view of a large house.

It was boxy in the most modern design, gray stonework along with the entire house aside from the gold detailing around the tall entryway. A golden chandelier glittered with gems above the massive double doors that swirled with gilded bars over gray wood. The guard next to me got out first, stepping aside so we could follow.

The lawn stretched on for yards, perfectly landscaped with manicured bushes and flowers that weren't native to Divez. We were in our quiet pocket of rural life here, far enough from the nearest structures to stay private. It was the perfect home for a fellow rebel or whatever the guard's master called his profession.

"The front sitting room," a man said from the entrance. He was dressed well, with fine slacks and a button-up complete with a gray blazer. He matched the surrounding brick so well he looked like he belonged to the house, and he likely did in a sense. He led our group through the double doors and past the entryway where we weren't even allowed a moment to pause and look at the polished cases of basketball memorabilia. We'd been apprehended by a ballplayer?

"Take a seat," the man said, motioning towards the soft-looking couches around the large coffee table. "The kitchens are open to you," he said, "We will have finger sandwiches out in a moment along with drinks. The master of the house likes to share whiskey with other members of the rebellion. How many glasses shall I bring?" Barker was quick to raise a hand, interrupted as the large screen against the far wall bathed the room in red and blue light from a news report.

"Sorry," August said, searching the couch around him for the remote.

"It's under your ass, Merkwood," Barker said, turning back

to the butler and signaling for five glasses. The man inclined his head and moved towards the kitchen behind us.

"Whose house is this?" Angel asked, looking at the guards who were positioned against the walls around us. None of them said a word.

"Will you turn that off already?" Barker asked as August finally extricated the remote from under one tree trunk-sized thigh. I looked up at the screen and froze. My face flashed in one corner with the words *Kieran "the Wolf" Grace* underneath.

"No," I said, scooting to the edge of the couch, "turn it up." August gave me a surprised look but turned the volume up anyway.

"The youngest of President Grace's children is now being called a wolf in sheep's clothing as more details about the young man's upbringing are coming out," the reporter said, "The President's team released sealed documents to the public in hopes that his son can be brought to justice. Kieran Grace is no stranger to the law. He was imprisoned in the arena's prison here in Gallaterra City by his father after he displayed terrorist-like behavior. President Grace explained in a tearful defense that he and his wife had tried everything from setting strict rules to weekly counseling services to try controlling their son's behavior before finally being forced to seek legal counsel. Kieran Grace, like most of his siblings, attended the highest educational facilities here in the city, though Kieran was pulled from the program after an incident his father was quoted saying "called for swift action" occurred."

"I got caught with a banned book," I blurted, looking from the screen to see that Angel, Sissa, August, and Barker were all watching me anxiously. I looked back at the screen.

"When the news of Kieran Grace's betrayal came out, some members of the public suggested the First Family tried to hide the teen's actions. Now, it's clear that the Grace family did everything that they could to reeducate their son and curb his behavior but were failed by the legal counsel and members of prison security who promised to keep Kieran Grace confined. After breaking out of the Arena, Kieran along with Aldierian Kenna Riley were able to lead attacks in several desert cities as well as raise an army of Aldierians that now pose a threat to all of Gallaterra. While leading an attack outside of the East Sea, the Aldierian forces were decimated. It was first believed that only Kenna Riley escaped alive, but we can confirm tonight that Kieran Grace was among those who survived the battle. He was taken into custody after discovery in a hospital where a team of surgeons fitted his left arm and leg with robotic prosthetics. We first announced his capture this morning, but the military would like us to add to that report now that Kieran Grace was able to escape along with these inmates and they are considered extremely dangerous. If you have any information, please call the tip line listed below."

All five of our faces and names flashed on the screen along with a phone number. Descriptions were given for each of us that included hair color, height, weight, my robotic arm, and my leg. I was aware now that I had stood up, mostly because I felt weak. Was there any hope of reaching Kenna now? How the hell could we walk into the capital city with police on high alert?

"I think you've seen enough," a deep voice said from behind. I turned and saw Senator Andre Covas. I'd seen him only one other time when my father told him during a gala at the capital that he wasn't welcomed there anymore. He was always the tallest man in the crowd and walking around the couch to greet us now I felt small in more ways than just physically. He was still dressed for work, a suit so finely tailored that it likely cost him a thousand dollars at least. My stained military uniform paled in comparison, though he didn't look at me with disgust like I anticipated. He smiled and took my hand, giving it a firm shake that conveyed admiration.

"You've made quite the impression on Gallaterra."

"I'm not the one responsible for all of this," I said and

pointed to the blank wall where the screen had been projected before, "I'm not the one you should be thanking."

"If you're talking about Kenna Riley, the sympathizers are well aware of her movements." Covas unbuttoned his blazer and took a seat next to Barker.

"Who are you?" Sissa asked, Angel, slapping her arm beside her in response. Covas wasn't offended by her brashness at all.

"Senator Andre Covas. I've been in politics since I left pro-basketball about twenty years ago, I guess it's been. My platform has always been about serving minorities and making sure people of all backgrounds have their viewpoint seen, so I became known real fast as being empathetic towards our relations with the Aldierians. A couple of years ago, President Grace banned me from working in Gallaterra City, so I try to video call in from my office here as much as I can. I've lost a little bit of my credibility in politics for what Grace did to me, but the scandal connected me with the sympathizers in Gallaterra and even though I was able to quiet the rumors in a few months, I grew my status with them at the same time. My connections in politics have enabled me to help the sympathizers out there doing all the work get a little further than before."

"A rich guy throwing money at whatever and instantly is the face of the revolution. Refreshing," Sissa said as two women came in with trays of crystal tumblers. Again, Covas wasn't taken aback by her comments. He thanked the woman who handed him a glass and filled it with the crystal bottle on the table before leaning over to do the same for Barker and August.

"I'm not the face of this at all and I wouldn't be the right person for it, neither would you," he said and looked up at me. I was glad someone agreed with me. "I've seen the coverage from the beginning, but the media only has time for the gossip about the president's son gone rogue, not the half-Aldierian girl who grew up poor and never knew her real parents or anything about her heritage. Her story was swept aside, but it's obvious who has the most to lose here."

"Kieran lost everything when his father put him in prison," Angel said.

"Kenna never had anything to lose, but her life," I said, "The most that would've happened to me had we been caught was getting a life sentence in a prison wing for high profile criminals, you know, the kind of place where my mattress would be brand new for me and the food better. Kenna wouldn't get that. She wouldn't even make it to prison and my father proved that when he put her in the arena for execution." Angel shrunk a little, sitting back in her seat and twisting her tumbler of amber liquid between her hands as she slowly nodded in agreement. I knew she didn't mean anything by it. When you grow up separate from how the average person lives, you have no idea what it means to advocate for your rights. I never had to advocate for shit.

"My team was working on the logistics of reaching out to the Ida when the attack on the beach happened. I'd seen her photo enough times, so I knew exactly who she was when she showed up at my office to see me, but I had no idea she had survived the attack until then," Covas said. His words sent a jolt through my body, stunning me to silence for a long moment.

"You saw Kenna? She came here?" I asked. The senator nodded.

"She and her brother stayed overnight. They left this morning for the capital. It wasn't until after they left that it was released that you had escaped prison. They were both so honed in on their mission that I doubt they know you're still coming if that's what you are doing." No one around the room spoke up, everyone was waiting on me. I can't remember making a plan with my new comrades other than needing to get to Kenna before she tries killing my father on her own. We'd been doing it all on the fly, as we needed to make moves and countermoves, and no one seemed to question that. Everything I'd been doing the last few days directly contradicted all the military training I got back in Varillia, and I was so focused on getting to Kenna that I never thought about leading a troop or whatever it was the five of us were now.

"We need to reach her before she tries following through with the plan," August said. Angel nodded next to him.

"I bet I can hack into the street cameras to find their pod if you remember the license plate number," she said.

"Tell me we're all going to kill the bastard after we get to them," Sissa said, "We'd be too close not to." Barker raised his glass towards me.

"You remember what I said," he started, "Fight together..." I remembered. His words, along with the encouragement from the others, my new troop, my friends, all of us arena-bound... I raised my glass towards him in agreement and we both downed the last of the amber liquid, the burn on the way down energizing.

"I'll make sure you reach her," Covas said, "President Grace has no idea what he's up against."

The senator's residence was expansive. He had one of his guards show us to a wing of the house upstairs especially for guests. There was a huge sitting room with several rooms branching off from it that sent our troop into a frenzy. I chose the first room while they all scrambled to search the rest.

The room was huge considering the bed against the far wall was king-sized. Everything was a muted gray color with splashes of navy blue in the form of throw pillows and a plush blanket that was tempting me to settle in for a long nap. Before I could decide, a knock came at the door, and I turned to see Andre Covas standing in the doorway.

He took up the entire frame, his bald head brushing the top. He glanced behind him to make sure the others weren't watching. I could hear them talking loudly in the next room, the usual argument between Barker and Sissa occupying the group. They wouldn't notice my disappearance and Covas must have thought the same, because he shut the door behind him a moment later.

"Something wrong?" I asked. I felt knots form in my stomach at the privacy. Maybe something bad had happened to Kenna that I hadn't seen on the news before. Covas shook his head and removed a folded piece of paper from his blazer.

"I did some research of my own on Kenna Riley," he said, "I hope you know that I didn't mean any harm by it. I researched you both and found nothing more than what you've told me, except for where Kenna is concerned."

Kenna had shared everything with me, at least I thought she had. Covas unfolded the paper and looked down at it as if making sure it said what he knew it did. He looked up at me and held it out.

"There's no way she knows. There's no way anyone knows other than us," he said. I took the paper and hesitated before finally flattening it between my hands and looking down at it. It was a background check, details going back to his apprentice-ship at one of the best hospitals in Gallaterra City, his research on brain activity and effects of the device, even a journal about the missing link in thought technology and the Aldierians that was flagged for harmful content by the government. The most recent marks in the search were his capture and trial with the Gallaterran High Court and his employment with the vice president.

"No," I said and looked up at Covas who nodded once. I looked down at the page again, noticing the photo in the top-right corner. He had her red hair. "He's alive?" I asked.

"Do what you think is right," Covas said. He left me standing in the middle of the room with the paper in my hands.

CHAPTER 23

I t took us most of the morning to drive to our destination. The security guards parked the pod behind a warehouse. We waited another hour before anyone approached us. It was a man on foot. He was young, so young in fact that I thought he was just some kid walking to a friend's house until he tapped twice on the window.

"Get out," one of the security guards said. The other sat forward in his seat and held out a thick wad of bills to me. I took it, my stomach tight knowing that it was likely a year's worth of combat lessons. I shoved it into my pocket and got out after Naja. The boy didn't wait long before he was walking down the alley ahead of us. Naja and I jogged to catch up, falling into step next to him.

"Are you coming with us?" Naja asked him, keeping his voice low. The boy didn't say a word. He didn't even act like he'd heard Naja. He walked on, slightly ahead of us, as if we weren't all together at all. We caught the hint and kept up the ruse, walking for another thirty minutes before we followed the boy into a fairly busy sandwich shop. We kept close behind him as he fell into line, staring up at the menu.

"You have to be kidding me," I said, "We don't have all day." Naja grabbed my hand.

"He knows that."

I could feel the nerves pulsing through him despite his assurance and my body felt like it would explode as we waited in line. Finally, the boy reached the front where a burly man was taking orders. He looked tired as if he'd been there since they had opened and spilled half a jar of mustard on his white apron from the look of him.

"I want to order off the menu," the boy said, his words making the man's hands pause over the tablet. It was a gesture so subtle that no one would've noticed if they hadn't been watching closely. "I'll have a meatball sub with two pickles on the side," the boy said.

"Sure," the man said, tapping the order into the tablet, "Two pickles. Fork or spoon?"

"One fork. One spoon," the boy answered and handed over a bill. The man nodded and promised to have the order out in a moment. Naja and I stepped to the metal counter next, the man's eyes looking us up and down for a split second before focusing on the tablet.

"What can I get for you?" he asked and let out a cough.

"Two meatball subs," I said, watching as he rang up the order. I paid him from the stash of cash in my pocket and we moved over to join the crowd around the pick-up counter. After a few minutes, the boy got his sandwich and I watched him closely as he took a seat near the window alone. Our sandwiches came out next. Naja carried them to the last table by the door while I followed with two paper cups of water.

"That was a code for sure," Naja whispered as we sat down.

"You think we were the two pickles?" I asked him.

"I think you're the fork and I'm the spoon," he answered, "or the other way around. I just want to know what stopping for lunch is supposed to get us." I wondered the same thing. It didn't seem like the boy was the one responsible for stealing the pod. He probably wasn't old enough to have a license, not that many people in the cities needed a pod license to get around anyway. He was a messenger boy, had to be. The sandwich shop was working for Covas. This was where the pod was, or it was where we got the keys. I lifted the sandwich with my index finger, some of the marinara sauce seeping onto the table and under the bun. Sitting square in the middle of the paper boat underneath was a small metal box with four silver buttons on top. I ran my ankle along Naja's until I felt his skin against mine.

"*I got it.*" I lifted the entire paper tray with the sandwich to take a bite.

"*What?*" He froze for a moment with his sandwich inches from his lips.

"*The key.*" I took another bite, motioning for him to do the same. He nodded and continued eating.

"This place looks like that kind of hole in the wall that will either serve the best sandwich you've ever had or give you a rare disease," he said, his voice thick from the meatballs.

"Oh, it's definitely the best sandwich in the world," I said, taking another bite. He let out a hum of agreement. We continued eating until it wouldn't look strange to get up and leave. Outside the sandwich shop, I began clicking the pod remote as we walked down the street and hoped we were going in the right direction. After a block, I could hear it beep.

"Down here," Naja said, leading the way down the street on our left. I clicked the remote again and the lights of a sleek silver pod flashed once. I unlocked it when we got within range and the door next to the curb slid open. It was small inside, but nice. The seats were brown leather and the tablet at the front a modest size.

"Do you know how to operate one of these?" Naja asked me as he pressed a button on the door so that it slid shut.

"I think so," I lied. I knew the key had to go somewhere. After scanning the dashboard, I found a metal slit just to the right of the tablet. After clicking the right button, a key slid out of the remote. I pushed it into the dash and turned right. Lights turned on inside the pod, all of them fading a moment later aside from the tablet mounted before the front windshield.

"Please, state your destination," a female voice said.

"Gallaterra City," Naja said as he settled into one of the leather seats.

"I have located Gallaterra City," the voice said, "Where would you like to go within Gallaterra City?"

"The government plaza," I said. A beat later, the voice announced that the location had been found and to take our seats. I sat next to my brother, the pod not moving until I had clicked my seatbelt into place.

"What do we do when we get to the government plaza?" Naja asked. I was hoping he had thought a little further than just getting there, but it seemed like neither of us had a good idea. I pulled out Kieran's note from my pocket and began looking over the directions again with Naja at my shoulder. We didn't speak for a long time, studying the words and drawings until we had them memorized.

"Maybe we should scope out the location before we make any moves," Naja said. I wanted all of this to be over. I couldn't think about President Grace without my entire chest feeling like it would cave in. I wanted to get off this pod the moment it stopped and find the man as soon as I could, but I knew better. Strong emotions were the quickest way to death if left unchecked.

"Did you bring your merchant coat with you?" I asked. Naja nodded. I began unraveling the scarf from around my head, letting the braids fall down my back. "I think we do a sweep of the plaza and then develop a plan for escape after we go through with the assassination," I said. Naja let out a breath.

"I thought you and I agreed to this mission," he said, looking at me with cautious eyes, "This is a suicide mission. We are going to kill the president so that the sympathizers can sweep in and overrule his administration and begin rolling back the destructive mining expansion. You and I won't survive this. I honestly believe that we can kill Grace, but I know that once we do we will follow him to our graves. I thought you knew this."

"I do," I said, my voice firm enough to keep him from questioning me. "They won't kill us on the spot. They will capture us. You don't understand what I do about Gallaterra. Everyone gets a device when they turn eighteen and I think that Grace has done something tyrannical to abuse his power over the device operations. If they implant devices into us afterward..." I let the words sink in, Naja's expression going tight and his hands clasping themselves together so that his knuckles turned white over his knees.

"You think Grace's closest followers will use the device against us, against our mother, our people," he said. I nodded. The thought hadn't crept into my mind until this morning when I began dwelling on the coming day. I was sure I would die today. I'm still sure of the fact. I didn't want Naja to die with me and prolonging our attack was the only thing I could see buying me time to plan his escape.

"I know where Mama Abraham works," I said, "We can go there after we search the plaza, and she can arrange for something with her high profile contacts."

"There's no way she has enough spies or even one person with enough power to get us out of there alive," he said, the anxious look gone from his eyes. My heart jolted in my chest, but I tried to make my face appear serious.

"We should at least try," I said, "We can't go in without a plan anyway."

"Sounds to me like you already got one," he said. His tone was so cool that it sent chills over my arms.

"I'm not abandoning the mission," I told him, looking directly at him. He smirked.

"You aren't hijacking the mission on my watch either," he said, "I won't let you go alone." He had hardly finished the words when my fist connected with his nose. Blood showered down the front of his shirt as he fell back against the wall with a loud clunk. I grabbed the front of his blazer and wrenched him to the ground. There wasn't enough space for him to roll to his back fast enough, so he reached for the weapon belts we left near the front of the pod. I dropped onto his back, flattening him and sending all the air from his lungs with a muffled grunt.

He moved his hands from the belt inches away and drew them to his chest. With a thrust, he rolled to his side, and my back connected with the door. The handle jabbed my ribs hard enough that it stunned me just long enough so he could pin me to the floor. The top of my head pressed painfully into the metal undercarriage of the seat in front of us.

"I'm not going to lose you after everything," Naja said, slamming my wrists to the floor behind my head for effect.

"I lost Kieran," I said, "Illya can't lose you." Naja froze, staring back at me with glassy eyes. A single tear fell from his left eye and onto my cheek. He took a deep breath and tightened his grip on my wrists, making my hands feel numb.

"You can't do this without me," he said. I didn't have his experience in combat. I might not even be better at hand-to-hand than he was. There was one area that I was better equipped for than he was though.

"Celina, recline front seats all the way," I said. Naja's expression changed from intensity to confusion just before the seat behind us whipped back and smacked him hard against the back of the head. His full weight fell against my chest. He was unconscious, but still breathing softly in my ear.

"Seats are reclined," the AI voice said. I crawled out from under my brother and took the scarf, which was exactly where I had set it, and began tying his arms and legs behind his back. I went to the tablet to check our distance. I gave the AI instructions to dock at a charging station and stay until the battery was at full capacity. Once at full charge, the pod would begin the trip towards the East Sea. It wouldn't have enough juice to get to Varillia, but it would get him out of Gallaterra City and then some. He was skilled enough to untie himself with time, but I hoped by then that he would at least be across the city with no other choice but to go back to Varillia.

Thankfully, I found a vial in the pouch of Naja's belt that would make him sleep longer. I turned his head and let the liquid trickle down his throat. I found a length of rope in his pouch as well, which meant I could use the scarf I'd used to restrain Naja to cover my hair and not need to make another stop for a disguise. Dawn Covas was right about a lone merchant looking out of place so close to the government plaza, but the idea of leaving the roomy coat behind made me nervous.

"Docking at Grand Street Charging Depot," the AI voice announced. I heard the mechanical whoosh of the port cover sliding away at the back of the pod. We backed up until there was a click and a green icon with a lightning bolt replaced the map on the tablet screen. I finished wrapping my hair in the scarf. I clipped my belt around my waist again, taking just one extra knife from my brother. There was no guarantee that I could even sneak the weapons I had into any of the buildings, and I didn't have the heart to leave Naja without a way to defend himself despite how much closer to danger I'd be than him.

I pulled the merchant coat on and got out of the pod. My breath hitched when I looked back and saw my brother lying on the floor. My chest was tight and my throat thick and I thought I would fall into a full-blown panic until I forced myself to think of Kieran. I could still see his face so easily. His blonde hair was pushed back so carelessly it almost looked intentionally styled. His blue eyes pierced through all the nerves and centered me once more. I let out a final calming breath and leaned back into the pod just far enough to press my lips to my brother's cheek and promise that when he woke, we would all be free from tyranny.

I shut the door and started walking down the street, the few people on the block not even batting an eye as I passed. The street led towards the government plaza, just a cluster of tall buildings behind the coffee shops and bookstores on this block. I felt determination building in my chest, making my tired feet feel light as I recognized one of the tallest buildings like the one I was first brought to after being arrested. Kieran and I were held in an open cell within that building. A rounded building half the size butted up against one side, steel-plated and shaped almost like a soup bowl. I was sure the arena looked like an architectural wonder to the general public, the citizens who had no idea about the elitist club that was the last stop for many high-profile criminals in Gallaterra.

I stopped at the end of the street where a group of at least twelve people was waiting at the crosswalk, talking excitedly about visiting the plaza. On the other side of the busy street, the concrete was whitewashed, making the grey sidewalk we were on look dirty in comparison. The entire plaza was bathed in white stone and marble steps. The only exception was the dark metal statue of President Grace standing in the center of the plaza.

The pods on the street slowed and we were allowed to cross. There were a lot of people milling about the plaza, way more than I had planned for. Most of them looked like tourists, only a few dressed up like Dawn said they would be. I went unnoticed, even when a man bumped into me because I'd stopped walking to take in my surroundings.

Alright. Search the plaza. Search the plaza. I didn't have to attack or even go inside any of the buildings for now. I just needed to get an idea of where I was. I felt exposed as I walked aimlessly down the sidewalk next to the busy street. I could see the center of the plaza from here between the buildings, a large circular area that would be perfect to get a good look at the place. I didn't have the guts to head in that direction yet.

I wanted to pull my hood over my head and after deciding that no one was paying me any attention anyway, I decided to do it. I saw a thick man in the traditional Conduit robes just ahead with a crate filled with pamphlets. He had his large hood pulled down like I did, his robes the same sandy tan color. I could hang around the center of the plaza unnoticed easier with a cover and street preaching would be a good cover, especially with one already present here. They never worked in groups of less than four.

I snagged a thick stack from his crate, fumbling and dropping most of them back into the stack. I paused to gather more, the man looking down at me. He had a nasty scar under his left eye and a dark beard thick as wool.

"Hey," he said, tone accusatory. His expression changed, something in his eyes making my heart jump. "Hey," he said again like he wanted to say more as he recognized me. I scooped up as many pamphlets as I could and began speed walking towards the center of the plaza, losing the man quickly as the crowd grew thicker near the center.

"Are you familiar with the Conduit of Christians from Earth?" I asked people as I passed. Most were eager to avoid me and gave me a wide berth with which to draw closer to the statue. I noticed as I grew closer that there was a podium set at the top of the steps of the largest building just beyond. Three rows of barriers were set at even intervals on the way up the marble stairs. I stopped ministering to people as I passed and focused instead of squeezing through the crowd to get as close as I could. Lights to my right made me stop.

A giant screen mounted on the side of one of the buildings projected the podium along with a single-file line of security guards as they walked out of the building. Sandwiched between the first half of guards and the second was President Grace himself. He wore a navy suit with the seal of Gallaterra pinned to his lapel. The sight of him had me rooted in my spot, just staring at the screen across from me.

The crowd hadn't noticed him yet, at least the people this far back in the plaza hadn't. Their faces were happy, excited as if seeing the president speak was some kind of a perk of their vacations. A father held his toddler on his shoulders while a woman stepped back to take a picture of her teenage daughters posing next to the statue just feet from me. It felt so large and threatening, the way Grace seemed when he towered over Kieran in the prison. If things had been different, maybe the Ida stone on my finger would've been placed there during a real wedding ceremony of our own.

I looked up at the screen as Grace approached the podium and the microphone squealed. It sent groans through the crowd and then silence as they waited for him to speak. He adjusted his collar and then his tie, his hands sliding to the chain hanging around his neck. Resting over his chest was the Heart of Aldieria. My heart stopped dead in my chest for a moment and I felt my body go weak. How did he get it? How the hell had anyone found it?

"I came here to speak with the citizens of Gallaterra today not to announce another Aldierian attack, but the success of an attack of our own," he spoke with a smile, "A special forces team was dispatched months ago to gather intel on the Aldierians and their movements after the escape of two extremely dangerous persons from our custody. I can tell you now that those two people were killed in an attack just outside the East Sea, led by our forces. We sustained very few casualties but were able to not only execute every Aldierian terrorist present but gathered information that will ensure the Aldierians won't be a major threat to us anymore."

The crowd exploded in such a cacophony that Grace had to stop talking. He stepped back from the mic and looked at one of the senators that had come out with him, exchanging words that left them both laughing. He was lying yet again to the entire country. Every member of our troop died before anyone could question them, so there was no way he got any big information out of us. The importance of the Heart of Aldieria died with the gold soldier, so the fact that he was wearing it now had to be seen as a show of power. He had something that was taken from us. He had taken so much from us, from me. Blood pounded loudly in my ears.

"We can all live in peace now, knowing that we no longer have to fear random attacks. We are safe from terrorist plots. We are safe thanks to the work of our special operations team and the sleepless nights of my administration that has worked on a new bill against Aldierian terrorism that is on the ballot when I run for reelection next fall. Gallaterra is strong," President Grace said and stepped away from the podium. The guards followed him back into the building. I knew where he was now. I was moving through the crowd before I realized where I was heading. Maybe I could skirt around them and find a way past the barriers.

I walked, picking up speed as I went, the urge to sprint growing so strong that I could hardly contain it. That's when I felt the presence of someone after me. I chanced a glance behind me and I saw a hooded figure a few yards behind me. Maybe I was paranoid. I mean, I had pulled my hood up and stolen a bunch of pamphlets out of fear of being noticed. There was no reason for someone to follow me. I told myself it was fine, but my body reacted much differently, scurrying across the street when the light turned red, and the pods all slowed to a stop.

I went another block from the plaza before glancing back again, seeing the same figure following me. I jumped into a sprint, my hood flying off my head as I moved. I ran past a few people before darting down a less busy street and then running down an alley behind a shopping center. I tugged at every door as I went, hoping that I could hide in the storage rooms. By the time I reached the last door, the figure had already seen me. The door opened easily with a rusty squelch. I knew before even going inside that this store had been abandoned long ago. The windows were mostly boarded up, just small slivers of light peeking in from the tops of the windows. The back room was filled with naked mannequins that only heightened my terror as I began taking random aisles that were stacked with dusty boxes and broken crates. I ran down an aisle, not even knowing what direction I was headed in at this point, and ran right into the chest of the hooded figure. I let out a girlish scream that he cut off with a hand to my mouth a second later.

"Falle etwva," he said, holding tight to me until I stilled a few seconds later. He lowered a hand from my mouth, towing me around the corner where the door of an office was. The window inside was left uncovered, sending natural light over the man's face. He was middle-aged and lean, almost too lean, and I could see the edge of a tattoo under the collar of his Conduit robes.

"Who are you?" I asked him when he finally let me go. He stayed awkwardly in the doorway like he was willing to keep me from escaping him, but not like he wanted to use any real force.

"James Barker," he answered.

"Who?" I asked again, looking out the window to make sure I could still see the plaza but was only able to see the brick wall of the alleyway. A couple more hooded figures blurred past the window, startling me. I heard a couple of plastic-sounding pops as more than one mannequin was knocked over

"Shit," a woman said, her voice echoing in the storeroom outside. The group wasn't trying to keep quiet anymore, the sound of feet slapping away at the concrete floor growing closer.

"I got her," James Barker yelled from the door. The feet stopped directly outside a moment later and James slipped out of the room.

"Kenna," he said. Kieran slammed the door shut behind him and pulled me to his chest a second later. I didn't care where we were or who those people were with him. He was here, alive, my Kieran.

CHAPTER 24

We kissed for a long time and then I was sitting on top of the desk with Kieran between my legs, his lips pressed to my neck. He felt more muscular in my arms and from this angle, I could see that he was leaner than before. His left arm combed into my hair, tugging my head to just the right angle so he could lead a trail of kisses to my collar bone. When he moved his hands to frame my face, his left hand felt much colder than his right. It was strange enough that it pulled me back to reality for a moment and I noticed it.

Now that the sleeves of his Conduit robes had ridden up his arms, I could see that his left arm had been replaced with a silver bionic replica. I don't know how long I'd sat there, completely transfixed, but it was long enough that Kieran backed away from me and began removing the robes. He wore a plain white t-shirt underneath and a pair of tan pants. The shirt made it easy to see that the arm was connected at the elbow. He moved it around for me to see, flexing his fingers one at a time and curling his hand in a fist.

"That's not all my new hardware," he told me, looking down at his feet. Where his left foot used to be was a curved running blade that connected to a thick bar that disappeared into his pant leg. I felt myself settle back into my body. I looked over the rest of him, happy to see that he looked exactly as he had the last time I'd seen him other than the missing leg and arm.

"What happened to you?" I asked him. I was glad he was still just feet away or he may not have heard my breathless words. He shrugged.

"I had to piece it all together with some help, but I think I got lucky and the trees in that ravine slowed my fall enough that I just broke a few things on the way down," he said, his voice surprisingly calm considering the horrors he'd experienced. He told me about the hikers who found him and took him to a small town with a hospital where he was able to get medical care. After surgery and a short recovery in the hospital, he was found out and soldiers arrived to arrest him.

"All those people out there," Kieran said and pointed at the closed door, "they were in prison with me. We were in a high-profile wing just waiting until we were shipped out for the arena. The important thing is that we were able to escape, and they've been helping me this whole time, to find you, and get to you before you tried anything." I couldn't believe it. Kieran had been on the adventure of a lifetime while Naja and I stayed in a million-dollar house and rode in private pods. There was so much I wanted to ask him, but I was so overcome with emotions that all I could do was pull him back to my chest by his shirtfront.

After another round of kissing that made me especially thankful for the locked door, Kieran sat with me on the desk and told me everything he'd faced up until now, sparing no detail past the event of his amputations. He got so excited by some points in his story that he stood up to reenact. I laughed in amazement when he showed me the way he was able to kill a Gallaterran soldier with the newfound super-strength his bionic arm possessed. The display of such uncharacteristic strength paired with his shirtless chest led to an intermission for kissing again that left us breathless and sitting on the floor where the light from the window fell across us.

"We decided Conduit missionaries were the best disguises since it hid my arms and our faces well and we could go for the most part unnoticed in the plaza while we kept a lookout for you. I mean, no one really wants to talk with the religious zealots on the streets, right? So, August was so stunned that you not only approached him but stole pamphlets from him, that he didn't think to chase after you. I wanted to be there when we found you. I hope Barker didn't scare you. He's a rough-looking guy, but he's probably been the closest to a friend as I've had during all of this," Kieran told me, glancing back at the door. I wondered how long we'd been in this office. Kieran told me all about his new crew, but it felt strange that I didn't know any of the people who had been fighting so hard to try and find me the past few weeks.

"We should probably go and talk to them," I said, standing up, "I want to meet your new friends." Kieran smiled back at me and let me pull him to his feet.

"You're going to like all of them," he said and led the way back into the storeroom. We followed the sound of voices to a break room near the boarded-up loading dock. Inside was a long table, a stained green couch, and a refrigerator with a sign taped to the front that asked all employees to clean up after themselves before returning to work. Around the table were the members of Kieran's crew.

"You met Barker," Kieran said, pointing to the skinny middle-aged man. Like the rest of the people in the room, he had tossed his robes onto the floor so I could now see that almost every inch of his body from the neck down was covered in tattoos, but the black ink looked more fashionable on him than it did a sign of prison toughness. There was a bandage around his chest that looked like it hadn't been changed since they arrived in the city, only adding to his rough persona. He gave me a nod from his seat at the table. Next to him was the large man I recognized as the missionary I stole pamphlets from.

"That's August Merkwood," Kieran told me. The man smiled so brightly that there was no way he had been arrested and imprisoned for anything overtly nefarious. A blonde woman sat at the end of the table with an array of knives and guns spread over the table in front of her. She lowered the cleaning cloth from the gun she was working over to wave at me, but a dark-haired girl strode through the door behind us before Kieran could introduce us.

"I tried finding Naja Petrek, but there's no sign of him or a single Aldierian in the plaza," the girl said and sank into the green couch with one leg propped up across the cushions and the other resting on the floor. She tugged her robes over her head and dropped them on the floor. She looked from Kieran to me now. She had dark hair and the tanned complexion of an Aldierian.

"Sissa Tamlot," Kieran told me. She smiled a little as she realized who I was.

"Falle etwva, Idava Kenna Riley," Sissa said, the formal greeting sounded strange considering her relaxed posture.

"Etwva Ida," I replied, "Call me Kenna, just Kenna."

"My name is Angel Torsney," the blonde said, drawing my attention from Sissa. Torsney wasn't a common name, so she had to be related to the Torsney Engineering Development family.

"As in TED?" I asked her. She nodded but didn't get a chance to explain before Sissa spoke.

"She's a super genius, probably even smarter than any of the TED guys working for her mother," she said, "It's a damn shame they cut her out of their perfect family." Angel's cheeks were turning pink, and she looked back down at the gun on the table.

"They'll realize how stupid they are when she's leading the way in new technology in Varillia," Kieran said, bringing a smile to her face. I laced my hand in his and he squeezed it. I never thought I could love Kieran more than I already did, but he was so sure of himself and strong in a new way.

"The sooner we discuss the plan for tomorrow, the quicker you two can get behind a closed door," Barker said, "The way you two are acting, I think we'd all rather you be in private now." I let go of Kieran's hand, noticing the pink that tinged his cheeks now. Everyone in the room sat up a little more to listen. Every eye was on us, throwing no doubt onto who was in charge of the mission.

"President Grace was wearing the Heart of Aldieria," I said, "We have to make sure that whatever we do, the priority is making sure we get it back."

"I thought getting rid of Grace was the priority. He and his administration are poisoning the entire planet, not just Gallaterra," August said.

"Yes, but the Heart of Aldieria will put us a step further than just that in preventing the collapse of the planet," Kieran said, "It's all connected, so we have to do both. If we don't kill my father, it won't matter if we can get the Heart of Aldieria into the converter. He will probably remove it anyway just out of spite. The only way we get the stone back is if we get close enough to kill him." I slipped my hand into his again, but not solely out of affection this time.

"I hope you know how we can get close to him," I said.

Kieran looked at me, a flash of fear in his eyes before he looked back at our new troop. They waited in silence as he took in the room. I worried that he didn't have a plan and was stalling to come up with one.

"My sister Cora," he said, "She never spoke up, but she was always on my side. I think she'll help us, but we have to make sure that we can protect her if things go wrong. I don't want her getting in any trouble because of me." His tone was cool enough to impress upon everyone in the room how important this was.

"I can keep her safe," August said.

"No, I want Sissa to make sure of it," Kieran said. Sissa sat up straight, looking from August to Kieran.

"I'm the strongest one here. I was a part of the Aldierian military," she said, adding on what were surely a few Aldierian curse words at the end.

"That's how important it is that Cora stays out of this mess," Kieran yelled over her, "I know you're stronger than all of us. I won't agree to contact her unless I do everything to make sure she won't be punished for it."

"Which is only half the problem here," I said, putting an end to the fight as they all looked at me. "We can plan to keep her safe, but we can't do anything at all if we can't contact her. How are we supposed to do that?" I asked. Kieran's shoulders slumped a little and Sissa muttered under her breath and sunk back onto the couch.

"I say we go back to the first plan and just sneak into the building," Barker said.

"I can hack into her device," Angel said.

"Most of us will die if we just storm the place and that includes you and Kenna," August said.

"Not to mention that we don't have that damn Ida stone that you said was so important," Sissa said.

"I'd gladly die for just an opportunity," Barker said with a laugh.

"Wait a minute," I spoke over the room, waiting until they all settled to point to Angel. "You can do what?" I asked. She shrugged.

"I can hack her device," she said, "All we need is a tablet or something with communication capabilities and I can get a message to her device. If she receives it and we can bridge contact with her, I can set up a call so we can talk to her just like you do with a normal device." Wow. I had to take a moment to process what she wanted to do, but I stopped trying to make sense out of it when it hit me that she needed a communication device.

"Could you still do that if the device is Aldierian technology?" I asked.

"Yes," she said, "Do you have one?"

"Here. Take it," I said, tugging the tablet from the pack on the belt and crossing the room to give it to her. She held it in her hands, not moving. Her eyes went from my face to Kieran's nervous gaze.

"Kieran," I said, pulling him out of his thoughts, "If we don't do this, I don't see a way in." After a moment he nodded and asked Angel to start working. She pulled out a weathered notepad and began flipping through pages of numbers and letters, some kind of code that only she likely knew.

"What do you want the message to say?" Angel asked. I moved to the front of the room again to stand next to Kieran. He stood tall and with all those new muscles, he looked strong, but his eyes told me just how afraid he was.

"Tell her I need her help," Kieran said.

"I'll let you know when I've sent it," Angel said, not looking up from the tablet.

"Thanks, Angel," he said and then looked to the rest of our new troop, "Thanks to all of you for sticking with me this long and sacrificing-"

"Save the big speech," Barker said, "we're not going anywhere." Sissa and August both nodded. I squeezed Kieran's forearm, though he didn't seem any more relaxed.

"I think we should all get some rest before… whatever comes next," I said, tugging Kieran towards the door. After the initial pull, he followed me back into the storage room and towards the office. I closed the door behind us and pulled him into my arms. I pulled back to look at him, seeing that he wasn't trying to conceal his worries anymore.

"I can't get Cora involved," he said.

"She won't be," I said, "She doesn't have to do any more than tell us what your father is up to, where he is now, and when our best chance of getting into the main building is." I gave his shoulders a shake and he relaxed a little, more like a stiff rubber band that might snap if I tugged too hard. I left him at the door and moved to our spot on the floor. After a moment, he joined me with his legs crossed under him.

"Naja didn't leave me," I said. His face turned to panic, prompting me to clarify. "He didn't die. He's alive and far away from here, I hope," I said and laid down on the floor. The cool concrete was strangely relaxing, despite how hard it was. "He found out that I wanted to go alone and leave him behind. I knocked him out, tied him up, and drugged him so he wouldn't wake for a day. I set the coordinates on our pod for as close to the East Sea as I could and sent him on his way. After that, you saw me in the plaza."

"You stole a private pod?" Kieran asked, lying down next to me.

"No," I said and started laughing, "Senator Covas did." I could hardly contain my laughter at how ridiculous the whole story was. Kieran propped himself up on his side.

"Senator Andre Covas helped you?" he asked.

"Yeah, I know. It all sounds crazy," I said between my laughter. He nodded, not able to speak through his snickers. We lost it, laying on the floor staring up at the stained ceiling tiles above us until Kieran took my hand. He gave me a small smile, the gesture begging for a distraction. There weren't many memories I hadn't shown him now, but I used the Ida stone on my ring finger to show him Naja and I's boring trip from the beginning. We had shared a lifetime of adventure already, but we still had tomorrow. At least, we still had tomorrow.

———

I was just halfway into my memory of how Naja and I found our way out of the forest when Angel knocked on the door to tell us she had sent Cora a message. Kieran buoyed between welcoming my distractions and turning away from them for the next hour until Angel returned. We followed her into the break room. Sissa was asleep on the couch and August snored on the floor, slumped against a vending machine with his head lolling to one side. Barker was the only one left at the table, sitting as if ready for a meeting of the utmost importance.

"He's here, Cora," Angel said. Kieran darted to the far side of the table where the table sat.

"Cora? It's me," he said, leaning over the tablet as if his sister could see him through the voice call and the mass of tiny code displayed on the screen.

"Kieran? God, father told us you died in the prisoner escape in Hendale," she said. Kieran sunk into the seat before the tablet. I sucked in a breath as the chair next to him squealed against the floor when I dragged it. Kieran didn't even look up, his sister continuing to ask questions. "Where are you?" she asked, "How many people are with you?"

"Cora, I need to get father in private," Kieran said. We could hear her suck in a breath.

"I can't believe I'm saying this," she whispered, "Are you going to kill him? Please, tell me you're going to kill him?" Her voice broke at the end.

"Cora, has he done something to you?" Kieran asked, holding the tablet in his hands now.

"Not me," she said, "Mother. You know how they are. He made her... I saw them in the living room weeks ago. He forced her to... Kieran, I don't want to be here anymore. I can't live here, and Leah and Oliva don't believe a word I say and you know Eli would tell father to do something horrible."

"I won't let that happen," Kieran snapped, "but you have to tell me if there's a way to get into any of the government buildings in the plaza. It doesn't have to be our living quarters. I just need to get close to him." Cora went silent on the other line. For nearly a minute, we didn't hear a single sound. A door closed and Cora began whispering again, this time her voice sounding small despite how close she was to the microphone on her device.

"Father is meeting with the engineering team in the energy complex about creating another massive generator to sustain Ida stone mining expansions. He wants to use the energy from it to create a fleet of ships for the military," she said. Kieran, Angel, and I all exchanged anxious glances. He was going to go further than just blame his terrorist attacks on the Aldierians. He was going to use them as an excuse for war.

"Bastard," I said.

"The energy complex is where the converter is," Kieran said, "Cora, is there any way we could get in there while he's there?" The room was quiet. I swear Kieran didn't even breathe until she replied.

"You know where the loading dock is?" she asked.

"Yes," he said.

"Be there at six. The door will be unlocked," Cora said. The call ended and we sat in silence for a moment until the sound of a chair scraping against the floor drew our attention to Barker.

"Well," he said, "I'll see you in the morning." Kieran nodded in agreement and Barker left the room.

"You should get some sleep too, Angel. Thank you for doing all of this," I said. She flashed a smile perfect enough to gloss magazine covers before taking the tablet from Kieran.

"Kenna and I will finalize the details," Kieran said and stood up.

"We'll let the whole crew know the plan in the morning," I said before he could add anything else, "No use in waking anyone up now." Kieran nodded and let me lead the way back to the office. The shadows from the moon were cast along the floor where the rays of the sun had filled the room with light hours earlier. There was no comfortable place to sleep, just the thin carpeted floor. We sat down where the moonlight was brightest.

"So, we all go to the loading dock like your sister said," I started, "and from there we make our way into the control room.

You drew me a map, so I know you can get us there. I think we should plan to take as many of your crew with us and just have them split off as we see the need, even if that means going into the room without anyone to cover us at the end." Kieran nodded, still staring out the window. All we could see from this angle were the stars. They looked just like they did the night we were fake married, sans fireworks bursting red, green, and gold against the dark sky.

"I love you, Kieran," I said, pulling his attention away from the window, "You are so much smarter than me and…" I stopped talking when he put a hand to my cheek and pressed his lips down onto mine.

"I love you too, Kenna," he said, "and you are smart. You are so much more than you think you are." I felt my face heat.

"How did you know I'd come here and not go back to Varillia?" I asked. He smirked.

"I guess I just know you too well, Kenna Riley," he said and laid down on the floor. I laid next to him and picked up where we left off in my memories but found myself thinking about the first time we shared a room under the stars.

CHAPTER 25

The air was filled with a nervous buzz as we all got ready, dividing up weapons and going over the plan more than enough times. We were all going to the loading dock, assuming the door would be unlocked like Cora said. From there, we would follow Kieran's lead through the building, breaking off into groups when the need arose. I could tell everyone was nervous about staying unseen. We discussed the possibility of stealing uniforms or trying to pass as delivery personnel from the loading dock, but there was no way we could firmly plan for this step. We planned for the worst instead.

If we couldn't get disguises or travel unnoticed, we would split off to take care of anyone that tried apprehending us along the way. We had no other options. We either go along with the plan now or start the journey home to Varillia. Kieran and I knew that the chance of dying during this mission was high, but we agreed that there was too much at stake to wait any longer.

Angel refused to go with us, which surprised no one but me. She said that she was working on something that would help us along the way and had found a way to hack the security cameras in the building. She didn't have to tell Kieran and I anything more than that. Kieran trusted her abilities and if he trusted her, then I did too.

After everyone had said their piece, mostly short speeches about the greater good, we donned our Conduit robes and started back towards the government plaza. It was practically abandoned compared to the day before. There were a few people, mostly well-dressed, who hurried along the sidewalks on their way into work. None of them gave us a second glance, despite our numbers. Kieran led us around the plaza to one of the tallest buildings with no other distinguishing features aside from the emblem of an Ida stone over the main doors.

There were even fewer people on this side of the plaza. We rounded the building where three loading docks were on the first three floors, a large cargo ship butted against the top section. As we got closer to the first-floor dock, I could see a single door next to the giant garage door. We stopped before the ledge of the dock, Kieran and I the first to climb onto the landing.

"So, we just try the door?" Sissa asked, a hand resting at her hip where I knew she had stashed a knife this morning. I checked my watch. We were right on time, just like Cora said. Before I could say a word to Kieran, the door opened and a girl with a blonde pixie cut, and blue eyes peaked her head out.

"Cora?" Kieran said, pushing the door open and pulling her to his chest, "You shouldn't be here. They probably have you on camera letting us in."

"I think it's more important that you get in," she said and pulled back from him. She led the way inside the large store-room. There weren't any workers in the room, but we could hear a few voices in the halls and side rooms. We walked past rows of empty shelves where a closet was. Cora opened the door and there were racks on every wall of the same black coveralls.

"The engineers working the floors wear these," Cora said. Sissa was already slipping into a jumpsuit in her size, buttoning the front over the gun strapped at her hip. Cora took her

Conduit robes and draped them over one arm, waiting for the rest of us to do the same.

"Thank you for helping us," I said and took a hanger off the rack. Cora nodded, taking August's robes and then Barker's. I made eye contact with Kieran as we both slipped into the pants. He couldn't hide his nerves, fidgeting with the buttons as he snapped them together. His anxiety worried me. My mother had warned me about letting him get in the way, but I wouldn't let him die this time for the sake of the mission. I couldn't do it a second time.

"You have to move fast," Cora said, taking our robes, "There's a shipment of parts coming in this morning."

"How did you get here?" Kieran asked. She looked just like him when he was frustrated with the same tight jaw and tense shoulders.

"I told father I was taking the internship here," she said.

"No. Cora, no, you didn't. If you take that internship, then you'll be sucked into his regime like all of Gallaterra is. You'll be trapped," Kieran said.

"Take care of the problem today and I won't have to," she said, ushering us all out of the closet and giving us no other option but to follow her towards the double doors at the back. They opened into a wide hall. A woman dressed in the same dark jumpsuit passed us without looking up from her tablet. Cora wished us luck and went to the elevator across the hall. She blew Kieran a kiss before the doors shut.

"Alright, kid," Barker said, "Which way?"

"Right," I said, drawing everyone's surprise, "Right and up two floors." I memorized Kieran's instructions the same night that Naja and I agreed to continue the mission. Kieran nodded and the rest of our crew fell in step behind us. I slipped my hand into Kieran's as we walked long enough to project my feelings of confidence. His chest swelled a little with every step now and he looked stronger than he had in the closet.

"Go," Sissa said behind us. I turned around to look at her, her expression angry. "Get the hell out of here," she yelled at me, "run." I saw a man down the hall withdraw a gun from his hip, but Sissa had already whipped around with hers raised. A bullet punched into his chest and sent his shot smashing into the row of lights above us. The darkness gave us cover as two more guards appeared down the hall to face off with her.

"Looks like we'll have to branch off after all," August said as we ran. No one spoke as we raced down the hall. Kieran's shoes squealed on the concrete floor as we nearly raced right past the stairs. He led the charge upstairs, ducking on the first landing as an electric arrow shot over his head and embedded in the wall with a zap that sent sparks showered down his back.

"Out of the way," a woman yelled ahead of us. Several people shouted down what must have been a busy hall. August pushed past me, his weight tossing me against the banister and offering him no help if he needed someone to watch his back.

"August," Kieran called as his friend ran into the hall. He fired three shots as he ran from the stairs to the hall opposite us. Back pressed safely against the wall, he looked back at us and motioned us forward.

"He cleared the way," Barker said and was the first to emerge into the hall. Engineers were cowering against the walls, three guards in silver uniforms lay spread-eagle in the middle of the hall. We quickened our pace, the silence strange after all the noise that still left my ears ringing slightly.

"Left," Kieran told Barker when we reached a fork in the hall. This hallway was abandoned, likely thanks to the shooting.

"You don't think your father left after the first round, do you?" I asked. Kieran shook his head.

"No," he said, "All the government buildings have sound-canceling technology. I bet only the halls aren't." I hoped he was right. Still, he wouldn't be there for long if any of the guards we encountered had alerted anyone.

"Shit," I said as he rounded another hall. At the end was the sliding metal door where the converter and main generator were. Hanging from the ceiling halfway down the hall was a metal box that swiveled its dark orb towards us. "We're on camera," I said.

"Not camera," Kieran said, "Kenna, move." Before it dawned on me what was happening, Barker stepped in front of me. A red ray shot from the device and soundlessly met the man's chest. He let out a groan and crumpled just as his gun fired a shot that shattered the device across the floor. His eyes were still blinking as he sprawled over the floor, looking from me to Kieran and the door.

"It's a stunning gun," Kieran said, "Come on. We have to move." He grabbed my hand and tugged me towards the door. I glanced once back at the man who likely had just given his life for me just as I was tugged into the room beyond. The silver doors slid shut and cut off my view.

It was silent in the new space. The entire room was much lighter than the dark concrete of the halls behind us. The walls were white and there was another metal door across the room. The Gallaterran flag hung over the center of the room and the walls had a variety of historical paintings all depicting scenes important to the mining industry.

"What's behind the door?" I asked.

"I don't know," Kieran admitted, the words sending a pit to my stomach, "but I know this is the complex we needed to be in. I just hope the converter isn't that much further and that no one has told my father we're here yet."

"Then we better keep moving," I said and strode ahead. I sucked in a deep breath and pressed the red button next to the door and stood firm as it slid open. The doors opened to a giant catwalk raised high above a completely abandoned floor. Two large machines sat beneath us with thick tubes and wires coming out the top. One had a clear bulb between the machine and the wires leading to the ceiling, a filament inside the glass flickering with bright blue light as the machine hummed. The next machine looked less strange to me, reminding me of the grey transformers attached to large buildings. That one had to be the generator.

"We'll have you nice and comfortable in the panic room in just minutes, sir," a woman said. Kieran and I both pulled out guns from beneath our coveralls just as a group of guards rounded the corner. I could just barely see President Grace behind the human shield.

"There," one of the men yelled. The sound of guns cocking and electric arrows zapping to life echoed off the metal surroundings as a dozen silver armored men and women pointed weapons at the two of us.

"He's right there, damn it," Kieran hissed, his gun held firmly aloft next to me.

"You lied to the entire nation," I yelled, "You told everyone we were both dead and that the Aldierians have been attacking Gallaterran cities when you were the terrorist all along."

"Stand down," the woman at the front of the pack called to us.

"Can't even successfully be a criminal, can you," Grace said, moving so he was standing just behind the woman so he could see Kieran past her shoulder. "You are a disgrace, and I knew I should never have claimed a bastard. I should've tossed you out and been done with you like I got rid of your filthy father," he said.

"You killed him," Kieran said, lowering his gun a fraction, "You didn't pay him off or make him any offers. You had him killed in one of your terrorist attacks just like you do anyone else who tries to take you down." I could see a few of the soldiers glancing sideways at Grace. The steadfast formation was cracking the more we spoke. Scott Grace was an asshole and anyone who met the man knew it. All we were doing was giving the guards a reason to hate him more.

"You weren't suited for this life, boy," Grace said, "You were always a risk that I took for your mother's sake."

"And you hit her just as much as you hit me," Kieran said, gesturing from his father to the door with the gun.

"Kieran," I warned, "Don't let your guard down."

"Listen to the Aldierian bitch, you-" Grace was cut off when Kieran took his shot, the bullet sinking into the front guard's chest. The entire group took their positions now, training their weapons on us.

"Kill them," Grace said, that same malicious smirk on his face that he'd worn when he visited Kieran in prison. The guards had started to relax though, a few groaning and some fainting. I noticed one pressing a hand to the device behind her ear before she collapsed. In just seconds, President Grace stood in the center of a ring of bodies.

"The device," I said as Grace looked around him in confusion and began pressing a finger to his device.

"Thank God for Angel," Kieran said, "She hijacked the device just like he did. Looks like he's not the only one who can play mind games on his people now." Grace looked up at us, fear clear in his expression even at this distance. He turned and ran, picking up two guns from the unconscious guards before rounding the corner. A hole appeared in the wall where President Grace just stood. Kieran lowered his gun and started running, not bothering to scoop up any extra weapons along the way.

"Kieran," I called after him, stopping just long enough to grab a crossbow with an electric arrow already loaded. The floor sloped around the corner, leading in a spiral to the bottom floor where the machines were. It was louder than I had anticipated down here, and I couldn't hear either Kieran or his father as they yelled. Kieran pointed the gun at his father before casting the weapon aside. President Grace's head popped up from behind the converter and I barely dragged Kieran behind the generator before he took a shot at us, sparks flying above our heads where the bullet scraped the metal.

"Is he wearing the Heart of Aldieria?" I asked, keeping my grip tight around his forearm.

"I... I don't know," he said, acting as if he'd just come out of a daze. He looked a little lost like he was running through the plan once more when we didn't know if we had even a second of time to spare.

"Face me like a man," Grace yelled.

"All I have are knives," Kieran said, looking back at me. His eyes landed on the crossbow. I handed it over, taking note of the four bullets left in my gun. I peeked around the generator and saw Grace run from behind the conductor. I tried shooting him, but the bullet just missed his left shoulder and pinged off the metal wall.

"He's running," I said, taking chase. I stopped halfway across the floor to take another shot, this one hitting the metal railing of the stairs. Sparks shot off the railing and made the president flinch before he started up the first set of stairs. Two bullets left.

"I can't cover you," Kieran shouted from behind. It was too late now. I couldn't lose sight of Grace now. I had to follow him. I took the stairs two and a time, never getting a clear enough shot to chance using my last two bullets. The stairs brought us to another catwalk on the opposite side of the room from the first, this one surrounded on one side by long skinny windows. Grace was running towards a door at the end of the catwalk. When he reached out and pulled the handle open, I took another shot. This one hit the door inches above his head and ricocheted into one of the windows with a crash that was sure to attract anyone in the plaza who hadn't been knocked out by Angel's hijack.

I wanted to toss the gun aside, wishing I had one of the knives that Jacob used to forge. I wasn't nearly as good of a shot as I was hand-to-hand. I felt my chest heave as I willed my feet forward and through the door. Jacob was dead. He was dead because of this man. We all could be dead thanks to this man.

"It's over," I yelled, hardly recognizing my voice. My gun was pointed at Grace who stood across the room looking at me with a smug expression. The room overlooked the engineering floor with the generator and converter on one side and a giant window behind Grace that looked down into the plaza. A loud alarm started to go off outside and the few people walking the plaza began looking around, a few running towards the nearest building.

"Yes, it is," Grace called back, "In minutes, security will be all over this place and you'll be arrested and executed, you and that bastard."

"I can still kill you first," I said, keeping my grip firm on the gun. I aimed my gun towards the door that just burst open to my left, faltering when I saw Kieran emerge with the crossbow. His eyes were set on his father, paying me no attention. He raised the crossbow and slowly began to approach.

"I'm sure you can kill me," Grace said with a humming laugh, staring directly at me. The crossbow in Kieran's hands lowered a little. His hands were shaking too much with anger to use it properly anyway.

"Look at me," Kieran said, his voice firm in ways I'd never heard it before. The president looked annoyed.

"So, what exactly were you going to do once you got onto the engineering floor? I'm curious," he said, taking his eyes off me and moving closer to the giant windows over the plaza. "You're not going to let me live long enough for security to reach us," he said and turned to face me again, "So, it's probably safe for you to tell me."

"Look at me," Kieran yelled, this time the ferocity surprised me, "I'm the one who's going to kill you. Look at me." Grace laughed, finally looking at his son.

"No," Grace said, "Not you," He winked at me and that's when Kieran charged. Grace dodged the tip of the crossbow just before Kieran set it off. The bolt pierced the window and left behind a web of cracks. Kieran got in a few jabs before his father gained the advantage with a sweeping kick that sent him to his back. I wanted to intervene, but I knew Kieran wouldn't want me to. No way could I get a clear shot to try shooting anyway and with one bullet left, there was no telling what we might need it for.

I ran to the doors instead, trying to ignore the cries of pain from both Kieran and his father as they fought. I made sure each door was deadbolted. It wouldn't keep us from getting arrested, but maybe Kieran could kill Grace and we could at least accomplish that much of the mission.

Kieran let out a terrible scream that forced me to turn from the door. He was halfway to his knees, a gash in his black coveralls revealing the bleeding cut underneath. I pulled the trigger before thinking it through, the bullet hitting Grace's outstretched arm. He backed away from Kieran with a scream, looking up at me in fear. I tossed the empty gun aside and the president lunged for it.

"It won't help you," I called to him. He ignored me and started towards the windows again. Kieran and I followed him, taking measured steps in case he decided to try running or attacking again. He stopped when his back met the window, a smile pulling across his face so sinister that my skin felt cold despite the sun that fell over us. I looked sideways at Kieran and could tell he worried the same thing. This had to be a trap.

"If you wanted to kill me, you'd have done it by now," he told me, "I was just feet from you and you missed the shot."

"It's not my fight," I said. I pulled the retractable knife from under my coveralls. It had been with me through everything like an old friend. Holding it felt comfortable. It made me feel powerful. It reminded me of everything I lost and gained along the way, the fights I had won and tragedies I'd survived even when it felt like they would swallow me whole. This knife had been the beginning of all my trouble, and it was only right that it would be the end.

I held it out to Kieran and he took it, the muscles in his forearm tightening when his fingers grasped it. Scott Grace laughed again, holding his arms open as if for a hug.

"You can't even do this, boy," he said.

"You will never hit me or my mother again," Kieran said, pointing at him with the knife. The blade popped out as he did so, extending it so the tip was just a few feet away now.

"Your traitorous mother was lucky I didn't cast her out and ruin her the way she nearly ruined me," the president said, "She would've been on the streets and you with her. My generosity saved you and you've spent your whole sorry life repaying me by fighting against me."

"Because you're wrong," Kieran said, "You're wrong about the Aldierians."

"What have you gotten out of fighting me all these years? Every time you reject what I've done for you, you slip further and further into the dark. I could've given you everything. You could've followed in your brother's footsteps and risen to greatness," he said, his voice rising the way it had when he yelled at Kieran in prison. Kieran wasn't going to just bear the brunt of his insults this time.

"What you've done with Gallaterra isn't greatness, it's fascism," he said, "You intimidate people into your beliefs and threaten their lives and the lives of their families if they speak against you. You blew up a bunch of people who challenged your ideas and blamed it on the Aldierians who aren't actually enemies of Gallaterra. They're trying to preserve the planet and you are in the way. What your administration is doing is going to kill all of us and you refuse to listen to your scientists because it means losing money and the power that you get from the mining business and their overlords."

"So, you're going to kill me and then do what?" Grace asked. I looked at his breast where the Heart of Aldieria was during his speech in the plaza. Where was it? It wasn't hanging around his neck and I couldn't tell if it was tucked under his shirt or not. He wouldn't hide it like that, would he? It was a show of power that he wore to address the people yesterday. It wouldn't make sense to hide it now unless he wasn't wearing it at all. My stomach sank.

"We'll rebuild Gallaterra without you," Kieran said, "There are more sympathizers than you think and the Ida of the Aldierians is prepared to make an alliance. You may have brainwashed many people against them, but love is stronger than hate." President Grace eyed me now, his gaze looking me up and down.

"You think you have so much power now because you fell in love with an Aldierian?" he asked.

"It's the love I feel for her and my mother that keeps me fighting against you," Kieran told him. He laughed, looking back at his son.

"Real power isn't earned," he said, "It's taken. Are you prepared to take what you need? Are you willing to kill for it, even if that means sacrificing innocent people? Power is what you need here, not love. You need power to overrule my administration. Killing me won't kill my politics. It won't destroy my legacy." I felt sick as he spoke, not because of the disgusting ideas of death and destruction he so casually mentioned, but because he was right. It would take a lot of work to overturn the brainwashing and the politics he'd put in place during his entire term. It would take more than a bunch of sympathizers. It would take putting one of the sympathizers in a position of power. It needed to be credible. The science needed to be front and center and undeniable. We could start the change and we could maybe even save the planet if we were lucky enough to find the Heart of Aldieria, but it would take much longer to undo his rhetoric.

"I'm right here in front of you with a knife and you're asking if I'm ready to take power?" Kieran asked with a laugh of disbelief.

"That's exactly what I'm asking, son," the president said. His tone was softer now, almost paternal. There was a beat of silence between them, long enough for the blaring alarm to remind me of what little time was left.

"After everything I've done, breaking your laws, surviving attacks, and escaping prison twice. I'm more than prepared," Kieran said, "I'm not just going to kill you. I'm going to take your power away from you too. After you're gone, everything will change. Your legacy will be forgotten and the people who do remember you, will only remember how you destroyed the country," Kieran said. Grace looked down at the gun in his hands, turned it a few times, and then looked up at us.

"You can't take my power away," he said.

"You never did believe I could do anything," Kieran said, "I didn't expect this moment to be any different, but it is. That's exactly what I'm going to do."

"No, it's not. You're the same cowardly bastard," Grace said, tossing the gun in the air and catching it in his right hand.

"I may be a bastard, but I've never been a coward," Kieran said. Grace smirked and tapped the end of Kieran's knife with the gun as if he was clinking glasses after a toast.

"If you weren't a coward, you would've asserted your power and killed me already," Grace said, "Now, you'll never have any power. Nothing." Before either of us could react, he turned and smashed the gun into the glass, sending thousands of shards raining down on us. When I lowered my arms from my head, Grace was already out the window.

"NO! NO! NO!" I ran to the broken sill to look towards the ground. I heard the smack before I saw him spread-eagled on the concrete. People began screaming, making the sound of the alarm sound distant. "The stone," I said, looking back at Kieran. He didn't look shocked like I'd expected, but angry. I'd never seen him so mad before.

"I pulled it off him before," he said, holding up the stone.

"How is security not here yet?" I asked, running past him to check the door. The engineering floor was still clear of any people.

"We have to get the stone down there," Kieran said, already

halfway out the door before I could stop him. I ran after him, surprised at how fast he was moving.

"We have to go," I called to him, "We can form another mission to put the stone in place, but if we are caught here with it, they'll take it away. We may never get another one. We're the only people who know how to get in here." Kieran was at the converter now, already pressing buttons and pulling levers as if he worked with the machine every day.

"We have to do it now," he said, "We can do it."

"Kieran, we can get out if we go now," I said, trying to tug him away. He shrugged me off and pulled a lever that opened a glowing compartment. There were three blue tubes with liquid Ida stones swirling inside. He pulled all three out and tossed them onto the ground. The lights went out around us for a second and the room was silent aside from the clinking sounds of the converter as Kieran worked. The lights came back on, and the whir of machines filled the air again. I saw the glittering stone suspended inside the compartment as if pulled in two directions by equal force.

"It's done," Kieran said and stepped back with a smile, "We did it. I can't believe it." His eyes glittered with tears. I could hear shouts coming from the catwalk that led to the hallway. We had just moments left before who knew what kind of torture we'd endure. We were kissing now, Kieran's grip on me so tight that it was almost painful. I was so engrossed in the feel of his body against mine that I hadn't heard her voice until Kieran pulled away.

Standing just outside the door to the overlook room was Sissa, a cut on her cheek but otherwise unharmed. She held her arms up in disbelief and motioned towards the room.

"I said, let's go. Move a little quicker," she yelled, trailing off in what I knew now as Aldierian swear words. I tugged Kieran towards the stairs, and we were already in the room when I heard soldiers yelling from the engineering floor. Outside the broken window was one of the cargo ships, the loading doors down with August hanging out the back with a bazooka he'd gotten from God knows where. He pointed it at the doors in case anyone came in after us.

I jumped in first, Kieran landing next to me. Sissa and August came in after us, the automatic door sliding shut before a single soldier ever made it to the overlook room. Sissa ran past us to the front of the ship and slid a small window open. I could see Barker's head behind the ship's control panel.

"We got them both. Let's book it," Sissa said. The ship lurched hard enough under us that Kieran and I fell. August lowered himself to the floor using the dark wall of the cargo hold. Sissa held onto a bar on the side of the wall, a tablet lighting up her face in the dimly lit ship.

"You good, Angel?" she asked.

"Yes," the soft voice replied, "I left for Varillia half an hour ago in a private pod I was able to hijack. Did you disconnect the main server with the code I sent you?"

"Yeah. Barker did it just like you said," Sissa told her.

"Then no one can track you. As long as you fly outside of normal airspace and move in at least double speed, you should make it to Varillia without a problem," Angel said. August laughed and let out a single whoop, Barker's own muffled cheering came from the driver's quarters.

"We'll see you there, Angel," Sissa said and hung up the call. She looked from Kieran to me. "Did you do it?" she asked, focusing on me now. Kieran was in tears. He was trying to control his emotions, that much I could tell, but a single soft sob escaped him before he buried his head into my chest. I wrapped my arms around him as he cried and looked up at Sissa.

"Yeah," I said, "We did it."

CHAPTER 26

When we made it to Varillia and reported the mission's success to Ida Imara, the entire city of Varillia and all the East Sea villages erupted with celebrations. Naja burst into tears the moment he saw me, breaking the ranks of soldiers there to greet us so he could pull me into a tight hug.

Kieran had kept to himself since we climbed into the cargo pod and escaped, only saying a few words when necessary. I wasn't surprised by his silence. I believed that he wanted his father dead and I believed him when he said he'd be the one to do it, but things hadn't gone the way he'd planned and the death of your father, even a father like Scott Grace, was still a loss. In a lot of ways, Kieran was starting over while I was just getting started in life. There was so much ahead of us, so many opportunities, and the Aldierians finally had a real chance of freedom now.

Our entire troop was booked for interviews and parades and fancy dinners for days before the celebrations faded and the conversations turned to what we should do next. The politicians in Varillia met to discuss how to go about reaching out to the sympathizers in Gallaterra. Things were already in motion, and I was happy for once not to be included in every detail.

Kieran and I were given raises, which allowed us to move into an apartment in the capitol building along with the rest of the small group of assassins we both considered friends now. We moved slowly at first, waiting a whole two weeks after the last of the celebrations to start our transition from Kieran's one-room apartment into the spacious five-bedroom compound. That's when I began feeling strange, like an imposter. I knew what we had done was nearly impossible and historic, but I didn't feel comfortable yet with all the finery surrounding me and understanding that brought me to the sad facts that Kieran had to be feeling the same sense of loss. It wasn't the loss of his old life or his father. It was a loss of self. We'd been focused for so long on surviving the day and the mission that it was weird for it to be all over. What came next, not just for me or Kieran, but for us?

"It always feels that way when you come back from a long mission," Naja told me, handing a mug of Aldierian tea to me and another to my mother on the couch. We'd been having afternoon meetings every Tuesday and Thursday since I got home exclusively for family time. I'd grown closer to my mother in the last few weeks, and she felt less like the Ida and more like… not quite a mother. I couldn't see myself as anyone's child other than Jacob's, losing him still a heavy feeling I tried not to visit too often.

Usually, we would all sit together and hold hands. We would use our Ida stones to express feelings and show each other memories. Today was different. I needed to feel contained in my own body, so I was better in control of my emotions. My mom and Naja seemed to understand.

"What do I do though?" I asked after wrestling with myself. I tried to find all the words to express it, and despite feeling like I wasn't explaining myself enough, it was as plain as I could put it.

"You move on," Naja said with a shrug. I snorted.

"Easy for you to say," I said, "You come home from your missions with life already here for you. Before, having a life after the mission was like a dream to Kieran. I don't think he ever planned on surviving it, not even when we first started. I think he's coming to terms with his mortality, like, survivor's guilt or something." Naja had started talking again, but I didn't hear his words. My mother placed her hand over mine and I could feel her sympathy so strongly that it drowned everything out. I felt the emotions from her mission with my father, his death, her grief, and then a cold nothingness that hung in silence as I stared back into her soft eyes.

"You can't take away his pain or show him how to navigate out of it," she said, *"but you can be there with him as he finds a way for himself."*

My body warmed as I realized what was next and she gave me a small smile, signally that she knew it too. I felt something cool slip into my other hand. I tucked it into my pocket and pulled away from my mother and back into the moment.

"He'll be okay," Naja finished with his speech to the empty room, "Give him some time is all." I agreed with him, my mom smirking at our secret. I stayed long enough to finish the tea and then left for my apartment, where I knew Kieran would be. He spent most of his free time there these days. We had a large balcony with a domed roof that allowed the sea to flow around us. It looked down on the beautiful coral garden in the center of Varillia and we could see the web of subs and smaller water pods, the part that Kieran was fascinated by.

Just like I thought, he was sitting at our little table on the balcony, a half-eaten sandwich and a glass of water sitting next to him as he fidgeted with a folded sheet of paper between his hands. It reminded me of our night under the stars watching the fireworks explode. Before he could notice me, I changed directions and went to our bedroom. I changed into a flowy dress and tried my best to braid my hair into the traditional Aldierian warrior style. I took my jacket with me, my mother's gift stowed in the pocket, and slipped into the seat next to Kieran. He offered a small smile and looked back at the sea.

"I like your hair like that," he said, folding the paper into smaller sections and slipping it into his pocket.

"I know," I told him. We were quiet for a while, watching as a sub moved directly under us and past one of the clear tubes where people walked. "Back in the arena," I said, turning to face him and placing my hands on the table, "What made you decide to give up everything for me? You weren't just saving my life and you know that. You were leaving everything behind at that moment for a chance of more," I said. He turned slowly in his seat, taking my hands and keeping his eyes on them.

"When I said that you are more," he said, "I didn't mean just more for me." He looked up at me. "You are an Aldierian who grew up Gallaterran. You are so strong physically and mentally. You were everything the planet needed and more to make things right. I never would have beaten you, even if I had wanted to try. I only escaped with you because, well, I was with you. I always want to be with you. Being with you makes me feel like the best version of myself. I've never felt as much like myself as when I'm with you," he said, lowering his eyes again. I slipped my right hand away and gave his left a tight squeeze to keep him from pulling away while I fished for the gift in my jacket.

"You're more too, you know that?" I asked. He smiled a little.

"I didn't feel that way when Grace jumped. I wanted to do it and I still don't know if I could've and I don't know what that makes me," he said.

"It makes you different from him," I said, "He didn't make you who you are, Kieran. You did that. Despite the hate you grew up with, you decided who you were going to be. You could've accepted all the power and money your father wanted to give you just like your brother did, but you didn't. You are strong because you chose to do what is right instead of what was easy."

"It sounds so heroic when you say it like that," Kieran said.

"That's because you are a hero, you idiot. You're just too modest to realize that," I said, taking both his hands in mine and tugging on them. He smiled, his body relaxing. He looked more himself than he had in weeks, like that same beautiful blue-eyed boy that stood up to the gold soldier in prison. His fingers grazed the Ida stone in the ring on my left hand. I pressed the cool metal of the wedding band my mother had given me into his hand. It was my father's wedding ring. I knew it from the emotions she felt when she'd slipped it into my hand. Kieran smiled as he held the ring between his hands.

"Kieran Grace," I said, slipping out of my chair and onto one knee, "will you marry me?" He laughed and I couldn't help but join in. He wrapped his arms around my waist and pulled me to my feet. It felt exciting, like it was the first time all over again. He kissed me, holding my face between his hands as he pulled back an inch and said, "yes."

ACKNOWLEDGMENTS

I can't believe this book is finally out in the world. Wow. It's taken a lot of hard work and it's been a learning process to make it all happen, but I didn't do it all alone. I want to thank all the friends and family in my life who have always encouraged me to follow my dreams. A special thanks to the friends who read the early drafts of this book and gave me their honest feedback. This book is what it is today because of you.

I think the most gratitude goes to my wonderful husband. Without your encouragement and support along the way, I might have let my self-doubt get in the way. This wouldn't have been possible without your love for me and my crazy ideas. Thank you for riding the highs and the lows of this project with me and for easing the headaches that came along with last minute cover design elements. Without your technology abilities, I don't know where this project would've gone.

My editor Dr. Sarah Stewart was a huge part in helping me smooth out the story. Thanks for highlighting my strengths, and my weaknesses, in order to shape this story into the best version I could.

Thank you to my wonderful cover designer, Lena Yang. She was amazing and I am so thankful that she could swoop in to save the day with her designs after my first cover designer couldn't finish. She was great to work with and did far more than I dreamed possible with the time we had. I am so grateful for her hard work and for making me feel comfortable.

I want to say a final thanks to you, the person reading this right now. I hope you enjoyed this book and will continue to follow my adventures writing more stories in the future. I have so many to tell, just waiting to get into your hands. Thank you.

ABOUT THE AUTHOR

Amy Prokopis is a fiction author from Oklahoma who writes books for young adults. She loves writing everything from science fiction and fantasy to contemporary romance. She graduated from Oklahoma State University with a bachelor's degree in English and a minor in German before obtaining a master's degree in school counseling. Besides writing, Amy enjoys distance running and spending time with her husband, their son, and their Havanese, June.